Sacred Love

A NOVEL

Cheryle Fisher

For Wendy

To our fantasies and to
the Sacred Love
only He can give.

PART ONE

"In Italy, when a woman blushes,
it is said that the angels in Heaven have told her a secret
that no man may ever know."
- Giancarlo Giannotti -

Chapter 1

HE REMEMBERED HOW beautiful she was, even in death. Though her stunning dark eyes had closed forever, the thick lashes that swept away from her lids, the porcelain skin of her face and her full alizarin lips testified to the fact that God had gifted her generously. Her gloriously thick brown hair draped her cold shoulders like an expensive fur stole. Death could not erase the beauty of her perfect form, and even the slight blemish on her cheek had only enhanced her charm. He had thought himself fortunate to have been her husband, but her death and the weight of the guilt it left him had become too much. She was part of the memories he wanted to leave behind; he was looking for new ones.

Now at fifty-one years old, he'd come to the United States for a new life and to find her family; he felt it his duty that they should know what had happened to her. And there was someone else, someone he couldn't stop thinking about. He knew her name and couldn't get her face out of his mind. And so, he'd given up his old life and was searching for her too. That search had led him to Cape Narrows, a small town by the Pacific Ocean, and to a new job as trauma surgeon.

He'd studied medicine at the Università degli Studi di Milano in Milan, Italy, a renowned school and teaching hospital with over twenty-five hundred professors and as many as sixty-five thousand students. After graduating near the top of his class, he'd been offered a staff position. He was eventually offered a professorship in the surgical program, but after the death of his wife, he'd declined, moved back to his home town near Florence and had worked at L'Ospedale della Sacra Famiglia. Finding no peace even there and knowing that there was something he had to do, he'd followed what clues he had and had come to this town and to Memorial Hospital.

A hospital, especially one as small as Memorial, is a microcosm of the community it serves. Employees know each others' names, establish relationships, form alliances and harbor enemies. Many of the staff at Memorial had worked there for many years owing to excellent benefit packages, competitive wages, challenging continuing education classes and upper management staff who were approachable and caring.

The CEO, Dr. John Hazleton, had been awarded honors for his hands-on, quality-driven efforts on behalf of patients and employees alike, and Dr. Giancarlo Giannotti was his newest addition to the surgical staff. From Giannotti's résumé and first interview, he seemed to fit perfectly with the Medical Board's expectations for strong leadership in the emergency department. Even the Ducati he drove implied skill, mastery and new direction.

After the initial meet-and-greet with Hazleton and the Medical Board, Giannotti was given a tour of the hospital. Memorial was a newer facility, small but adequate for the town it served. There were a total of eighty-five in-patient beds. The building consisted of three floors, encompassing three main wings which were joined to form a 'U' shape, leaving an open garden area in the middle. There were all the standard departments including labor and delivery, pediatrics, emergency and surgical services and ancillary services, to include radiology, pharmacy, laboratory and an office for the pathologist, who was also the town's coroner.

During the tour, Dr. Giannotti was introduced to each department head, always aware that he was the new man, untried and under scrutiny. The staff he met seemed very cordial, welcoming and genuine in their pleasure at meeting him, especially Gayle Matthews, the head nurse in the emergency department.

At the end of the tour, they returned to Hazleton's office on the first floor. "You'll need this," he said and handed Giannotti a laminated identification card. "We'll see you here tomorrow at seven, then. Please feel free to stay as long as you like. I'm sure you will find the staff very helpful." They shook hands, Hazleton insisting Giannotti call if he should have any problems or questions. "My door is always open to the staff here at Memorial," he said.

Giannotti walked back toward the main entrance. As he neared the cafeteria, he realized he was hungry and went in. It was busy and bright, decorated in muted colors, and the smell of the day's special was too hard to resist. He ordered his meal and found a table near the windows.

He was halfway through his meal, wondering if this town too would lead to a dead end, when he noticed her, three tables away and sitting alone. He remembered he'd seen her in the patient accounts department on his tour. She hadn't even looked up from her work when they'd come in, but her blond hair had caught his attention.

Now he studied her. Her eyes were fixed on her lunch while she picked at her food. He noticed there was a sadness in her posture and in the way she seemed unaware of the activity and noise around her. He realized she was prettier now than she was in the photo. There was something else, too, something that he noticed immediately: she was not wearing a wedding ring. Aware that his search was now over, he walked to her table, taking his cup of coffee with him, hoping that she would be part of the new memories he wanted to create.

"Hello, I am Giancarlo and you are…?" He held out his hand, waiting for hers.

She looked up, fumbled for a response and came out with a hesitant and confused "I'm Windy…no, not Windy! I'm Wendy," sounding the 'e' with extra emphasis. Her face flushed red, her usual response to embarrassment. It happened so often that she had even given it a name: 'lobster face.'

For a moment, she was stunned by his good looks, especially the easy smile revealing his perfect, white, beautiful teeth and his extraordinary ebony eyes and the way the light danced in them. In those first silent seconds of uncertainty, the kind that beg for a comment to redeem oneself, she was speechless. She felt the flush again and was aware that he'd noticed.

"Forgive me. Perhaps in America, women do not shake hands with men. Is this so?" She recognized his accent as Italian. It floated across the air like the scent of the jasmine that grew in her garden, sweet and sensual. She now knew that everything she had ever fantasized about Italian men was standing right in front of her in a tailored suit, his arm outstretched, waiting for her to take his hand. Summoning her courage, she took it and was unable to ignore the warmth of his skin and the firmness of his grip.

"I'm so sorry," she apologized. "Yes, of course women shake hands. It's just that I was preoccupied for a moment." For now, that little lie would have to do. She could think of no other response and she surely wasn't going to tell him that she was totally caught off guard by his looks, the kind Gayle would describe as "drop dead gorgeous." She felt giddy, like a love-struck school girl, but admitting that to herself increased her heart rate.

"May I join you? I am new here and do not know anyone."

She nodded and he sat down opposite her. She thought of herself as shy, but she didn't want to tell him 'no' and that surprised her. "I know what that's like. I'm sure you'll make new friends in no time," she offered. She remembered when she first came to Cape Narrows. She was new to the people who lived here, to her job at Memorial and also new to being single again, a widow after eighteen years of marriage. It had taken her a while to adjust and while she now had friends, she still sometimes felt lonely and lost.

This man looked like that: definitely out of place in what she thought might be an Armani suit, his white shirt accentuating his tan skin. His hair was black and thick, somewhat wavy, with only a hint of gray at the temples. His nose was straight, his jawline square and strong. When he smiled, the creases at the corners of his eyes made him all the more handsome. There was perfect symmetry in his face. She guessed he was in his early fifties, like herself. As unobtrusively as she could, she glanced at his left hand; there was no wedding band. She had never done that before, checked a man for a wedding band, and she wondered why she had done it now. She realized she was now staring at him.

"How long have you worked at Memorial?" he asked. He searched her face, admiring her natural beauty and her eyes the color of the Adriatic in summer, a mix of crystal blue and turquoise. He knew how old she was and that her husband was dead, but he would keep that to himself for now. He was happy that she was staring at him, but then she averted his gaze and went back to her lunch.

"Oh," she replied, "I've been here almost seven years. I started as a medical assistant in the emergency department, but they needed someone in Patient Accounts. They promised to train me and offered me a nice bonus, so I accepted." Her voice trailed off for a moment as she remembered happier times working with Gayle.

"You are sad about that I think," he responded, noticing the faraway look cross her face. The intimacy of his statement surprised her. She didn't really know him after all, and his comment was personal. She wondered why she didn't feel ill at ease, puzzled that she felt comfortable with him. She sensed a gentleness in his manner, a softness to his voice and his presence made her feel very calm and relaxed. She realized then how tense she'd been all day, how upset she was about the lack of advancement in her department. She'd been seriously considering finding a new job in bigger town, but now wasn't so sure she wanted to leave Cape Narrows. Besides, she could put up with Tanya and Mr. Dellette for a while longer.

"Not really, I mean it was just that the ED was so interesting and I have always wanted to be a nurse. Working there was as close as I could come to my dream." She steered the conversation his way. She was feeling too comfortable with him and that scared her. "Do you work here or are you visiting someone?"

"Forgive my manners, Signorina, I should have introduced myself better. My name is Giancarlo Giannotti and I am the new surgeon in the emergency department. Today is my first day. I have been in meetings with Dr. Hazleton most of the morning, but the smell was so wonderful coming from here that I could not resist having some lunch."

She felt her pulse quicken at the knowledge that he would be working at Memorial.

"The food here is very good. We have an excellent chef. He makes the most wonderful lasagna." She knew she was running at the mouth and embarrassing herself.

Dr. Giannotti just smiled and said, "I'm sure I will like it. Lasagna is one of my favorite dishes, but the best lasagna is made by my mama. She is a wonderful cook!"

Wendy was charmed that he referred to his mother that way. She had loved her mother dearly, but had lost her several years before to a stroke and only two years after losing her father. She wanted to keep the conversation about him, partly because she was interested in him, but also because she had always been hesitant to give her life history to people she didn't know. She didn't need and didn't want pity for her losses.

"Where does your mother live?" she asked.

"She and my papa live in Bivigliano. That is where I was born. It is a small town not far from Florence. Have you ever been to Italy, Wendy?"

"No," she admitted, "but I would like to go someday. How did you end up here at Memorial?"

"I worked at a very large hospital in Milano. It was very busy and the hours were many. I did not have the time to know my patients and it was very *insoddisfacente*…." Here he hesitated, looking for the right word in English, "…how you would say, unsatisfying. I wanted to work somewhere not so crazy." He tapped the side of his head. Wendy smiled. "And tell me how you came to Memorial."

She didn't want to reveal her past to him, at least not yet. She felt there were some things that were best kept close to her heart. She checked her watch. If she was late getting back to work, Mr. Dellette would surely say something about it; he always did. She wasn't close to being late yet, but she was starting to feel vulnerable. She got up, grabbing her purse off the back of the chair.

"I'm sorry, but I must be getting back to work. It was very nice meeting you, Dr. Gian…" She stumbled over his last name.

"Giannotti," he coached. He rose and extended his hand to her again, and this time she took it without thinking. "It is a pleasure to meet you Wendy, not Windy," he said jokingly, placing the emphasis on the 'e' just as she had done. "However, you must call me Giancarlo. *Siamo amici ora*. We are friends now, are we not?"

She was momentarily caught off guard by his directness, but recovered quickly and said, "I know you will have many friends here at Memorial." It was a polite and sincere remark and thankfully, far removed from she was thinking: 'Anybody who looks and sounds like him can be my friend anytime!' She had to smile at that voice in her head that was always saying crazy things, things she wanted to say but wouldn't. Wendy knew for certain that she was going to look forward to coming to work from now on.

She left the cafeteria knowing that she had lied. She had another ten minutes before she had to get back to Patient Accounts. She decided to sit in the chapel for a while so she could think.

The chapel was tucked at the rear of the hospital, down the hall from the cafeteria. There were comfortable pews and windows with heavy draperies. A table near the wall displayed religious pamphlets and two chandeliers adorned the ceiling. She did her best thinking in here; it was quiet and like being in church. It helped her to make confessions to herself and to sort out how she felt about things and why. It was empty today and she took a seat toward the back of the room.

It weighed on her that she had lied twice in less than ten minutes, something that was not her habit, and that she had lied to *him*. She couldn't quit thinking about him. Was it his startlingly good looks that so captured her attention or was there something else, something she couldn't quite put her finger on but rather felt, like 'woman's intuition?' That's what Gayle would call it. He was definitely charming, but it appeared natural, not put-on, and he seemed totally unaware of his looks, as if he'd never seen himself in a mirror. Maybe it was the inner calm she felt in his presence, a peace that could even override her erratic heartbeat and feelings of vulnerability. She had hungered for that sense of peace in herself for so long. Sometimes she had it for short moments, but it never lasted. It eluded her like a firefly's light: first visible, then invisible, here then there and never constant.

She didn't want to admit it to herself, but there was something else too. She realized that she suddenly felt alive, like she was waking from a very long, dreamless sleep. Something was beginning to stir in her and it was a feeling that she hadn't even realized had been missing, a feeling she hadn't had since she'd first met Mark.

"Code Blue, Emergency Room!"

The loudspeaker announcement broke her train of thought. She checked her watch. She was going to be late. She grabbed her purse and dashed back to Patient Accounts.

Chapter 2

HERS WAS THE desk next to the windows. She got it as a bonus for her promotion to Assistant Accounts Manager two years ago. The pay increase was minimal, the work load heavier, but she did get that desk by the window. She wasn't going to allow herself dwell on those things though, to give in to negativity. She had a job, it paid the bills and for that she was thankful, even though she was having to give herself pep talks more often. She was frustrated and felt stagnant, going nowhere in a boring job.

Mr. Dellette came out of his office as she walked in. She locked her purse in the bottom drawer of her desk and waited for the lecture.

"Little late getting back from lunch, aren't we?" he scolded. It annoyed her the way he put everything into plural pronouns.

He was sixty-seven, somewhat short and pale like his skin had never seen sunlight. What was left of his hair was steel gray and never seemed to lay down flat. His reading glasses hung off the end of his nose as if they were perched on a cliff, ready to commit suicide. He was going to retire in a few months and felt no compulsion to ease up on his dictatorial management style. He had no plans to relinquish his authority in Patient Accounts until the day he walked out for good. He was boss and he wanted everyone to remember that. He was particularly hard on Wendy, having heard rumors that she would be promoted to his position once he retired. He had no intention of giving her any slack before then.

"I'm sorry, Mr. Dellette," she said. "It won't happen again." Experience had taught her that no further explanation, no matter how legitimate, would change anything. She had quit trying to explain herself to him long ago.

"Well, see that it doesn't and bring me that file on Ed Jones. I'm going to call Premera and give them a piece of my mind." He turned and went back into his office. The negative thoughts came rushing back at her, crowding out all the pleasant ones from her encounter with Dr. Giannotti. She couldn't wait until Mr. Dellette retired. It couldn't be soon enough as far as she was concerned.

Working in the ED had been fun because Gayle was a great boss. She was charge and never asked anyone to do anything she wouldn't do herself. She wanted things done her way, but there was always a sound reason for it. She never berated anyone if they'd done something wrong, never got mad, but made sure they understood the error and why it needed correcting. She always reminded the staff that so much depended on proper procedure in the ED. "Lives are at stake," she would say.

The remainder of the day went quickly for Wendy, especially since she'd taken her lunch later than usual. She tried to concentrate on her accounts, making lists of whom she had to call about which problems, but her efforts were half-hearted at best.

Mr. Dellette never reappeared from his office until quitting time. She'd heard most of his angry phone conversation through the wall that separated her area from his office and felt sorry for whomever had picked up that call at Premera and had to explain policies to Mr. Dellette. When he thought he was right, there was no convincing him otherwise and she'd heard the phone slam back down on the cradle at the end of the call. He had sounded even more obstinate than usual, which was saying a lot.

She finished the last of her list, grabbed her purse and headed out the door. Annie was still at it, talking to someone on the phone, but she waved as Wendy left. Tanya had slipped out a few minutes before.

Her car, The Beast as she referred to it, was parked in the parking lot along the east side of the building. She didn't notice the motorcycle parked in the spot to her left until she was inside, putting the key into the ignition.

It was red, spontaneously combustible red, and like no other she had ever seen in Cape Narrows. Even though she was no cycle expert, she knew it wasn't a Harley Davidson. It had a more enclosed body, a small angled windshield and a trim black seat sloping downwards toward the handlebars. Everything about it screamed "speed." On the side, a silver decal read '1098' and on the gas tank was another that read 'Ducati.' Wendy had never heard of that brand, but then the only brand she really knew was Harley Davidson.

A tap on her side window brought her to attention and she was surprised to see Dr. Giannotti standing there. She turned the key in the ignition, allowing her to roll down the window.

"Uh…hi," she stammered. She was surprised by his presence, but excited to see him again. She noticed her pulse rate accelerating just as it had done earlier.

"I was leaving and saw you. I wanted to thank you for allowing me to share your table at lunch." He wouldn't tell her that he had waited for her shift to end so that he could speak with her again. He reminded himself to take his time with her.

The tone of his voice was so sincere it made her feel special, a feeling she hadn't had in a long time. She felt her face warming at the thought; she was having an attack of lobster face and recognizing that fact just made it worse. This time he commented, his voice gentle, his smile warm and inviting.

"In Italy, when a woman blushes, it is said that the angels in Heaven have told her a secret that no man may ever know. I think you must have many secrets that I will never know." She was too flustered to answer. Lobster face was full-blown now, but thankfully he said nothing more about it.

"I must go now. I have kept you too long. Your family is waiting for you at home, yes?"

"Oh, that's all right. Nobody is waiting for me." The rapidity of that admission shocked her. She was never that open with people. It made her vulnerable and she didn't like that feeling. What she didn't want to admit to herself was that she wanted him to know that she had no husband or significant other waiting for her, that she was unattached. "Well, nobody except for Dexter. He's my fox," she offered.

"*E'vero? Avete una volpe?*" His face lit up like a child with a new toy. "Oh, *mi scusi!* I fall back to my Italian when I am excited! It is true? You have a fox?"

He needn't apologize; she loved hearing him speak Italian. His excitement made owning a fox sound like winning the lottery.

"Yes, I found him as a kit, a baby fox, and I raised him. He's like a pet dog except he catches birds and mice. He's a good hunter."

"This is amazing to me! I like animals very much. Perhaps sometime I could see him?"

Wendy couldn't believe it. He was genuinely excited about Dexter! But the need to protect herself, the uncertainty, left her wondering if he was really just a nice guy who got excited about foxes or if his motives went deeper. After all, she wasn't unattractive for her age; she'd been told that before. Since Mark's death, she hadn't been blind to the fact that men were noticing her and she thought of herself as smart, independent, intuitive and loyal in her friendships. Was he just another guy hitting on her and if that was the case, was she ready to take a chance on another relationship? She was having a hard time reading him. For now it was better to leave him hanging, just until she could tell.

"Well, I'll keep that in mind," she replied, hopefully ending his interest in meeting Dexter for now. She changed the subject, not wanting him to leave. "How was your first day at Memorial?"

"I could not wait to…how is it said in English…to 'get my hands dirty?' Is that correct?" Wendy laughed. Maybe Dr. Giannotti was just some crazy Italian workaholic. She knew that most Europeans were not as driven as Americans and she'd always envisioned the Italians as being much more laid back.

"Yes, that's right. Excuse me for laughing, but as nice as it is to work at Memorial, most people aren't quite so eager to come to work."

A haunting look passed over his face, its meaning she couldn't discern, except that she suddenly felt sad when she saw it.

"You will forgive me if I presume on our new friendship, Wendy?"

'New' was an understatement! She had spent all of twenty minutes with him today and had impulsively given him permission to treat her as a friend. Now she was afraid he was going to confide something personal to her and she wasn't sure she wanted him to do that. She didn't want him to be open with her; she barely knew him. She had her own ghosts to deal with, but the sadness in his face tugged at her heart and somewhere inside her, she wondered why.

"We agreed to be friends at lunch, remember? There's no imposition between friends." She couldn't believe she had just given him permission, but then she had never been able to override her soft heart. Even so, she regretted her decision the minute the words were out of her mouth. She needed time to decide if she was ready to be close with a man again, even if he was just a friend.

He started hesitantly, unsure of revealing too much, too soon. "You see the Ducati? It is mine." He nodded toward the red bike next to her car. She'd already figured that out: hot Italian surgeon, hot bike with an Italian-sounding brand. One plus one equals two! And she'd noticed the helmet he was holding.

"Five years ago, there was an accident," he continued. "My wife was killed."

She was momentarily stunned. She knew what that loss was like and she didn't want him to remind her of her own pain. It was too close to the surface. But he went on and she didn't stop him.

"She wanted to drive the Ducati, but I would not let her. It is a very powerful bike. I was called to do surgery at the hospital, but that day it had rained. The streets were *scivoloso*…um… slick, so I took the car. After I left, she took the bike. She could not resist. She was always like that." He paused for a moment as if trying to find the right words or was he was judging her reaction? "She was brought to my hospital. I tried to save her, but her injuries were too serious."

From her own loss, Wendy knew that there was nothing she could say. She knew in situations like this, the less said, the better. A friend would understand that and she suddenly realized how much she wanted to be his friend. She reached out her window and placed her hand on his arm. She wanted to connect with him, to let him know he was not alone. "I'm so sorry, Giancarlo," she said.

"I am excited to come to Memorial because I love my work," he continued. "It is my life now. I suppose I try to make up for not saving Donnatella. Do you believe this is so?"

Wendy never claimed to be a counselor, but she knew enough about psychology to know that this guy had figured it out on his own. After Mark's death, she had left his father's vet business and moved to Cape Narrows, pouring herself into her work at Memorial. She understood where he was coming from.

"Yes, I think you're right. But that would be a natural reaction to what happened, don't you think?" He nodded and seemed to recover in that acknowledgement.

"*Grazie*, Wendy. I have taken enough of your time. Dexter will be waiting for you, yes?" He smiled remembering that she'd said there was nobody at home waiting for her.

"Yes, he will. He gets very upset with me if I'm not there to feed him on time."

"Then I will see you tomorrow. *Ciao*, Wendy."

"*Ciao*, Giancarlo." It was all the Italian she knew. He smiled again and walked around her car, putting on the helmet as he went. He mounted the Ducati and Wendy heard its engine start, the noise sounding like the buzzing of a giant mosquito. It was nothing like the Harley's she'd heard. He rode off with a wave in her direction.

'A powerful bike,' she mused, a grin forming at the corners of her mouth. 'Very powerful!'

Chapter 3

GAYLE WAS WORKING intently on the morning's paperwork when Dr. Giannotti wandered into the emergency department. She saw him out of the corner of her eye and wondered if he too, was going to be as short-lived as the past two surgeons she'd had to endure. The Board was having a run of bad luck recently finding a head surgeon for her department. Gayle figured that the good wages and benefits attracted the good candidates, but also the lazy ones who were more interested in filling their bank accounts and then moving on to bigger hospitals and better positions. She remembered that the past two recent docs were young and from cities in other states.

Gayle had lived in Cape Narrows all of her forty-two years and her heart was here in this small town. Her passion was her work at Memorial. She loved the patients and staff, most of whom she knew, and she had no time for and gave no leeway to slackers and incompetents. He looked good on the outside, but she was skeptical about Dr. Giannotti and he was an outsider to boot: not only not native to Cape Narrows, but not even native to the United States. She would give him a fair chance, but she would be keeping a microscopic eye focused on him.

"Your name is Gayle, yes? Sometimes I am not so good with names, but nice smiles I always remember." He was standing at her desk now, wearing a pair of blue scrubs, not the nice suit she had seen him in yesterday. She noticed that he was very fit, just under six feet tall by her estimate and well-muscled. 'Well,' she thought, 'I'll give him a point for the compliment.' Gayle believed in her point system for gauging people.

"That's right, you have a good memory." She was hoping she'd have some time to wrap up an ongoing problem with the purchasing department, but she wasn't having much luck accomplishing that task.

"I am eager to familiarize myself with the department and to know the staff better," he said.

"We have three staff this shift, counting myself. They're all in a CME class, but they should be back any time now." When she used the acronym CME, she saw the puzzled look on his face. Not only was he not native, he didn't understand English very well, she thought. "The other staff are in a continuing medical education class. You're a little early, Dr. Giannotti."

"Yes, I know. I hope you will excuse me for that. It is because I am excited to be working here. I have worked in big cities and in hospitals with three and four hundred beds. The work is too impersonal for my taste. I want to know the staff and particularly my patients. Memorial seems like the correct fit for me."

'Okay,' she thought. 'That's point two for him.' She was beginning to like the way this man talked, but then the others had all sounded good their first day too. She wasn't going to get too excited about this one, at least not yet.

"Well, it's a little slow around here at this time of day," she offered. "It should pick up a little later in the morning, but weekends are really the busiest times for us."

He smiled and Gayle noticed that he seemed very confident. After all, he was new here and she expected him to be a little unsure of himself. She prayed he wasn't one of those cocky, self-assured, take-command kind of surgeons, the ones who couldn't pass a mirror without admiring themselves, even though he *was* easy to look at!

"With your permission, I would very much appreciate if you would show me your emergency department. I see you are busy, but may I have a few minutes of your time?"

Now she wondered if this guy was for real! He was the head surgeon, for goodness sake. He could do whatever he wanted and yet, he was asking permission of *her*! He'd just earned his third point. She shuffled her paperwork into a pile. Purchasing could wait. "I'd be happy to show you around, Dr. Giannotti. Um...did I pronounce that correctly?"

"*Si signora, molto bene!* But please, you will call me Giancarlo when there are no patients. I think this is customary, yes?"

Gayle grinned. That was point four for him. Dare she hope he was for real? "Actually, it is more customary to use your title at all times, Dr. Giannotti, but thank you."

The emergency department was located on the first floor and was small, but designed to be efficient. It could accommodate ten patients. The nurse's station was centrally located and sided up to the medication and supply rooms. Any patients entering on foot, by ambulance, or by other vehicles passed the nurse's station first. Only three of the beds were located in a bay, separated by privacy curtains. The other seven rooms were accessed through double-wide doors bordered on either side by large, curtained viewing windows. There were two double doors located on the interior back wall, allowing convenient access to the hallway. Two elevators were located in the hallway, one at each end, along with the ED's waiting area, which was comfortable and was kept stocked with fresh coffee.

Gayle was showing her new boss the med room when Jeff and Monica returned. They had all been introduced to Dr. Giannotti yesterday on the grand tour, but she thought it prudent to remind him of their names. They both shook his hand again, Monica hanging on just a little too long, Gayle noticed.

Monica was in her late thirties, a competent nurse, but just coming off a bad divorce. She couldn't tolerate her husband's long road trips for his sales job and it had caused a lot of arguments and bad feelings in their marriage. His trips had gotten longer and longer as the arguments had increased in hostility. She had finally had enough and walked out, taking their two children. Gayle had known Monica since high school and knew she was looking for someone who wanted to be planted in Cape Narrows and take care of her and the children. It looked like she had just set her sights on Dr. Giannotti to be the next candidate. Gayle could see it in the way she was drooling over him, but that was just like Monica. Even in high school, she'd managed to run through at least twenty different steady boyfriends and that was just her junior year. Gayle knew that not much had changed with Monica. Monica warranted watching too.

Jeff, on the other hand, had been happily married to his high school sweetheart for eight years and had two children. He'd just turned thirty. After high school, he'd enlisted in the Navy where he trained as a medic, did his four years, married Lindsey and then had gone to the same school for his nursing degree as Gayle had. He was bright, a hard worker, compassionate and one of the funniest people Gayle knew. His sense of humor was legendary at Memorial and Gayle couldn't think of one staff member who didn't enjoy being with him. He was definitely a bright spot in the ED.

As they were talking, a taxi pulled up outside the ambulance entrance and Gayle saw Mr. Hutchinson get out of the back seat, followed by his wife. "Oh, dear," she sighed. Everyone turned to look as Lillian Hutchinson tottered toward the big double doors, hanging on to her husband's arm.

Monica was the first to speak, her eyes fixed on Dr. Giannotti. "Those two are always in here for every little ache…"

Gayle interrupted her. "Jim and Lillian Hutchinson are a sweet couple. We've tried to explain to them that they should come here only in an emergency and contact their doctor for non-emergencies, but they always come here first. I think they just like visiting and need the company. They're really no problem." Gayle shot a look at Monica, who pretended not to notice.

Dr. Giannotti approached Lillian and took her arm, as it looked as though Jim wasn't very steady on his feet either. They both had that slow shuffle of very old age, the frail appearance, the dim eyes and thinning, white hair. Jim though, seemed to have more hair than Lillian. "Gayle, where would you like me to direct Mr. and Mrs. Hutchinson?" he asked.

Gayle pointed to the middle bed in the bay and grabbed an extra chair so that one of them could sit while the other was being examined. Usually it was Lillian who had health problems.

Dr. Giannotti started in a slow but clear voice and asked Lillian what had brought her into the emergency room.

"I haven't ever seen you before. What's your name?" Lillian was looking at him, her eyes squinting as though she might have seen him before, but couldn't trust her memory.

"My name is Doctor Giannotti and I am pleased to meet you."

"What did you say?" He repeated his last name again, this time more slowly. "I don't think I can remember that. I'm going to call you Dr. Notti." She smiled and winked at him. He laughed, knowing full well she knew exactly what she had done; it was the smile that gave her away. "Now what did you ask me?"

"Tell me what is troubling you today."

"Oh, my dear young man," she exclaimed. "There's nothing wrong with *me*!" Her voice was as small as she was, but strong. "It's Jim this time. He can't pee! He waits and waits and nothing comes out!" She leaned closer to Giancarlo, her hand near her mouth, a serious look on her face and whispered, "Dr. Notti, I think he's having trouble with his prostitute gland!"

Everyone overheard and they all knew that Lillian believed she'd used the proper word.

It was too much for Jeff. He tried to stifle a laugh and made for the hallway doors. Before the doors closed, he could be seen doubled over, his hand over his mouth, his body convulsing while he tried to restrain the laughter. Gayle almost had to join him for fear of embarrassing Lillian, but kept her composure. Monica feigned a look that said, "Really?" Gayle had never seen a sense of humor in Monica.

She did give Dr. Giannotti his fifth point for keeping his composure, though he couldn't hold back a very wide grin. At that moment, she realized that she was going to like this man and after only giving him five points. Usually it took at least seven or eight before she made up her mind. This man though, was different!

Monica got Jim undressed, in a gown and on the gurney while Dr. Giannotti resumed his history, this time getting his information directly from Jim. He palpated Jim's abdomen and felt a full bladder, wondering if there might be a prostate cancer growing, cutting of the flow of urine. Just the thought of the word made him smile again. He asked Gayle to bring up Jim's past records on the computer so that he could take a look at them.

Jeff was back in the room, still grinning and throwing an occasional wink in Gayle's direction, which had her trying to suppress a laugh all over again. All in all, thought Gayle, not a bad way to start off the new kid in town. Dr. Giannotti was going to do just fine; she knew it.

Chapter 4

WENDY WOKE UP earlier than usual on Tuesday morning. The sunlight made its glorious entrance between her bedroom curtains like a symphony conductor at the opening of Beethoven's Fifth. She felt energized, a feeling which had escaped her lately. She was excited that spring had finally made an appearance and she could start planting her garden, but she also admitted to herself that she was excited to get to work for the first time in many months.

She hurried through her morning routine, giving Dexter some extra affection as she checked his food bowl. He lived outside in her fenced yard, which she referred to as his 'hunting grounds,' and seemed happy with his status as 'head dog.' He'd never displayed any yearning to return to his wild roots, although Wendy would have allowed it if he showed those tendencies. She would let him go if that's where he would be happiest. For now, he seemed to think of himself as the pet dog and Wendy treated him as such.

She pulled into her usual parking spot at Memorial and didn't want to admit to herself that she was thrilled to see the Ducati parked where it had been yesterday, right next to her spot. He was already here, but then she reminded herself that his shift started at seven, while she wasn't due in Patient Accounts until eight.

When she arrived at her desk, Mr. Dellette walked by without even a 'good morning' to her. It was typical of him, she reminded herself, but today she wouldn't think about her boss. There was someone else she had her mind on.

She wondered if she would see him today. The ED was down the hall from Patient Accounts, a short distance, but she had a full day's worth of work and only two coffee breaks and a half hour for lunch. The chances of her running into Dr. Giannotti were pretty slim unless of course, she had a sudden life-threatening medical emergency. Unfortunately, she'd already had her appendix removed three years ago. It was during her convalescence that she was offered the job in Patient Accounts. She had paid sick leave, but she also had her insurance deductible and out-of-pocket requirements to meet. The increase in salary with the move to Patient Accounts, though small, would help pay off her medical bills.

Wendy's phone rang. She'd just stashed her purse and hadn't even had time to organize her day's tasks. "Great," she sighed. It was going to be another one of 'those days.'

If it weren't for Tanya, the remainder of Wendy's morning wouldn't have been too bad. She surprised herself by getting quite a few major problems either resolved or chipped down to a manageable size. She'd forgotten to take her ten-minute break, which was all right with her, even though it meant that she may have missed running into Giancarlo. She didn't like to drink coffee this late in the morning and if she didn't drink coffee, the temptation to eat some chocolate was always too great; the vending machine was only a short trip down the hall in the ED waiting room. Besides, Tanya was in perfect form today, very disruptive as usual, and Wendy needed the extra time to do her paperwork. It was all she could do to keep from throwing a stapler in the direction of Tanya's fat head.

Tanya seemed like the fun type, always joking and pulling practical jokes, but Wendy had shared this office with her long enough to be more annoyed by her antics than entertained. She knew that there was animosity behind the jokes, that they weren't done in fun, and over the last two years, Wendy had come to dislike Tanya immensely.

Tanya's specialty was calling Wendy's extension pretending to be an angry patient. Wendy always had to be on guard for that one because she never knew if it was Tanya or a real patient; Tanya was good at voice impersonations. She'd made that mistake once too often and had been reprimanded by Dellette for being rude to a legitimate patient. Wendy had spoken to Dellette about the problem several times, but nothing was ever done about it so Wendy had finally given up.

Her plan now was to ignore Tanya, hoping Tanya would get bored and leave her alone. It was all she could do to push on with this current plan; it wasn't working so far. Between Tanya and Dellette, Wendy wasn't surprised that her attitude had been so negative recently, but after yesterday, she was hoping it would change.

The only other person who worked in Patient Accounts right now was Annie. She was hired after Jayne quit and had the desk nearest the hallway door. Annie was quiet and a diligent worker, but kept to herself and seemed unaware of the office tension pooling around her. Wendy liked Annie, liked her friendly smile and how she talked to patients. She was sincere, compassionate and very smart when it came to sorting out problems with patient accounts. She was especially good at dealing with delinquent payments, always respectful and kind with the debtor, who always seemed to respond by sending the payment immediately.

At twelve-thirty, her usual lunch time, Wendy went to the cafeteria, ordered a burger and found her favorite table near the wall. It was always busy at lunchtime, owing mostly to Chef. Even on the slim food budget the kitchen was allowed, he managed to turn out the most flavorful and delicious meals.

The hot entrée this day was braised beef with vegetables and was one of the chef's best dishes. Any staff who'd ever ordered it raved about it, but today it was a little pricey for Wendy, so she passed on it. Payday was almost a week off and she needed to get some minor work done on her car. The burger was excellent and much cheaper. She paid and sat at her usual table.

"I am so glad you are here, Wendy." It was Giancarlo. He'd walked up behind her and she hadn't noticed in her reverie about the braised beef. "I have something I wish to discuss with you." He had a tray with a plate of Chef's entrée of course and Wendy could smell its succulent aroma. "May I join you?"

"Yes, please do," she said and added, "That beef is delicious, you know. Everybody loves it." He was a surgeon, she told herself; he could afford it. She had no idea what he could possibly want to talk to her about, but was elated to be having lunch with him again.

She waited while he cut some of the beef and she could tell that Chef had succeeded again. The meat fell apart with the first cut of the fork; knives were not required for Chef's braised beef.

She was salivating and thinking to herself, 'Okay, I'm drooling and it has nothing to do with this guy! I need to get a life or take out a loan to afford lunch!' She was grinning at the thought and noticed Giancarlo looking at her.

"Those angels, are they talking to you again?" he asked, the warmth in his smile raising her heart rate.

"Oh, I was just thinking of something." She felt the blush, but knew it wouldn't be very bad this time; at least, that's what she hoped. She quickly changed the subject. "What was it that you wanted to talk to me about?"

He got right to the point, but did so with the same relaxed familiarity that he'd shown the day before.

"You told me yesterday that you once worked in the emergency department." He ate another piece of the beef and Wendy decided her burger wasn't as good as it was before that beef showed up at her table. 'Well, actually there are two pieces of beef at my table!' It wasn't 'politically correct,' but it was funny and she couldn't help smiling, thankful she had managed not to laugh out loud.

He was looking at her again, shaking his head and grinning. "*Vorrei darle le mie Ducati di sapere quello che vi dicono!*"

She waited for the translation; none was forthcoming, but he had a sparkle in his eyes and so she ventured to ask for one. "In English, I said I would give up my Ducati to know what they are telling you!"

"But the angels say I must keep their secrets. Isn't that what you told me?" She was enjoying talking to him even though being with him still made her heart beat fast.

"Yes, but that does not mean that I do not want to know what they say." He winked at her and went back to the beef.

When his mouth was empty, he began again. "If it could be arranged, would you work in the emergency department again?"

Her excitement was immediate. She loved the ED! She was fed up with Patient Accounts, with Tanya's jokes and Dellette's heavy-handed control. She was in a dead-end job and she knew it.

"I'd go back quicker than you can say *clostridium perfringens*!" She laughed out loud, partly at her irreverent answer, but mostly out of sheer joy at the prospect.

Her enthusiasm captured him and he laughed too; fortunately she'd caught him with his mouth empty. He knew the words of course. *Clostridium perfringens* was a bacteria, one that could cause food poisoning with its symptoms of diarrhea, nausea and vomiting. He was pleased at her obvious medical knowledge.

"Well," he shot back, "let us hope *this* meal has no *Clostridium*. But if it did, it would be well worth the misery, no? This is *molto squisito!*" Their laughter joined together and Wendy realized that she was now perfectly relaxed being with him, except for tachycardia!

"Then, my friend Wendy, I have a proposal for you." He was focused now, making eye contact with her and her mind was stuck on the word 'proposal.' She knew he wasn't talking marriage, but even so, she felt the dreaded rush of blood to her face and she knew that this time, it was going to be a full blown lobster emergency!

"Since you are in agreement, I will make arrangements and you will work with me in the emergency department."

After the first few seconds of initial shock at hearing his 'proposal,' her head spun with questions she wanted to ask him. Didn't they have all the staff they needed in the ED? Who would replace her in Patient Accounts? Would she take a pay cut? What kind of pull could he exert at this point to get her transferred?

Giancarlo was finished with his lunch now and was looking at her, waiting for her answer. She tried to calm herself down, but wasn't succeeding.

"Um…well…," she stammered. The questions were crowding out any ability she had to make an immediate decision and she just couldn't find the words to answer him.

"Please my friend, say yes," he encouraged. "I hope you are not angry with me, but I spoke to Gayle and she told me that you are an excellent nurse."

"But I'm not a nurse. I'm just a medical assistant," she corrected. She didn't want him thinking she was more than she really was, more educated and better trained. Maybe they didn't have medical assistants in Italy and he didn't know how lacking she was in those areas.

He was smiling at her and she knew that she was blushing: not out of embarrassment this time, but because the thought of getting out of Patient Accounts and working with him intrigued and excited her.

"*Ascoltare i vostri angeli,* Wendy," he said. "Listen to your angels."

She took his advice, realizing that it certainly had turned out to be 'one of those days!'

Dellette was standing outside his office door, arms folded across his chest and a scowl on his face when Wendy returned to the office. She knew she was in trouble again. The prospect of a tongue-lashing from Mr. Dellette, though, wasn't about to dampen her mood. She was still on a high from having spent lunch with Giancarlo and now she might be moving into a much better job: a job away from Dellette and Tanya, a job back in the ED doing what she liked most. Pleasant thoughts twirled around her brain like square dancers doing a do-si-do. She was having a difficult time trying to hide the smile on her face.

"That's twice in one week, Wendy!" Dellette was furious. The veins in his temples were distended and pulsating. She could have determined his heart rate just by watching them. The thought occurred to her that he might have a stroke. She was seriously worried about Dellette's blood pressure. She knew he took medications for it. What could she say that would satisfy him and get him off her case?

"I'm very sorry, Mr. Dellette. Perhaps you would like to call Dr. Giannotti and speak to him. He wanted to talk to me and since he is head surgeon of the ED, I didn't see how I could refuse." She felt suddenly bold and assertive and she liked it! Giancarlo was having a good effect on her, all except for lobster face!

"Maybe I'll do just that," he shot back, walking toward his office and slamming the door behind him. She knew he would never do it. He had no power to take on a doctor. He might be the reining Hitler in Patient Accounts, but if he had a problem with Giancarlo, he would have to follow the chain of command. That meant going to the Medical Board. Wendy knew he didn't have the guts to do that, but it probably made him feel better to make the threat, hoping he'd put the fear of God into her.

She settled into her chair and checked her 'to do' list. Line three of her phone lit up green and she answered it with her usual greeting: "Patient Accounts, this is Wendy. May I help you?"

The voice in her ear was almost a whisper and she strained to hear. "I saw you. I saw you with *him*. You'd better keep away or there'll be hell to pay." The line went dead.

She knew it was Tanya. First thing back in the office and she had to deal with Dellette and now Tanya. She was quickly losing the euphoria she'd experienced at lunch and Tanya would pay for that. Obviously the 'ignore it and it will go away' tactic wasn't working. This call however, was unusual for Tanya; she hadn't impersonated a patient this time.

She glanced in the direction of Tanya's desk. Until the call, she hadn't even noticed that Tanya wasn't there, wasn't even in the office. She was using a phone in an empty patient room, Wendy reasoned. Tanya would do something like that, had done it before in fact.

"Annie?" Annie's head was buried behind her computer screen. "Do you know where Tanya is?"

Annie looked up from her work and shrugged. "She left about twenty minutes after you did. She said she'd be right back, but didn't say where she was going." She went back to her work.

Wendy decided that she would find a way to get back at Tanya some other time. For now, she let the matter go in favor of remembering lunch and that didn't mean she was thinking about her hamburger!

Giannotti headed back to the ED, mentally rehearsing. He was new here. He didn't want to cause problems by requesting that Wendy be transferred back to the ED. He knew that Gayle liked Wendy, but there must have been valid reasons why she was transferred out in the first place. What reason could he give? The truth? That he was working at Memorial because he'd come to Cape Narrows to find her? He didn't think that would carry much weight. He would have to think more about this before he approached Gayle.

There was only one case in the ED when he came in. Jeff had gotten the patient into a gown and had taken her vital signs. Joan was restocking the instrument cabinet and Monica was nowhere to be seen.

"What do we have here, Gayle?" he asked, joining her at the nurse's station. The patient looked familiar. He guessed she was in her forties and very obese. She was sitting upright on the gurney, rubbing her stomach and belching.

"I was just about to call you. That's Tanya Winston. She works in Patient Accounts. She's complaining of chest pain and nausea, no vomiting. Says it started a few minutes ago. According to her there's no radiation of the pain. Her blood pressure is one forty-two over ninety, pulse is ninety-six, respiration's eighteen and her pulse oximetry is ninety-seven." Tanya belched loudly, then excused herself. Gayle continued. "She has no family history or past history of cardiac problems. She's borderline type two diabetes, but on no medication for that as yet. Her PCP is Dr. Costa. I've pulled up her past records on the computer." She lowered her voice and said, "We've had numerous talks with her about her need to follow a low-fat diet and watch her weight. It doesn't seem to do any good." Dr. Giannotti nodded and walked over to the bed.

"Gayle tells me you work in Patient Accounts. Tell me what is bothering you." As he questioned her, he listened to her heart and lungs, but heard nothing out of the ordinary. Tanya winced and rubbed her stomach. "Have you ever had this pain before?"

She belched again and said, "Only once, right after I ate at McDonald's. I'm pretty sure that was just heartburn. This is different though."

"And how is this different?" He was holding her wrist, feeling the strength and rhythm of her pulse. Jeff had placed the leads of the cardiac monitor on her chest and the tracings indicated a normal sinus rhythm.

"Well, I kinda felt out of breath when it started and I almost threw up."

"Have you had your lunch today?" Giancarlo was watching the monitor, which continued a steady sinus rhythm. Her blood pressure reading was heading back to normal.

"Oh yeah, I ate."

"Tell me what you ate."

"I had a pepperoni and sausage pizza."

"Anything else?"

"Yeah…some bread sticks, a Coke and banana cream pie for dessert."

"Are you having any stomach pain, especially here?" He gently pressed her abdomen on her upper right side. She shook her head 'no.'

"Do you think I'm having a heart attack?" She didn't appear to be worried.

He smiled at her. "No, I do not think so. I think you may be suffering from heartburn again. To be safe, we will do an electrocardiogram and order some blood tests to make sure we are not missing anything." He turned to Gayle and said, "And give her ten milligrams of Pepcid." He patted Tanya's arm, then went to check her records on the computer.

The EKG reading continued showing normal sinus rhythm. The blood results were back from the lab in thirty minutes.

Except for a high cholesterol and a blood glucose of two hundred-ten, all the other values were normal, including the cardiac enzymes. He would try the advice again, but was pretty sure Tanya would continue to do exactly as she had in the past.

Tanya remarked that she felt much better after taking the Pepcid. He approached the subject of diet and exercise and as he spoke, Tanya nodded her head. She was impatient for the lecture to end; she'd heard it all before.

"I suppose if I see you in the hallway, you'll be checking on me to see if I've taken your advice. Right?" Her tone was full of sarcasm, but he chose to ignore it. He just smiled pleasantly and told her to check back with him if her symptoms should reoccur. Gayle liked the fact that even Tanya couldn't ruffle his feathers and gave him another point.

When Tanya returned to her desk, she was met with an icy stare from Wendy. She was well aware that Wendy had pretty much marked her with a bull's eye, but she didn't care. She thrived on causing trouble and was so good at it that Jayne had walked out of the office one day, never to return. She'd never liked Jayne; she was too efficient, too perfect and too cute. So Tanya had taken care of the problem. She was going to take care of Wendy too; she promised herself that.

Chapter 5

THE REST OF the week seemed to drag on forever. Wendy and Annie were given a detailed and highly exaggerated account of the "heart attack" when Tanya got back to the office on Tuesday. She played up her episode of heartburn with so much drama that the only thing Wendy thought the story needed were some special effects done by Industrial Light and Magic. She went on for a full ten minutes and by the time Tanya was finished with the story, Wendy thought it deserved a Pulitzer Prize for fiction.

Her story, though, left Wendy with a big question: if Tanya was in the ED, who made that threatening call? Wendy spent the rest of the week a little unnerved and rattled, but shook those feelings off by Friday, dismissing the call as a prank or a new tactic in Tanya's arsenal.

Every day she had hoped she would see Giancarlo at lunch, but never did. She was eager to hear any news about her transfer, but also she enjoyed the time she spent with him. She would sit at her usual table in the cafeteria, picking at her food while watching for him through the glass doors. She assumed the ED was keeping him busy. She hadn't even seen Gayle, which was unusual because she and Gayle almost always ended up with the same lunch period at least three times a week. She didn't want Gayle to know how interested she was in Dr. Giannotti, but Gayle might have some tidbit of news about him, about how his first week in the ED was going. She might also have information about the transfer.

❧

The weekend weather was beautiful: sunny and warm. Spring had made a tentative arrival after weeks of rain and wind, and Wendy spent Saturday afternoon in the backyard playing with Dexter. He seemed as excited about the sunshine as she was. He was pure, unbridled energy with a fluffy tail and two huge ears. Those ears picked up every sound and every sound needed investigation. Wendy had come home more times than she could count to find little 'gifts' from Dexter: a robin here, a mole there, usually hidden in his favorite cache, the tool shed. Wendy fed him a high-protein dog food, but Dexter liked his 'treats' and as long as it didn't border on mass killings, Wendy was okay with his hunting trophies. He was an animal after all and a wild-born one at that, and she loved animals.

Playing with Dexter brought her memories of Mark flooding back, memories of all the animals they cared for together and memories of the black stallion, Envy. She would never forget Envy or what had happened, but those memories made her tears come too easily. 'Don't go there, Wendy,' she told herself. There was already a tear, which she wiped quickly with the back of her sleeve and then gave Dexter an extra scratch behind the ears. He always made her smile.

It was a productive weekend, one that Wendy spent tilling the soil in her garden space, anticipating the vegetables she would grow. The weeds and wild grasses were already firmly entrenched and by Sunday afternoon, she was tired, sore and ready for an early dinner. By four o'clock, the air had cooled considerably and the clouds had moved in from the ocean. It was too chilly to be outside.

She put a frozen TV dinner in the microwave and headed for her bedroom to get into her favorite pajamas. She would make a fire in the fireplace and cocoon in her quilt, she decided. And she would finish the book she was reading. She thought of Giancarlo and about how nice it would be to be wrapped in that quilt with him, but wouldn't let her imagination dwell on that. It only made her miss the times she and Mark had done that and those memories made her sad.

She did think about Giancarlo though; she couldn't help herself and she knew she was beginning to like him more than she wanted to admit. The more she thought about him, the more she realized that even though he was devastatingly handsome and charming, it was something entirely different about him that kept him in the forefront of her thoughts. True, she had been alone for almost ten years, but she was fairly certain she didn't see him as just a nice 'package,' one that she would like to unwrap, even though that thought had crossed her mind. She wondered if it was empathy. She felt sorry for him, for the tragedy of losing his wife. She knew how badly that hurt. His loss made her want to hold him and tell him everything would be all right. Or was that what *she* needed: somebody to hold *her* and make everything all right?

Regardless of the reason, she knew she was spending too much time thinking about him and wanting to be with him. It was all a fantasy anyway, she told herself, a romance movie she liked to watch in her mind. He didn't feel that way about her, had never given her any reason to believe he did. He'd said they were "friends" and that was all.

For now, she would keep her mind occupied with the possibility of working in the ED again. She went into her bookcase and located her medical assisting text books, determined to brush up and hoping there would be some news in the coming week. It was smart to be prepared.

Chapter 6

CHEF'S SPECIAL ON Wednesday was barbecued pulled pork sandwiches and Wendy couldn't pass them by. Besides, they were the same price as a burger. She paid for her meal and noticed Gayle at a table near the windows.

"Hey there, Gayle! Long time, no see." She hung her purse over a chair and sat down.

"Hi, Wendy! What have you been up to?" Gayle also had the pork sandwich. "I guess we've missed each other the last few days."

"Yeah, we have. Has the ED been busy?" Wendy was eager to get some news about Giancarlo, but reminded herself to play it cool.

Gayle desperately wanted to fill Wendy in on Tanya's visit the previous week, but due to privacy rules, she bit her tongue. Besides, she knew Tanya well enough to know that Wendy had heard the entire story, probably in graphic detail and with dramatic embellishments.

"Oh the usual, you know: a bloody nose, broken finger, some lacerations and a cardiac scare that turned out to be pizza and banana cream pie overload!" Gayle winked and Wendy couldn't help but laugh. That conversation however, ended right there. They both worked on the pork sandwich for a few seconds.

"How's the new surgeon working out?" Wendy hoped she'd sounded very nonchalant, but Gayle's look told her otherwise.

"Dr. Giannotti? Oh he's fine…and I do mean *fine*!" Wendy laughed so hard, a piece of pork fell out of the bun and landed in her lap. Gayle was happily married after all and it seemed so out-of-place for her to talk about another man like that. But that's what Wendy liked about her; she was fun.

"Come on, girl!" Gayle teased. "You must have some kind of hold on that man for him to go to bat for you, trying to convince me that we need you back in the ED. He told me he even cornered Dr. Couch coming out of a Medical Board meeting yesterday and explained how, and I quote, "cost-effective and prudent" it would be to have a medical assistant in the ED. He told Couch that it would take some of the ancillary duties off the RNs and free us up to concentrate on patient care. And let me tell you, Monica is all for that idea. She hates any task she thinks is below her station as an RN." Gayle's expression changed. Her tone was serious. "I think she's got her next guy lined up. Just watch your back, okay?"

Wendy got the message and was relieved that Gayle knew; nothing got past her. "Believe me, Gayle. I had no idea Giancarlo was going to ask me to come back to the ED, no idea at all." Wendy sponged the barbecue sauce off her skirt with her napkin, thankful that she'd worn black.

The fact that she had called Dr. Giannotti by his first name didn't escape Gayle's notice. "Well, I know nothing about that. All I can say is that you should be getting a call from Human Resources any time now. Dr. Giannotti told me Couch said that it was as good as done. And you know that I have always wanted you back in the ED."

"Thanks, Gayle. To be truthful, I hate Patient Accounts. I like the work, but between Tanya and Dellette, it feels like an asylum. I'm always ducking a verbal assault by Der Fuhrer and being physically assaulted by Lizzie Borden!" Now it was Gayle's turn to laugh.

"So…is there anything else you want to tell me about?" Gayle was never subtle, but she and Wendy were good friends and she knew Wendy wouldn't be upset. The gossip was that Wendy and Dr. Giannotti were seen having lunch together twice and it was out of the ordinary for a brand-new doctor to request an employee be transferred to his department. Gayle was happy about it, though. She hadn't seen a ring on Giannotti's finger and she had been trying to convince Wendy that it was time to start dating, that she needed somebody in her life besides Dexter.

"Like what?"

"Like…what's up with you and Dr. Giannotti? Is he married or what? Give me some details!" Gayle's face was bright with anticipation.

"There's really nothing to tell, Gayle. No, he's not married and we're just friends, that's all. We have a lot in common." Wendy tried not to give too much away, tried not to let Gayle know often she thought of him.

"Well, yeah! You're both pretty to look at! But there must be more than that!"

Wendy didn't care about the gossip or what people thought of her, but she didn't want rumors spreading about Giancarlo. She didn't know if he wanted everyone to know about his wife. She looked at Gayle, making direct eye contact with her, and said, "Please, Gayle, if you're my friend, let it go for now. Okay?"

Gayle was momentarily taken aback. She knew she had crossed a line.

"I'm sorry, Sweetie. Consider the topic closed. Forgive me?"

"Well, of course. You know I can never get mad at you!"

Their lunch plates were empty. Wendy was so engrossed in their conversation that she hadn't even realized she'd eaten the entire sandwich and hadn't even thought about how it tasted. She knew it had to have been good, but knowing she would be back in the ED and working with Giancarlo was even better.

Gayle checked the clock on the wall and got up, Wendy following her. "Well, I've got to get back," Gayle said. "I have to make sure Monica hasn't put the 22-gauge needles in the same drawer as the 22 French urinary catheters again. You know, I just realized something. Every time Monica has some new, hot guy on the hook, she can't keep her mind on anything. But you're not like that," she paused, picked up Wendy's purse and handed it to her, "are you? Looks like you forgot this!" She smiled, threw a knowing wink Wendy's way and said, "See you soon!"

At two-thirty, Wendy's phone rang. She'd been working intently on a particularly difficult account and was startled by the ring. She grabbed the receiver excitedly, hoping it was the call from Human Resources. She used her most professional, pleasant voice. "Patient Accounts, this is Wendy. May I help you?"

"You had your chance. You won't have any more. Say good-bye." The line went dead. She hung up the receiver, feeling scared for the first time. She couldn't ignore the voices in her head telling her this was serious and she needed to call the police. She tried to calm herself by taking a deep breath, but it didn't help. She argued with the voices: 'It's a hoax, nothing to freak out about,' but she wasn't convinced.

Looking up, she saw that Tanya wasn't at her desk. There was an opened can of peanuts balanced on top of a sack of paperwork as if she had just left. "I knew it was Tanya!" she exclaimed under her breath, the fear loosening its grip on her. Everything seemed to fall into place. Tanya had been in the ED when Wendy had gotten the first call, but she could have made that call on her way there. Maybe she faked the chest pain. Maybe she faked everything to give herself an alibi so she could make that first call. And now, here she was gone again, somewhere in the hospital pulling her damn practical jokes! 'What has she got against me?' Wendy wondered. Well, this time Tanya had crossed the line and Wendy was going to make sure it never happened again. She'd go to Dellette again and if nothing was done, she'd go all the way to Dr. Hazleton. There were laws about making threatening calls.

She was calmer now but nearly jumped out of her seat, banging her knee on her desk, when the paging system came to life, blasting its message: "Code Blue, Emergency Department!" Wendy knew the switchboard operator, Joyce, who was always calm, having worked as a 911 operator for several years. She was not calm now. Wendy could hear it in her voice. Something big was happening.

Giannotti dropped his freshly poured cup of coffee into the wastebasket and rushed back to the ED from the waiting area.

His nostrils were stung by the unmistakable odor of vomit and he sidestepped to avoid it. Gayle, Monica and Jeff were all working furiously on a patient in bed five and one look at Gayle's face told him things were very serious.

"It's Tanya! She's tachycardic! Her blood pressure is dropping!" Gayle was panicked and that surprised him. Jeff had the cardiac electrodes applied and the monitor was spitting out ventricular arrhythmia. Tanya appeared confused, unable to respond to questions, but at least she was talking. She was diaphoretic, the beads of perspiration forming on her face.

Gayle continued. "She walked in here a few minutes ago, complaining of severe abdominal pain. She vomited before we got her into a bed. She was diaphoretic so we were expecting it was her heart." Tanya was already getting oxygen through a nasal cannula.

As Gayle talked, Giancarlo watched the spikes on the monitor plot out a fluttering heartbeat, one incapable of circulating enough blood to sustain life for very long. The respiratory therapist had arrived. Monica had gotten an IV started, though she wasn't happy about the difficulty of finding a good vein. Not only were Tanya's veins collapsed because of her hypotension, but the veins were deep due to her obesity. "Should have taken that advice about diet and exercise," she said, not caring who heard her.

"We will give her Pronestyl, Gayle, and see if that converts her," Giannotti ordered. Gayle rushed to the med room to get the drug. He would try the less traumatic route to stabilize her heartbeat, knowing that conversion with electric shock would, in effect, stop what heartbeat she already had in hopes of restarting the heart again in normal sinus rhythm. He talked calmly to

Tanya, knowing that she probably didn't understand what was happening.

Gayle returned and the Pronestyl was injected into the IV line. They were all watching the monitor, waiting to see the heartbeat convert to sinus rhythm. The seconds passed and Tanya's heart continued its irregular rhythm.

Suddenly she went quiet, her body still, the cardiac monitor sending out its shrill alarm. She had slipped into unconsciousness. The respiratory therapist checked the monitor; Tanya's heartbeat was nonexistent and her oxygen level was plummeting. He tilted her head back and inserted an endotracheal tube, hooking it up to a resuscitation bag. He would breathe for her now, forcing air into her lungs as he squeezed the bag.

Gayle grabbed the defibrillator and thrust it at Giancarlo. He applied the paddles to Tanya's chest, shocking her failing heart, all the while keeping watch on the monitor. He was relieved to see the tracings reverse their jagged up-and-down pattern and settle into a weak sinus rhythm. She had converted. Her blood pressure was still too low, but not going lower for the moment and her oxygen level was coming up. There were looks of relief from everyone in the room; everyone except Monica. Giancarlo noticed that she looked uninterested.

"Gayle, please get her blood drawn and labs ordered. I know she just had them done, but something is not right here and I want to be sure we are not overlooking something from her last visit." Giancarlo had that feeling that experienced doctors sometimes got and good doctors wouldn't ignore: somewhere in his brain, a red flag had been raised. Something was not right.

Gayle nodded, got the supplies she needed and drew the blood, handing it to Jeff, who ran it off to the lab. The respiratory therapist had stopped resuscitating, but left the endotrachial tube in place, assuring a good airway. Giancarlo stayed at her bedside, checking the monitor. He listened to her heart. He couldn't shake the feeling that something didn't add up about all of this, but try as he might he couldn't pin it down, at least not yet.

After five minutes, Tanya's vital signs were not improving. Giancarlo wanted to see the lab results, but knew Tanya couldn't wait; she needed to be admitted to the ICU now. He asked Gayle to call the unit and let the nurses know they would be bringing her over. When everything was in order, Jeff wheeled Tanya down the hall to the intensive care unit and Giancarlo went with them. He knew Gayle would have him paged if he was needed in the ED, but for now he wanted to stay with Tanya until he could determine what was going on.

✌

"I'm not the one who's going to be in trouble with Dellette this time!" Wendy said under her breath. She knew nobody could hear her. Dellette was in his office and Annie had her head buried in a large insurance binder.

In those private places where her thoughts were born, those places she didn't want to admit she had, she knew she was looking forward to the inevitable confrontation between Dellette and Tanya. This was going to be very satisfying. Dellette didn't like Tanya any more than he liked her. Annie seemed to escape Dellette's wrath, but then Annie stayed invisible.

Tanya had been gone for almost an hour. Wendy had argued with herself about how to let Dellette know that Tanya was away from her desk. She decided that she would ask him if he knew where Tanya was, telling him that she needed to go over some files with her. Wendy congratulated herself on having the perfect revenge plan and the best part of it was that Tanya had brought it on herself.

In the middle of enjoying her plan for revenge, Gayle came into Patient Accounts, went straight to Dellette's door, knocked and went in, not even waiting for his response. Wendy heard the muffled voices coming from his office, but couldn't make out what they were saying. She hoped Gayle would let her in on it later.

After five minutes, Gayle emerged with Dellette close behind. They both wore the same expression, a look that chilled Wendy. He escorted Gayle to the outer door, then turned to Annie and Wendy. "Could I see you both in my office please?"

'Oh boy,' Wendy thought, 'this has to be serious! He said please!' Wendy looked at Annie, who was mirroring Wendy's same expression: 'What's this all about?'

Emory Dellette was head of Patient Accounts, but his office wasn't much to look at. His desk was strewn with paperwork, files scattered in disarray on every flat surface and nothing in the way of decorations, not even a photo of his wife or a green plant. It wasn't necessary to keep it neat; no one of any importance ever came to see him. He motioned for the women to sit. He took his seat and leaned forward, his hands folded on top of a ream of computer printouts, a pencil behind his ear.

"I have some bad news, ladies," he began. This was the first time Wendy had ever heard him refer to any one of them as 'ladies.' He continued. "Tanya is very ill. She's in the ICU. Apparently she's had a heart attack." He paused, waiting for a response, but Wendy and Annie were shocked into silence, trying to process the news.

"Right now, her condition is very guarded. We don't know when, or even if, she will be coming back to the office. The ICU has called her family and they are on their way. Wendy, go through her desk and box up her personal items. See that her family gets them." Wendy was silent, too shocked to respond. She nodded her understanding as he continued.

"I'll get in touch with HR and have them send a couple of replacements." Here he directed his attention to Wendy again. "I've been informed that you will be transferring to the ED at the beginning of next week, so tie up any lose ends you have with your accounts." Wendy noticed that the look on his face was anything but congratulatory.

She sat, too stunned to say anything. This was terrible! Even hearing that she would be starting in the ED made her feel sick. She wanted her revenge on Tanya, but not like this. She felt the guilt creeping up on her, covering her like a heavy blanket. She felt as though she was being suffocated, but mostly she felt like a traitor, like she was abandoning ship while the ocean gushed in through a hole in the hull. Annie would be the only person in the office until replacements could be hired.

"Well, we all have work to do," Dellette was saying as he stood up. Wendy heard his words through the weight of that blanket. "We're just going to have to plod through these changes the best we can. That's all for now." With that, he got up and opened the office door. Annie and Wendy filed out saying nothing and went back to their desks.

An oppressive silence hung in the air as Wendy went through the disorganized mess on Tanya's desk. She started with the can of peanuts, half of which were gone, and threw it into the wastebasket. She didn't want to see it, didn't want to remember Tanya at her desk, always snacking, putting on weight with every bite. 'She should have taken better care of herself,' she thought, trying to take off some of the weight of the blanket. Wendy thought about how angry she had always been toward Tanya and the jokes she played. She tried to convince herself that Tanya was just relieving the boredom of dry numeric charts, endless insurance regulations and day after day of sameness. It didn't matter what rationalization Wendy used even if it was true. It didn't make her feel less guilty for wanting revenge, for hating Tanya.

It was the same after Mark died. That wasn't her fault either, but knowing that didn't make the guilt go away; nothing did. She carried it to this day and now it was heavier than ever. Now she hated herself for all the times she had fantasized how she would get revenge on Tanya, even the plans she wasn't serious about, the decidedly illegal ones. She forced herself to quit thinking about it. She had to concentrate on what she was doing. Maybe she would visit the ICU after work; maybe Tanya was going to be all right.

She found Tanya's purse and car keys in the bottom drawer, along with two Snickers bars, a small bag of potato chips and some Oreo cookies in a zipped plastic bag. She put these into an empty box, along with a blue sweater which was draped over the back of her chair.

There was a small, gold-framed photo on the desk, almost hidden by stacks of binders. Tanya had shown it to Wendy quite a long time ago. It was a photo of her older brother, a typical military photo: serious-looking young recruit wearing his dress uniform with the American flag as a background. It was his boot camp graduation photo. Now the thought of that soldier being told the news Wendy had just heard brought a sadness that made her heart ache. She knew that ache, lived with it, wished she could push it away, but it was always there. She knew then that she had to go to the ICU.

She left the box on the seat of Tanya's chair and looked at the clock on the wall. It was five. Annie was putting on her jacket. Neither of them had said a word to each other since leaving Dellette's office. An impulse quickly engulfed Wendy and she wrapped her arms around Annie and hugged her. All Annie said was "thank you" and then left.

Wendy grabbed her purse. She felt she should say something to Dellette, let him know she was leaving, so she knocked on his door and heard his "Come in." She stood in his doorway.

"I'm going now, Mr. Dellette. Tanya's things are in a box on her chair. Did you want me to take them to the ICU?"

"Yes." He hadn't even looked away from his paperwork.

"Goodnight then," she said. He waved his pencil in her direction, eyes still on his work. She closed the door, picked up the box on Tanya's chair and headed out into the hall.

It was a few minutes past five when Wendy passed the ED on her way to the ICU. She wished Gayle was still there. Gayle sometimes worked late, inputting notes into the computer, especially after an emergency code. She needed Gayle, needed someone to hug her, to tell her there was no reason she should feel any guilt. Gayle knew all about Mark and the accident and knew why Wendy felt guilty. She understood. But right now, carrying the box of Tanya's things, Wendy just needed someone to hold her, someone to take away the emptiness she felt.

She passed by the ED without stopping. Even Gayle wouldn't stay two hours past the end of her shift. Wendy just wanted to get this over with: drop off the box, maybe talk with Sandy, the evening shift charge nurse, and then go home. The shock and guilt were making her nauseous.

Chapter 7

THE WAITING AREA for the ICU was located between two sets of double doors, just past Radiology, on the main floor. The outer doors were glass, but provided a privacy buffer against the noise of the hallway. The second set were metal with only a small window in the middle of each door and they led into the ICU proper. Both sets opened automatically with the push of a metal plate located on the wall near each door.

Wendy had been to the ICU many times, but not since transferring to Patient Accounts, and remembered the color of the walls: a pale misty lavender. It made the ICU seem so calm and peaceful. She was hoping those feelings would rub off on her because as she approached the first set of double doors, she was anything but. She took a deep breath and reached for the plate, hesitating.

She recognized him immediately through the glass doors, sitting in the waiting area speaking with an older woman. The sight of his Army uniform stabbed her heart; it was the boy in the photo, but he was a man now. It was Tanya's brother and the woman must be Tanya's mother. She looked like Tanya: same color hair, same eyes. He was trying to comfort her, his arm around her shoulder as she sobbed quietly, clutching a wilted cotton handkerchief.

Wendy felt her legs giving out, felt the nausea starting. She had to leave, she told herself. She would bring the box back later, some other time. It could wait, couldn't it?

The second set of doors opened and she saw Giancarlo enter the waiting area. He knelt in front of Tanya's mother and brother, taking the woman's hand. Through the glass, she faintly heard him say he was sorry; they had done everything they could to save her. Tanya's mother wept aloud now, her left hand clinging to his, her other wiping her eyes with the handkerchief. Giancarlo let her cry. Watching them, time seemed to stop for Wendy. She remembered a similar scene only the faces were different, but the pain on those faces was the same.

Giancarlo stood up and Tanya's brother joined him. They shook hands and Wendy could tell Tanya's brother was thanking Giancarlo. They spoke more, but Wendy couldn't hear what they were saying. She saw Giancarlo nod and then he pressed the button to open the doors. Tanya's brother and mother filed past him into the ICU. Giancarlo was now looking at Wendy. She hadn't realized that he had even noticed her.

He looked tired and stressed. The same sadness she had seen in him when he had told her about his wife hung on him again like an oversized coat. He motioned for her to come in. She was relieved that the waiting area was now empty, except for them. She could give the box to Giancarlo and not have to go into the ICU, especially now that Tanya's family were in there. Especially now that… Her thoughts trailed off into a black space, like a train passing from daylight into an endless tunnel.

She didn't know what to say to him. For a long moment, she looked at the box in her hands, finally speaking. "These are

Tanya's things. Mr. Dellette wanted me to bring them here…to give to her family." She felt the heat radiating to her face, felt her eyes filling, the tears inching down her cheeks. She could find no other words.

Giancarlo took the box from her and set it on a chair. He wrapped her in his arms, holding her tightly. She felt the security of his embrace, felt it pushing against her guilt, crowding it out until she was aware of nothing but his strong arms around her. His embrace gave her permission to let go and so she cried for Tanya, for the soldier, for Mark, and she cried for herself.

Harborview Boulevard ran from the hospital down the hill toward town, where it ended in a right turn onto Shoreline Avenue. Shoreline then ran parallel to the ocean and was rimmed by typical beachfront houses, packed closely together to maximize every inch of real estate. The lots here were pricey, not like the forested area across town where Wendy lived. The road hemmed the homes in front, effectively cutting them off from the sandy beachfront, but there was a large community park on the ocean side. In the summer, old men would spend hours sitting at the concrete chess-and-checker tables, while kids played or swam and parents unpacked picnic lunches. Today it was empty except for an old woman walking a small dog on a leash. It was almost six o'clock. The sun had just set on the horizon and it would be dark soon. She wondered if she was making a mistake.

At the end of Shoreline, the Ducati made a left turn onto Pacific Way and she followed it in The Beast. Pacific Way continued along the beach, but here the houses were on the ocean side of the street, giving them direct access. The traffic in this part of town was always lighter, except during summer. The only business out this way was Pirate Joe's Marina and Eats. Most of the traffic came from tourists who rented jet skis or sailed their boats into the marina, tied up and wandered into town. The locals moored boats here also. The moorage and rental fees helped sustain the little store and cafe.

Wendy liked Joe, who wasn't a real pirate, of course, but a personable former merchant marine who'd sailed most of the world's oceans and had a riotous story for each port he'd ever visited. The gold earring in his left earlobe was the only resemblance he had to the pirates of legend. It was a merchant sailor's 'badge' and signified that he had crossed the Equator.

She had only been to the end of Pacific Way once, when she was new to Cape Narrows and was getting to know the town. The houses at this end of town were large for the most part and expensive. They all tended to be Mediterranean in design, probably built by the same developer, Wendy guessed. She wondered if Giancarlo lived in the mansion at the end of the road. She could only imagine how beautiful that house was on the inside. On the outside, it was Spanish in design. Arches wrapped the house around a central courtyard. A large marble fountain sat in the center of the courtyard like a giant topper on a wedding cake and a rainbow of flowers grew around the base. Yes, she could see him living in that house. It was commanding, just like he was.

The Ducati pulled into Number 455. She parked The Beast in front along the curb and got out. Well, she thought, it wasn't the Spanish mansion, but it was nice and definitely Mediterranean in style. She could see a second-story patio with vines growing over a wooden pergola. The outside was a terra cotta colored stucco and the roof was made of half-round clay tiles. The windows were all shuttered and she could see a garden area along one side of the house.

"I'm so happy that you accepted my invitation, Wendy." He had dismounted the Ducati and removed his helmet and was ushering her to the front door. "I call this house 'Villa Bella'."

Once inside, she knew for certain that Giancarlo belonged in *this* house, not the Spanish mansion. The house was masculine and solid, just like him. The spacious entry led directly into the living room with its strong, Mediterranean-style furniture. An entire wall consisted of large windows framing a beautiful ocean view. She could see the yard behind the house and a swimming pool. To the left of the entry was a staircase leading up and a small hallway that seemed to lead to another door into the back yard.

"Your house is beautiful," she said.

"It is not my house. I rent it. But someday, I hope to have a house like this. Would you like some wine? I have Chianti." He motioned her toward the kitchen, which was located off the entry to the right. He was getting some wine glasses out of a cupboard. She noticed the wine rack next to the wall. It was about as tall as she was and well-stocked.

"Yes, that would be nice," she said. He poured two glasses, handed one to her and positioned his to make a toast.

"To new friendships," he began, fixing his eyes on hers. "May they be as strong as the oak tree, as fruitful as the olive tree and last as long as the cypress. Per la salute."

"Cheers," she said and they clinked glasses. The wine was full-bodied, sweet and delicious. 'Just like him,' she told herself, the wine helping her blush this time. For a split second, the events of the day slipped away and she smiled.

"They love you very much," he said softly, the same intimacy in its tone that she'd heard before.

She took another sip of the wine. He was filling a pot with water at the sink. The kitchen wasn't large, but looked well-equipped. The table had enough room for a large family. She wondered if he had children. Did they visit here? Did he ever go back to Italy?

"Who?"

"Your angels...they speak often to you." He was peeling and dicing fresh garlic, which he added to a smaller pot, along with some diced onions. She could smell the aroma of the fresh garlic. It mixed with the smell of her Chianti and she realized she was very hungry.

After meeting in the ICU, after the comfort of his embrace, he'd told her he needed to talk to her and his tone implied that it was important. He suggested they have dinner in the cafeteria. She knew she couldn't eat anything; the nausea still lingered and she had no appetite, but she didn't want to be alone, so she agreed.

The minute they had walked into the cafeteria, they both realized that it was a bad plan. The evening dinner rush was in full swing, the cafeteria full of hospital personnel and visitors. It was too bright, too busy and too noisy. Before they'd even checked Chef's special, he'd suggested they go somewhere more private. He'd asked her if she liked *gnocchi quattro formaggio*. She'd admitted she didn't know what it was and the decision was made: she would come to his house and he would cook for her. They would have privacy and could talk openly.

His little fantasy about her 'angels' charmed her. "I don't think it's angels. I just have a lot going on in my head," she explained.

"There are many happy things then, but there are sad things too I think."

She watched him add the small pillows of pasta into the boiling water. The cheese sauce bubbled daintily on low heat. Maybe it was time to tell him about Mark. He'd been open with her about his wife, open about her accident. She wanted, no, *needed* him to know. Maybe if he knew, her guilt would go away. There was something about him that told her he was surviving better than she was. But the angels spoke to her, telling her 'not yet!' and she chickened out. She didn't want to spoil this time, this delicious smelling dinner in *his* house. She wanted to pretend like she had been transported to Tuscany, far away from Cape Narrows, away from Memorial and away from what had happened today. She would tell him later. She took another sip of the wine.

"This wine is excellent," she said, redirecting the conversation.

"I am happy you like it. The wine we grow in Italy is much different. In America, it is bottled and sold too soon. We Italians let our wine rest much longer than Americans do."

"Well, it's very good. What was it that you wanted to talk to me about?"

He dumped the pasta into a large pottery bowl and covered it with the cheese sauce. The plates were on the counter and he dished up portions on each plate, carried them to the big, family table and then held her chair for her. "After we eat," he said, his tone momentarily serious. "For now, we will enjoy this meal." He saw it in her face every time they were together. She was interested, but he held back. He knew it was too soon. He would wait a little longer.

"Of course," she agreed. "Tell me about Tuscany. I've always wanted to go there."

The first bite was culinary ecstasy. It was rich and satisfying, the sauce caressing the pasta pillows like a silk gown clinging to a beautiful woman. Watching the satisfaction on her face, he told her again in Italian what it was called and then explained what is was. The pasta was made from potatoes, eggs and flour and the sauce from four different kinds of cheese. Wendy didn't even want to think about the calories. In the pleasure of its seductive richness, Cape Narrows disappeared and there was nothing but Tuscany, Villa Bella and dinner with him. She never wanted to leave.

Chapter 8

IF IT COULD ever be said that there were quiet days in the ED, Mondays would surely be at the top of that list. This Monday was no exception, even though the morning had been busy. There were enough patients to keep the staff continually involved, but working efficiently. There were no critical emergencies, no need for a SWAT team presence, no chaotic screaming from patients or staff and no major disasters that played havoc with the smooth operation of her ED. Even the patient who had come in with a plastic Cool Whip bowl of ice containing two fingers from his left hand was triaged with calm efficiency. Dr. Giannotti had examined him, re-wrapped his hand, ordered morphine for the pain, reprimanded him for removing the safety shield from his table saw, notified the hand surgeon and had the patient and his 'finger bowl' sent to surgery all within thirty minutes of the patient's arrival.

The only real problem today as far as Gayle could see was Monica. She was distracted, surly at times and bordered on being rude to the patients. Gayle was having none of it. She pulled Monica aside in an empty exam room and gave her fair warning. One, correct the attitude, two, take an unpaid leave, or three, quit. Those were her choices. Monica offered no explanation, but understood her options and had been eerily contrite from then on.

Where Giancarlo was concerned though, Monica was overly helpful, overly attentive to his every need and followed him around like a Justin Bieber groupie. Gayle had notice that Monica was wearing much more makeup than she normally did and had a new, tight-fitting scrub top, about two sizes too small, Gayle estimated. Monica was not bad-looking by any means and Gayle was purposefully keeping an eye on Dr. Giannotti's reactions. She could see that he was paying no attention to Monica's little performance and that scored him three points; his total now numbered nine.

Problems with the staff were the last thing Gayle needed in the ED today, especially in light of Tanya's death. It was troubling enough that Dr. Giannotti seemed to be so preoccupied. She knew he was bothered about something, but so far he hadn't mentioned anything to her. He had asked her several times if the autopsy results had come back on Tanya. Gayle couldn't even understand why he had ordered one. Tanya was borderline diabetic, morbidly obese, middle-aged and never exercised. A cardiac arrest in a person with that history was not unusual; case solved, to Gayle's way of thinking. And yet, he had gotten permission from the family to do an autopsy.

The bright spot of the morning was having Wendy back in the ED. She seemed more relaxed than Gayle had seen her in quite a while. She flowed back into the department routine as if she had never left. She had already restocked the supply cabinets, put away the clean linens, packaged and sterilized instruments and helped take several patients to other departments, including the unlucky guy with the severed fingers. She calmed a four-year-old while Dr. Giannotti put a few stitches in his scalp and was able to catch the little guy's mom in mid-faint before the poor woman hit the floor!

Dr. Giannotti seemed happy to have Wendy in the ED too, although Gayle still had no idea why he'd pulled strings to get her transferred. He took every opportunity to explain procedure to her, throwing in an anatomy lesson if warranted, and invited her to assist him with procedures so that she would feel more confident in her abilities. He took it upon himself to be her personal mentor, which was okay with Gayle, who had other problems to deal with, namely Monica.

Monica left no doubt about how she felt about Wendy, especially about the amount of time she and Dr. Giannotti spent working side-by-side. If looks could kill, Monica would be serving a life sentence for capital murder and Memorial's ED would be down one medical assistant! Gayle, though, was pleased to see them together. She liked them both and was happy to see their friendship growing.

Shortly before lunch, Dr. Mauritzen limped into the ED with a file in one hand and a cane in the other. He'd broken his ankle for the third time while snow skiing in Colorado at the end of February. It was a bad break requiring surgery and he knew the limp was going to be permanent this time.

He was tall and slim, about thirty-eight and what he lacked in skiing ability, he made up for with his brilliant intellect. He graduated from high school at sixteen and did pre-med in three years instead of four. After medical school and internship, he chose a pathology residency. He wasn't just the pathologist at Memorial either, but the coroner as well and there was nothing under a microscope or in a Petrie dish that had ever escaped his notice. He found Dr. Giannotti at the back desk working at the computer.

"Sorry these took so long, Dr. Giannotti. I sent the tissue and blood samples to the state forensics lab and asked them to fax the results as soon as possible. I wanted to make sure I was on the right track. I've never run into anything like this before." Dr. Mauritzen laid the file in front of Dr. Giannotti. In his eleven years at Memorial, he'd only done twelve autopsies. This made Tanya Winston unlucky number thirteen.

Dr. Giannotti poured over the file, his eyebrows knitted together in a scowl. Dr. Mauritzen continued. "Are you familiar with sodium fluoroacetate?" he asked. Giannotti shook his head and continued reading. "It's an extremely toxic rodenticide." Giannotti didn't know the English word. "Rat poison," Mauritzen explained and continued. "It grows as a plant in Australia, Brazil and Africa. The only company producing it in the United States is the Tull Company in Alabama. Most of it is exported to Mexico, Israel, New Zealand and Australia and is used to control invasive animal species like rats, possums and rabbits. Here in the U.S., it can only be used in collars on domestic herbivores, like sheep, to kill coyotes."

"So someone would have to travel to one of these other countries to purchase this rodenticide?" Giannotti spoke the unfamiliar word carefully.

"Yes, probably, or have it shipped or brought to the U.S., but that would carry heavy risks. Fluoroacetate is a white powder, just like some other highly illegal substances. It would not be overlooked by security and customs agents." Mauritzen rubbed his leg where it ached. He'd been putting in extra hours on Tanya's autopsy. This was the first time a death with suspicious overtones had made it into his morgue. "And I believe it would be highly unlikely that anyone would accidentally ingest a chemical as tightly regulated and hard to acquire," he continued.

"If a person could come by it, the toxicity warnings are pasted all over the product and are quite extensive."

"What are the symptoms once it has been ingested?" Giannotti asked. It was the fact that Tanya had exhibited neurologic symptoms in the ICU that had made him suspicious in the first place: muscle twitching and seizures that were uncontrollable even with anti-convulsant medications. She had gone into ventricular arrhythmia again and they were unable to bring her back.

"The initial symptoms would be nausea, vomiting, abdominal pain, sweating. That would be followed by cardiac arrhythmia, hypotension..." Mauritzen's voice trailed off. He could see Giannotti nodding in affirmation. "...then CNS symptoms as the toxicity progressed: agitation and muscle twitching. Seizures would follow. Fluoroacetate produces a metabolite that halts the citric acid cycle in the blood." Mauritzen knew that Dr. Giannotti could follow the pathology from there: too much citrate in the blood, no energy for the cells. "That's my report in a nutshell." Giannotti looked puzzled again and Mauritzen added, "The short version."

"Is there an antidote?"

"Not at that dose. Sometimes supportive measures work if the dose is very small. Your patient was doomed as soon as the fluoroacetate entered her body. It's my opinion that she was murdered, although I can't put that on the death certificate. I'm going to list the primary cause of death as cardiac arrest with a contributing factor of ventricular arrhythmia due to ingestion of sodium fluoroacetate. Oh, and another thing," he added as he stood up to leave, "sodium fluoroacetate tastes a little like table salt. It's lethal in doses as small as half a milligram. Her blood level was ten milligrams. If you look at my report there on page two, you'll see that I found undigested peanuts in the stomach contents. They were the last thing she ate before her symptoms started. Symptoms will present in about thirty minutes to three hours, depending on the amount ingested. With the amount found in her blood and tissues, she would have had symptoms even sooner."

Giannotti got up and extended his hand to Dr. Mauritzen. "Thank you, doctor. I appreciate your help in this matter," he said, shaking hands. He walked with Dr. Mauritzen toward the hallway doors.

"It would be a great help if we had some of those peanuts. That is, provided she didn't eat all of them," Mauritzen added. "I mean, it would help establish murder. You understand that I will be notifying the proper authorities?"

"Yes, of course," Giannotti said, his mind racing with everything he'd just heard. He almost followed Mauritzen out of the ED, but caught himself and turned to find Gayle behind him.

"Can we get a discharge order for Mrs. Keyes? She's hell bent on getting home to watch her favorite soap opera." Gayle was eager for her to leave too. The patient was an alcoholic and not a nice one. She was loud, obnoxious, a "frequent flyer" and caused an uproar every time she came in. Today was no exception.

"Yes, of course, send her home. Where is Wendy?"

"I think I saw her in room eight. She was cleaning up after Mr. Rosenthal left." Gayle was dying to know what Dr. Giannotti and Dr. Mauritzen had discussed. It wasn't very often that the pathologist came into the ED and she knew that Dr. Giannotti was expecting autopsy results. But it was a private conversation, so she said nothing.

He headed to room eight. Wendy was just finishing. "Would you have lunch with me please? I must talk to you." His expression was serious and the tone of his voice made it sound more like a command rather than an invitation. She wondered if she'd done something or said something wrong. Maybe he was going to tell her what he had wanted to tell her last week, when she had had dinner at his house.

Even after the gnocchi was gone, even after the second glass of wine and the innocent chit chat, he still hadn't told her why he needed to talk to her. She'd asked him again, and again he told her it could wait, that he was enjoying the evening too much and didn't want to spoil it. *"Questa notte è per gli amanti e gli amici,"* he had said. It was the way the words slid effortlessly off his lips, like butter on a stack of hot pancakes, making her hungry for maple syrup, that persuaded her not to ask for a translation, but after another sip from his wine glass, he'd said, "This night is for lovers and friends." Wendy had wondered which he considered her?

The two conference rooms were located on the second floor, west wing of the hospital, and were joined to the north wing by a skywalk; the only other departments in this wing were the pharmacy and laboratory.

Each room was decorated with typical executive-style furnishings: six expensively upholstered high-backed swivel chairs clustered around a massive oak table. There was a coffee station equipped with the latest coffee maker, the kind that brewed individual cups. There was an abundant variety of coffees of different flavors and roasts, and teas: flavored, regular and herbal. All the condiments that anyone could possibly want completed the station. It was almost like a private Starbucks. The potted plants up here were real, not silk as in most other areas of the hospital. These were executive digs and she was more than just a little nervous about eating her lunch here.

They were using the bigger of the two rooms, the one with the floor-to-ceiling windows. She chose the chair nearest the windows, the one that was bathed in sunlight, and wondered what could be so important that he'd insisted they eat here.

"I am sorry to have to bring this up to you, Wendy," he started. "I know how very upset you were last week outside the Intensive Care. I assure you I would not speak of that time to you again if it were not necessary." She was picking at the chicken piccata on her plate, impatient for him to get to the point, all the time feeling the sun's warmth on her back and enjoying his cologne.

"Tanya died from an overdose of poison." He paused to judge her reaction and saw her eyes widen, her lips parting as she inhaled sharply. "I am so sorry, Wendy. I tell you only because I need your help." He put his hand on her shoulder as if trying to steady her.

"No, no…it's okay. It's just that I'm so…so surprised! I mean…shocked! We all thought she died of a heart attack!" It was hard for her to gather her thoughts. "I don't understand. How did that happen?"

"Her cardiac arrest was not typical. Her heart was very unstable, then she started to exhibit neurological symptoms. I could not stop the seizures she was having. Then her heart started fibrillating again. I tried everything to save her." She saw that look again, the one he'd had when he told her about Donnatella, the one that made her sorry for him.

"That's why you ordered the autopsy, isn't it? I saw you talking to Dr. Mauritzen. What did he say?"

He had his elbows on the table, arms drawn up to his chest, his hands together as if in prayer. "He said the poison was very toxic, that she had no chance as soon as she had eaten the peanuts." Silence followed. His head was bowed, resting on his hands. Was he praying? He looked at her and continued. "In my country we have a saying: '*A tutto c'è rimedio, fuorche all morte*. There is a cure for everything except death'."

"Peanuts?" she blurted out. She remembered tossing out a can of peanuts when she cleared out Tanya's desk. Tanya must have died eating *those* peanuts! "I threw them out! They were on her desk and Mr. Dellette wanted me to box up her things. I threw them out!" A thousand questions fought for her attention, begging for answers and leaving her confused. Then it came to her. Tanya didn't make that second call. She couldn't have. She was dying at the time! Wendy was suddenly overwhelmed with emotions, fear being uppermost, all pressing in on her at once. She felt like she couldn't breathe.

"I am so sorry, Wendy," he said again, regretting that he'd had to speak to her.

"How can I help you?" she asked. She felt her eyes fill with tears. She didn't want them to win, not this time. She didn't want to be some helpless, emotionally fragile woman needing to be comforted, draining the life out of those around her, draining the life out of *him*.

"You already have. Where did you throw them? Do your remember?" He was looking directly at her, the intensity in his dark eyes throwing her off guard.

"Um...yes, I threw them into the wastebasket by her desk. Why?"

"Dr. Mauritzen told me that it was unlikely that she had ingested that poison accidentally. He said the peanuts were the last thing she had eaten before her symptoms appeared. If we can find the peanuts and have them tested, we can prove that Tanya was murdered."

Murdered! The word hit her as if she had been punched in the chest, all of the air forced out of her lungs. She hadn't even considered that! She had been so unnerved remembering the phone call that she had assumed the poisoning was accidental. Giancarlo was standing now. She got up too, unable to sit still any longer. She was feeling faint.

"We need to find the peanuts," he was saying. "Will you show me where you threw them?"

She didn't hear him. She was picturing the soldier again. This new information would deepen his wounds and leave him in greater pain and she knew there were no drugs that would relieve it. The tears won at last and rolled down her cheeks. She felt the warmth, not just on her back now, but pressing all around her, making her feel safe. As she mourned for Tanya, she let his warmth hold her.

Chapter 9

BY ONE-THIRTY, everyone in the ED had heard about the autopsy results and the associated implications. By two, the entire hospital staff knew and theories were being created faster than apps for an iPhone. After lunch, Giancarlo and Wendy had gone to Patient Accounts, only to discover the wastebasket at Tanya's desk had been emptied. It was a lot to hope that the can of peanuts would still be there; the maintenance staff cleaned regularly. But Giancarlo had insisted they look anyway.

Annie seemed happy to see Wendy. She nodded her head toward Mr. Dellette's door and whispered, "He's interviewing a new temp. They haven't found anyone to replace you yet." In her normal voice, she added, "How goes it in the ED?"

"Things are good, Annie. I'm where I belong and I'm happy," she answered earnestly.

"I'm glad. You deserve some happiness." She aimed a fleeting glance toward Giancarlo, smiled and said, "I miss you. Let's have lunch soon, okay?"

"It's a date," she promised and realized that this was about the longest conversation she'd ever had with Annie, not to mention never having had lunch with her.

༲

Giancarlo and Wendy were filling Gayle in on the autopsy results when Detective Brantmeier walked through the main doors of the ED twenty minutes after Dr. Mauritzen had called the police department.

Brantmeier was in his early forties, a little heavy with short, cropped, brown hair and a look that said ex-military from his spit-shinned shoes to his perfectly pressed clothes. He had over fifteen years on the Cape Narrows police force. He'd enlisted in the Army after high school, spending his four years as an MP. After his discharge, he attended the police academy, started working traffic detail and eventually got promoted to detective. There weren't many homicides in Cape Narrows, hence his extra weight, but he liked his job.

He approached Giannotti and Gayle, hand extended. "Dr. Giannotti? I'm Detective John Brantmeier. Is there somewhere we can talk?"

There were only three patients in the ED: a woman Giannotti suspected of having gall bladder disease who was on her way to radiology; a very unhappy two year-old who had fallen and put his top teeth through his bottom lip and a woman who had a nasty cut on her hand that had required sutures. She explained that she was boning a chicken while watching a culinary instructional video and as she put it, "The chicken tried to make an escape and my French knife slipped." Giancarlo had closed the wound with several sutures and Jeff was just applying a dressing and giving her instructions for home care.

The mother of the baby was holding an ice pack on his lower lip. He was not happy about that, but Giannotti had looked at it and told the mom it didn't need suturing.

"There's a vacant office across the hall," Wendy offered. She knew about this office, had dreamed about it at one time. "You can talk in there."

"And you are…" Brantmeier was looking at her, checking her out from head to toe.

"This is our medical assistant Wendy. She worked with Signorina Winston," Giancarlo offered.

Brantmeier shook her hand. "Pleased to meet you, Ma'am," he said. 'Definitely military,' Wendy thought and remembered the photo of Tanya's brother. "Maybe you should join us then." She got a sudden sinking feeling in the pit of her stomach. She had never really like Tanya. Did that show somehow?

Gayle caught Giancarlo before he left. "What about the baby?"

"He can leave. Have his mother keep ice on the lip if he will allow her, just for a while." He looked at Brantmeier and said, "I hope this will not take much time. As you see, I have patients I must attend to."

"Don't worry, Dr. Giannotti. I'll be as quick as I can."

They settled themselves in the vacant office, Giancarlo and Wendy taking the chairs facing the empty desk with Brantmeier sitting on the edge, facing them. It was the power position, Wendy realized. Brantmeier was above them, like a lion who rests on an outcropping of high rock where he can spot his prey more easily. She was feeling more guilty than ever now.

The office was bare except for the furniture: a desk, chairs, bookcase and file cabinet. It was going to be her office. There was talk around the hospital that when Dellette retired, his replacement would occupy this office so that there would be more room for new staff in Patient Accounts. The talk was that Wendy was going to get the job. She would be the new Director of Patient Accounts. It was her ticket away from a boring job and Tanya, but everything was different now.

Brantmeier got right to the point and asked Giancarlo to give him the details leading to the death. Giancarlo started at the beginning, relating the details of Tanya's symptoms in the ED and her rapid decline in the ICU. The neurologic symptoms, he said, were the reason he became suspicious that this case was more than a cardiac event. He had spoken to the family, specifically Tanya's brother, about his reservations and a permission was given for an autopsy. Her brother had said Tanya had always had a healthy heart and he wanted to know why she had died.

"Did Dr. Mauritzen do the autopsy?" Brantmeier had a notebook and pencil out. He had met Dr. Mauritzen previously during another investigation. Giannotti confirmed that. Brantmeier turned his attention to Wendy. "You worked with the deceased?" he asked.

"Yes, I was still working in Patient Accounts when she...when she died." Wendy had a hard time saying it; it brought up her feelings of guilt, not just about Tanya, but about Mark too. "I just transferred to the emergency department." She saw something change in his expression, but couldn't quite figure out what it was. She realized she was scared. Did her guilt show? Could he see it in her face?

"So when did you transfer and why?"

"Today is my first day in the ED," she said, not liking the way this was going. She felt a chill, shivered and noticed Brantmeier looking at the goose bumps on her arms.

"I asked Wendy to transfer to the emergency department two weeks ago. I am the head of the department and this was a move to realign the staff for more effective staff coverage. This was done with the full knowledge and consent of the Medical board." Brantmeier may have thought he had the power position, but Giancarlo had just set the limits of that power. Wendy hadn't heard that tone in Giancarlo's voice before this moment. Had he dealt with the police before?

Brantmeier backed off, put his notebook in his coat pocket and got up, extending his hand to Giancarlo. "Thank you, Dr. Giannotti. I think that's all the information I need right now. I'll let you get back to your patients. If I have any more questions, I'll get in touch with you." Giannotti stood up, acknowledged him with a nod and Brantmeier left.

"I apologize, Wendy. I felt that he was being...*difficile*... difficult. This is the word, yes?" Giancarlo walked beside her down the hall, his hand on the small of her back.

"Well, in America, we might even had said he was being an ass!" Wendy said. They smiled at each other and headed back to the ED. There was that matter of the screaming two-year-old.

Brantmeier was busy the remainder of Wednesday and for several hours on Thursday interviewing anyone and everyone who had even spoken to Tanya. He didn't have any other cases on his desk, hadn't had any for months, so he was free to give Tanya's murder all of his time and energy.

He brought in his "forensics team" consisting of one man who spent time taking samples from Tanya's wastebasket, looking for any residue of the poison. The poor guy also went dumpster diving out behind the kitchen searching for the elusive peanut can, but it wasn't there.

The only bit of pertinent information Brantmeier obtained all week came from Annie. When he interviewed her, he asked her if she remembered seeing the can of peanuts. She said she had. She told him she distinctly remembered it because she had gone to the restroom and when she returned, had noticed the peanuts on Wendy's desk. He wanted to know where Wendy was at the time and Annie said she was at lunch.

Annie told Brantmeier that she thought it was very strange because she remembered hearing Wendy tell someone once that she had a severe allergy to nuts. Annie told Brantmeier that she had mentioned this to Tanya and said she wouldn't have had another thought about it except that before Wendy got back from lunch, Tanya took the can and told Annie, "If she's allergic, she won't mind if I have these." Brantmeier had asked her a few more questions and then left.

That information led the detective right back to the ED and a serious, one-on-one interview with Wendy. Brantmeier had cornered her in an empty room; she was cleaning up after a procedure. Giancarlo and Gayle were in another room dealing with a hysterical teenager who was hyperventilating. She'd just gotten tickets to a One Direction concert from her parents and the excitement was overdone to the point of rapid breathing, dizziness and tingling in her hands.

Brantmeier had escorted Wendy back to the vacant office and had grilled her for twenty minutes. Where did the peanuts come from? How did they end up on her desk? Didn't Wendy have a peanut allergy? Did she get along with Tanya? Where was she when the code was called? Did she have any enemies, people who might want to hurt her? He finally let her go, telling her that he was sure he would need to talk to her again and warned her to stay available.

She was nervous. He must think she had something to do with Tanya's murder and even though she had no idea where the peanuts came from, he didn't seem to believe her. She had left the interview shaken, confused and needing anti-anxiety medication or better yet, needing to sit beside Giancarlo at his house, drinking Chianti and watching the gulls flying above the ocean.

Chapter 10

IT STARTED RAINING on Saturday morning, not a hard rain, but a timid drizzle that bathed everything in somber grayness and turned buildings into foggy apparitions. Wendy had finally gotten an appointment to drop her car off at the shop and was told they would call her in an hour with an estimate. She got her gym bag from the car and walked the three blocks to the aquatic center. She needed to exercise, to work off her fear, her anxiety and her confusion, but mostly to work out how she felt about Giancarlo.

The aquatic center was relatively new with an Olympic-sized heated swimming pool on the main floor, along with a small cafe tucked into a back corner of the building. Only soups, sandwiches and drinks were listed on the menu, but the food was made fresh and was excellent.

The exercise equipment was located on the second floor. The entire room looked out over the pool below, with nice locker rooms and showers on both floors. Wendy appreciated that there were enough treadmills that she'd never had to wait to use one. There were also several weight benches.

She climbed the stairs, changed into her workout clothes and chose a machine that looked out a front window. The traffic on the street was light and the cheerless sky mimicked her mood.

She hit the treadmill at a sprinter's pace. She didn't feel like warming up. She wanted to feel the pain of her muscles burning, to concentrate on that and not have to think about the past week. So she ran, putting all her effort into it, running from her fears, from her guilt, from the interrogation and from her loss. She ran until there was nothing but the pounding of her heart and the aching in her chest, her lungs ravenous for oxygen.

After eight minutes she stopped, exhausted but in a better mood. She showered, dressed and decided to treat herself to lunch in the cafe. She ordered a turkey sandwich on foccacia bread and a diet Pepsi and chose an empty table near the back windows. She preferred the patio outside in the back, but the rain wasn't permitting that today. She ate in silence, watching several drenched little sparrows picking at soggy crumbs on the patio.

She heard the familiar accent. He was at the counter, ordering a coffee. He turned to pay the cashier and saw her, smiled and approached her table.

"*Buon giorno,* Wendy," he said. "May I sit here?" He was waiting, holding the styrofoam cup of coffee, and she wondered why she wanted to tell him 'no.' She wanted to be alone, to think…about *him*, that was it. She knew her feelings for him were getting more serious, but she also had no indication that he felt the same way about her.

"Sure," she lied and then added, "I didn't expect to see you here." He was wearing a black, long-sleeved tee shirt and sweat pants and she had to admit that he could make even a tee shirt look classy. It was fitted and accentuated the contours of his toned body, the black color complimenting his olive skin. He sat opposite her, sipping the hot coffee.

"I had planned to take the Ducati for…a…spin. I think that is how it is said in English. But the weather is not so good. So I came here to see this place. Jeff told me there is exercise equipment and I am used to lifting weights. I have been so busy with my new job that I have neglected my exercise." If that were so, Wendy couldn't see that his fitness had suffered any. For a man his age, he was in surprisingly good shape. "And you, do you come here to exercise or for the sandwiches?"

"The sandwiches are wonderful," she said, knowing she was about to lie to him again. "My car is at Al's Auto Repair. I'm waiting for a call about the estimate. I just need something to do while I wait." It was just a small lie. He didn't need to know why she was really there, that she was trying to clear her mind, trying not to think about him.

He sipped the coffee, making eye contact with her, never letting his gaze wander. She'd never met anyone who could bore into her soul the way he did. It made her feel like he could see right through her and right through her lies, like he knew what she was thinking. Her head told her to keep quiet, to keep him at arm's length, but her heart was telling her the opposite. She desperately wanted him to know all about her and all about Mark. She wanted him to know how attracted she was to him. If she let it all go, emptied herself, maybe then she would feel better. Maybe she would know if he thought about her as often as she thought of him.

"They speak to you, but they speak of serious matters...your angels." How did he do that? Were her thoughts written all over her face with a permanent ink marker or something? His hands had assumed the prayer pose that she'd seen that day in the conference room and she fought the wave of her imprisoned emotions, fought them from escaping from her heart and leaving her broken and at his mercy. "But I forget, Wendy. No man may know what the angels say to a woman. Please forgive me."

Just that one sentence and all that she had struggled with, the pain and guilt of losing Mark, Tanya's death, the loneliness and aching for someone to hold her, overwhelmed her and left her despondent, struggling not to go to that place where she feared she would not return. She jumped. Her phone was ringing in her purse, jolting her back to reality.

"This is Wendy," she began, her voice shaking a little. "Oh…Yes, I understand. When can I pick it up?…Not until then?…Will you call me when it's ready?…Fine. I'll be waiting to hear from you. Thanks." She pushed the 'end call' button and slid the phone into her purse. His eyes were still locked on her. "That was Al. My car needs more work than I thought. He says it won't be ready until closing, about five-thirty." She looked at her empty plate, trying to avoid his gaze, remembering that just a short while ago, she had not wanted to be with him at all and now she didn't want him to leave.

"Is there somewhere I can take you until your car is ready?" he offered.

"I don't want to impose on you. I'd like to go home, but then I would have no way of getting back into town to get my car. I'll just wait here until it's ready." She felt the grayness of the day covering her like a shroud, leaving her chilled.

"I will take you home. When your car is ready, call me and I will drive you back to town to get your car. That is simple." His offer brightened her mood, but she was hesitant.

"That would be too big an imposition, Giancarlo. I can't ask you to do that. My house is at the other end of town."

"Wendy," he said, the firmness in his voice again, "we are friends. I will take you home and stay with you until your car is ready, if you will permit me. Then I will bring you back when your car is finished. This is less imposition, yes? Please allow me to do this for you."

They were telling her to say yes, the voices in her head. Her 'angels.'

"Thank you," she said. "I'm lucky that you're here."

"No, I am the lucky one. I get to meet Dexter at last!" They both laughed and walked out into the rain to his car.

They drove through town on Harborview Boulevard, turned onto Evergreen Way and drove past the Army Reserve Center. They were both silent. She didn't want to talk, not yet, not in the car. Somehow he knew that and remained quiet. She wanted to go home, but part of her wanted to be alone when she got there. Did her angels lie to her? Should she have stayed in town and waited until her car was ready? 'You can trust him,' she told herself, or were those her angels again?

As they approached Cedar Road, she instructed him to stay left and told him the pavement would end in about a quarter mile. He could park at the end of the road and they would have to walk to her house.

Diamond Falls cascaded almost one hundred feet down, jumping over the series of great boulder dams that tried to prevent its union with Fraser Lake below. It originated in the high mountains that boxed in Wendy's property on three sides. By no means would anyone classify it as grand. It filled the modest lake, which then generously fed a stream that snaked its way out of the trees and back toward the ocean.

The land was heavy with large cedars and other coniferous trees. Her house hugged the north side of the lake and sat alone; there were no neighbors. Wendy liked it that way. She loved the solitude, the forest and her privacy. Giancarlo parked the car and they walked the two hundred feet of path that hemmed the west side of the lake and led past her garden. When they approached the house, Giancarlo ended the silence.

"You did not tell me you live in a tree house!" His face glowed like a kid opening Lego's on Christmas morning. She laughed, letting her desire to be alone slip away. "I have said something wrong again?"

"Yes, but it's okay," she said, still laughing. "In a way, what you said wasn't completely wrong. A tree house is a little house built *in* a tree. They're made for kids to play in. This is a log home, a house built *from* trees. You're just having some trouble with your prepositions." She laughed again and decided she was glad he was with her.

"*Grazie*, Wendy," he said, returning her laugh. "I will try to remember that. But it is wonderful, your house of trees! I have never seen one before!" Wendy laughed again. Sometimes his face reminded her of a child discovering a new world for the first time. His dark eyes glistened and every facial muscle was dedicated to that broad smile framing those white teeth.

Dexter's 'hunting grounds' were near the house and the fox greeted Wendy with his usual enthusiasm as they approached. He was pawing at the fence, waiting for attention.

"Hey, Dex. You been a good boy today?"

"*La volpe!* Can I touch him?" The Christmas-morning look hadn't left his face and it made Wendy forget about everything except being a child with him, seeing the world through his eyes.

"Sure. He won't bite, but let him smell your hand first. Just hold it in front of him." Giancarlo did as she instructed. Dexter sniffed, looked up at Giancarlo and decided to give him the official fox welcome: he licked Giancarlo's hand.

"*Mi piace!* He likes me!" Giancarlo was thoroughly enjoying the attention from Dexter, who was doing an extraordinary job of lick-washing his hand. Dexter turned, went to the far end of his pen and returned with a dead, thoroughly rain-soaked mouse, which he dropped in front of Giancarlo.

"Wow! That's the first time I've ever seen Dexter present a gift to someone else! He usually saves them for me!" Wendy was truly astonished, but Giancarlo was taking it in stride, as if this sort of thing happened to him all the time.

"I thank you for your gift, Dexter, but I cannot accept. We would not want our Wendy to become jealous, would we?" He was petting Dexter now. "He is truly like a dog, is he not?" he asked.

"Well," Wendy replied, "he does seem to have the same fickle loyalty!"

Wendy loved her home, loved the solid cedar logs it was made of and the comfort she felt here. It was small but more than adequate for her needs. Its A-frame provided room for a cozy living area with a stone fireplace, a kitchen with small eating area, bathroom and room for her washer and dryer. A narrow stairway led upstairs to the only bedroom, under the pitched roof, and another bathroom. Her favorite feature though was the deck that ran the entire length of the front of the house and jutted over the edge of the lake. When the weather permitted, she spent most of her time there, reading or working on her tan.

It was almost one o'clock. Giancarlo seemed enthralled with the house's structure: how it was built, how the spaces between the logs were filled. Wendy explained it to him while she fed newspaper and kindling into the fireplace. It was cold outside, the rain coming down harder now, and it was chilly in the house. She needed warmth. The fire ignited easily and soon was spitting and popping as it consumed the wood and gave its welcomed heat in return.

"I don't have any wine, but could I get you something else? I have coffee, tea, lemonade and San Pellegrino sparkling water." She had the door of the refrigerator open, looking in as she listed his options. "Did you have lunch?"

"*Grazie*, Wendy. Yes, I ate before we met today, but I would take the water." He was seated on the sofa, facing the fire, and it seemed such a natural thing to see him, like he had always belonged there. He looked so relaxed, the plush cushions of the sofa cradling his body, his eyes fixed on the fire. As she brought the glass of water, she realized that it wasn't him her mind was picturing there. It was Mark. And it wasn't this fireplace, but the one at the home they'd shared together. The image had caught her off guard. 'He isn't Mark,' she reminded herself, 'and he doesn't love me.' She was trembling as she held out the glass. She was cold outside and inside she felt like she had died along with Mark and would never be warm again.

Giancarlo took the glass and when his hand touched hers, the loneliness and longing she had for someone to comfort her rose up from deep within her and she could no longer hold back the tears, forcing her to the sofa. With her hands covering her face, she felt the warmth of the fire, of her tears and of his arm around her shoulders. He said nothing, but held her until he felt her muscles relax, heard her breathing become regular again.

"I'm so sorry," she said at last, wiping her face with her hand. "It seems like I'm always crying when I'm around you. You must think I…"

He cut her off before she could finish. "I will tell you what I think," he said softly, "if you will allow me." He wiped the last tear from her face with his thumb. "I think your heart is wounded and you will not let it heal. I think the pain is always there and you would like it to go away, but you are afraid."

He was right. He'd seen her clearly again, but could he also see that she wanted him to make the pain go away? And if it would never be him, if he wouldn't return her affections, she knew the pain of loss would be added to what was already in her heart and she didn't think she could survive that. 'It's time now, Wendy!' the voice in her head told her: the angel voice. 'Tell him and let it go away!'

She began hesitantly. "I lost my husband ten years ago." She took in a slow breath and continued, realizing as she always did that it seemed like only a month ago. "Mark was a veterinarian and he was treating a large horse, one that was very high-strung." She paused for a long moment, wondering if she could continue. Giancarlo had taken both of her hands. She looked at him, the tears filling her eyes again when she felt the warmth of his skin.

"I was supposed to hold the horse for him, but I wasn't strong enough. He knew that." A gentle smile formed on her lips for a few seconds. "He was like you in that way. He encouraged me to try things. But I couldn't hold that horse. It was wild from fear and too strong for me and because of that, Mark died."

She had finally said it. In telling him, in hearing it spoken, she understood in her heart that it was an accident and that it wasn't her fault. Out of love for her, Mark had allowed her to help him, even knowing she might not have the strength to restrain Envy and because of the resulting accident, guilt had overtaken her heart and mind, leaving the grief fresh and keeping her tears flowing.

"You have thought all this time that it was your fault. Is that not true?" She nodded and wiped her face with her hands. "I too believed that my wife's death was my fault. Sometimes I still feel that way, but I know that these things happen and we must forgive ourselves. It is how we honor the memory of the ones who have died. Do you believe this is so?"

She thought about that, thought about what Mark would say right now if he could see her crying and living closed off from life and happiness, afraid to give her heart away and to love again. "Yes, I think you're right."

She knew she looked a mess. Her mascara was running, her nose was running. She needed to go to the bathroom and put herself together. "Will you excuse me for a minute?" She headed for the bathroom, already starting to feel better.

Chapter 11

HE PLACED ANOTHER log on the fire, waiting for her to return. He had planned to get to know her slowly, to reveal who he was once they both were comfortable with each other. Now he knew why he had impulsively approached her that first day he'd seen her. It was her sadness, a sadness he knew intimately, one fed and sustained by guilt. He had come to terms with his guilt years before, when he'd found out where Donnatella was going on the day of her accident. He'd left his guilt in the past and was now waiting for his future.

He noticed the framed photos on the mantle, each one fighting the one next to it for space. That one was very old: sepia in color, a turn of the century couple, perhaps her grandparents. And this one: more modern, most definitely her parents. Wendy had his electric blue eyes and her shy smile. And this one: the handsome man and Wendy together, maybe the last photograph of them as a couple? They were close, holding each other, smiling, celebrating, with champagne glasses held up to the camera. And this one...crowded behind the others. He picked it up, a small photo: two children, a toddler being held by a girl of about seven years, her face partially hidden behind the baby's head. She looked familiar, the blemish on her cheek, the way she seemed to hide purposefully.

"I'm sorry," she apologized again. "I know I haven't been very good company for you. I just didn't realize how messed up I've been lately." She had come out of the bathroom. The redness in her eyes was fading and her hair was brushed away from her face and he saw her natural beauty, saw how the guilt had hidden who she really was. He saw the other Wendy, the one in the photo with the champagne glass, the one in the photo he had in his wallet. His heart was captured by her face: the soft curve of her cheeks, the golden shoulder-length hair framing her perfect skin and her gentle eyes and smile. Seeing her now, he admitted to himself that he had wanted to be with her from that first day, to take care of her, to take away the sadness he saw and to love her.

"Is the little girl you, Wendy," he asked, "with your brother?" He held the frame out to her, knowing the answer already, but wanting more information.

"Um, no, that's Mark and his sister. It was a very special photo to him. He told me it was the only picture ever taken of him and his sister together."

"That seems strange," he said, trying to elicit an explanation. There was so much of her early life that he didn't know about, the little girl with the blemish.

"I never met her. She left home before I met Mark. She was adopted about two years before that picture was taken. Mark's parents didn't think they could have children, so they adopted her. Then his mother got pregnant with him." She smiled. "Isn't that the way it always happens?"

He nodded and said, "Yes, I know this happens often. But why is there only this photo?"

"She refused to have her picture taken. She would go crazy, screaming and kicking. His parents had a very hard time raising her. They took her to all kinds of doctors until she was finally diagnosed with attachment disorder. Have you heard of that, I mean the English term?"

"Yes, I remember learning about this. It is a terrible thing to cut oneself off from the affection of others," he said, knowing Wendy was in that place, wondering if she would come back and see that he was waiting for her.

"She never bonded with Mark or his parents," she continued, "and they loved her so much. When she turned eighteen, she left home and never came back. It was devastating for all of them."

"Did she ever contact them?"

"She lived all over Europe for many years. They did get postcards from her, I believe. I'm not sure." Wendy looked thoughtful for a moment. "I wish I could have known her. I could have told her that most of the time, the best things are found right where you are." Her thought trailed off. She was thinking about Mark again. "Tell me something about you. Do you have brothers and sisters?"

"Yes, I come from a very large family! I have three brothers and four sisters. They are all married and live in Italy and they have many children. My mama and papa still live in the house where we were raised."

"Do you have any children?" she asked.

"Donnatella never wanted to have children. She was much like your husband's sister, I think. She was too much concerned about herself."

"Yes, she sounds a lot like Mark's sister." She had no words to tell him how sorry she was for him, that he deserved to be loved, that he was special in the way that Mark was. She had had a fulfilling marriage with Mark and she knew Giancarlo deserved that too.

The room was warm now, the fire burning down. They were both quiet for a moment, each caught up in their own thoughts.

"She was American," he said. "Did I tell you that?" He'd deliberately given her a hint.

She was surprised. No, he hadn't mentioned that. "But isn't Donnatella an Italian name?"

"Yes, I called her that, but her American name was Donna." He searched her face intently, looking for a sign of recognition and he saw it, the concentration drawing lines in her forehead.

A long forgotten memory, buried so deep she didn't even know if it was real, stabbed at her brain, making her head ache. What was it? A letter maybe? Did she read something in a letter? But what letter? She couldn't remember and she wanted to remember more than anything.

His cell phone chimed. He was on call at Memorial this weekend. "*Mi scusi*, Wendy. I must take this." He paused, then said, "Start Lactated Ringers. Get a CBC, PT and PTT and call respiratory immediately! I am on my way." He stood as he pushed the phone's off button.

"I'll come with you," she said. "I can walk into town and wait for my car." She knew he could be tied up for several hours. It was almost four-thirty; she wouldn't have long to wait. Besides, she had to try to remember.

She was intubated, the respirator breathing for her. He saw it immediately in the color of her skin, the posture of her body. He lifted her eyelids and shined the pen light into the blackness of her pupils. There was still a weak response, but it would not be there much longer. The lines on the monitor confirmed what he already knew. Death had made its claim and he would lose this time, but he would fight for her regardless, unwilling to let Death win easily. He would fight for Monica.

"Have you called her family?"

Deanna handed him a stethoscope. She was in charge on the evening shift. It was on her face too, the look of inevitability. Doctors, nurses and paramedics could see it. They dealt with death often enough to recognize it. How they knew couldn't be explained to an outsider, but they saw it in the patient when Death had marked them.

"Only her husband was listed as her emergency contact on her application, but that was before their divorce. His number has been disconnected. The paramedics said the police have her children and will try to contact her family."

The Ringers was going in Monica's left arm. Labs had already been drawn and Giannotti was anxious for the results. "Do we know what kind of snake it was?" He put the stethoscope to her chest, hearing the respirator fighting against the muscle paralysis, then to her heart, hearing the irregular rhythm, knowing that Death was winning.

"Not yet. Animal Control was notified by the 911 dispatcher. Monica told the paramedics that she opened a box and the snake bit her before she even saw it. She didn't know if the snake was still in the house. The EMTs found her outside with her children. She was pretty panicked and already having respiratory problems."

Giancarlo was looking at the puncture wounds on her arm. There were two very small marks located on the inner side of her right upper arm, but very little swelling or redness. Too close, he thought. Too close to her heart. The venom would circulate much quicker.

Deanna didn't wait for his next question. "The nearest Cro Fab is over two hundred miles away. We don't stock it. There aren't any poisonous snakes in this area." Giancarlo looked up to see two men in olive colored uniforms come though the entrance.

"Was the snake found?" he called to them. If they could get the anti-venom here by helicopter, Monica might have a chance and Death might not win this time.

The taller of the men looked rather shocked as he approached Giannotti, handing him a small, paper-bound book. The page was marked and as he opened the book and found the place, Giannotti saw the photo. Underneath it read: *Dendroapsis Polylepsis*. Black Mamba.

"Are you sure of your identification?"

The other man opened a paper bag. He carefully pulled out the snake's head attached to about six inches of its body, which was small and slender. He took his pen and lifted the mouth open, revealing the black color inside. That's when Giannotti knew his chance was gone. Monica was bitten by the second most deadly snake in the world, the one whose bite was called the 'kiss of death,' and he knew that even if the Cro Fab arrived in time, it would do no good. She would need anti-venom specifically for the mamba. Finding mamba anti-venom in the United States was almost impossible and the bite of the black mamba was one hundred percent fatal, unless treated immediately. It could kill in as little as thirty minutes. Monica was out of time.

Sacred Love

The cardiac monitor alarmed. A male nurse positioned himself and started CPR. A second nurse had the defibrillator ready, waiting for Giancarlo to take it, but he decided he would not do that to Monica, would not put her lifeless body through the trauma of a resuscitation he knew was already hopeless. The snake's venom had paralyzed the muscles she needed to breathe and there was nothing that would undo that. He looked at the clock on the wall and said, "I am calling the time of death at five-ten." Giancarlo had a hundred questions and he knew the police would too.

Chapter 12

AT FIVE, AL came into the customer waiting area and told Wendy her car was ready. She was surprised Al had finished early; that wasn't like him. Wendy wondered if maybe her pacing in his waiting area had anything to do with it, but she was thankful for whatever motivated him. She paid him with her VISA card and left, The Beast now purring like a pampered house cat.

She still couldn't remember the letter, if it even was a letter. Had Mark told her about it? Had she seen it, read it herself? These questions paled in comparison to the underlying question she couldn't ignore: what were the chances of something like this happening? And then, there was the question she refused to confront. She put it away. She locked it up because it would change everything between them and she didn't want anything to change, not yet and maybe not ever.

Memorial was on her way home. She drove out Harborview Boulevard and when she got to the turn off onto Evergreen Way, she didn't take it, but continued on Harborview toward the hospital. It was like The Beast had a mind of its own, keeping her hands from turning the steering wheel, driving her toward her fears, telling her she would be miserable until she knew for sure. But she had to remember first. She needed more information about Donnatella, about what she may have told Giancarlo about her family in the United States.

She pulled into the parking lot, noticing the unmarked police car parked by the main entrance. 'It must be Brantmeier,' she thought. Wendy was very uncomfortable the last time he had talked to her and she didn't want to show up now and give him another chance to grill her. But her need to talk to Giancarlo overruled her intimidation and she headed for the ED entrance, finding Brantmeier and Giancarlo having an animated discussion in Room One. The door was closed and she couldn't hear what was being said. Giancarlo, though, didn't look happy.

She saw Deanna at the nurse's station, working on the computer, but didn't want to talk to her. How would she explain why she was in the ED after her shift had ended? There were already those knowing looks passing between the staff in the ED whenever she and Giancarlo were together, on the day shift anyway. Wendy had noticed them and didn't want rumors to start on evening shift too.

The door to Room One opened and the men walked out, Brantmeier giving her a nod as he left. No smile, but then no accusatory looks thrown her way either.

"Wendy, what are you doing here?" He wasn't smiling and Wendy heard something in his voice that made her suddenly cold. Was he angry, mad at her for following him to the ED?

"I was just on my way home." She was hesitant, so she opted for a partial truth. "I wanted to thank you again for all you did today. I really appreciated it."

He was still in his black shirt and sweat pants and she realized then that she had spent most of the day with him. She searched his face, waiting to see if his expression would change, wishing she had just driven home.

"You do not need to thank me. I am happy that you allowed me to help." She was relieved to see his face soften, the tension leaving. "Have you had dinner?" She shook her head 'no.' There was still something there in his face, but she couldn't tell what it was. The brightness of his eyes was gone. He looked exhausted and worried. Maybe it had something to do with the call he'd gotten at her house. "I am finished here for now. Would you like to get something to eat?"

"Yes, that would be nice. I'm really hungry." At least that was the full truth.

It had been such a long day. Maybe the rain made it seem like that, but as they walked outside, Wendy saw that the sky was clear. From Memorial she could see Cape Narrows below the hill where the hospital sat. The stars were just now starting to appear above her as the sun touched the edge of the ocean, escorted by wisps of pink and dark purple clouds. The light breeze from the ocean reminded her that spring had only just arrived; it was cold, almost biting.

Her phone rang and she thought seriously about not answering it, but reached into her purse anyway and looked at the screen. All it said was 'private caller.'

"Hello?"

And then the same muffled voice spoke, sending a shiver throughout her body. "Your time is up." The line went dead. Her breathing was shallow and rapid, her hands trembling. She couldn't even put the phone away, but stood looking at it as it shook in her hands, afraid to move, unable to speak. She felt the blood draining from her face and her legs becoming weak.

"Wendy, what is it?" He was facing her, his hands on her upper arms, holding her up. "Tell me what is wrong." She felt his grip, but couldn't talk. Her mouth was too dry to form words. "Come back into the building."

He started to lead her back toward the ED entrance, but she didn't want to go there. She didn't want to have to explain about the calls with Deanna and the rest of the staff there. She didn't want to be treated like a patient. She broke free of his grip.

"Please, just walk me to my car. Please, Giancarlo!" she pleaded.

She couldn't get the key in the lock. He took the keys and unlocked the door for her. She sat in the driver's seat while he got in the passenger's side, waiting for her to calm down, not pressing her for an explanation.

When her heart rate slowed, she took a deep breath and looked at her hands. This was her problem. She could work it out. After ten years without Mark, she was used to handling her own problems. But she was more scared than she had ever been in her life and she needed Giancarlo.

"I've been getting threatening calls." She waited for his response, but he remained quiet, letting her work through her thoughts. "That was the third one and I'm really scared." Her hands were still shaking as she brushed the hair out of her eyes. His hand gently caught hers.

"Do you know who is doing this?" Her hand was cold, the kind of cold that reminded him that Monica was in the morgue and her hand was cold too.

"I thought it was Tanya when I got the first call. She was always doing things like that, making anonymous calls, using different voices. She thinks it's..." Wendy caught herself and began again. "She *thought* it was funny. But then I got the second call and realized later that it was made just a few minutes before I heard the code from ED. Tanya was...dying when the second call was made. That's when I got scared, but with Tanya's death and then finding out it might be murder and Brantmeier questioning me, I just…" She couldn't finish, didn't want to relive the bad memories of the past two weeks.

"So you think it is a woman? What does she say?" He was still holding her hand, noticing she was not shaking as much.

"I can't tell if it's a man or a woman. The voice is almost a whisper. The first time, the voice said, 'I saw you with him. You'd better keep away.' That was the day Tanya was in the ED with heartburn. The second call said, 'You had your chance, there won't be any more. Say good-bye'." Just repeating the caller's threats caused a fear that clutched her throat and made it difficult to breathe. Giancarlo held his next question until he could see she was a little more relaxed.

"And this call. What did the voice say?" He saw the color leave her face again and her hand got colder.

"Your time is up." Wendy's heart was pounding in her chest again. She couldn't go home; she was scared to be alone. She didn't know what to do.

"We must call Detective Brantmeier, Wendy. These calls may be related to the murders." As soon as he'd said the plural form, he knew he'd made a mistake. He didn't want her to find out like this. He planned to tell her over dinner, somewhere warm and quiet. "Wendy, I am very concerned for you, for your safety."

In her shock, she barely had the breath to ask him. "Was there another murder? Who was it?" Her eyes were now pleading with him.

He started slowly, telling her only the details he thought she could bear to hear. "It was about Monica, that call I received at your house. She was bitten by a very deadly snake and did not survive." He waited for the information to connect, hoping she would be satisfied with only what he had told her.

"Why do you think it was murder? There are snakes around here, aren't there? Rattlesnakes? Couldn't it have been an accident?" He remembered she hadn't lived in Cape Narrows very long and the subject of snakes had probably never come up. He had to say more, to distress her even further and he hated doing it, but she needed to know. She needed to protect herself, to find out for sure if the murders were connected to her menacing calls.

"Wendy," he began as gently as possible, "it was a black mamba that bit her. It is a snake that is native to Africa. She told the paramedics that she found a box on her doorstep and when she opened it, she was bitten." He could see that it was sinking in now. She understood how impossible it was that being bitten by *that* snake in Cape Narrows could ever have been an accident, especially since it arrived in a box.

She locked on to his eyes. "I don't want to be alone." She said it simply, the full realization of her predicament finally clear in her mind. "We have to call Brantmeier."

Brantmeier was not happy about being called to Memorial for a second time in as many hours. Homicides were rare in Cape Narrows and he now had two unsolved cases on his desk and he was getting nervous. He knew the pressure would be on to get them solved quickly and the perpetrator locked up. News of Monica's death had already leaked out to the media, setting a record for the quickest news leak in Cape Narrows's history, even having made the evening news at the state level. Black mamba bites were almost nonexistent in the United States as a whole and this one made for good ratings for the news media. He had noticed the network news vans gathering outside his office building already. He wasn't used to this kind of pressure, even when he was in the military. Back then, it was a few drunken fights between GI's, maybe a stabbing or AWOL, but nothing like this. It was almost six o'clock and he wanted to go home.

He met Giannotti and Wendy in the empty office once again and had Wendy give him details about the calls. In order to connect the harassing calls with the murders, he told her he needed to establish some kind of link between Tanya, Monica and herself. Who and what did they have in common? Was it coincidental that they all worked at Memorial or relevant? Had Tanya or Monica ever spoken about receiving threatening calls? What relationships with other people did they have in common?

Brantmeier wasn't hopeful that he'd gotten any usable information that would help him link her calls with the murders, but told her he wouldn't discount the connection yet. He would work on that angle. He was going to try to trace the calls and asked if he could see her cell phone. He needed to check every possibility he could; the media would be watching.

At the end of the questioning, he reminded Wendy that even in light of the murders of her co-workers, the calls could be just a prank. Kids especially were known to do this and in case Wendy wasn't aware, Brantmeier reminded her that it was spring break. Prank call complaints always increased during spring break. He advised her to be cautious, inform him if she had any information or further calls, but to go home and try to maintain some normalcy until there was clear evidence that she was in danger.

Wendy left the hospital not feeling at all comforted by anything Brantmeier said. At least, the detective's attitude toward her was better than the last interview. He seemed genuinely concerned for her safety.

It was much colder when Giancarlo walked her back to her car; the wind had picked up considerably. She shivered and hugged her lightweight coat to her body, processing the conversation with Brantmeier.

When they approached her car, Giancarlo took her arms as he had done before and turned her so that she faced him.

"You should not be alone tonight," he said, his grip firm, holding her in place like the wind might blow her away. She didn't know what to say to him. She didn't want to go home, not by herself. She was sure of that. "I hope you will not think that I am taking liberties with our friendship Wendy, but I would like to stay with you tonight, to make sure you are safe. May I do that?"

Now she was literally speechless. Her brain screamed at her, telling her to tell him 'yes' and her fear agreed. But there was that part of her that she heard the loudest, that told her there was more danger in having Giancarlo stay with her that there was from whomever was making the calls. That fear was real too: fear of becoming too involved with a man she hardly knew, fear of giving herself away only to end up alone again, fear that she could not trust herself with him.

He waited patiently for her answer, realizing that he had just put her in an awkward position, but he was worried about her. He had just found her and didn't want anything to take her away from him. He couldn't save Donnatella or Tanya or Monica. He didn't have the power to stop what happened to them, but he could protect Wendy before anything happened, stop a tragedy from happening in the first place.

Her thoughts quieted until there was just one left, speaking to her clearly. Maybe it was reason or maybe it was her angels. She told him 'yes' and it was done.

Chapter 13

IT WAITED IN the background of their conversation, between the bites of barbecued brisket and potato salad they'd picked up on the way to her house. Wendy and Giancarlo held it back until there was no food on their plates, no other pleasant conversation and only an uncomfortable silence between them. She watched him hold his half-empty cup of coffee, running his fingers on its smooth surface. She was like that cup, she told herself: half-empty.

He finally broke their silence. "I think you are uncomfortable that I am here tonight."

His look reminded her of a child caught stealing the proverbial cookie. It wasn't punishment that was uppermost on the child's mind, but the regret of having broken the trust of his parents. She had felt his reticence at suggesting he stay the night and now it only made her desire him more. She refused to lie to him and if he could deal with her honesty, he could keep her friendship. If not, it was better that he leave now before she fell completely in love with him.

"Yes, I am," she replied. "But I believe you understand why that is."

"Yes, I know. It is not right that I stay the night with you. We have both been hurt and carry that pain with us and we are both lonely. Because of that, it is too easy to become intimate with each other, believing it will make the pain and loneliness go away." His directness made her ashamed of the desire she had for him, the thoughts of making love to him.

"I know that you are concerned about my safety. I appreciate that and…"

He interrupted her, locking eyes with her. "Do you trust me, Wendy?"

She heard the angels, heard what they were saying to her, but could she say it to him? She could feel her heart pumping hard in her chest. "Yes, I trust you Giancarlo." She swallowed. "I don't know if I can trust myself."

He smiled at the honesty of her confession, taken by her openness and aware that it was getting harder to control himself and to wait for the right time.

"My Papa taught us children what it means to have a sacred love, to give yourself to one person only. When that person is gone, you wonder if you can give yourself again, if love can be sacred the second time. Someday you will find the answer to that question, Wendy, but you will not find it tonight."

She wanted to tell him she was ready tonight, ready to find the answer with him. She knew he liked her and thought of her as a friend, but she wanted him to be in love with her. She didn't want him to be the knight in shining armor ready to rescue her from a lonely, miserable life. She knew that could never turn into the sacred love he spoke of. More than anything, she wanted his commitment to love her.

"I will go, if you want," he said, "but if I stay, I promise that I will protect you, even from yourself."

The seriousness of his promise was all over his face; she could see it. She felt relieved that it was out in the open. She had to smile though, picturing herself running through the house after him and him with his eyes wide, saying something like "My Mama warned me about women like you!" She laughed at the absurdity of that vision and then looked at him. He was shaking his head, his entire face lit with a smile.

The house was cold. She had fed Dexter when they arrived, got him set for the night and then they both had gotten right to the barbecue. It was now just past eight and Wendy was starting to feel the effects of the day's stress. Her thigh muscles ached from her overly strenuous workout that morning. She'd had the shock of the phone call and Monica's death and the paralyzing fear that followed and now, she'd had to come to terms with her feelings about Giancarlo staying the night. She needed Ativan or maybe Valium, not that she ever considered taking medication for anxiety or to relax, but that didn't mean she didn't think about it once in a while. For now, a nice fire going in the fireplace would suffice.

She had no more formed the thought than Giancarlo got up from the table and said, "I will make a fire, if you would like." How did he do that, she wondered?

"That would be great," she said. "Everything should be right there. If you need more wood, the stack is out behind the house. There's kindling already cut."

While he was outside, she tossed the empty take-out containers in the trash and wiped the kitchen table. She reprimanded herself out loud. "You should have come home and cleaned house when you had the chance but no, you had to get all involved in murder, mayhem and a sleepover with every woman's fantasy lover!" She laughed, then blushed. She knew she was feeling better, more relaxed. She was smiling when he came back in. She looked directly at him standing there, his arms loaded with wood, and said, "It's not my angels this time, believe me!"

By ten, neither of them could keep from yawning. They were too comfortable, swaddled in the plushness of the sofa, the fire burning low before them. "I have to get some sleep. I'm sorry, but all I can offer you is the sofa," she said.

"This will be wonderful, Wendy," He replied. He'd slept on a sofa many times when Donnatella forbid him to share their bed. He didn't mind Wendy's sofa at all.

"I'll get some blankets and a pillow." She climbed the stairs to her bedroom and found the extra blankets and a pillow tucked far back in her closet. As she picked up the blankets, she saw it where the closet light never reached: a familiar box, one that she remembered had belonged to Mark's parents. In an instant she felt her heart skip a beat. She remembered what was in the box!

The temptation to open it right then was unbearable, but he was downstairs, waiting for her. He would see it in her face. He would see that she had a secret and more than anything, she didn't want him to see that tonight, not this night. She would open it tomorrow when he was gone and she would have a chance to think about the contents.

She made her way down the narrow steps cautiously, making sure of her footing, the blankets and pillows blocking her view. She set them down and looked up just as he was crossing both of his arms in front of himself, grabbing the hem of his T-shirt and pulling it off over his head. In that glorious instant, seeing the contours of his perfect chest, the dark hair covering it and trailing down the middle of his taut abdomen, Wendy realized just how long ten years really was!

Chapter 14

BRANTMEIER'S MURDER INVESTIGATION was not going well. There were no clues where Tanya's murder was concerned, absolutely none. He followed every possible lead, always arriving at a dead end. He learned that after the trash was collected that Friday, it was taken to a burn plant in Eatonville, twenty miles away. The plant could burn eight hundred tons of waste a day, turning it into sixteen megawatts of sellable electricity. The peanut can was gone...for good.

The forensics guy had found a minute amount of the poison in Tanya's wastebasket, but not even enough to kill the rodent it was designed for. Brantmeier had called the manufacturer in Alabama, asking about unusual orders for the sodium fluoroacetate, but was told there were none that were out of the ordinary. All of their orders so far this year had been shipped out of the country to established customers. They had checked their records back two years with the same result.

Tanya's apartment had been thoroughly searched, the neighbors interviewed and everyone she knew or who knew her questioned, with no new leads uncovered. The thing that bothered Brantmeier most was that there didn't seem to be any motive. He'd interviewed a few people who admitted that Tanya's personality was grating at times, Wendy being one of them, but none of them seemed to be overtly upset by her sense of humor. They all said she was a good neighbor, minded her business and didn't cause any trouble. He got almost the same opinions from the staff at the hospital. It seemed like the only person who had any animosity toward Tanya was Wendy, though even that seemed superficial. He decided to put Wendy on his 'possible suspects' list. You could never tell, he told himself.

Monica's murder was still new, so there were more possibilities of finding some good leads. The department had been called by 911 after receiving Monica's call and two officers were dispatched to her home. They made sure no one had access to the house until Animal Control arrived. At that point, it was a safety issue. After Animal Control had killed and identified the snake, the officers called Brantmeier with the news that there might be another homicide.

The crime scene was a disaster. Animal Control had gone through the house, beginning at the front entrance, and overturned everything in sight hunting for the snake. The box was found lying on its side on her kitchen floor where it had fallen. It was plain brown, no markings or labels. Even Brantmeier, seasoned cop that he was, got the willies imaging Monica putting her hand into that box and feeling the sting of the fangs piercing her arm. The reptile was found behind Monica's refrigerator and promptly dispatched by one of the Control officers.

His interview with Dr. Giannotti had gone well up until the time Brantmeier had insinuated that Giannotti was a newcomer to town and nothing was known about his background. Giannotti was defensive, but became downright mad when Brantmeier got around to questioning the doctor about his past. Brantmeier had backed off. He could find answers to all of his questions about Giannotti's background elsewhere, but wanted to see how Giannotti would react.

He turned his attention to the snake, checking off his mental list of questions. How would someone go about getting a mamba? How closely were exotic animals like that tracked in the United States and was it legal to own one?

He started by calling Animal Control and spoke to the same guy who'd killed Monica's snake. He was told that keeping venomous snakes in their state was illegal, but each state had its own laws. The states that did allow it required permits, licenses and insurance and not just anybody could own them. Of course, he told Brantmeier, regulations didn't preclude someone having an illegal venomous reptile. The control agent advised Brantmeier to contact the state Fish and Wildlife Department; perhaps they had records of licenses and permits.

That trail too, led him to a dead end. They had only one permit, issued fifteen years ago to a research facility, but the permit had not been renewed for the past eight years; the facility had gone out of business and their venomous snakes sent to other labs. Brantmeier's assumptions were correct: tracking the snake was going to be a long process, but there was a possibility that couldn't be overlooked. Both the snake and fluoroacetate could have been acquired by illegal means and concealed from the authorities, if a person knew what they were doing.

Giannotti and Wendy were the only two suspects on his list at the moment and even then, Brantmeier knew he had no hard evidence to link either of them to the murders and the fact that either of them was guilty was unlikely.

Chapter 15

THE NIGHT HAD been quiet: no threatening phone calls, no prowlers and no rain. The circumstances were perfect for a sound sleep, but Wendy had tossed, turned and paced until she was worn out. Who was she kidding when she told herself she wouldn't look in the box until Giancarlo had left? Delayed gratification had never been her strongest personality trait. Yes, she had waited until she'd changed into her pajamas, brushed her teeth and gotten into bed. She'd even read two chapters in her current book, but the expectation was too much for her and she had succumbed.

It was an old cigar box belonging to Mark's dad who, she remembered, allowed himself only one cigar a week. In it were several dog-eared postcards, neatly stacked with the photos facing up. She hurriedly thumbed through the photos: the Eiffel Tower, the Louvre, Buckingham Palace, the Tower of London, the Alhambra in Spain, the Ponte Vecchio in Florence. She turned that one over quickly and read the message: 'Love Italy! Drivers are crazy! Weather is beautiful! Artwork is sublime!'

Wendy put that card aside, looking at the photo on the next one. She recognized the cathedral in the center of the city. The card was from Florence. On the back, the photo description read:

'*Santa Maria del Fiore*' and this time, the card started: 'Dad, Mom and Mark,' and continued, 'Got married last month! Met a wonderful guy and am in love! His name is Giancarlo. He's a doctor. No need to worry about me now. Miss you all. Love, Donna.'

Wendy was dizzy now, her head spinning. Giancarlo was her brother-in-law! She knew she was falling in love with him. She hoped that he would eventually love her in return, but now she didn't know how she should feel about their relationship. It felt wrong, morally wrong, to be in love with him, even though she knew they weren't related by blood. But she wanted him. Being with him made her feel special, but also close to Mark again. She still loved Mark, but she loved Giancarlo too.

And lurking behind all of these confusing emotions was a cold apprehension as she imagined how Giancarlo would take the news. She was afraid that they would always be just friends. Would she have to spend her life wanting him, but not being able to have him? That's how she felt about Mark every day, knowing he was gone and she could never be with him again. She wasn't sure she could survive the rest of her life feeling that way.

She would keep her secret a little longer; she was too afraid of losing him. There was too much going on and besides, maybe Giancarlo didn't ever need to know, at least not until she knew if he was falling in love with her and maybe not even then. She'd finally fallen asleep at one-thirty, at peace with her decision.

Sacred Love

He was still asleep when she padded down the stairs in her robe and slippers at seven-fifteen. It was Sunday, a day of rest. She longed for rest, not for her body, but for her heart.

She slipped past him as quietly as she could, went to the kitchen and brewed a pot of coffee. She poured herself a cup and headed for her favorite chair by the fireplace.

Sitting with her legs pulled up under her, she watched him. Sleep had erased the tension from his face and he looked peaceful. She watched the rhythmic rising and falling of his chest as he breathed, wondering what he dreamt about. She noticed the way his hair curled at the ends, the gray just now appearing at his temples. She looked at his strong jawline and told herself that Michelangelo's 'David' had nothing on Giancarlo. Her thoughts turned to his gentleness, which she loved and which existed equally with his commanding control.

Sipping her coffee, she let herself imagine lying next to him every day for the rest of her life, feeling his warmth next to her and the strength of his arms around her. With her heartbeat increasing, she thought of making love to him and wondered if he would ever love her, wondered if he would ever give her that sacred love he spoke of.

She took another sip of the coffee, looking into the darkness of the cup and when she looked up, he was staring at her, his intense eyes fixing her in place so that she couldn't move.

"*Buon giorno*, Wendy," he said, the smile spreading across his face like light chasing shadows away at sunrise.

She nearly choked on her coffee. "How long have you been awake?" she asked, the surprise obvious in her voice.

"I heard you come down the stairs. *Le scale scricchiolano.*" She understood without a translation: 'The stairs squeaked.' "You are not mad, are you?" He was grinning at her, enjoying his little joke.

He pushed the blankets away and sat up, his smooth skin taut over the muscles beneath. No, she wasn't mad, just relieved that he couldn't read her mind, or could he!

"You startled me," she said with mock anger, "...again!" She was smiling, trying to hide her face behind the coffee cup, knowing that he'd know exactly what she had been thinking if the dreaded lobster face made an appearance right then. She finished up the last bit. "I'll get dressed and then make some breakfast," she said at last.

He was standing now, putting on the long-sleeved shirt, looking relaxed and rested. "Yes, you get dressed and *I* will make some breakfast. I must repay your hospitality. And do not even think I will let you clean up afterwards!" She knew that tone in his voice. It was no use arguing with him.

She did her best imitation of Marlon Brando. "You just made me an offer I can't refuse."

"*Non si scherza con il padrino*, Wendy," he said, his imitation much better than hers. "Do not mess with the godfather!"

He made scrambled eggs and they were as dazzling with color as the Sistine Chapel: red and yellow from sweet peppers and tomatoes; green from zucchini and scallions; earthy brown from mushrooms and white morsels of feta cheese. It was Heaven with a side of buttered wheat toast! She knew she had all those ingredients in her refrigerator, but had never imagined they could be joined together to create such ecstasy. He watched her enjoying the eggs, her head back and eyes closed, concentrating on the pleasure of their taste.

"*Come una piccola cosi che porta tanta gioia.*" She stopped in mid-bite, waiting. He was smiling. "Such a small thing that brings such great joy," he translated. "You are always happy over such small things. I watch you with Dexter and I see how happy he makes you. I see the happiness in your face when you help the patients. I cook eggs for you and your face...*esso si illumina como se averte visto Dio.*" He searched for the English words. "'It glows as if you have seen God.' And my cooking is ordinary."

"You're a wonderful cook, Giancarlo!" she said.

"Well, my cooking is only good, but you should taste my mama's. It is wonderful!" Then he did that Italian thing that Wendy had seen in the movies: he brought his fingertips together, put them to his lips and kissed them, throwing the kiss away. She imagined the kiss landing on her lips: warm, moist and sweet.

There was a loud knock at the front door. It startled both of them, Wendy especially. It was a rude assault on the perfect experience of being with Giancarlo. She opened the door and was annoyed to see Detective Brantmeier standing there. 'It's Sunday, for Pete's sake! Doesn't that guy ever take a day off?' she thought.

"Sorry I have to bother you again, but I'd like to talk to you." He glanced past her, saw the blankets on the couch and Giancarlo sitting at the kitchen table. "There are some things I'd like you to clear up for me."

"I've told you everything I know, Detective. Can't this wait until next week?" She was mad now. How dare he interrupt her beautiful morning with Giancarlo? Tanya and Monica were dead and questioning her on a Sunday wasn't going to bring them back.

"I want you to come down to the station with me." His tone had changed. Wendy knew he was serious and it worried her. Looking past her at Giancarlo, he added, "Alone." Brantmeier wasn't surprised to see the doctor. A deputy had driven by the house at midnight, saw Giannotti's car parked at the end of Cedar Road and as instructed, had reported it to his boss.

Giancarlo joined Wendy at the door. "Is this absolutely necessary, Detective?" He was mad too, but Brantmeier wouldn't budge.

"This is a murder investigation," he said, his eyes locked on Giannotti. "I have the authority to question anyone at any time. I suggest Wendy get her coat. It's chilly today."

Wendy's face was pale now and Giancarlo hated Brantmeier for that. He wanted this time with her, wanted it to be healing for her. He had seen such joy in her smile, had seen how relaxed she was eating breakfast. He'd seen the beauty of her soul in the excitement of his cooking as it filled her senses. He didn't want any of their time together to end, especially not like this. But he knew that legally, Wendy couldn't refuse; she had to go.

"It's okay, Giancarlo. Will you wait for me?" She would need him by the time Brantmeier was finished with her. If she knew Giancarlo was waiting, she could tolerate whatever accusations the detective would throw at her.

"We will drive my car," he said and looked at Brantmeier, "Is that permitted?"

Brantmeier didn't like that idea at all. He didn't want to take the chance that they would make a quick exit out of town. "You're welcome to come in your car, but Wendy will ride with me." There was nothing else to do. Wendy got her coat and followed Brantmeier to his car. At least she knew Giancarlo would be there to take her home...*if* she was allowed to leave after the questioning!

The room was small with only a table and three uncomfortable-looking chairs. There was a square mirror on one wall that Wendy assumed was two-way glass. She wondered who was on the other side watching. She realized that the room was just like the ones in the true-life crime dramas she liked to watch on TV. But this was real. Brantmeier sat down across from her.

"Let me lay my problems on the table for you so you'll know why I called you back in. I think that's fair, don't you?" His tone was civil. She was expecting that he would be more forceful, but she knew the session was young. This was her third interview with him and with each one, she felt more and more like a rope was tightening around her neck.

"Let's start with Tanya's murder and the can of peanuts. I have a witness who saw the peanuts on *your* desk." He emphasized the word 'your' and she felt the rope tighten ever so slightly. "I also know that at no time was the office completely empty of people, which means that if somebody from outside the office had come in and put that can on your desk, somebody would have been there to see it. So I'm left wondering how that can got on your desk. Any ideas?" He had never taken his eyes off her. She knew he would be watching her eyes, evaluating her body language.

"I told you before. I have a peanut allergy, a bad one. I won't even get near them and I don't know how they got on my desk." She was trying to stay calm and focused. "Maybe someone else, someone in the office, hid the can under paperwork or binders or something and carried them to my desk and left the can without it being seen. That's possible, isn't it?"

"So you're telling me that maybe someone wanted you dead, right? That would have to be someone who didn't know about your allergy. Who would that be? I mean, who in your office?"

She thought about this for a while. "It could have been Mr. Dellette. He never paid attention to any of us in the office, never asked about our families or pastimes. Stuff like that. I don't remember telling him that I had a peanut allergy, so it could have been him." Wendy hadn't thought of this before, but then Brantmeier's questioning hadn't been this intense before.

"You told me before that you didn't have any enemies, anybody who would want to harm you." He made a mental note to re-interview Dellette.

"I told you I didn't *know* of anybody who wanted to hurt me. That doesn't mean there wasn't someone who did. It just means I didn't know." She was feeling more confident, but she knew that Brantmeier wasn't going to let up. He looked like he was trying to collect his thoughts. Maybe she had momentarily detoured him.

"You hated Tanya though, didn't you? You're the only one on my list who had a motive. You told me about the jokes she used to play on you and how frustrated you were with her behavior. I got the same story from the other woman in your office." He was talking about Annie and Wendy was surprised to find out that Annie had even paid attention to Tanya's behavior. She always had her nose buried in her paperwork. Wendy knew Brantmeier's questioning was building in momentum; she could feel the noose tightening by increments.

"Seems pretty convenient that you were the one that threw away the can after you knew she was dead." He waited to see her expression.

"Mr. Dellette asked me to clean out her desk. I'm sure he told you that, providing you thought to ask him." If he wanted to play verbal war with her, she was ready. She'd had enough of his suspicions. She just wanted to go back home and be with Giancarlo.

"Where did you get the rat poison? Was it something your husband used in his practice?" He'd switched tactics on her so fast, she was caught totally off guard. The intensity of his stare increased and she knew others were watching through the glass.

How dare he bring Mark into this! She was mad at him now, but she also realized that he'd been checking her background...thoroughly. She willed herself to calm down, fearing she would say something that would tighten the noose even more.

"What proof do you have that I have ever had or used rat poison or that my husband had either? I want to see the proof!" Her voice was starting to tremble, the tension getting to her.

"Believe me, I can get proof." Brantmeier seemed cocky now, confident of his interrogation methods.

"So you don't even have proof, nothing you can show me." She was beginning to discern his methods. It was the same way suspects were questioned on the crime dramas. Keep the suspect off guard. Don't let them relax. Don't let them have time to make up answers. "Show me your proof and I'll answer your question." She hoped her self-assured demeanor was successfully hiding the fact that she was scared to death. Her stomach was tied in a knot and she didn't know how long Giancarlo's scrambled eggs were going to stay put.

"You didn't answer me. You hated Tanya, didn't you?"

"You didn't give me a chance to answer!" She was losing it. She could feel her anger burning, feel the nausea building. 'Keep calm! Keep calm,' she kept repeating to herself. "I didn't hate Tanya. I didn't like her, but I didn't hate her." No matter what she said, Brantmeier was never satisfied with the truth.

"Did you ever think about how good it would feel to get revenge for what she did to you?" His questions were getting too personal, too dangerous to answer. But she still believed that the truth would clear her…wouldn't it?

"Tanya made me mad sometimes. I admit that. And I admit that I wanted to get revenge, even thought of ways to turn the tables on her. But I never hated her or ever considered killing her!" All she had to give Brantmeier was the truth and the truth wasn't loosening that rope around her neck.

"You hated Monica though, didn't you?" He was good at keeping her off-guard. It was getting harder to think clearly, to edit her answers mentally so the he couldn't trip her up.

"I had only been working in the emergency department for one week before Monica died. Do you really think I could learn to hate her enough in one week to want her dead? What was my motive? I hated her because she could restock shelves better than I could? Really, Detective, that seems pretty far-fetched even for you." On the outside, she fought to sound in control, but inside it was all coming apart and she couldn't stop it.

Brantmeier didn't appreciate that comment at all. He didn't want her to think she had the upper hand or any kind of advantage in this interview. He was damn well going to get his confession no matter how dirty he had to play.

"Oh, you had a motive all right, a motive as old as the human race! Monica had her sights on Dr. Giannotti and you decided you didn't want the competition. You already had your hooks into him, didn't you?"

It wasn't working any more. She tried to coach herself to stay calm, but it was useless. The knot in her stomach was now as tight as the one she imagined around her neck. She couldn't breathe; her body heat was rising like a thermometer left out in direct sunlight. She fought to keep her breakfast down. She knew Brantmeier would notice her hands shaking, but she couldn't stop them and Brantmeier just kept charging at her, over and over again.

"He started at Memorial three weeks before Monica was killed. You saw him and decided you wanted him. Three weeks was plenty of time for jealousy to motivate you to get rid of her, wasn't it? You would have gotten rid of anybody that had their sights on him. Isn't that true?" Brantmeier was on a roll and he was eager to put these murders behind him, but even more eager to get the press off his back. He knew that his reputation was on the line and maybe even his job. "How long have you been sleeping with him?"

"I need to go to the bathroom! Please, let me go to the bathroom!" Wendy was about to taste breakfast again, but this time it wasn't going to be good. Brantmeier saw her go pale, saw her break into a cold sweat and motioned toward the glass. In a few seconds, a female officer entered the room and escorted Wendy down the hall to the restroom.

Chapter 16

BRANTMEIER WAS FRUSTRATED. All the momentum he'd worked so skillfully to build, trying to get Wendy to give up something usable, was gone. There had been an irreparable break in his questioning and his experience had taught him that once it was broken, the momentum was almost impossible to get back. Well, he consoled himself, better to lose momentum than have the suspect lose lunch with both of them trapped in that small room!

Wendy was escorted back, not looking much better. She was still pale and shaky and Brantmeier didn't think she'd tolerate much more of his drilling. Yes, he wanted to solve these murders, but he didn't want a false confession borne out of browbeating and intimidation. That wouldn't look good on his résumé either.

"Feeling better?" He could see that she had been crying. She didn't answer him, but dabbed at her nose with a tissue. He tried again, this time speaking to her like a concerned big brother.

"I'm trying to help you, Wendy. You can see how this looks for you, right? You had motive and opportunity." He waited for her response. There was none. He was certain that at any minute, she would ask for a lawyer and then his chance would be gone for good. He decided to target her weak spot, but with a softer approach.

"Tell me about you and Dr. Giannotti. I know that both of you are widowed so you must have a lot in common. Both of your spouses died in accidents, is that right?" She was relaxing a bit now and making eye contact with him.

"Yes, that's right," she said, the color returning to her face. "We have a lot in common and because of that, we've become good friends." These questions seemed innocent to her, but she was still cautious. There was nothing illicit about her relationship with Giancarlo, nothing to be ashamed of and she wanted Brantmeier to understand that. "I have never slept with him and it insults me that you assume that I have."

"It's my job to ask those questions. You understand that, don't you?" Yes, she understood, but that didn't make it any better. "Didn't he spend last night at your house?"

"He slept on the sofa. I was scared to be out there by myself. You said you'd have a deputy drive by, but Giancarlo offered to stay in the house. I told you, we're friends." The nausea was gone for now, but the noose was still tight.

Brantmeier wasn't getting anywhere and decided to try ramping up the questioning once more, hoping to bring her to a breaking point where she would give him a confession.

"Dr. Giannotti is a very handsome man. I'm sure a lot women have fantasized about making love to him. So you're asking me to believe that the relationship between you two is solely platonic? That you've never felt like that about him and given in to those desires?" Brantmeier could see that Wendy was getting pale again, the tears filling her eyes, ready to cascade down her cheeks. He might still have a chance to salvage this interview.

"Yes, I'm asking you to believe that because it's the truth!" she protested.

"But you want to sleep with him, don't you? You've always had that goal in mind and Monica was getting in your way. Isn't that why you killed her?"

"I didn't kill her! I don't know why you won't believe me!"

He kept hammering away, waiting for her to break and give him the confession he needed. She had motive and opportunity as far as he was concerned and he had no other suspects. His reputation depended on closing this case.

"Monica wanted Dr. Giannotti. I have witnesses who will testify to that. You wanted him too. I know that you and he had lunch together the first day he showed up at Memorial and even after that. I know you had dinner at his house. He was with you this morning at your house and you admit that he slept there last night. You were working on him from the very beginning and you weren't about to let another woman take him away from you. Why don't you just admit that and we can all get this over with?"

Wendy's eyes couldn't hold the tears any longer and they flowed down her cheeks and dripped into her lap. She saw now how her love for Giancarlo was nothing but a selfish and one-sided fantasy that she wanted to be true. It had no value. Brantmeier's questions had forced her to confess that to herself.

She didn't answer him; she couldn't. She didn't kill Monica, but she felt guilty all the same: guilty of using Giancarlo, of using his friendship to be near him and to entice him to fall in love with her. She hung her head and cried, great sobs heaving from her soul.

Brantmeier could see it; he would get nothing more out of her. He had no new leads and he had no evidence to bring charges against her. He had pushed her hard and she had turned a corner, one from which she wouldn't come back. The interview was effectively over. His instincts told him she was innocent, something he had suspected all along, but wouldn't accept. Her face, her eyes, her body language all told him that she was hiding nothing except her true feelings about Dr. Giannotti. He didn't need to be a detective to know that Wendy Alexander was a woman who was very much in love. He needed to close these cases, but underneath the cop was the soldier and the soldier's honor.

"That's all I need, Wendy," the big brother in him said and the soldier added, "I'm sorry I had to put you through this."

Giancarlo was waiting for her at the front desk. She looked terrible, her eyes red and swollen from crying, her face pale from nausea. He put his arms around her, but she pulled away from him. "No, just get me out of here, please!"

He walked her to his car, held the door for her and then got in the driver's side. She couldn't look at him. She kept her head down, picking at the disintegrating tissue in her trembling hands. He pulled out of the parking lot and made a left turn on to Pacific Way. She looked out the window and noticed he was going in the wrong direction.

"I'm taking you to my house, Wendy," he explained. She didn't want to go, didn't want to be with him where she would remember their delicious meal at the big family table, the Chianti and small talk sitting close to him on the sofa, watching the gulls fly over the ocean. She didn't want to remember how good she felt being with him. But she didn't have the strength to tell him to take her home. If he took her home, she knew he wouldn't leave her alone, that he would stay with her until she had to explain to him how she had used him. She turned her attention back to the tissue, her mind rehearsing what she would say to him.

He tried to steady her as she climbed the steps to the front door, but when he took her arm, she pulled away again. She couldn't let him touch her any more, but she couldn't bear to be away from him. She didn't want to talk to him, but she ached to hear his voice. She could never have him, but she wanted him with her entire being. She was being torn apart and she knew she would not survive the pain.

He led her to the living room. She sat on the sofa, still quiet, still torturing the tissue until there was nothing left of it but bits of white fuzz. He poured her a glass of red wine.

"Wendy, please drink this. It will be good for you." He held the glass out to her and she took it without a word. He sat down next to her and waited, not wanting to push her, knowing that when she was ready, she would tell him what had happened.

He was puzzled that she had pulled away from him, that she wouldn't let him comfort her as he had done before. He wanted her to know that all he ever wanted to do was to love her so much that she would never be sad again, never have another reason to cry.

She now realized that she had been lying to herself. Brantmeier had shown her that. She had allowed, even encouraged herself, to fall in love with a fantasy, that of loving Giancarlo and believing that he would love her in return, just as Mark had. She needed from him what Mark had given her: peace, comfort and security. She was tired of coming home to an empty house and eating meals alone. She saw no pleasure in a future by herself with just Dexter for company. She longed to feel a man sleeping next to her, to feel the heat from his body warming hers, to feel his skin on hers and know that he desired her.

But it was *her* dream, not Giancarlo's. She had let the dream grow out of control and she now knew that it grew from selfish desires. The reality was that he had given her his friendship, a precious thing, and nothing more and it had not been enough for her. Worst of all, she had taken his friendship and used it to fantasize that he was something more than he was: not a knight in shining armor, but her savior. He would save her from her guilt and fears. He would save her from a life lived alone.

She realized now that he was just a man after all, just like Mark: just a human being. He was not perfect no matter how much she wanted him to be. She had convinced herself that Mark was perfect and had taken that perfection and put it on Giancarlo and that was unfair to him. That hurt most of all: that she believed that she loved him so much and yet, had not honored who he really was. She had used him and he didn't deserve that.

Her heart was utterly broken, the pain unbearable. It pressed on her chest until her breathing came in staccato bursts. It overpowered every other sense in her body until there was nothing left of her but the pain and the realization that she would never have the love she wanted from Giancarlo, the sacred love he spoke of.

All of the sadness she had been carrying, all of the loneliness, came spilling out of her eyes in hot, salty tears. She was crying for her selfishness and she was crying for the way she had dishonored him. She was losing a dream that would never be and that hurt the most.

She let him hold her now, feeling his arms around her, holding her body tightly as if he were afraid her trembling would cause her to fly into a million pieces. She knew then that it was time to confess to him, to tell him everything that she had been keeping locked up in her heart. She wanted him to know so that he could decide if he would continue to be her friend. She would start with her secret about Mark and Donnatella.

"Giancarlo, I have something to tell you. It's about Donnatella..." He put his fingertip on her lips, his eyes boring through her as though he saw the degradation of her soul. She couldn't hide from him and she was afraid.

"*No parlare*, Wendy. Do not speak." His voice was gentle, almost a whisper. He reached into his pocket, pulled out a photo and handed it to her. A great ache coursed through her as she recognized the photo: it was her and Mark, so many years ago and so young. It was taken on their wedding day. She stared in disbelief, trying to blink the tears away so that she could be sure of what she was seeing.

"Where...did you get this?" She could barely get the question out.

"It belonged to Donnatella. She showed it to me and told me that Mark sent it to her. Do you want to know what she told me when she saw it?" Wendy nodded her head, still trying to believe what she was holding in hand and to understand how Giancarlo had come to be in her life, bringing Mark back to her.

"She was sad," he continued, his voice still just a whisper. "I had never seen such a great sadness in her like that. She told me that she wished she could meet you because she would like to be your friend. And I saw that she loved you because you loved her brother. I think she was sad that she had left her family behind." Giancarlo gently lifted Wendy's chin so that she was looking directly into his eyes. "Wendy, you cannot understand what happened to me when she said that." He paused, choosing his words, his voice strong now so that she would hear him and know.

"I did not understand her until you told me about the attachment disorder. I loved her for a long time, but I knew that she did not love me as much. She was unhappy, but I was lonely and I knew this was selfish. I became very angry with her and she could not live with my anger and so she found another man. Then the photo of you and Mark came in the mail and when I saw her face, I was able to see her differently. I realized that she could love very much. I believed that I was the cause of her unhappiness and so I tried to love her better. I forgave her for being with the other man and I stayed with her."

She saw his pain and felt his guilt. "You've known all along that Mark was her brother?"

"Yes, Wendy, I knew. When I told you about the accident with the Ducati, I did not tell you something else about it." His lowered his head, his eyes closed for a moment. He forced himself to say the words. "She took the Ducati because she was going to meet with her lover. Before I left to go to the hospital, she told me she didn't want to be married to me any more and she was leaving. And I thought it was my fault that she wanted to go."

She had nothing to say to him. They shared the same sin, that of selfishness, and she'd been unable to say anything to herself that made her feel better, so what could she say to him? She could see him clearly now, who he truly was and she saw him even better than she had imagined him. He was looking at her now.

"I came to America to look for Donnatella's family. I wanted them to know that she loved them and missed them. I needed to tell them how much I loved her. But I found out her parents and even her brother had died. So I went looking for the woman in that photo and God led me to you! I saw you that first day, in the cafeteria. You looked so sad, but I knew you were the woman in the photo. I didn't think it was possible that I had found you. That is why I wanted you to work in the emergency department with me."

He was holding both of her hands tightly, holding her so that she could not get away from him, like he would never let her go if she tried.

"I have loved you since the first time I saw you. I wanted to make sure and as I came to know you more, I loved you more. I saw your heart then, just like I saw Donnatella's heart when she saw the photo. I did not want to tell you because I wanted to see if you would love me. Vi amo con tutto ciò che sono. Wendy, I love you with all that I am. I do not want to live without you."

He took her in his arms, feeling her body yield to his embrace. He was drawing her to himself and she couldn't pull away from it. It filled her with something new, something she'd had with Mark and wanted to have again with Giancarlo. He kissed her and she let his lips press hard against hers, giving her heart to him hoping it would be secure in his love.

"Can we have it, Giancarlo? You and I? Can we have it again…together?"

"What do your angels tell you?"

"They tell me 'yes.'"

"Then it is so; the angels never lie, Wendy. We will have a sacred love."

Epilogue

FOR AS CLEVER as he had been in securing the sodium fluoroacetate and black mamba, the double murderer made the most elemental, amateurish mistake and even months after the sentencing, Brantmeier still wondered how something so obvious had been overlooked.

He had never murdered before, but he was highly intelligent and detailed in his planning. He might have gotten away with killing Tanya and Monica had it not been for that last phone call from his office. The first two calls had been made from his office to Wendy's desk. They couldn't be traced. He'd made the last call after work hours, to Wendy's cell phone. That was his mistake. It hadn't taken long to trace the call back to his office; cell phone technology had made police work much easier. But even so, Brantmeier wanted to catch him in the act of making a call, to get hard evidence before making the arrest.

Wendy had been eager to help, even though Brantmeier knew how terrified she'd been about the calls and upset about the murders of her co-workers. He felt guilty for the way he'd questioned her, especially about her relationship with Dr. Giannotti, but he was a detective and at that time, she was his only suspect. He wanted to make that up to her. Because of the direct threats made against her, he wanted Emory Dellette locked up as soon as possible.

After securing a court order, Brantmeier had Dellette's office phone tapped. Then it was just a matter of waiting for the next call and Brantmeier hadn't had to wait long. He hadn't had to wait long for the confession either after he'd presented Dellette with the evidence.

During questioning, Dellette had told Brantmeier everything, had not held anything back. He'd secured the rat poison from a friend, a guy he fished with. This friend had traveled extensively, including a recent trip to Mexico where he'd bought the poison after being told how effective it was on rats; his tool shed had a long-standing rat problem, but the problem was now taken care of. He was only too happy to share the fluoroacetate with Dellette, who saw the benefits of it as a murder weapon and also had a rat problem: the two-legged variety.

He'd meant the peanuts for Wendy, not knowing she had an allergy to them. He'd never liked her, was jealous and had felt threatened by her competency. Something in him had finally snapped when he'd heard the rumors that she was going to be promoted to Head of Patient Accounts after he retired. He wasn't going to let her have his title, even after he no longer worked there. He couldn't control Wendy and that's why she had to go.

He was frustrated that Tanya had eaten the peanuts. He didn't like Tanya any more than he did Wendy, but Tanya knew her place; she was afraid of losing her job and he could control her.

Monica was dead for an entirely different reason. Hospital gossip was going around that she was after the new Italian surgeon. It hadn't taken her long to go after him either, but Dellette had been interested in her in for quite a while and had approached her and told her so. She'd snubbed him with a demeaning put-down that had so trampled his ego, he'd decided that if she wouldn't have him, she'd never get the opportunity to have anyone else.

Dellette's story about getting the snake was convoluted and disjointed. He told Brantmeier that he had forged papers to represent himself as the head of a research facility doing studies on the medical use of snake venom as an anti-coagulant. With a common graphics program he was able to create a very official-looking letterhead. In the papers, he'd reported that the research done at his facility was underwritten by a large drug company; he was making great headway and the drug was almost ready for trials. Stockholders were set to make a fortune once the drug was on the market.

He'd sent the paperwork off to a venomous reptile farm, one that he knew from the Internet had been fined for selling endangered and illegal species of snakes. With expectations of rising stock prices in the drug company and large returns on any investments they would make, the reptile farm had been only too happy to sell him a mamba with the condition that their name never be mentioned. They charged him an exorbitant fee for the mamba and for an extra fee, they had offered to deliver the snake personally. Dellette had agreed.

There was no trial. Dellette knew the evidence of his guilt was conclusive and by the time he'd signed his confession, he'd given up and had gone into a deep depression, not even interested in the insanity plea suggested by his attorney. His life was over and that was okay with Emory Dellette.

The murders of Tanya and Monica were solved, Wendy and Dr. Giannotti were getting engaged and Brantmeier was happy. Things at the station would go back to their usual routine and Cape Narrows would go back to being the quiet, pleasant town it had always been.

He leaned back in his chair, put his feet up on his desk and decided it was time to spit-polish his shoes again.

PART TWO

❧

For Doug
Thank you for forty-five years
of Sacred Love

Chapter 1

HE WAS DREAMING he was going fast, very fast. The trees were shooting past him in a blur, but there was no wind on his face and he wondered how that could be possible. He saw something up ahead and he knew he was going to hit it. He couldn't stop. Then there was nothing but blackness.

In the blackness, though, he knew he was dreaming, but he couldn't wake up. He tried. He was fighting so hard to move that he was totally exhausted from the effort, but no part of his body obeyed his commands. He heard voices, but he couldn't understand what they were saying. He couldn't talk, couldn't tell them he didn't understand. Why couldn't he talk? He tried, but heard only a moan like a wounded animal and wondered if it was coming from him.

Then there was just the blackness all around him. He knew it was drawing back over him again like someone pulling a sheet over a dead body. It came quickly until it covered him and then there was nothing.

Wendy felt a hand on her back. She had been sitting by his bed for hours and had finally folded her arms on the bed and put her head down. She hadn't left his side since he was brought in on Wednesday and had fought off all advice that she should go home and get some sleep. His family, especially his mother Lalia, understood. She would have stayed too, but the family were expecting her. Most of his siblings had rushed home when they heard the news and they would have to be fed. It was her duty to them. Now it was Thursday morning and it worried Wendy that Giancarlo was still unconscious.

"Wendy?" She looked up to see Dr. Rossi, his pleasant face reassuring. Wendy liked him. She'd heard Giancarlo mention him one day at Memorial before they'd come to Italy. He and Giancarlo were good friends and had worked together many times. He was about sixty, with gray hair and a heavy, solid build. From the short time Wendy had spent with him, he seemed calm and in control, just like Giancarlo. Wendy appreciated that about both of them; it made her feel secure.

"I have arranged for a cot to be brought in for you," he said quietly. "The nurses may ask you leave from time to time, but otherwise you may stay. Is this acceptable to you?" She was exhausted and still hadn't be able to shake the jet lag.

"Yes. Thank you so much."

"Gianni is my good friend and I know he would do the same for me if our circumstances were reversed. You will see, Wendy. He will be all right." Dr. Rossi smiled, patted her back and left.

She had requested to stay with Giancarlo in the intensive care unit and was told that it was not usually allowed. She knew she couldn't be separated from him, not now. She wanted to spend every minute she might have left with him, just as she had done with Mark. She was relieved when they had made allowances for her. The staff all knew she was the fiancée of Dr. Giancarlo Giannotti and that title carried some privileges with it.

She still had to remind herself who 'Gianni' was. It was his nickname. Giancarlo was a combination of the names Giovanni and Carlo. The nickname for Giovanni was Gianni. Since being in Bivigliano, she hadn't heard anyone call him Giancarlo; it seemed so formal on him now.

His siblings and their spouses came to see him during visiting hours, all except his youngest sister Analisa and his brother Marcello. Both of them lived out of town and had planned to drive down with their children on Friday, the day before the wedding. His mother had called both of them, told them there was nothing they could do and, since they had jobs, to stay put and she would call them daily and give them a report. They could come for the weekend to visit Gianni and meet Wendy if they wanted. The rest of the siblings lived near Bivigliano scattered within a ten-mile radius of the house where they were raised.

Bivigliano was a small town, tucked up against the mountains, about ten miles northeast of Florence. It consisted of very narrow, winding streets, a nice park, small family-owned stores and the typical stucco houses with shuttered windows, neat yards, plush gardens and stone fences. There seemed to be stone everywhere, Wendy thought. To the southwest, the land leveled somewhat and was farmed. It was a sleepy place, a place most tourists never visited, and she had liked it the first time they'd driven through it on their way to his family home.

Only two family members at a time were allowed in the intensive care unit and so Wendy would sit in the waiting area while his brothers, sisters and in-laws came to see him. After visiting hours, when his family was gone, it was Wendy's time to be with him. She could touch him, talk to him and pray for him. She wouldn't let go of his hand. She held it firmly and told him how much she loved him.

She remembered the first time she'd met him, in the cafeteria at Memorial Hospital, how when she had blushed, he had told her that her angels were telling her secrets. She thought about their first kiss at his house when he told her that he did not want to live without her, when he promised her they would have a sacred love. But would they ever have it now? Would she have to live without him and the love he'd promised her?

When she would reach the lowest point of her despair, imagining her life without him, she would put her lips up to his ear and tell him the secrets the angels had told her. Her tears came easily during those quiet times beside his bed, listening to the heart monitor's steady beep.

She had been able to manage only snatches of sleep here and there. She told herself that she was doing okay, but she knew she was lying. The look on Lalia's face when the call came kept flashing back to her, denying her any rest.

They had all been sitting at the big kitchen table, the siblings having come to meet Wendy and have dinner. Wendy was being entertained with stories of Giancarlo's childhood by Pietro, his father, when the phone rang. Lalia had answered it and Wendy had seen her face and knew instantly; her intuition had told her the call was about Giancarlo. He had been in an accident, the police told Lalia. It was bad. He was being taken to L'Ospedale della Sacra Famiglia and the family should come right away.

Giancarlo had taken Emiliano's Ducati into Bivigliano to buy extra milk for the children, even though she'd asked him not to, telling him that she had a bad feeling about it. He told her she was just nervous because of the wedding. He had borrowed

Emiliano's leather jacket, gloves and helmet, promising her he'd be careful. He'd kissed her, put on the helmet and then had driven off toward town.

What happened after the call was a blur, her recollection mercifully dulled by shock and jet lag. She had only flashes of memory: Giancarlo's family showing up in the emergency department, doctors and nurses in and out of the trauma room, his mother tearful, wiping her eyes with a cotton handkerchief. And then the thing she remembered clearly. It was another woman with a cotton handkerchief, crying. It was Tanya's mother outside the ICU. That was almost five months ago.

All of Giancarlo's siblings spoke English very well and Cristiano, his youngest brother, had taken it upon himself to act as translator for Wendy. She thought he looked a lot like Giancarlo: same build and same smile and he was a doctor too, a pediatrician. He had an innate kindness and a gentleness about him that Wendy felt when she'd first been introduced to him

Time seemed to slow down and turn into agonizing, endless minutes. The minutes turned into one hour and then another, with the third hour looming ahead before the doctor had finally come out to talk to them. Lalia took a handkerchief out of her purse, preparing for the worst. Pietro never let go of his wife's hand. Wendy sat in shock, her mind reeling; it was three days before their wedding was to take place and her joy had been instantly changed to horror with one phone call.

The doctor introduced himself to the family. He told them Giancarlo was unconscious, that he had three broken ribs on the right side, one of which had punctured his lung. They had inserted a chest tube to re-expand his lung and had placed a breathing tube into his throat to make sure his airway was maintained.

There were many abrasions and contusions to his body, he had said. They were worried about an injury to his liver, but the worst injury was to his right leg. He had suffered a fracture of the thigh bone. The doctor explained that fractures of this bone caused injury to the surrounding muscles and tissue and the bleeding from the tissues and the bone was extensive, so they had ordered blood to replace what he had lost. He told them that they would not do surgery to fix the broken bone until Giancarlo was more stable. For now, he said, they had splinted it as a temporary measure. The doctor called it an 'external fixation.'

He warned them that Giancarlo might not regain consciousness right away, that it depended on how badly his brain had been shaken inside his head, but said that because he had been wearing a helmet, it was hopeful that the trauma to his brain would be minimal. They had done a CT scan and it looked encouraging, but even so, he doubted Giancarlo would remember anything just prior to the accident.

A scan of his abdomen indicated that he had a tear in his liver, but it was felt that it would heal on its own and did not require surgery. They would be keeping an eye on that for any bleeding into the abdomen.

At the end of his report, he told the family that he believed Giancarlo would make a full recovery, but that it would take some time. He also said that he had always admired Giancarlo and wanted the family to know that they would give him the very best of care; they should not worry about that. He informed them that Giancarlo would be taken to the intensive care unit. There wasn't anything else to say. Pietro told him '*Grazie*' and the doctor had left.

That was on Wednesday morning. They had been allowed to see him after he had been taken to the ICU. When Lalia first saw him lying so still, the breathing tube protruding from his mouth, she broke down and cried for several minutes. Giancarlo was her first-born, holding those special memories for her that all first-born children hold. She kissed his forehead and spoke to him in Italian.

Before they left, Papa and Mama told Wendy they would talk to the family and tell them they should all return home, that she would keep them informed of Giancarlo's condition. They all had jobs and children in school.

Wendy was alone with him except during visiting hours and when the nurses came in to check him and change his position. There were many large, dark-blue bruises appearing on his body, especially on his right side. His right elbow was bruised and swollen, but she was told they had x-rayed it and that there was no break. His right leg was uncovered and she could see how swollen his thigh was, the skin shiny and very tight. The pins of the external fixation rod were coming out of his skin and were attached to the stabilizing rod. She couldn't even imagine how painful that must be and she thought maybe it was better that he was unconscious for now. She'd heard him moan and knew that even the narcotics they were giving him for pain would not take it all away. In his unconscious state, he would be aware of pain, but hopefully would not remember it once he was awake.

It was especially hard when the nurses would reposition him. They would work in pairs. One would roll him so that he was off of his back and hold him in position while the other one would prop him with pillows, adding extras to support his leg. They would do this every two hours and Wendy was relieved when they asked her to leave the room. It made her lightheaded to see him like this and at times she'd had to fight some nausea.

There were tubes and lines attached to him or coming out of him everywhere: monitor wires, pulse oximetry, the endotrachial tube, IV line with bags of saline and blood, a blood pressure cuff and a urinary catheter. And above everything else was the steady beep of the monitor, always in the background, reminding her that life is fragile and nothing is promised. She remembered that he'd once told her that there was a cure for everything but death.

She sat next to the bed holding his hand, whispering to him. The nurses told her that he could hear her and that if she talked to him, it would help him wake up. So whenever the nurses were out of the room, she would tell him stories about how their life would be after they were married.

They would keep both houses in Cape Narrows, she told him. They would live in her house during the fall and winter so that they could snuggle on the sofa, wrapped in her quilt, warmed by the fire in the fireplace. She would read books to him.

They would sleep upstairs in her 'house of trees' under the steep, pitched roof, snuggled together in her warm bed, listening to the rain. They would make love all night, and in the morning he would make her scrambled eggs with Feta cheese and peppers and they would eat it in bed and not get up until noon.

In the summer, she told him, they would live at his house by the ocean. She would help him grow tomatoes, basil and garlic in the garden. He would make gnocchi quattro formaggio and they would eat it at the big family table in the kitchen. They would drink Chianti and talk until all hours of the night.

On Saturdays, they would go to Pirate Joe's cafe and sit outside on the dock, eating hamburgers and watching the tourists sail their boats into the marina. They would sit on a blanket behind his house and watch the gulls flying above the ocean waves and at night, with only Orion in the sky able to see them, they would make love on the beach.

She told him how she would make love to him and how happy they would be together.

The cot had been brought in after morning visiting hours. It was a roll-away bed, made up with sheets, a blanket and a pillow. It didn't look very comfortable, Wendy told herself, but at least she would be lying down. She had finally kissed his forehead and had told him 'goodnight.' She pulled the privacy curtain between his bed and the cot; the light coming from the nurses' station in the hallway would keep her awake. She slept fitfully, but she slept.

Chapter 2

HE KNEW HE was awake even though he couldn't open his eyes, or maybe his eyes were open and he was blind! The panic hit him hard; he felt nauseous. He was aware of the pain, aware that his right leg hurt, but he didn't know why. He tried to move it and felt fire shoot up into his body. He heard the animal moan again, but knew this time that it had come from him and with the moan came even more excruciating pain in his chest. He thought he was crying, but he couldn't be sure.

"Giancarlo, open your eyes." She was talking to him, but he didn't know who it was. Her voice was gentle, but familiar. He wanted to obey her. He wanted to see who it was, but his eyelids were so heavy and he had no strength, but she kept talking to him anyway.

He would try for her. With great effort and to prove to himself that he wasn't blind, he opened his eyes and light appeared for an instant. He saw her blurry outline. Was she smiling? His energy was spent and the blackness and silence covered him again quickly.

By Thursday morning, she was starting to feel the effects of sleep deprivation. She hadn't left his bedside except to use the restroom and buy some snacks from a vending machine. A nurse came in to check the IV. Wendy couldn't remember her name even though every nurse caring for him had introduced themselves and told her how much they admired him. She was glad they wore badges. This one was pretty: beautiful skin, stylish haircut and dark eyes. She was young, maybe very late twenties, but she seemed confident in her tasks. Her badge read 'Rosabella.'

"His eyes opened for a moment!" Wendy was excited. Dr. Rossi had told the family what to expect as Giancarlo came out of the coma. "That's a good sign, isn't it?"

Rosabella was checking the monitor, reading the blood pressure and checking the heart rhythm. She checked the chest tube that kept his right lung inflated. With her stethoscope, she listened to his lungs.

"Yes, that is a very good sign! He will be able to keep his eyes open for longer periods of time as he recovers from the coma. He may also wake up all at once. Keep talking to him and encouraging him. But you must realize that sometimes he will be asleep and sometimes he will be awake, even though his eyes are closed. Talk to him anyway. He can hear you, but he may not yet understand what you are saying." She watched him breathing, the endotrachial tube strapped to his face to keep it in place. "Very soon we should be able to pull this tube out. That also is a good sign."

Rosabella took his hand. "*Stringermi la mano, Giancarlo.*" She wanted him to squeeze her hand. There was no response. "*Stringermi la mano.*" Still nothing. "*Apri i tuoi occhi.*" She watched his eyes. They fluttered open for a few seconds. She smiled at him. "*È buono, Giancarlo!* That is good!"

Next Rosabella took her knuckle and pressed into his chest, rubbing hard, waiting for the response. He groaned, his hands attempting to raise in defense of the assault.

"That is a very good sign!" Rosabella said and added, "He is responding to commands and reacting to pain. He is doing very well!" She seemed as excited as Wendy, but of course she would. All of the staff here knew Giancarlo, liked and respected him. He had worked at Sacra Famiglia after moving away from the huge teaching hospital in Milan. Bivigliano was his hometown and almost everybody knew both Doctors Giannotti: Giancarlo and his brother, Cristiano.

"If you need anything, please let me know. I will be here until this evening." Rosabella smiled and Wendy thanked her.

The clock on the wall showed seven-thirty. Papa and Mama would be in when visiting hours started at eight. She longed for a time when she could be alone with him, with no place to go and nobody to see. Just the two of them, alone for hours on end. That dream seemed so far away now.

"*Buon giorno, Wendy.*" It was Dr. Rossi. "And how is our patient this morning?" His English was excellent. While packing for the trip to Italy, she had asked Giancarlo if she would be able to understand anybody once they arrived. She didn't speak any Italian, though he was trying to teach her. He'd told her that English was taught in Italian schools and was an important language to learn everywhere in Europe. The United States was a premier world country, he'd said, and she remembered how proud that had made her feel. He assured her almost everybody she'd meet would speak some English.

Wendy got up from the chair where she had been sitting. "He opened his eyes! Rosabella and I both saw it!"

"That is wonderful! I had expected that it would take much longer to come out of the coma. Perhaps he is just eager to get married, yes?" He smiled at Wendy and continued.

"He is much more stable now and it is time to fix his leg. Dr. Allesandro DeSanti will be doing the surgery. I am sure he will be in soon and introduce himself. Gianni is a strong man and everyone here wants what is best for him. We will do everything possible to make sure he gets the very best care."

"Yes, I know that and I'm so grateful for all of you, especially you, Dr. Rossi."

"Wendy, you must call me by my first name. It is Enrico. Gianni would insist on it. He is a very lucky man to have found you."

Pietro and Lalia arrived at eight and were relieved to hear that Giancarlo was starting to respond. His mama spoke softly in his ear, always touching him, letting him know that he was not alone. Pietro, too, stroked Giancarlo's hair and spoke to him.

Pietro's English was very good, better than Lalia's. Before he had retired, he was a distributor for Illy coffee and sold to customers in many countries. He spoke several languages and was tall with thick gray hair. It wasn't hard to see where Giancarlo got his good looks. For a man who was pushing seventy-two, he was fit and energetic. Wendy filled him in on the upcoming surgery and then left the room so that they could have time alone with their son.

At eight-thirty, Dr. DeSanti appeared in the doorway and asked everyone to step out into the hall. He introduced himself and told Pietro and Lalia how happy he was to have received the wedding invitation and how much he admired Gianni. He told them they had worked together many times in surgery and said that he intended to do his very best to have Gianni back on his feet so that the wedding could take place as soon as possible.

He turned to Wendy. "And you are the woman who has stolen Gianni's heart. It is a pleasure to meet you." He shook Wendy's hand, the strength of his grasp reassuring. He looked younger than Giancarlo and was slim, but athletic, his brown hair shortly cropped. He had an easy-going manner, but an intensity in his blue eyes that said he was intelligent and focused.

Dr. DeSanti told them Giancarlo would be given anesthesia, even though he was in a coma, to ensure that he would feel nothing and would not wake up during surgery. He explained how he was going to repair the break, that a metal rod would be placed down through the center length of the bone and then held at both ends with screws. He drew a picture so that everyone understood. Giancarlo was on the surgery schedule for nine-thirty and he would come and talk to them after the surgery was finished. "Now I must see my patient," he said and they all filed back into the room.

He uncovered the sheet on Giancarlo's leg and inspected the external fixation hardware. "It is time to make this repair permanent. I have seen his x-rays," he continued, speaking to Pietro and Lalia, "and it is a bad break, but fixable. I expect to find damage to the tissues and muscles in the leg, but that will heal with time. After surgery, he will go to the recovery area."

He shined a pen light into Giancarlo's eyes, then took the stethoscope from around his neck and listened to Giancarlo's heart and lungs. He checked the chest tube and nodded his head in satisfaction. "He looks good. Surgery will go well, I am sure, and we will have Gianni up in no time."

He turned his attention to Wendy. "He will be on crutches for at least four weeks. He will be allowed to put his weight on the leg, but gradually. In my opinion, you could have your wedding in three weeks, two at the earliest and knowing Gianni as I do, he will be ready even before that! He will be using crutches though." Dr. DeSanti was smiling broadly. "I must go now and as I said, I will speak with you after we are finished with the surgery." They all thanked him. He smiled and walked out of the room.

Pietro and Lalia had decided to wait in the surgical waiting area. They were told it was a comfortably large room and could accommodate the family. It was located on another floor and the family headed down there leaving Wendy in the ICU.

She wanted to be alone for a while, to have time to think. The tension of the past forty-eight hours had left her totally exhausted and about to fall asleep on her feet, but she refused to lie down yet. She wanted to be awake when the surgery was finished. When she knew he was okay, then she would sleep.

She noticed a woman wearing scrubs standing outside the room watching her. Wendy had not seen her on this floor before. Getting up from her chair, she went to the door and asked, "Are you looking for someone?"

"Gianni." she replied. "I thought he was here." She was about Wendy's age, maybe younger, not plain-looking but not beautiful either. She was pretty, though, in her own way. Her brown hair was pulled into a tight bun on top of her head and accentuated her long neck and oval face. Even without makeup, Wendy noticed her pretty hazel eyes and long eyelashes and noticed that her scrubs were perfectly ironed. She thought that was odd; nobody ironed scrubs! She wasn't wearing a name tag and seemed nervous.

"He's in surgery. Are you a friend of his?"

"Not really a friend, but I know him. I was told he was in an accident." She avoided making eye contact, glancing at the floor occasionally as if she were counting the tiles. Wendy extended her hand.

"My name is Wendy Alexander. I am Giancarlo's fiancée." The woman hesitated for a moment, then took Wendy's hand. "I'm sorry you missed him. Will you come back later?"

"I have something I need to tell him. I do not know if I can come back again."

This was getting mysterious and Wendy definitely didn't need a mystery right now. What she needed was sleep, but her interest was piqued. If she wasn't Giancarlo's friend, what could she possibly have to tell him...no, '*need*' to tell him?

"You didn't tell me your name," Wendy probed.

"Sofia Amato," she responded hesitantly.

"Did you work with Giancarlo?" She noticed that the woman's hands were shaking ever so slightly, that her gaze returned to the floor when she wasn't speaking.

"No, I work in the laundry," she answered.

'That might explain the ironed scrubs,' Wendy thought. She had called him 'Gianni' and Wendy thought it odd that if she wasn't a friend, but only 'knew' who he was, that she would refer to him by his nickname. It was unusual too, for someone who worked in the laundry to refer to any doctor that way.

"If you'd like, I can give Giancarlo a message. Would that help?"

Sofia considered this for several seconds. At one point, she looked so nervous that Wendy thought she just might leave at any second.

"May I speak to you in the room?"

Wendy sensed something foreboding in the way she had said it. Her eyes were pleading and she was looking directly at Wendy as though whatever she had to say was going to come spilling out at any moment. Turning back into the room, Sofia followed her and sat down, her eyes still counting the tiles on the floor. "There is something I think Gianni needs to know. It is about Donnatella, about her accident."

Now Wendy was very interested. She had always had the feeling that Giancarlo hadn't told her everything about Donnatella's death, but she had never pressed him for details. She knew it was hard for him. Donnatella was gone after all and it didn't matter to Wendy if there were parts of his life that he kept to himself. She was also keeping parts of hers secret from him.

Sofia hesitated, as if she was trying to decide if she should tell what she knew, trying to decide if she could trust her. "Do you know about Donnatella?"

"Yes, I know about her and about the accident. Giancarlo told me."

"Did Gianni tell you that she was having an affair?" Wendy didn't know where this was going and she was starting to feel uneasy.

"Yes, he told me."

"But I do not think he told you she was having an affair with my husband Nicolò." Wendy was immediately uncomfortable. No, Giancarlo had never told her that he knew the name of his wife's lover. Wendy's sympathy went out to Sofia. Donnatella may have been the victim of an accident, but she was dead and felt no pain. Wendy could see that Sofia was a victim too and had to live with pain every day. There wasn't much she could say.

"No, he didn't tell me that. I'm very sorry, Sofia."

"I must tell Gianni what I saw. I think it was not supposed to be Donnatella who died."

Wendy felt her stomach tie in a knot. "What do you mean? What did you see?" All she could think about was Giancarlo, about the implication of what Sofia had just said and she was worried, concerned for his safety.

"My husband Nicolò was very much in love with Donnatella. He wanted her to divorce Gianni, but Gianni would not do it."

Wendy saw the hurt in her eyes and wondered how Sofia knew Giancarlo wouldn't grant a divorce. Her husband surely hadn't told her.

"You knew who your husband was having an affair with?"

"Yes, I knew. Women know these things. I would smell her perfume on him or see lipstick on his neck and know I had not kissed him. He would leave many times at night and tell me he was going to the hospital, but I knew he was lying because he would smell like her when he came back home."

"How did you know it was Donnatella, that it was her perfume?"

"I met her at parties many times. She was very beautiful. I saw the way Nicolò looked at her and the way she looked at him. I saw in their eyes how much they wanted to be together." She looked down at the floor. "Women know these things," she repeated.

"What about the night before the accident? What is it that you want to tell Giancarlo?"

She started slowly. "I wanted to tell him after the accident, but I was afraid and I did not know for sure." She hung her head, her hands covering her face momentarily and said softly, "I did not want Gianni to get hurt."

Wendy was impatient. Why wouldn't this woman just spit it out?

"I followed Nicolò the night before her accident. I wanted to know for sure if it was Donnatella he was seeing. He parked down the street and waited. I saw Gianni leave the house and get into his car." Wendy could see the hurt in her eyes and the tears forming.

"When he was gone, Nicolò and Donnatella met at the front door and were kissing and...he was touching her." Sofia whispered the last part. "He stayed for only a short time and then I saw him come outside with her. They kissed and after she went inside, Nicolò went over to the bike and I saw him kneel down beside it. I could not see what he was doing. I thought he might have dropped something."

"Do you think he did something to the bike, something to cause the accident?"

"I told you, I could not see. I do not know what he did." Wendy realized that Sofia was falling apart. She was trembling and there were more tears falling.

"Did you tell the police about this?"

"No. I read in the paper that the police said it was an accident." She pulled a tissue from the pocket on her scrub top and wiped her eyes. "You do not understand about my husband. Nicolò has a very bad temper. If he knew that I followed him, it would be very bad for me. Now that Donnatella is dead, he has been faithful to me. I believe this and I do not want to cause trouble with him."

Wendy could understand her fear now, but something needed to be done. If Nicolò had purposefully tampered with the Ducati, causing the accident, then the police must be notified.

155

But there was something else bothering Wendy, something she needed to know.

"Sofia, how did you know that Giancarlo wouldn't grant Donnatella a divorce?" She waited, watching Sofia's face and body language, looking for truth in her answer.

Sofia made eye contact and said softly, "You must ask Gianni." She paused for a moment, wiped the last remaining tears and then said, "He is a very good man. You are fortunate to have him."

With that, with Wendy unsatisfied and hungry for an explanation, Sofia got up and turned to go. "Please tell Gianni that I hope he will be well soon and I congratulate you both on your marriage." She turned, saying nothing more, and walked out of the room, disappearing through the main doors.

Chapter 3

SHE STAYED IN Giancarlo's room after the talk with Sofia. Donnatella was gone and that part of his life was over. But if Nicolò had done something to the Ducati, the police would have to be notified.

Pietro and Lalia came to the ICU and told Wendy that Dr. DeSanti had spoken to them after the surgery was finished and said that Gianni had done well; the fracture had come together perfectly and now it was just a matter of healing. Dr. DeSanti had suggested that it would be better for Gianni if the family would come back tomorrow during visiting hours. Lalia and Pietro stayed only a few minutes and then hugged Wendy, telling her to get some sleep, that they would return home, wait for her call and when Gianni was back in his room, they would return to see him.

Wendy could hardly keep her eyes open. When she couldn't concentrate enough to put together a coherent thought, she laid down on the cot and fell asleep.

She awoke to the monitor's beep, its constancy reassuring to her now. Two nurses were with him, sorting out all the tubes and wires, getting them hooked back up and making sure that everything was operating properly. They listened to his lungs and heart and checked the monitor to see his blood pressure. They made sure the IV was dripping at the proper rate. They changed his gown and positioned him. The metal fixation rod was gone and there was a large dressing on his hip, extending halfway down his thigh. As part of their assessment, they told him to open his eyes, but there was no response. He was still sleepy from the anesthesia, they told Wendy, assuring her that it would wear off soon.

He was finally settled to the nurses' satisfaction and they left. Wendy pulled the chair up close to the bed and took his hand in hers, rubbing the back of it absentmindedly with her fingers. She saw his chest rising and falling and remembered watching him sleep on her sofa early on that Sunday. She was completely in love with him even then. She remembered telling herself that she wanted to wake up next to him every day for the rest of her life. She had come so close to that dream, until yesterday when the dream had taken a painful detour.

She thought about the masculine, sensual smell of his cologne and how it had captured her the first time she'd noticed it. He smelled like iodine and antiseptics now, smells she was familiar with, but seemed out of place on him. *He* was out of place, lying in the ICU, his body broken, hooked up to monitors, his life reduced to numbers and tracings on a screen.

All the sorrow that she had been successfully controlling up until now washed over her like a high tide, taking her breath away and drowning her. She put her head down, resting her cheek on his arm, feeling his warmth and smelling the iodine, and cried.

He was choking. He felt like he couldn't breathe, like his throat was closed. He was confused and was trying to touch his face, trying to find out why he couldn't breathe, but he couldn't lift his arms and he couldn't see. He fought to move and knew that someone was holding him down. The pain was excruciating. Maybe he didn't want to breathe any more. He just wanted the pain to stop. He wanted to go back to sleep and not wake up if the pain would be waiting for him. He wanted the blackness to cover him again.

"*Calma, Giancarlo!*" Rosabella held his wrists; she was having a hard time restraining him. She knew his exertion was causing him pain, despite having just given him a heavy dose of morphine. She was thankful that she had asked Wendy to step out of the room.

She kept talking to him, her voice soothing. "*Apri i tuoi occhi.* Open your eyes." His eyes opened. He saw her, but Rosabella could tell he didn't recognize her.

"You're doing fine, Gianni. Just relax. We're going to extubate you." He couldn't talk to her, but she saw the questioning mixed with panic in his face.

"You were in an accident on the motorbike. You had surgery. You are doing well. We are going to take this tube out of your throat and you will feel much better. Do you understand?" He nodded his head, his body finally giving in to the exhaustion.

Dr. Rossi came in and was surprised to see his patient awake.

"*Gianni, si guarda molto miglio!* You look much better!" Rosabella had released her grip on his wrists. Dr. Rossi unfastened the strap that had been holding the tube in place.

"Rosabella is going to suction your throat. I want you to relax and she will be as gentle as possible. Then I am going to pull out the tube and when I do, I want you to cough. Do you understand?" He nodded again, the anxiety evident in his eyes.

When Rosabella snaked the suction down inside the endotrachial tube, he winced, his eyes shut tightly against the discomfort. He was gagging and choking. The panic was returning, making him breathe fast and every breath was agonizing. He heard the gurgling of the secretions as she suctioned them out.

"Cough now, Gianni." Dr. Rossi pulled on the tube and it slid out as Giancarlo coughed. His discomfort was intense. Rosabella suctioned his throat again and he gagged.

"There, it is done. You will feel much better now." Dr. Rossi checked the monitor while Rosabella placed an oxygen mask over Giancarlo's mouth and nose. The oxygen was running and the oximetry was reading ninety-seven percent. He was still coughing, trying to clear the secretions from his throat.

The blood pressure reading was high, but that was due to pain and anxiety and Dr. Rossi knew it would normalize as soon as the narcotic took full effect.

"You will be wanting that chest tube out too, I suppose." Giancarlo closed his eyes, still unable to talk, the pain in his throat making him wince whenever he tried to speak. He heard the words again in his head: chest tube. Did he have a chest tube, he wondered? He was still confused.

Dr. Rossi listened to his lungs and decided to leave the chest tube in and remove it later in the evening.

Giancarlo tried to speak, but his voice was weak and unintelligible even to him.

"Your throat will be sore for a while. Just stay quiet." Rossi took his pen light out of his coat pocket and shined it into Giancarlo's eyes. Both pupils were equal and contracted when exposed to the light. "Squeeze my hand, Gianni, and now with your other hand. That is excellent! You have good strength."

Giancarlo's heartbeat was fast, but regular and strong. Dr. Rossi smiled and turned to Rosabella. "How much morphine did you give him?"

"Twenty milligrams in the IV," she said.

He put his hand on Giancarlo's shoulder. "I am very pleased with your recovery. Get some rest and I will come back later and we will talk then. If you are good and do not give Rosabella any trouble, I will make you a wedding present of that chest tube." Rossi smiled and Giancarlo did his best to return it.

He tried to remember having an accident. The first thing he could remember was being at the airport waiting for Papa and Mama to pick him up and he was with Wendy. Was she the one who had been talking to him? He couldn't concentrate. The morphine was working and he was finally comfortable. He knew the blackness was coming to him again, but it came slowly this time. It was different now; there was very little pain and he was relaxed. He fell asleep and didn't dream.

ॐ

Afternoon visiting hours began at two and Pietro and Lalia were right on time. Wendy watched them as they got off the elevator.

She had immediately liked his parents. Before he'd even had time to introduce her at the airport, Lalia had greeted Wendy with an enormous bear hug, then a kiss to each cheek: the typical European greeting. She had insisted that Wendy call her 'Mama' and then after hugging and kissing her son, Lalia had scolded him saying, "She is *more* beautiful than you said, Gianni!" Wendy had looked at him and he had winked back at her, smiling.

Pietro had given her the same hug and cheek kisses, had told her she must call him Papa, but his comment had been for Wendy. "If my son ever breaks your heart, he will answer to me! It is my promise to you." He had smiled warmly at her, but the Godfather movie had flashed in her head and she had giggled.

She and Giancarlo had arrived on Monday. Dr. Hazleton was allowing them three weeks for their wedding and honeymoon, even though Giancarlo was new to Memorial and didn't have a lot of vacation time accrued. But true to his philosophies toward employees, Hazleton had granted their request. He liked Giannotti and liked the changes he was making in the ED. Memorial would hire temporary replacements for them.

Wendy was so happy for him, knowing how much he had been looking forward to seeing his family again. As soon as they had made their plans for the wedding and had ordered the airline tickets, he'd talked of nothing else but his family and had called them almost every day telling them about her.

Giancarlo told her stories about his mama. Wendy had surmised that he was a bit of a rebel as a small child and was in trouble with Mama quite often, but could always charm his way into her good graces with his engaging humor and gorgeous eyes. He hadn't changed much from that little boy, she mused. He sometimes used those tactics on her, not because he was in trouble with her, but when he wanted something from her. His eyes would get larger and he would give her his 'puppy dog look,' as she called it. She could never resist him when he did that!

Most of Giancarlo's seven siblings, plus children of all ages, shapes and sizes, had come to the house to meet Wendy and see Giancarlo. He'd been in the United States almost nine months and they had all missed him. Wendy was introduced to each one of them, including the children, and knew from the beginning that she would not remember many of their names, but that was okay; she would make Giancarlo bring her to Italy every year to visit. She was already in love with the country and his family.

There was a huge family dinner on Monday and Tuesday. Giancarlo's sisters and sisters-in-law were in the kitchen with Mama, cooking and chatting away in Italian and English. They had insisted that Wendy join them. It was a chaotic blend of conversations, laughter and good-natured teasing, most of it aimed at Wendy and having to do with Giancarlo's virility. It was the first time she could remember having lobster face when she was with a group of women! She enjoyed these woman. She loved their passion for life and for their men and children.

The men congregated outside on the large patio at the front of the house and talked while loosely supervising the children. Wendy could hear quite a bit of laughter coming from their direction and wondered if the subject of their conversations with Giancarlo matched those of the women with her.

It was a busy, noisy, loving homecoming and Wendy and Giancarlo had enjoyed every minute of it. Now everything had changed. Pietro and Lalia were in the ICU visiting their oldest son, trying to be brave and trust God, but worrying nonetheless. The worry showed in their faces.

Wendy met them at the door. "Look!" She pointed at Giancarlo, who smiled at them and said something in Italian. Even the oxygen mask was gone now.

They were overjoyed, particularly his mama. She crossed herself and exclaimed *"Grazie Maria, Madre di Dio!"* She kissed both of his cheeks, her smile lighting up the room. Wendy told them that Dr. Rossi was going to remove the chest tube later in the day and this news too, was followed by another round of thanks to the Blessed Virgin.

Wendy stayed for a short while, then told them she was hungry, that she hadn't had a full meal in two days and that she was going to the cafeteria to get something hot. She *was* hungry, but more than that, she wanted them to have their time alone with him.

Coming back up to the floor, she passed them as she got off the elevator. Mama said nothing to her, but gave her an especially long, affectionate hug and then kissed her cheek. Papa followed suit, then they told her "Ciao," stepped into the elevator and the door closed. Wendy was puzzled, wondering what had prompted their unexpected show of affection.

Rosabella was in his room when Wendy got there. She didn't look happy.

"Wendy, would you please tell Gianni that it is time for his pain medication? Dr. DeSanti has ordered it to be given every four hours today and then…" she locked her eyes on him, her voice more stern, "…whenever he asks for it starting *tomorrow*!"

"I think you should do what Rosabella says. She sounds pretty serious." It was meant to be a light-hearted comment, but she knew he needed the morphine. Although he was trying to appear comfortable, she could see by the tension in his face that he was miserable. He was clenching his jaw. Wendy got serious now too. "Giancarlo, you need the morphine. Please let Rosabella put it in the IV."

He was serious too; she could see it in his eyes. "Not yet, it puts me to sleep. I will take it in a few minutes." She didn't want to force the issue or argue with him; it would only intensity his discomfort.

Rosabella knew that he had the right to refuse any medication he did not want. She gave Giancarlo a scowl and Wendy a look that said, 'It's out of my hands,' and then left with the morphine.

"Did you eat?" he asked.

"Yes, it was good, but not as good as Chef's food. I met your mama and papa as I got off the elevator. They were especially affectionate with me. Do you know what that was all about?"

"They asked me how I felt and what they could do that would make me feel better. I told them that I would feel much better if I could hug you, but it would hurt too much. I asked them to do it for me." He was trying to smile through the pain.

"Well, both of them hugged me *and* kissed me."

"That is strange," he said. "I only asked Mama to give you a kiss for me. Papa? Well, I think that was his own idea."

"Your papa! He's just like you," she laughed.

"Yes," he said, "but I am a better kisser!"

He was quiet for a long moment and then his expression changed. "I am so sorry, Wendy. I wanted your time here to be happy. Now this accident has caused you worry and that is my fault. I did not mean for this to happen."

His eyes were getting red and glassy. She knew he had no emotional reserves left. She understood how pain and stress could bring a person to a place where there was nothing left to sustain them. She knew this; it was the same for her after Mark's death.

"You have nothing to be sorry for. None of this was your fault. It was an accident." She paused, hoping he wouldn't remember that she had asked him not to take the bike into town.

She didn't want him to feel guilty and now she regretted having said it in the first place. He said nothing and she continued.

"I *have* been worried about you. But you need to know that at the same time, God has blessed me." He looked puzzled, his face pale now.

"I watched your family, all of them. It made me happy to see how close and loving they are toward you and they have been so welcoming and nice to me. I have met so many staff here who care for you and respect you. I see how they treat you with such compassion and gentleness and it humbles me because I wonder if I am worthy to love a man who is so admired by others." The last sentence caught in her throat.

"And I'm so thankful for Dr. Rossi. I don't think I could have stayed sane seeing you only during visiting hours. He let me stay with you, to sit beside your bed, to touch you and talk to you and to know that you were still with me. My only comfort was to be able to hold your hand and rest my head on the bed. That's when I could pray and then I could sleep."

She grabbed a tissue. He reached up and caught a tear before it dripped, wiping it away from her face with his thumb. Then the corners of his mouth turned up ever so slightly.

"Do you think we should tell her?" he asked, his voice weaker now.

"What do you mean?"

"Mama. Do you think we should tell her that we slept together?"

She smiled. They had both been through so much the last two days and he had found a way, as he usually did, to lighten her mood. At that moment, she loved him more than she ever thought possible, but he was waiting for her answer, his face tense now.

"No, let's not tell Mama. You know how she would feel about that," she said, the light-hearted moment gone.

"Wendy, would you tell Rosabella I will take that morphine now?"

It was then that she realized he'd deliberately refused the morphine in order to be awake for her, to be with her so that he could apologize. Now he was paying the price.

Chapter 4

DINNER DIDN'T STAY down, but he had absolutely no appetite anyway. Fortunately, Dr. DeSanti dropped by his room just after and ordered something for the nausea. Wendy had stepped out of the room when she saw Dr. DeSanti. She needed to go to the restroom and felt that Giancarlo would be more open with DeSanti if she weren't there.

"Feeling a little better now?" Dr. DeSanti pulled the sheet back, uncovering Giancarlo's leg. He noted the dressing was dry. He took a quick look at the monitor, nodding his head in approval.

"*In un po 'di tempo.*" His stomach was still unsettled and he hoped there was nothing left in it. He was still waiting for the pain in his chest to settle down. He could feel the ends of the ribs grating against one another when he retched, giving him a new appreciation for every accident victim he had ever operated on.

"You are making a remarkable recovery. You do not appear to have any lasting trauma from the concussion and…"

"How long was I unconscious?" he interrupted. He didn't realize until that moment that he didn't even know what day of the week it was and didn't remember what day the accident had happened.

"Two days. The police came to the emergency room with the ambulance and gave us a report. A witness told them a stray dog ran out in front of your cycle just as you were going around that corner on Via Salicotto. She said you lost control of the bike. You hit the stone wall and then went over the embankment on that turn and landed very hard. She said you 'flew' off the bike. She called in the emergency. You were very lucky. Had you been going any faster, I do not think we would be speaking together right now."

"I know I have broken ribs…"

"Yes, three."

"What about my leg?"

"It was an oblique spiral fracture. You lost much blood, which we replaced."

"How much?" Giancarlo wanted all the details. DeSanti understood exactly; he would want the same if the situation were reversed. Giancarlo wanted to be able to assess his injuries. Foremost in his mind was being able to estimate how long it would take to get back on his feet so that he and Wendy could have their wedding.

"Two units. I did an external fixation in the emergency room, then a medullary nailing. The bone went back together very well. Other than that, you have a liver laceration which is stable and many abrasions and bruises. The CTs of your head and abdomen look benign. As I said, you were very lucky." He changed the subject. Giancarlo didn't have to be told how close he had come to being another statistic.

"I have been told that you are giving the nurses a bad time. You refused your morphine?"

"Just waited a short time, that is all. I took it." He was getting tired and it was time for his next dose. This time, he wasn't going to delay taking it; he'd learned his lesson.

"I will look in on you tomorrow. Until then, give the nurses a break, *per favore*. They already think that we doctors make the worst patients and we do not need you to prove it!"

Giancarlo smiled. Whatever energy he had, was spent now; it took whatever was left just to breathe. He knew that the pain from his broken ribs prevented him from breathing deeply and that he would be susceptible to pneumonia. He wanted to cough and breathe deeply, but it was impossible with the pain that came with it. He needed the morphine, needed relief from the all-consuming aching in his body. It hurt to move and he couldn't get comfortable. The nausea still hadn't left him. He didn't want to think about it, but sometimes he just wanted the blackness to come back and cover him so that he felt nothing.

DeSanti put his hand on Giancarlo's shoulder. "I am glad to see you again my friend, though I would have preferred it be under happier circumstances. Take your morphine like a good boy, yes? I will be back to see you tomorrow." He smiled and left.

By the time Wendy had used the restroom, lingered at the vending machine to kill time and then returned to Giancarlo's room, the evening nurse had given him his next dose of morphine. His eyes were closed and she assumed he was sleeping, so she sat quietly in her usual spot next to the bed.

She listened to the monitor's steady beep, beep, beep and thanked God for every one of them. Now that he was stable, she'd had a chance to face the reality of how close she'd come to losing him. She wouldn't allow herself to think long about what that would have been like to be without him, to be standing in a cemetery reading his name on a headstone with her life gone. She remembered doing that, but it was Mark's name on the headstone. Thinking that way made the tears come too easily.

Instead she thought about his recovery, about being in his childhood home with Papa and Mama and all of them taking care of him. She would ask Mama to teach her to make his favorite lasagna and then she would make it for him. Between her and Mama, they would feed him good food and get him well. He and Wendy would walk outside and talk about the wedding. They would be alone in the olive orchard and feel the sun on their faces and hold each other, letting all the memories of this hospital fade away. They would thank God for his life and their life together and he would heal.

She took his left hand, kissed it and thought about lasagna recipes.

"Do that again," he whispered, startling her.

"Do what?"

"Kiss my hand." She smiled and obliged him. She would have kissed it a hundred times more if he'd asked her. He let out a long breath and she could tell he'd had morphine. He looked very relaxed.

"When I was in the coma I heard voices, but I could not understand what they were saying. Were you talking to me?"

"Yes, Rosabella told me to talk to you, that it would help you wake up."

He was concentrating, trying to remember. "You told me stories. I remember…" He was having a hard time and Wendy could see it was tiring for him.

"You don't have to think about all that now. You should rest." She ran her fingers through his hair. She caressed his cheek with the back of her hand and felt the stubble of his beard. She had never seen him anything but clean shaven and then only with a five o'clock shadow at the end of his shift at Memorial. The stubble looked good on him though. It gave him that masculine, outdoor look and she pictured him at her house, ax in hand, chopping wood for the fireplace.

"You told me a story about your house of trees. We would live at your house." A faint smile crossed his face and he squeezed her hand. "You told me you would make love to me all night. You promised and I will hold you to your promise."

She had talked to him for hours and *that* was what he remembered? He was definitely feeling the effects of the morphine.

"Oh, Gianni! You are *such* an Italian!" She blushed wanting to keep that promise and as always he noticed and had to say something.

"Wendy, I think I have just stepped on first base." Now he was smiling at her.

"You mean you've *gotten* to first base," she corrected. "What makes you think so?"

"You are not so formal with me now. You called me 'Gianni.' I am on first base, true?"

She loved his sense of humor, how his unfamiliarity with English idioms just made his humor all the funnier.

"Oh, yes," she said, smiling. "You got to first base!"

"That is very good because I am trying to get to home base, to your house of trees to collect on your promise!" The smile was spread across his entire face now and he winked at her. She could feel the warmth of the blush and she tried to hide her face in her hands, but he took them and pulled them away. His smile was gone, his voice soft and serious. His dark, beautiful eyes looked through her, accelerating her heart beat.

"Please, Wendy," he begged, his eyes pleading with her, "do not ever hide yourself from me."

The depth of his emotion stunned her, leaving her momentarily speechless, until she finally said, "I won't, Gianni. I promise."

❧

"Gianni, do you want my wedding gift now or should I come back when you are not trying to seduce this beautiful woman?" It was Dr. Rossi, standing by the door and smiling broadly. Wendy wondered just how long he had been there.

"Please, the wedding gift. The other..." he said, cocking his head toward Wendy, "...I will finish when you are gone!"

Wendy was lost. She had no idea what they were talking about. The doctor's hands were empty; she didn't see a gift.

"And should we send *la bella donna* out or do you wish her to stay?" Rossi continued.

"I think we should let *la bella donna* decide for herself. After all, it is her gift too." Wendy was beginning to wonder if she'd just been given a nickname. She liked it because she knew what it meant: the beautiful woman. She was slowly picking up some Italian words, thanks to Gianni.

Dr. Rossi looked at her. "Well, what is your decision?" He waited for her answer and she was trying to decide yes or no without a clue as to what this wedding gift could be. Then she remembered: he was going to remove Gianni's chest tube this

173

evening. She hadn't realized it was a little after seven o'clock already.

"I'll stay, Enrico, thank you. Gianni has been giving me nothing but grief since his last dose of morphine. Maybe your 'gift' will put him in a more serious mood."

"Then let us begin, shall we?" Dr. Rossi turned and walked toward the nurses' station, picked up a tray with the supplies and carried it back into the room.

He helped Wendy turn Gianni on his left side and showed her how to support him in that position. She'd always wanted to get back into nursing, but this was a little more than she had expected. Gianni was looking up at her with a look that made her wonder if she should have declined the offer to stay. But it was too late and if he thought she was going to go all weak and 'girlie' on him, he had another think coming. She could do this. She wanted to do this, wanted to show him she was strong and could take care of him, that he had taught her well.

Dr. Rossi tore several long strips of wide adhesive tape off a roll and stuck them on the bedside stand. Then he clipped the suture holding the tube in place. After he clamped the tube, he placed petroleum gauze at the insertion point on Gianni's chest and several layers of gauze on top of that.

"Now Gianni, you know how this works. We'll count three breaths and on the last one, blow it out and hold." Dr. Rossi pressed lightly on the dressing and counted the breaths. As Gianni held the last one, Rossi pulled the tube out, holding the dressing in place. He secured the dressing firmly, totally covering it with the tape.

She was relieved, expecting a much more dramatic procedure considering that they had just pulled a plastic tube out of his chest. When she helped roll him on to his back, she could see that it hadn't been as simple for him as it had seemed to her. Even with the morphine, his face was gray, his eyes were closed and his breathing was shallow and rapid.

The dizziness overtook her suddenly. It wasn't the procedure that bothered her, it was knowing how miserable it had been for him. She should have declined staying; what was she thinking? Isn't that why she had always escorted patients' relatives out of the ED when there was a procedure to be done? She was upset with herself for staying, but more upset that she had stayed only to prove to Gianni that she wasn't some fragile flower that needed to be shielded from the distasteful things of life.

"Try to breathe slowly and relax. Do you need more narcotic?" Rossi was arranging the covers back over Gianni while Wendy tried to look casual, the dizziness gradually subsiding. She could see that his color was improving. He opened his eyes. His breathing was slower.

"*No, grazie, Enrico. Mi sento meglio ora.* I feel better now."

"Good! Tomorrow we will move you out of here and find a bed for you on the orthopedics floor." Rossi looked at Wendy. He had noticed her getting pale, but decided she was better now too.

"Then, Gianni and Wendy, I will be on my way and let you get back to what you were doing when I arrived." He shot them both a sly smile. "You will be needing the curtain closed?" Gianni smiled broadly; there was still too much pain to manage a laugh. Wendy surprised herself by not blushing and Dr. Rossi left chuckling to himself.

❦

She left to get some dinner when Emiliano and Isabella showed up for visiting hours. On her way to the cafeteria, she realized that after Gianni was transferred to the orthopedics floor, his family would be able to visit more often and there would be more of them visiting. She wouldn't have her cot next to his bed any more, wouldn't have the time alone with him that she so jealously coveted. She told herself that she was being selfish. She couldn't monopolize his time. His family loved him and had been separated from him for nine months. They were going to be part of her family soon and she would always have to share him. Besides, she told herself, she'd had her time with him in Cape Narrows.

After everything that had happened, the murders and threatening phone calls, after he'd told her that he loved her, they had agreed to put everything behind them and just enjoy being with each other.

They were inseparable. In the ED at Memorial, he continued her medical training. She had always wanted to become a registered nurse and he was seeing to it that she was as well-educated as any licensed staff in the ED. They ate lunch together every day and spent whatever remained of their lunch hour in the chapel, a quiet place where they could talk.

The entire hospital was abuzz about the growing relationship and rumors flew that an engagement ring would be on Wendy's finger in no time. Gayle especially was happy for them, even though she and Wendy rarely shared lunch together any more. Gayle wasn't upset, though. If it were her, she'd rather eat with Giancarlo too and she told Wendy so, to much laughter on Wendy's part.

Off duty, they spent all of their time together either at her house or at his. They cooked, read to each other and took long walks. Sometimes they sat at Pirate Joe's watching the boats sail into the harbor, then walked along the beach and swam or worked out at the Aquatic Center.

During that summer, their love grew to such an extent that it was assumed between them that they would get married. He didn't need to ask her and she didn't need to be asked. They knew they wanted to be together and that was enough.

They both wanted the sacred, powerful fulfillment of consummating their marriage vows on their wedding night. They had discussed this often and Wendy knew that this was something his father and mother believed in strongly, as did she. She and Giancarlo had both had it with their first marriages and he had promised her they could have it again. When they needed to separate, to step back in order to keep their promise to each other, they would stay apart for a time and see each other only at work, honoring their decision not to make love until they were married.

It had been getting more difficult every time they were together, to be physically close to each other, knowing their passions were getting harder to control. Finally they knew it was time to take a leave of absence, travel to Italy and get married. She was overjoyed at the thought of being with him, with his family in their country and getting married in his hometown. She never could have foreseen all that had happened since then.

She had bigger problems now, namely her talk with Sofia and how and when she would broach the subject with Gianni. He was still so early in his recovery and she didn't want anything to upset him or delay that recovery. He had enough to do just getting well.

Gianni didn't even suspect that Donnatella's accident was anything but just that. She wondered how he was going to take the story that Sofia had told her. One part of her wanted to see justice for Donnatella; she was Mark's sister, after all, and she felt she owed that to the memory of Mark and his parents. On the other hand, she and Gianni were going to be married soon and she would be his wife. She wanted Donnatella put behind him, just like she would put Mark behind her and they could start their life together: a fresh start with no ghosts, no secrets and no skeletons in the closet.

Try as hard as she might to push it out of her mind, she had to face the fact that at some point, she would have to talk to Gianni about Sofia. There was no rush as far as she was concerned. Donnatella had been gone for five years and speaking with him about it could wait a few more days. But she worried about how it would affect him. She would need to listen to the little voices in her head; her angels. She wasn't sure what to do next, but hoped that as he got better, she could tell him what Sofia had said and get some answers for herself.

She finished her dinner, a somewhat tired-looking pasta dish and a salad, and headed back to the ICU.

He was asleep when she returned to the room. The morphine was working well and she hoped the nurses would let him sleep for a while before they found some chore they were required to do for him and there seemed to be so many.

She sat by his bedside for a while. Visiting hours were over and she needed time to think. This might be her last night sleeping in his room, but she would try to spend as much time with him as she could.

Maybe a break from the hospital would be good for her, though. She would stay at the house and get to know his parents better. Mama had already told her some funny stories about when

Gianni was a boy. She loved hearing them and there was always that lasagna lesson she hoped Mama would give her.

She was tired. When she slept, she heard every noise, every nurse that came in to check him and every beep of the monitor; at least that's the way it seemed. She badly needed uninterrupted sleep, regular meals and a good soak in a tub of hot water.

The steady beep of the monitor was making her sleepy. She kissed his forehead softly, drew the curtain between them and made herself as comfortable as possible on the cot. She would fall asleep thinking about the wedding, how beautiful it would be and how happy they both would be, crutches or no crutches. She would think about the food that Mama and Gianni's sisters would prepare for everyone, how they would drink Chianti and about the singing and laughter at the house. She would think about going away with him, just the two of them by themselves, and she would think about becoming one with him in sacred love.

Chapter 5

NICOLÒ AMATO WAS a man on a mission. He was a cardiologist and his mission was not to heal a diseased heart, but to stop a healthy one.

Ever since Donnatella died, Amato knew that someday Giannotti would prove her death was not an accident and would never give up looking for the person who had caused it. Someday he would know who Donnatella was having an affair with and he would get the evidence he needed to prove it and if that evidence was found, Amato knew where it would lead the police. If that happened, he knew that he would be facing charges of murder and conspiracy to commit murder. As it stood now, Donnatella's death was still listed as an accident, but as long as Giannotti was alive, that could change. He had no intention of being arrested for her murder now or ever, and Giannotti was the only one who stood in the way of his continued freedom.

It had all gone terrible wrong, a tragedy of errors equal to the plot of Romeo and Juliet. Donnatella was the perfect Juliet: radiant, beautiful and desirable. She was unhappy with her husband, complaining that he was too serious, too rigid and especially, too religious. She needed the freedom and money that Amato could give her.

Amato understood her, understood her passions and was willing to fulfill her desires for wealth, travel and social status just to be seen with her. He loved her and she loved the things he could give her.

But just as with Shakespeare's lovers, the love Nicolò had for Donnatella was being denied. Giannotti would not agree to a divorce, telling her it would be morally wrong, that they could work out their problems and love each other again, the way they loved when they first met. He promised her he would make her happy. She didn't want to be happy with him. She wanted to be happy with Nicolò. Donnatella had pleaded with her husband to no avail.

She and Nicolò had devised a clever plan. She had allowed herself to become pregnant with his child. As soon as the affair had begun, she had refused to let Giancarlo sleep in their marriage bed. Five months into the affair, she'd discovered she was pregnant. Giancarlo would know it was not his baby and that she had committed adultery. For that sin, he was sure to divorce her, but when she told him, he forgave her and told her he would raise the child as his own.

She told Nicolò that Giancarlo was adamant about his decision and wouldn't change his mind, that she knew her husband well enough to know that the only way out of their marriage was if he was dead. She told him all of this, never intending to set a plot in motion, never expecting that Nicolò would take matters into his own hands. As far as Amato was concerned, Donnatella and his child were dead because of Giannotti's righteous ideals. If he would have granted Donnatella a divorce, they would still be alive today.

That was how he had come to be at L'Ospedale della Sacra Famiglia on this Friday at two in the morning, outside the doors of the intensive care unit. He had decided it was time to take care of Giannotti when he'd seen the wedding announcement in the paper.

Giannotti had left Italy several months after Donnatella's accident. As long as he was out of the country, Amato didn't worry that the truth about her death would surface. But now he was back, had met someone new in the United States and was bringing her home to meet his family and have a private wedding ceremony. Amato's anger burned against him. Amato should be the one getting married, to Donnatella. He was going to be envied with her on his arm. She was the perfect woman for him: desirable, beautiful and free-spirited. She wanted the nice things money could buy and he wanted to buy them for her.

The second article in the paper, the one about the accident with his brother's Ducati, had made his plan even simpler. Giannotti was tall and strong. It would be easy to kill him while he was injured and unable to defend himself. Amato would solve two problems: he would once and for all take care of any future worry about indictment for murder and he would exact revenge for Donnatella's death.

He had planned the perfect alibi too. After Sofia fell asleep, he would set the clock back one hour. Then he would awaken her, tell her that he was needed at the hospital, tell her the time and that he'd be back in an hour and that she should go back to sleep. He would dress as he always did, kiss her and leave. After he returned, he would move the clock forward to the correct time and wake her, telling her he wanted to make love to her. She usually asked the time and if she were ever asked what she had been doing on that night at that time, he would make sure she would remember.

He chose to solve the problem with Giannotti with morphine, a deadly dose already pulled up into a large syringe, the remainder in a vial tucked into his pocket. He knew where to get it and from whom. In fact, because he was a doctor it was easy. Most doctors knew where to go to get what they needed and he was no different. He'd even had the occasion to acquire some for Giannotti after his knee surgery.

He'd also found Giannotti's room number in the computer. He knew the layout of the ICU; he had patients there frequently. He knew the shift schedules, knew the staff and about when they would be taking a break, when they would make rounds and how many nurses would be on. He could move around without being noticed. If he got caught, he could lie about why he was there. It was going to be easy. He'd even donned the perfect disguise: scrubs, a surgical mask, and gloves to eliminate fingerprints.

The windowed double doors allowed him to see into the unit. He didn't notice anybody at the nurses' station. This was going to be easier than he'd thought. He made his way quietly down the hallway, keeping close to the doors leading into patient rooms in case he needed to duck into a room in a hurry. As he passed the nurses' station, he could hear voices coming from the conference room behind. If they were all in there, he knew they would not linger long. The nurses in intensive care were regimented about checking on their patients. They knew which ones needed constant observation and were disciplined about making sure they kept on top of each patient's condition.

The more critical the condition, the closer the patient was located to the nurses' station. Giannotti's room was at the far end of the hall near the exit stairway. Amato's experience told him that it was only for a limited observation period that he had been taken to the unit in the first place, that and because he was a physician and physicians always got preferential treatment.

He found the room. Giannotti was alone, sleeping soundly, probably under the influence of the same drug he was about to use. The monitor was beeping rhythmically. He looked at the familiar tracing of the heartbeat, knowing it would soon be flat, knowing that the morphine would slow Giannotti's breathing down to the point that it would cease and he would become unconscious. Without oxygen, the heart would stop. Within five minutes after he stopped breathing, Giannotti would be dead. There would be no thrashing, no fighting against the drug, no seizures, nothing that would bring the ever-vigilant nurses down to this end of the hall. He turned the monitor off. He didn't want it to alarm, calling the nurses into the room.

He thought about Donnatella and remembered how beautiful she was. He loved her even now and he hated Giannotti for not taking the Ducati that evening. He found the injection port on the IV tubing and pushed the entire syringe of morphine into the tubing, still picturing Donnatella. Then he took the bottle from his pocket and drew up another syringe full. He began injecting the second dose.

The privacy curtain on the other side of the bed flew open and in the dark, he could only faintly make out the silhouette of a woman standing there watching him. Panicked, he pulled the needle out of the port, sped out of the room and to the stairway exit without looking at her and before she'd had a chance to speak. He was out of the hospital in less that one minute and in his car driving quickly away.

His hands were shaking as he gripped the steering wheel. He was worried about the woman. He wondered who would have been in that room and then he realized it must be her, the

American that Giannotti was going to marry. Amato was sure she would call the nurses. If she did, if they realized what had happened, they would use Narcan and all his work to end Giannotti's life would be in vain. As he drove farther away from the hospital, his thoughts turned darker, his hatred for Giannotti stronger than ever. If Giannotti lived, Amato would have to try again. At least he was relieved that he'd escaped tonight and that it was over, relieved until he realized he'd left the vial of morphine behind.

It had always been there in the background. At first, it scared and worried her. The constant beep of the monitor was telling her that Gianni was badly hurt and that his future was hanging in the balance. It told her how important it was to love completely, passionately and well because each beep was a second gone, a second never to be regained. She hated hearing it, hated that it reminded her that she might lose him.

In the quiet times when she was alone with him, she would hear it and it would tell her that life always struggles to maintain itself, to overcome everything that would seek to deny or destroy it. It told her that the human body was infinitely more fragile than anybody fully realized, but that it was also far more complex. The beep told her that the body's ability to repair itself was designed and set in motion by a healing God and that the human body always struggled to return to health and normalcy. At those times, the beep gave her faith.

As the hours of this day passed, it had been telling her to be patient, be steady just like his heart and Gianni's body would heal.

It assured her that their life would go on, that they should spend whatever cherished time they had together wisely and that they should be complete in each other. It told her that there would be times of trial in their lives, along with the times of joy, but they would see them through together. The beep encouraged her.

Then the beep stopped. There was no alarm, no shrill warning. It was the lack of noise, the lack of the beep she had become so used to, that woke her.

She went to the bedside and looked at him. She knew something was wrong. It was his breathing. It was too slow and he seemed to be struggling to get air into his lungs. She shook him and called his name, but she couldn't wake him up. She pressed the button to call the nurse, then turned on the overhead light. She saw it on the nightstand, the large vial, the word 'Morphine' printed on the label. She'd never known a nurse or anybody else to leave narcotics in the room. It terrified her.

A nurse came in. Her name tag read 'Fabiana.'

"Help him!" Wendy yelled at her, holding up the mostly empty vial of morphine. "Please, help him!"

Fabiana saw that the monitor was off and flipped it back on. That's when they both heard the shrill blast of the alarm. His breathing was slow and labored, his pulse was weak and his blood pressure was dropping.

The alarm brought in two more nurses, both speaking Italian rapidly, both with worried looks on their faces. One of them left, running to the nurses' station and within a few seconds, Wendy heard what she assumed was a Code being called over the intercom.

"Do you know what happened? How did this vial get here?" Fabiana asked.

"I saw a man in here, a doctor I think. He was putting something into the IV. I couldn't wake Gianni up. I saw the bottle on the nightstand."

Fabiana spoke to the other nurse, who flew out of the room, returning almost immediately with a smaller vial and syringe.

By now, there were two men in the room and Fabiana was speaking to them in Italian. Wendy didn't need to know what they were saying. She knew from her experience in the ED at Memorial what was happening. One of the men was from the respiratory department. He had tilted Gianni's head back and placed a resuscitator bag over his mouth and nose. There was oxygen being fed to the bag as the respiratory therapist squeezed it, forcing air into Gianni's lungs.

The other she assumed was the doctor on call. He lifted Gianni's eyelids and shined a pen light into his eyes. He put his stethoscope to Gianni's chest and listened, his face grave. After filling the hypodermic syringe, he inserted the needle into the injection port.

"Dr. Lissandro is giving him naloxone. It is also called Narcan. It will reverse the effects of the morphine." Wendy nodded at Fabiana, letting her know she understood.

Wendy knew about Narcan. Giancarlo had used it in the ED at Memorial one afternoon a few weeks before they had left for Italy. A young kid only seventeen years old had been brought in to the ED by his parents, who told Giancarlo that their son was a heroin addict and had overdosed. He gave the kid Narcan in small incremental doses every two to three minutes until the kid regained consciousness and started complaining that Giancarlo had robbed him of his 'high.' He was discharged into his parents' custody, complaining all the way out the door about how much that heroin had cost him. Wendy remembered the mother crying.

She also knew that Narcan was used after surgery to reverse the effects of anesthesia. She knew that in Gianni's case the doctor would know when the effects of the morphine were reversed because Gianni would regain consciousness. It was a definitive indication that the Narcan had done its job. The trick was to give him enough to wake him up, but still keep him out of pain; too much and he would have to endure until the Narcan wore off. It was an amazing drug, but she was scared all the same.

After the first dose was given, the waiting started. Two minutes after the first dose was given, the doctor injected another dose into the IV and the waiting continued. She thought his breathing was less labored, but it was still slow and he was not waking up. In another three minutes, another dose was given.

Within twenty seconds, Gianni moaned and opened his eyes, pushing the resuscitation bag away from his face. He looked confused which was understandable; the room was full of people all focused on him. Wendy had stepped back from the bed in order to let the staff treat him, but now she came over and took his hand.

"What is happening?" His eyes were searching her face for clues. She didn't know how much to tell him. She was thankful when the on-call doctor spoke to him in Italian and Fabiana translated for her.

"Dr. Lissandro tells him that there was a medication reaction and that his breathing was affected. He tells him that everything is good now and that he should try to go back to sleep." At this point, Gianni said something back to the doctor and Fabiana continued translating.

"Dr. Giannotti said he does not wish to have any more morphine. He says he would like something not so strong and Dr. Lissandro is saying he will give him oxycodone, but that he thinks that it will not be good enough. Dr. Giannotti is insisting that he does not want morphine."

"Gianni," Wendy said and he looked at her, "please take the morphine to help you sleep. You can take the oxycodone later."

"All right, Wendy, I will take the morphine again, but no more after this. I will be all right. Please trust me." He was already feeling the throbbing in his hip and leg, the sharp pain in his chest every time he breathed. He knew the effects of Narcan could last from thirty to ninety minutes and he realized that by the time he got another dose of morphine, the pain would be unbearable.

As the doctor was leaving, he motioned Fabiana and Wendy to follow him. They stood at the nurses' station, Fabiana translating as the doctor spoke.

"Dr. Lissandro wants to know how this happened and asks what you know about this."

Wendy related her story, how she had awakened because she could not hear the monitor's beeping, how she had seen a man putting something into the IV tubing. She filled in the rest of the details. Dr. Lissandro wanted to know if Wendy could give a description of the man and she told Fabiana that it was too dark, but that he was wearing scrubs and a surgical mask on his face. They would be notifying the police, Dr. Lissandro said. He then asked Fabiana to ask Wendy if she was all right and Wendy told Fabiana to thank him for his concern and that she was okay. With that, Dr. Lissandro spoke again to Fabiana and then got on the phone.

"Dr. Lissandro is notifying the police. He thinks it would be a good idea to have Dr. Giannotti moved into another room, but not into a patient room. He says they are too accessible. He suggests that we move Dr. Giannotti into the conference room. It is located behind the nurses' desk so that anybody who would go in there would have to come into the nurses' station. Dr. Lissandro feels it would be more secure. We will be doing that tomorrow in the morning. Until then, we have informed hospital security and we will all be keeping watch on Dr. Giannotti's room. You will be in there with him, so we feel he will be safe tonight."

"Thank you so much, Fabiana. Thank Dr. Lissandro for me too, please." She was still shaking inside, but the staff seemed to have everything under control. She just wanted to be with Gianni, to make sure he was all right.

When she got back to his room, he was still awake, though his eyes were shut tight against his discomfort. She didn't know how she was going to tell him what had happened and she was scared. She didn't understand why someone would want to hurt him. Then she remembered what Sofia had told her and the thought chilled her like someone had opened a door and an Arctic blast of wind had blown past her.

"What happened?" he asked, opening his eyes. "I know they used Narcan and I see your face and I know you are afraid." His eyes locked on to hers and wouldn't let her go. There was an edge to his tone that made her uncomfortable and nervous.

"You should try to get some sleep. We can talk about it tomorrow." She thought she'd try, but she knew he wasn't going to listen to her.

He wouldn't take his eyes off hers, wouldn't look away so that she could have time to think of a way to make this sound better than it was. His eyes would pin her down, hold her to the truth until she told him everything. There was no escaping his stare, no way of hiding from those stunningly dark, penetrating eyes.

"Tell me what happened, Wendy," he commanded.

"Someone tried to give you an overdose of morphine." She'd said it, gotten it out and now she waited, wondering how he would take it. His eyes were still focused intently on hers; he wasn't going to release her yet.

"Tell me all of it." His voice was firm and demanding and she didn't like how it made her feel, like he was her father and she was in trouble and about to be scolded. Had he used that voice with Donnatella too? There was nothing for her to do but give him what he wanted.

"I woke up because I didn't hear the monitor beeping. I drew back the curtain to find out if you were okay and I saw a man putting something into your IV. I thought it was a doctor, but before I could say anything he ran out the door." She was shaking again, but worse now, thinking about how close she'd come to losing him. "I tried to wake you up, but you were unconscious so I called for the nurse." She hung her head. She didn't have the strength to look into his eyes for one more second. He took her hand in his, his voice soothing now.

"I should not have been harsh toward you. I'm sorry." His gaze was soft and subdued now. His eyes had released her. "I owe my life to you."

Was it going to be like this, Wendy wondered? Would there be times when they would say or do something to hurt the other's feelings? Was it pure selfishness and disregard for each other, the newness of their relationship dimming? Or was it from past experiences, from their first marriages? She wanted things to be different for him this time. She wanted to love him in the way that he deserved, the way he hadn't been loved before, but there were those times like now that she felt like he was treating her as if she were Donnatella. She didn't like it. She was afraid that at some time in the future, it would steal away her love for him.

She wouldn't tell him about what Sofia had told her, not yet. There would be time for that later. "Can we talk about this tomorrow, Gianni?" She needed to step back, just for a short time. She needed time to think and some time to heal from the wounds of his harsh words.

"Yes, we will talk tomorrow. I'm sorry, Bella Donna. *Tu sei la mia vida.* You are my life." He pulled her down toward him, brought her face close to his and kissed her. She knew it was his way of asking forgiveness and so she forgave him well.

Fifteen minutes later, an officer came into the room. He was young and looked a little nervous, but his manner was professional. He was tall, but slight of build and Wendy wondered if he was even old enough yet to shave; his face was smooth without even a hint of a whisker. His uniform was neatly pressed, the navy sleeves of his shirt rolled up, his beret perfectly placed on his head. He introduced himself, intent on speaking his best English. She wished someone with more experience had been sent, someone like Brantmeier. This was serious and she was afraid for Gianni's life.

The officer took out a notepad and pen and asked her almost the same questions that Dr. Lissandro had asked and she gave him the same answers. He noted everything, told her an inspector would be out in the morning to investigate further and that he would be searching the hospital. Then he left.

As the minutes passed by, she sat silently at his bedside, anxious for the time when he could have his next dose of morphine. Beads of perspiration formed on his forehead as she watched him struggling to maintain control. After what seemed like an eternity, Fabiana finally came into the room and injected the narcotic into the IV. Within a few minutes his body relaxed, his eyes closed and he fell asleep.

She rested on the cot, aware of the nurses checking on him each time they came into his room. In the back of her mind, she kept close track of the monitor, listening to the beep. Now it was telling her something different, something hidden that she knew nothing about. He was keeping something from her; she knew it and it made her anxious. More than anything, she wanted to trust him, but now was wondering if that was possible. Someone wanted him dead for some reason and that was a secret he shouldn't be keeping from her.

She thought about everything that had happened since they had arrived in Italy until the steady beep of the monitor finally lulled her to sleep.

Chapter 6

THE POLICE INSPECTOR came at seven. He excused Wendy from the room, telling her that he would speak with her shortly, and then closed the door. She could see them talking and the longer they were together, the more worried she became. Gianni looked uncomfortable and tired and every so often, he would glance at her through the glass windows. She tried to smile, to let him know everything would be okay, but inside she was scared.

The Inspector finished and came out of the room. He introduced himself as Giorgio Iacopetti. His English was very good and for that Wendy was thankful. She didn't want anything she told him to be misunderstood. She still had bad flashbacks of her time with Brantmeier and she didn't want to go through that again with this man.

She guessed he was in his late sixties, tall and slim with a salt and pepper short beard, a receding crop of dark grey hair and deep lines etched around his eyes. There was an intensity in his manner, but also a congeniality toward her.

She related the same story she had given Dr. Lissandro, almost word for word. He was disappointed that she couldn't give any kind of description of the suspect, but he was very attentive when she told him that she might know who he should talk to. She told him about Sofia and their conversation. The Inspector seemed to know all about Donnatella and her accident and that she was having an affair with Nicolò Amato. She assumed that he had investigated that case too.

"Dr. Giannotti did not mention anything to me about Signora Amato. Do you know why that is?" he asked.

"Sofia told me that she had never said anything to Giancarlo about it. She said her husband had a bad temper and I got the impression she was afraid of him. But she wanted Giancarlo to know and asked me to tell him."

"But you have not told him."

"Giancarlo has been very ill. I didn't want to upset him. I was going to tell him as soon as he was feeling better. If I had known that an attempt would be made on his life, I would have told him right away."

"I will leave that up to you, Signorina. He has always suspected that his wife's death was not an accident, but we have never had enough evidence to charge anyone with her murder."

Inspector Iacopetti was less threatening than Brantmeier. He told her he would come back if he had any information for Dr. Giannotti and gave her his card. He also said that he understood that the staff were going to move Dr. Giannotti into a safer room and he agreed that that would be a good idea. He excused himself, saying he would keep in touch and then added, "It has been a pleasure meeting you." Wendy thanked him and he left.

She was mystified. Gianni *had* been keeping things from her. He'd never told her that he thought someone was responsible for Donnatella's accident, never told her that he'd gone to the police about it. She wondered why and wondered what else he was hiding.

After breakfast was served and the tray picked up, Rosabella and two other nurses came into the room and started moving his things over to the conference room. When everything else was in place, they moved Gianni's bed.

She knew he'd only slept two hours after the last dose of morphine and had asked for oxycodone during the night. She could tell it wasn't giving him the relief that the morphine had and when she'd mentioned it to him, he'd reminded her that he wasn't going to take any more morphine and told her again that she shouldn't be concerned, that he could handle it. He had used the same tone that he had the night before. When he spoke like that, she knew the subject was closed. She felt chastised by him again and hoped it was just his pain talking. In all that had happened, she had never heard him speak harshly to anyone, especially her.

Maybe it was his demeanor. Somehow it was different since the attempt on his life and she wondered if he was scared. Was he worried that at some point in the future, whoever wanted him dead would accomplished the task or was there something else bothering him?

When she thought about their time together in Cape Narrows, she had to admit that she really hadn't known him for very long; it had only been about five months from that first day he had introduced himself. She realized that she didn't know much about who he was in those secret places that everyone had, herself included, those places that were shared only on the most intimate level.

❧

The conference room was larger than the patient room he had been in. The staff had had to improvise in order to make sure everything needed for his care was available. There would be no call button, so it was decided that the door would be left open whenever there was no one in the room with him. The nurses could see clearly into the room from their desk at the nurses' station. A linen cart was brought in, stacked with clean linens and a bag for dirty linen was attached to a stand on casters. Wendy's cot was moved in, along with a larger chair and two visitor's chairs. It was an inner room, so there were no windows.

When everything was moved and organized, only Rosabella remained. She had given him oxycodone and he was enduring patiently until the drug took effect. He looked tense and uncomfortable.

"Dr. DeSanti wants you out of bed today," she told him. "I will return in one hour to get you up. If you feel you need morphine, tell me." He nodded and thanked her, and Rosabella turned her back to him and left, but not before she rolled her eyes at Wendy. Wendy smiled; she was beginning to see the effect Gianni had on people.

She pulled a chair up next to his bed and sat down, needing some answers and hoping he was ready to give them.

"Gianni, do you remember when I covered my face and you asked me never to hide myself from you?" He nodded. "I'm worried about you. Tell me how you are and don't hide yourself from me."

He closed his eyes for a long moment, long enough to make her uncomfortably nervous. When he finally met her gaze and his eyes locked on hers, she knew he was going to be truthful and it scared her.

"I am so tired, Wendy. I am tired of the pain." Somewhere in her heart, she knew he wasn't talking about the pain from his broken bones.

He looked away from her, trying to organize his thoughts, trying to go to that place that he kept hidden from her to spare her. He didn't want there to be any secrets between them, didn't want his relationship with Wendy to be like that. But he didn't know if he could trust her with what he'd done.

"In my coma, I could feel the pain. Everything was black and I wanted the blackness to cover me and never allow me to wake up again. But I heard you talking to me, telling me to open my eyes. I did not know it was you, but I could feel your love." He was looking away, afraid she could read what was on his face. "I am afraid someday you will not love me and that you will leave me."

"Gianni, look at me," she demanded. "I will never leave you. Don't ever worry about that. I love you more than I love my own life and I will *always* love you. You are everything to me."

Had Donnatella ever said anything like that to him, she wondered? Had she ever had the capacity to care about him enough to make him feel safe in her love, the wife who had vowed to cherish him? She wondered if he would ever feel secure with her or would he always have doubts?

Maybe his physical pain was worse. The muscles in his face were taut and his jaw set firmly. He wouldn't look at her, but kept his eyes turned down. She knew there was something else and the look on his face made her go cold inside.

"Wendy, I have something to tell you. I know it will hurt you and I do not want to do that, but you must know this thing I have kept secret from you." She felt her heart tight in her chest, its rate increasing until the pounding made her head ache.

198

Whatever he was keeping from her, she wanted it out in the open so that she could deal with it, but she was terrified to face it.

"*Gianni, che è successo? Perché si è mossa?* What happened? Why did they move you?" Mama and Papa were coming through the door. Mama looked worried, her voice a little louder than usual. Papa was shushing her, reminding her it was the intensive care unit and she should be quiet.

Wendy's heart was still pounding, her nerves frayed. Could there have been any worse time for his parents to show up? She knew she was unable to hide her frustration. The only thing to do was to leave before they noticed.

"Gianni, I'll get some breakfast and let you visit with Papa and Mama." Forcing a pleasant smile, she kissed his forehead and left. She would let him deal with his parents. She was upset and needed time to think. Besides, she wouldn't know what to tell them about the attempt on his life and he would.

She walked slowly toward the elevator, remembering every word he had told her before his parents had shown up. He knew that what he had to say was going to hurt her. That admission left about a million scenarios that sped through her mind like movie projector film unwinding off the reel, out of control, spilling in an irreparable, jumbled heap on the floor.

Her greatest fear was that he couldn't commit to her, that he didn't trust her to love him. Wouldn't that be the most likely problem, she wondered, when he'd lived through that very thing with Donnatella? He always seemed so self-confident, but she knew how Donnatella's unfaithfulness would have devastated him, robbing him of any confidence he had as a man.

She wondered if he wanted to back out of the wedding and if so, would there be anything she could say to him that could change his mind? He had a track record of making decisions and sticking to them, never backing down. Would his record stand? If she couldn't change his mind, could she live without him and could she survive the devastation it would cause her? She felt the tears coming and so she took a deep breath and forbid herself to cry.

There were other pictures flashing in her mind too. There was still something that nagged at her about her talk with Sofia. It was the feeling she'd had when Sofia had told her that Gianni was a good man and that Wendy was lucky to have him. It was the tone of her voice: soft, gentle and knowing. The 'knowing' part; that's what bothered her.

She told herself that whatever it was he wanted to tell her, she loved him enough to forgive him anything. If he wanted to back out of the relationship, she would let him go no matter how much it hurt her. Mark was gone and she had survived his death and if Gianni wanted to leave her too, she would continue to go on with her life. She loved him so much that she wanted him to be happy even if that meant that he was happy with someone else. It was decided, and she prayed she would feel at peace with herself.

By the time she got to the cafeteria, she had no appetite. She ordered a cup of coffee and sat sipping it, searching the movies playing in her head for the surprise ending, the one she could live with, the one that had them married and enjoying their honeymoon. She wanted the movie with the 'happily ever after' ending.

She walked slowly back to his room, telling herself that she wanted to give him time to talk to his parents, but she knew she was lying. She didn't want to go back, didn't want to talk to him and find out what it was that was going to hurt her.

Maybe she would tell him she was going home with Papa and Mama to take a hot bath. She needed one and wanted the relaxation it would provide her; he might let her go. She was looking for an excuse, wanting to believe she could find one, but knowing he wouldn't let her leave until he'd had his say. Facing him would be easier than avoiding him. There was nothing else left to her but to return to his room and get the pain over with. Even after drinking the coffee, she still felt cold inside.

When she returned, Papa and Mama were nowhere to be seen. He appeared to be asleep and she wondered if she'd gotten a reprieve.

"Wendy? Did you get something to eat?" He opened his eyes, looking more relaxed.

"I wasn't hungry. I just had some coffee. What did you tell Papa and Mama?"

"I told them that I had a reaction to the morphine and the nurses wanted to watch me and make sure I was okay. I know Papa did not believe me, but I will tell him the truth later."

"How are you doing? Is the oxycodone working?" She sat down on the edge of the bed and wondered how long she could avoid his confession.

"You are not going to try to talk me into taking morphine again, are you?"

"Would it do me any good to try?" She heard an edge to her voice that she'd never used with him and it bothered her.

"I can endure the pain," he answered flatly.

He wanted to make her feel better, to atone for speaking to her the way he had during the night. He pulled her down, folded his arms across her back and held her tightly, kissing the top of her head and breathing in the smell of her shampoo. He could never express to her how much he loved her, could find no words to do it justice. He held her and hoped she could feel how much he desired and wanted her.

"I am sorry about Papa and Mama coming in like that," he said at last, releasing her.

"Gianni, whatever it is that you want to tell me, I want you to know that I love you more than I have ever loved anybody." She knew as soon as the words came out of her mouth that in that statement, her love for Mark was included. "Tell me what you want to say."

He couldn't look at her. Instead, he concentrated on their joined hands: how delicate hers were and how gentle she was when she held his. When he finally spoke, his voice was strained and low.

"I was very angry at Donnatella when I discovered she was having an affair," he began. "She had not allowed me to share our bed for a long time. One day at the hospital, a woman I knew asked to sit at my table at lunch. She worked in the laundry."

Wendy almost gasped as the coldness inside her increased until she felt herself shiver. It had to be Sofia he was talking about and she knew where this might be leading. Her chest was already starting to hurt, her heart beating faster.

"We talked and I realized how good it was to have someone to talk to, someone who listened and was interested in me," he continued.

He had told her that what he had to say was going to hurt her, but she could see that it was painful for him too. She wanted

202

to stop him, conscious that they were both going to end up hurting, but she knew he had to continue. She understood that he could not be redeemed until he'd confessed. The heartbreak was already starting and somewhere deep inside her, she was afraid that she had lied to herself, that she wouldn't be able to forgive him *'anything.'*

"We would meet for dinner at places we knew we wouldn't be seen." He paused, looking for a way to soften his confession, trying to minimize the pain he knew was coming. "She was married, Wendy, and her husband was my friend."

The guilt was obvious in his face, so much so that she felt her eyes starting to sting and knew her tears were not far away. He was right. It did hurt, deep inside her. She didn't want to hear any more, didn't want to picture them together and didn't want to know how intimate they had been. She could see what it was doing to him though, could feel it in the shaking of his hands as she held them, in his beautiful eyes that out of shame, would not make contact with hers.

"Please Gianni," she pleaded. "you don't have to tell me any more. I don't need to know about this. Please just rest." Now her hands were trembling too and she wondered if he noticed how cold they were.

"How can I rest? Every time I hold you or kiss you, I know there is something that separates us, a lie that I told you and I cannot rest until you know what it is."

Wendy was sure of one thing: he would not stop until he'd told her his secret. This was his way. She didn't want anything to come between them, but the idea of forgiving him was becoming harder to believe in.

"One night, I asked her to come to my house. I cooked dinner for her and after dinner we drank wine and talked."

That admission hit her with a force so powerful that it surprised and stunned her, leaving what felt like a gaping hole in her chest and no air left in her lungs. He had cooked dinner for Sofia! They had talked over glasses of wine. Chianti maybe? She remembered when he'd cooked the gnocchi for her: how charming he was, how attentive to her. She felt violated, knowing that he'd done the same thing for Sofia and she wondered how many other women he'd cooked for, how many others he'd kissed and held, how many other women he'd made love to? She pulled her hands away, hugging herself so that she wouldn't fall to pieces. She felt herself slipping into some dark abyss. It all seemed so incongruous and mixed up: she loved him and wanted to forgive him, but she was so angry at him for destroying her belief that she was special to him. It didn't make sense; s*he* didn't make sense! Her head was spinning and he just kept talking, taking what was left of her heart and crushing it under his confession!

"It became late and we had nothing more to say, but I did not want her to leave. I knew it was not good for her to stay, but I needed to be with her." His head was down and his eyes closed. "I needed her," he whispered to himself.

Wendy couldn't listen to any more. She didn't want to picture them in her mind but she already had. She just wanted him to stop, but he wouldn't until it was out in the open and he had laid it before her for her to judge. She started to get up, to leave, but he grabbed her wrist and held tight.

"Please, Wendy. Please let me tell you." The pain she saw in his eyes was overwhelming and she felt dizzy. She sat down again, knowing only she had the power to relieve it. She had to let him continue.

"She was sitting next to me and she removed her blouse. She had nothing on underneath." He closed his eyes tightly, trying to push the vision away. "I kissed her and then I touched her. I wanted to make love to her and I started to, but I knew it was wrong. I knew if I were to let myself go further, I would be hurting her and her husband and hurting Donnatella. I could not do that, so I asked her to leave. I told her I could not make love to her."

She took a deep breath, trying to exhale the pain inside, telling herself that he had kept his integrity intact. Now she understood what Sofia had meant when she said that Gianni was a good man. He had chosen to deny himself knowing the suffering he would be causing others. But the betrayal she felt was still inside her and nothing she told herself made it go away.

"I know what I have done, Wendy. I wanted to make love to a woman who was not my wife. I know God says to do that is adultery. You hold me in such high regard, but I do not deserve it; I do not deserve you. How can you forgive me if I do not confess to you? How can God forgive me?" He finished and he waited in silence for her verdict.

She saw his beautiful eyes, his eyes that had always captivated her. She saw the shame in them and that hurt her more than his confession. She lay across his chest again, holding him tighter this time, willing their hurt to go away while her hot tears left wet spots on his gown. She knew that a trust had been broken, but she would not let it destroy the bond they shared. He had been truthful with her and had not hidden what had happened. He was right. She did hold him in high regard and he had just proven to her that he deserved it and her forgiveness.

"God forgives you, Gianni and so do I. I love you so much for telling me and I love your honor."

There was nothing else to say. They were both quiet in their own thoughts. After several minutes, Wendy sat up, knowing it was time. "I have something to tell you. While you were in surgery, Sofia came to your room to see you."

He was taken aback, his eyes wide and questioning. "She told you who she was?"

"She only told me her name and that she knew you."

"Donnatella was having an affair with her husband, Nicolò," he said. "I never told you that and I never told you that she was carrying his baby."

She was shocked. The thought that Donnatella may have been pregnant had never crossed her mind. She felt so sorry for Gianni, knowing that he had always wanted children.

"I do not think that Sofia ever loved me, Wendy," he said quietly. "I think she wanted to use me to hurt Nicolò in the way that he was hurting her and maybe I wanted to use her to hurt Donnatella."

Wendy had seen Sofia's eyes when she'd said that Gianni was a good man and she'd seen love in them. She could see now that it was his honor that Sofia loved and so she let it go without saying anything more; they were both carrying enough pain where Sofia was concerned.

"She wanted to tell you something important. She said that she had followed her husband to see where he was going and she saw him at your house with Donnatella."

"They met at our house?" There was another kind of agony that Wendy saw in his face now, one even more upsetting to her than seeing his physical pain. His wife was taking another man into their bed in their house. Did he wonder if she had become pregnant in his bed?

She took his hands again. "I'm sorry, Gianni. I know that hurts."

He was quiet for a moment. "I will be all right. Tell me what else she said, please."

"She said she saw Nicolò come out of the house. He bent down and did something to the Ducati. She said she couldn't see what it was, but that it was the night before Donnatella's accident."

He was alert now, looking directly at her, his eyes wide. "We have to notify the police. I always believed that her accident was unusual. She could ride and it is true that my bike was powerful, but the front brake cable was disconnected from the bike. If she used both brakes with no front brake, the bike would swerve badly when she tried to stop."

"Did the police investigate the accident?" Wendy was having bad memories of the two murders at Memorial.

"Yes, they checked it and they believed that I had disconnected the cable. They questioned me for many hours. They knew that Donnatella and I did not have a good marriage and they thought that I had tampered with the Ducati. But they had to let me go because they had no proof. We must tell them what Sofia told you."

"I've already spoken to Inspector Iacopetti and told him what Sofia told me. He said they would be talking to her and Nicolò." She hesitated asking him, but she needed to know. "After Donnatella's accident, did you tell the police you had been seeing Sofia?"

"No, I wanted to protect her and to protect her name. I had hurt her enough and I didn't want her involved in Donnatella's death." He was silent for a moment and then added, "And I thought if they knew about Sofia and me, they would suspect me even more."

She heard him inhale forcefully, his eyes wide again as if viewing some horrific scene. "Wendy, it was not Donnatella who was supposed to have the accident. It was me! I would not give Donnatella a divorce and if I were dead, Nicolò could marry her. He did not know that I would take the car that morning because it had rained."

He paused. She could tell he was fitting the pieces together, making sense of all that had happened. His hands were shaking harder. "I think it was Nicolò you saw in my room. I think he gave me the morphine. We must call Inspector Iacopetti and tell him."

Chapter 7

THERE WAS A quick knock at the door and Rosabella came in. She was carrying some scissors and a pair of gloves. "I am going to remove that catheter and then we will get you up." Wendy moved to the door and looked out, watching the nurses working at the desk.

It was a quick procedure; one snip of the tubing, a gentle pull and the catheter was out. "And you do not need these anymore," she said, turning off the monitor and removing the electrodes taped to his chest, the oximeter clamped to his finger and the blood pressure cuff wrapped around his arm.

When she turned around, she was happy to see that he was free of all the paraphernalia except for the IV. But in her excitement, she realized she would miss the steady beep of the monitor. At first it had driven her crazy, but now had come to symbolize his heart: strong, steady and true.

Getting him up for the first time was not going to be easy. Wendy and Rosabella could both see that the oxycodone was not providing enough pain relief for this step in his recovery. Wendy wondered if some of that had to do with his confession.

"I would like your opinion, Wendy," Rosabella said. "Do you think Gianni should be taking a milder pain medication so soon after surgery? It is a very painful surgery and our patients usually take morphine for several days before switching to oxycodone."

"Yes, I know it's a painful surgery. To answer your question, as a nurse who is being trained by an excellent doctor…" here she glanced at Gianni, "…I would say no. It's obvious that the oxycodone doesn't work as well as the morphine does." It was a simple way for the women to get the point across to him and Wendy could see that he had relented.

"Are you two women going to stand there all day talking or are you going to give me some morphine so that I can get up?"

"I will be right back," Rosabella said and she left with a wink to Wendy.

"Do not even think that you will try that after we are married, Wendy!" He was smiling at least, his face still pale.

"Thank you, Gianni. I can't bear to see you suffering any more." She meant every word of that statement; it showed in her face and he saw it.

From the first step of his good foot onto the hard surface of the floor, he was thankful he'd had the morphine. The pain in his right leg was miserable lying down in bed, but unbearable standing up, even with the narcotic.

Rosabella positioned the larger chair next to the bed. She and Wendy helped him stand on his good leg and then swivel his body so that he could sit down without having to put any weight on the bad leg. Both women could tell he was miserable. When he complained of feeling dizzy and faint, they put him back to bed. Rosabella decided to call Dr. DeSanti about the morphine issue.

Dr. DeSanti came soon after Rosabella's call. He was making rounds on the orthopedic floor at the time and Wendy was glad that Rosabella was worried about Gianni too and had made the call.

"What have you been doing to get two women in such a state?" As he spoke, he was feeling Gianni's pulse. "Rosabella told me that you did not look very good. If Rosabella is concerned, then I am concerned also."

DeSanti removed the dressing over the wound and discarded it. "Your incision looks good." Wendy could see the long line of staples in his thigh, the incision red, swollen and angry looking. "Tell me what is bothering you."

Gianni stole a sideways glance at Wendy and then looked back at DeSanti.

"Wendy, would you step out for a moment please?" DeSanti was smiling at her, but she was now even more concerned about Gianni. She left the room, hoping that whatever the problem was, he would tell her later.

"So my friend, tell me what is bothering you." DeSanti sat on the edge of the bed.

"I am sure I am having symptoms from the morphine."

"You have had morphine before and have had no problem with it. Am I correct?" It had been about seven years before that DeSanti had done knee surgery to repair the anterior cruciate ligament his left knee and had given him morphine after surgery.

"After you repaired my knee, I took the morphine too long after I got home. I tried to do without it, but the pain would get worse and I would end up taking another dose, but a larger one." He hesitated, contemplating if he should confess, knowing that DeSanti would remember just how much of the narcotic he usually prescribed and wonder where Gianni had acquired more and how much.

DeSanti was calm. He didn't feel it necessary to lecture. He knew that addiction in doctors was not uncommon and he wouldn't press for details, but he was surprised that Gianni had succumbed to the morphine. "Have you solved this problem?"

"When I realized it was out of control, I stopped. I stayed home until the withdrawal was over. I do not want to have that problem again."

"Tell me how you are feeling."

"I have a headache and my hands are shaking." He held his hands up to DeSanti.

"You should not worry. I believe your symptoms indicate you are having side effects of the morphine, not withdrawal symptoms. It is possible to have morphine and not be bothered with side effects, but then take it again at a later time, and have them. I know you are aware of this. The morphine works well for controlling the pain?"

"Yes, very well."

"Would you like me to prescribe something different?" DeSanti understood Gianni's concern. As an orthopedic surgeon, he'd seen it before: the dependency on narcotics to ease pain, physical and emotional.

"No, if you think it is safe to take it." He knew he'd come very close to being seriously dependent when he'd had his knee surgery. He'd had some withdrawal symptoms, but they were mild.

It was different back then. He was depressed about his relationship with Donnatella and the morphine helped him feel better, helped him deal with his life. It helped him forget that he lived with a beautiful woman whom he loved and yet was lonelier than he had even been in his life. It took away the pain he felt when she wouldn't allow him to sleep with her and showed no desire for him, making him feel less than a man. That was what was so dangerous about taking it: using it to feel better emotionally. That's where addiction was rooted and he'd realized that he was on that path.

"I think you will be fine with the morphine and we will take you off as soon as you feel you are ready. My concern is that you are comfortable, that you are able to rest and to be up and mobile. When you think you can be comfortable on oxycodone, tell the nurses, but I want you to take the morphine for now."

"*Grazie, Fabiano.* I think that will work." He was relieved. He could deal with the side effects and he was certain that he would not abuse the drug this time. He knew his life was different now, better and happier than it had been with Donnatella.

"I think the best medicine for you is waiting in the hallway." DeSanti was smiling. "I will come back later and perhaps we can get that IV taken out too. Then you will be free to walk in the halls and show off that beautiful woman, but I still do not know what she sees in a scoundrel such as yourself." He laughed and got up.

"Perhaps it is the scoundrel that excites her," Gianni called to him as he left the room and DeSanti waved over his head.

When she came back into the room he seemed more relaxed. His face was still pale and his hands were shaking, though not as badly. She was hoping he'd tell her what was going on, but decided she wouldn't push it with him. That was the last thing he needed right now.

"Did you talk to the inspector?" He was rubbing his forehead, his eyes closed.

"No, but I spoke to the person on the line and he said he would make sure the inspector got the message. Are you okay?"

"Yes, I am fine. I just have a headache."

There was a gentle knock at the door and Rosabella poked her head inside the room. "Gianni, I will come back in a minute and give you a bath." With that, she left.

He had a strange look on his face, an odd smile. Wendy knew something was going on in that brain of his. She could tell he was plotting and she didn't mind at all: it meant he was feeling better and after the emotional stress of his confession, she was happy about that. He was looking better now, too. She knew the morphine was starting to work.

"Wendy, I would be more comfortable if you would bathe me." He said it so innocently.

Now she knew the basic game plan and she could guess pretty accurately how this would transpire. As a medical assistant, she had bathed many patients, women and men, and she knew that sometimes for men, the intimacy of being bathed by a female nurse was uncomfortable and embarrassing. Nurses, though, thought nothing of it except to be aware of the patient's feelings and provide as much privacy as possible. The patient was usually always left to "finish" the bath himself after the nurse had left the room. Gianni would do or say something that would embarrass her and then just lie back and enjoy her discomfort, enjoying watching her face turn hot and red. She could always tell by the expression on his face that he loved her most when she blushed, when she seemed innocent before him. She liked that he saw her that way. This time though, she was going to turn the tables.

"Rosabella is a very good nurse. I'm sure she would do a good job." She wanted to play this for everything it was worth. She was going to toy with him, lead him by his nose like an old horse being led to the barn, play with him like a cat with a live mouse.

"Yes, she is, but it is awkward because I am a doctor and we have worked together and I do not want her to be uncomfortable. You and I will be married soon. We have nothing to hide from each other."

Oh, now he had them painted as an old, married couple who'd been together so long that all the magic of intimacy between them was long gone. "Of course, Gianni. If you'd rather I bathe you, then I will."

She got the basin from the bedside stand, left the room and came back with it filled with warm water. She closed the door and grabbed three towels from the linen cart and found a bar of soap.

She was already aware that linens in Europe were different from linens in the United States. Wash clothes were not terrycloth and were the size of a small hand towel. Bath towels were not as large and luxurious, but smaller and plain cotton. In hospitals in the United States, bathing a patient in bed always required a bath 'blanket': a very large, soft cotton sheet used to cover the patient for warmth, but also for modesty. She hadn't seen anything on the cart that looked like a bath blanket and she wouldn't have used it if she'd found one. He was counting on her 'innocence' in such an intimate encounter with him. She did not want to disappoint him.

"Please give me a towel so that I can cover myself," he said, the sparkle in his eyes obvious. She handed him one of the towels, the smallest one. He said nothing, but she saw that self-satisfied look on his face. He thought his plan was right on track. He worked under his gown, spreading the towel across himself, covering the place that needed to be covered.

"Are you ready now?" she asked and he nodded.

She pulled the sheet down to the foot of the bed, knowing full well she could have improvised a bath blanket using the sheet, but that would effectively end the competition. She would not have had the satisfaction of seeing *him* suffer lobster face.

She helped him out of his gown and for a split second, she almost lost the contest. It was after all, the first time she'd seen so much of him uncovered all at once. She knew he was in excellent physical shape, but she was taken aback just the same. He was very fit, with well-defined muscles and beautiful tan skin. In the face of seeing him like this though, she realized that she had successfully suppressed a blush and she knew right then that victory was hers.

He was watching for a reaction. She didn't give him one. She pretended that she bathed nude, Italian gods every day. She'd just upped the ante.

She wet and wrung out the wash cloth and washed his face. He supplied the requisite sighs of pleasure and she thought he should get out of the doctor business and become an actor. She could only imagine how he was going to express his pleasure when she washed the rest of him! She wasn't sure she could suppress a smile or a laugh much longer.

She did love looking at his face though. She always got lost in his large eyes with his full black lashes and dark eyebrows. She loved his classic nose, strong jawline and beautiful, perfect lips. The impulse to forget the bath and climb into bed with him was very strong.

"Wendy, are you daydreaming?" His question snapped her back to reality. She was determined to stay focused no matter how difficult it was.

Next she washed one arm, dried it and then did the other, then his chest and she realized it was getting very hard to stay focused! It was time to win this contest before she lost by default.

She could only wash the lower part of his right leg because of the incision, so she decided that the left leg was going to be the area where he would surrender to her and victory would be hers. She rubbed the bar of soap on the wash cloth until she had a good lather worked up.

"Bend your leg for me Gianni, so that I can wash underneath."

He did as she asked, but she noticed that a small chink was starting to appear in his armor. He was getting tense. She could see it in his face; he knew he was getting very close to being completely exposed to her, realizing that he'd probably thought she would have blushed by now and his joke would be over. He tucked the towel, making it more secure in the areas where it needed it and in doing that, she could tell he was rethinking his plan, deciding how best to call it off without giving himself away.

She took her time washing his leg, purposefully beginning at his foot, then working up his lower leg: front, sides and back. By the time she was ready to wash his thigh, the tension in his leg was causing a minor muscle tremor.

"Gianni, relax your leg." He tried, but the tremor just increased. "Relax your leg!" she repeated, this time more forcefully.

"I cannot. I have a muscle cramp!"

It took every bit of her will not to laugh out loud, but if that was the excuse he wanted to go with, she would move on. She knew victory was at hand. She had never seen him this close to blushing and even if he didn't blush, she was enjoying his embarrassment. The tables had already turned and she was happy.

She dried his leg, rinsed the wash cloth and applied more soap, watching him relax. "I'm ready to finish now." She saw those gorgeous eyes of his widen to twice their size!

"But you are already finished, are you not? Do you not want me to finish?"

He was beginning to look like a man who'd been defeated at his own game, but Wendy wasn't through with him yet. She knew he was close to blushing and she wasn't going to stop until he did. It was payback time!

"Gianni, you have spent the past several months teaching me how to be a good nurse. You have always told me how important it is to do the best job possible and to complete all tasks. Well, your bath is not complete and I am ready to finish it now."

She made a move like she was going to remove the towel, but he quickly placed both of his hands over it, holding it as if a gale force wind was approaching, a shocked look on his face and the blush appearing just as it always did on her: first the cheeks, across the nose and then total coverage of the face. On him, it looked *so* good!

She'd won at last! She'd gotten her revenge and it felt good. She laughed and noticed that he'd just realize he'd been beaten at his own game. He was shaking his head, the smile appearing on his face and his laugh starting.

The door suddenly opened and there stood Mama and Papa. Mama's face was instantly frozen in shock, then turned scarlet red. She threw her hands up over her eyes. She had not seen her baby boy this exposed in many, many years! Papa took her by the shoulders, turned her around and led her out of the room with not one word being said by either of them.

Gianni looked at Wendy, who now was also a victim of lobster face! He knew it was going to hurt, but he didn't mind at all. He laughed long and energetically and she joined him.

Chapter 8

PAPA AND MAMA came back after a few minutes. Mama still looked shaken. She had averted her eyes when she came in, avoiding Wendy altogether. Wendy wanted a chance to talk to her and tell her it was all a joke, that she was getting revenge on Gianni and that it wasn't as bad as it looked. She liked Mama and was afraid she'd compromised their relationship.

Papa however, greeted her with a gentle pat to her shoulder and a sweet smile that told her he held no animosity toward her. She hadn't had much time to get to know Papa, to spend time alone with him and talk. She needed that time with him now, to let him know who she was and that she was a good person, a person who could be trusted.

They were both so delighted to see Gianni free from all the medical machines. They had an animated conversation in Italian with him. She stayed in the background, watching and enjoying their affection toward him, wondering if they would continue to be as affectionate toward her and what they thought of her now.

She and Gianni had spoken many times about Papa and Mama, about their relationship and about the morals they believed in, practiced and taught all their children. It was Papa who had taught his sons what sacred love was and even though

Wendy had never heard it called that, she believed the same way. It was what she wanted with Gianni and she knew he wanted it too. Perhaps this time she could have it.

Every so often he would glance at her, gauging how she was reacting. She would look back and he would give her a knowing look, one that reminded her of her plan for revenge and she would feel ashamed. Then he would wink at her, all while Mama was speaking non-stop in Italian, hands flying in front of her for emphasis. Shortly though, they switched to English and Wendy became the topic of conversation.

"Mama, I think Wendy needs to go home with you and Papa. I know she has not had a good meal for days and she would probably love to have a bath, but she does not trust the other nurses with my care. Will you talk to her?" Wendy almost blushed again. He had the puppy-dog look on his face and she could see how he'd always be able to worm his way out of being in trouble with Mama as a child. It was his eyes, those beautiful, huge eyes that fairly danced with light, like he could turn their sparkle on and off any time he wanted and that gorgeous smile that always drew her in to him! She knew *she* could never resist that aspect of him and she knew why Mama couldn't either.

Mama looked at her. "It is decided, Wendy. You will come home with Papa and me. I will make you a meal *multo squisito* and you will have a hot bath and a good night's sleep. Let Gianni be by himself for a while. It will do him good and he will want you all the more when he sees you again!" She was smiling, a broad smile that told Wendy that all was forgiven as far as Mama was concerned. For Wendy, the emotional relief was immediate and welcomed. It was important that they like her because she wanted their approval for Gianni's sake.

"I would really like that, Mama, especially not having to eat from the cafeteria again tonight."

"*Bene, bene!* Papa and I have some errands to run. We will come back for you later, yes? Then you will have a good meal and a good sleep." She turned to Papa, whispered in his ear and then told Wendy to come out into the hall with her. Papa stayed behind with Gianni.

When Wendy returned, Papa kissed her cheek and joined Mama in the hall. When they had gone, she sat next to Gianni on the bed.

"I'm so embarrassed! I hope they don't hate me." She avoided his eyes and picked at a loose string on the hem of her blouse.

"They do not hate you, Wendy. They may be grounded in the old Italian traditions of their time, but they do understand our time. Besides, all that conversation in Italian? I was explaining what happened. Actually, they took your side! Mama said I needed to be put in my place. She said I deserved it and that I should not tease you like that."

She felt better immediately. "You did deserve it. Mama is right. But don't tell her that I love it when you tease me like that. Don't ever stop, okay?" He smiled, pulled her down close to himself and kissed her.

"Did you explain to Papa what was going on between us, about the bath?" She needed to know if his Papa was upset.

"He thought it was a good trick that you played on me. He said he liked you very much. What did you and Mama say in the hallway?"

"Your mama said she wanted to have a talk with me." Wendy planned to choose her words carefully, though why she felt she needed to escaped her, especially after what had just happened. They were engaged, for Pete's sake, and would have been husband and wife on Saturday. But then, maybe that was why it still felt uncomfortable to be totally open with him, especially in matters such as this. He waited for her to continue.

"She told me that she thought it was unfair that we had to wait to be married because of your accident and that she thought we might be..." She searched for the right word knowing she couldn't tell *him* the way his mama had told her. "She thought that we might be frustrated."

He was smiling. He loved her innocence, though after the bath he was now beginning to think she wasn't as innocent as he had believed. "What else did mama say?"

She felt it coming on her cheeks first, the heat spreading across her face. She had hoped that there would never be any reason to be embarrassed in front of him again, but it wasn't to be; not yet.

"Wendy?" He was waiting, an expectant look on his face.

"Well, it wasn't so much what she said as what she didn't say." He watched the concentration lines appear on her forehead as she tried to arrange her thoughts. "I think she was giving us permission." She'd said it and much more delicately than Mama had!

"Permission?" He played dumb, deliberately prolonging her torture for the pure pleasure he got in the beauty of her childlike soul. That she would be so shy with him only made him love her more and he breathed it in, his desire for her all-consuming. "What *exactly* did she say?"

"I don't know! It was in Italian!" She'd done it again. She was sure that God was keeping a list of all the lies she had told and here was another one to add to that list. She knew exactly what Mama had said by the hand gestures she'd used! They were women and women understood things like this. He was teasing her yet again.

"Let me help you then. My mama said, '*Si dovrebbe fare l'amore*' something like that, yes? Do you know what that means?" he asked.

"I'm not sure." She did it again…another lie for the list, but he deserved it. She would make *him* say it; she would not give him the satisfaction. Two could play his game; she'd won once and she could win again.

"Mama said we should make love." He said it matter-of-factly, but his grin was giving him away.

"How do you know that's what she said?" she shot back at him. She thought that if Mama were here right now, she would put him in his place.

"Wendy," he laughed, "my mama had eight children. I think I know what goes on in her head! What did you tell her?" He was intent now, but still smiling.

What did he want her to tell his mama, she wondered? But here, she was not going to lie to him. "I told her that we are going to wait until after we're married."

"And what did she say then?" His smile was gone. Maybe he didn't know his mama as well as he thought. Maybe he was hoping she had changed her mind after talking with Mama.

"She didn't say anything. She just smiled and gave me a big hug! She was happy and I think she was relieved."

"Yes, she was happy," he said, smiling. "*Questa è la mia mamma.* That is my mama! She knows how things are with people of our generation, but she did not raise her children to be like that."

"I think you have a wonderful mama, Giancarlo."

"Yes, I love her very much. But she would have done me a big favor if she had changed your mind!" He was giving her his come-on look, the smug smile pasted on his face, waiting for the reaction he loved so well.

And it did come. He pulled her closer to himself and kissed her cheeks, feeling the heat of her skin. "Ti amo, Piccola Aragosta!" he said. "I love you, Little Lobster!"

Rosabella came in with his lunch tray and Wendy thought the food looked much better than what was being served in the cafeteria. As he devoured the lunch, she could see that his appetite was improving and knew that it was one more step in his recovery, one more step until he could come home and they could be together and talk about the wedding.

At one o'clock, Inspector Iacopetti stopped by. He told them he had questioned Sofia and Nicolò Amato separately, but didn't have enough evidence to hold Nicolò with regard to Donnatella's death. He told Wendy that Sofia had denied saying anything to her about Nicolò tampering with the Ducati and in fact had denied ever following him anywhere or telling Wendy that she had. If the case went to court, he said, anything Wendy told the jury that Sofia had said would be classified as hearsay.

"Did you ask either of them about the overdose at the hospital? Does Nicolò have an alibi for that?" Gianni was upset. As he saw it, the evidence clearly pointed to Nicolò.

"I asked them both. Nicolò told me he was at home in bed at the time the intruder gave you the overdose. Signora Amato confirmed this and when I asked her how she could be certain, she told me that she knew exactly what time it was because Nicolò had awakened her and wanted to make love. She remembered looking at the clock."

"She's lying, Inspector," Gianni said, the exasperation obvious in his voice. Wendy could see that he was getting tired and decided to end the discussion. There was nothing more the Inspector could offer now anyway and she wanted Gianni to get his morphine and then sleep.

"We appreciate all that you're doing, Inspector Iacopetti. Please keep us informed of your investigation," she said.

"I will do that, Signorina, and please call me if you have anything else that will help." He turned and left, leaving Gianni angry and frustrated.

"We both know that Amato is guilty, Wendy. Why will he not see that?"

"He may very well see it, but he has to have evidence. He'll get it, don't worry. If Nicolò is guilty, he will make a mistake and the Inspector will have the evidence he needs to arrest him."

"You are always so sure. You always believe that good will win over evil. That is what I love about you, that and your lobster face." He pulled her down to himself again, his desire for her increasing, his body relaxed. He needed to know if she had truly forgiven him, if she still felt the same way about him. Did she still love him and want to make love to him? Feeling his heart pounding in his chest, he kissed her responsive lips and then her smooth cheeks. With her breath quickening and warm on his face, he knew she still wanted him and it increased his hunger for her. His hand searched between their bodies until he felt the silken flesh under her bra.

She pulled away from him sharply, a vision of him and Sofia on his couch flashing before her eyes, feeling an iciness seize her body.

"You can't touch me like that, Gianni! We made a promise to each other and to God!" She knew that she was just as guilty as he was. She longed for him, craved his touch on her skin, but she wanted his sacred love even more and she wasn't sure now if he wanted it as much as she did. It was the vision of him and Sofia that tortured her, that felt like that knife in her chest all over again. She believed that she had forgiven him until she'd felt the agony of that knife.

Neither of them spoke for several seconds, the implications of what had just happened heavy on them. The pain of his confession was still burned into her heart. How could he do this to her after all he had said?

"Did you love her when you touched her? Did you love Sofia?" The tears came instantly and spilled onto her cheeks, dripping off her chin. She didn't wipe them away and neither did he. She searched his face for the truth and saw such great sorrow there. She wanted to take her question back, knowing how much it hurt him. She had told him she would forgive him anything and now she was holding his transgression up to him, making him confess it again, but she couldn't get that picture out of her head. She felt betrayed, just as she had when she'd found out what Mark had done.

"No," he said softly. He didn't want to look at her, but had to. He had already dishonored her and he wouldn't dishonor her again by looking away. "I did not love Sofia. I needed to make love to her, that is all."

Sacred Love

"Do you love me or do you just need me to satisfy your lust?" Her anger toward him shocked her and she was afraid she would never see him as honorable again.

What could he say to erase the pain he had just caused her? Would she believe anything he said after this or ever again? He was terrified that he had lost her. "There is nothing I can say to you to make this better." His entire being ached for her forgiveness, but he would accept her condemnation. He understood it was what he deserved, from her and from God.

"I have to go." She could say nothing more and with that, she turned her back on him and hurried out of the room.

He lay there a long while, the guilt crushing him, wondering if it was all over now and how he would go on without her. He had caused her so much pain today and knew she would never be able to forgive him. He would never be able to forgive himself.

Why was it so difficult to restrain his passion for her, he wondered, when he respected her integrity and desire for a sacred love so much? She was saving herself for him, for their wedding night. He knew she had never given herself to anyone else except Mark. Had he lied to her and to himself? Did he only desire her to satisfy his lust, his selfishness in putting his animal needs above her honor?

He had broken his promise to her. It *was* selfishness; he knew it and God knew it. He prayed for her heart, that God would heal her and give her a love that was worthy of her honor. In his soul, he let her go, freeing her to find that love with someone else.

He was startled when Rosabella appeared in the doorway.

"Gianni, do you need anything?" She waited for his answer knowing it had been a while since his last dose of morphine.

The weight of his emotional pain joined that of his physical pain and he felt himself so burdened by it all that he could hardly breathe. It would be better, he thought, if he could stop breathing altogether. He didn't care about being in pain; it was his punishment for what he had done and he accepted it.

"No, Rosabella. *Grazie.*"

"You will call me then if you need something?"

"Yes, I will call." She left and when her back was turned to him, he buried his head in his hands and sobbed silently.

Chapter 9

WENDY WAS WAITING when Papa and Mama came back. Mama could see that she had been crying; her eyes were red and puffy and there was a sadness covering her like a mourning dress. They drove toward home in silence, Mama deciding it was best not to pry.

Perhaps Wendy was "frustrated." Mama knew that Gianni was. She knew about men and she could see it all over him when he and Wendy were together. She could see the hunger in his eyes. It was the same with Pietro when they were in love and waiting for their honeymoon night.

She had seen how unhappy Gianni was in his marriage to Donnatella and knew that Donnatella had shut him out of their bedroom. It grieved her to see how badly that had hurt him. He needed the love of a good woman, Mama told herself, and she prayed that Wendy *was* that good woman. She understood that Wendy was frustrated too.

Mama would talk to Papa when they got home and tell him that he should talk to her and find out what was wrong. It wouldn't do for their soon-to-be daughter-in-law to be plagued by anything that would steal her joy when she had a wedding to think about.

That first day she had seen them, Wendy loved the scarlet poppies that carpeted the ground under the cypress trees. Today though, their vibrant color only mocked her sadness. Pietro and Lalia had raised all eight of their children in this house and Wendy loved being there. It was a part of who Gianni was, a part of his childhood she heard about when Mama told her stories. Now it just reminded her of how much she didn't know about him and how much she knew already and wished she didn't.

When they had first arrived, Mama had arranged separate bedrooms for them upstairs, but she told Wendy that now they would be more comfortable in the larger bedroom with the private bath. It was the only bedroom on the main floor and Gianni would not have to manage the stairs once he came home from the hospital. It was Papa's and Mama's bedroom, she said, but there was another room upstairs with a bath that would be sufficient for them. Wendy protested, but Mama had a convincing argument: Gianni would need someone to help him at night and to give him his pain medication. Wendy was a nurse, Mama pointed out, and he should have the best care after he left the hospital. Wendy saw immediately that she needn't argue with Lalia; she was the matriarch of the Giannotti family and her decisions were final. Gianni took after his mom in that respect.

After what had happened at the hospital though, she wasn't so sure she wanted to be sleeping in the same room with him. She was upset at what he had done to her, but afraid that if he tried again, she would allow it. She couldn't trust him or herself and she knew that if that happened, she would hate herself for being so weak, for grieving God by breaking the pledge.

Mama led her to the bedroom, which was separated from the main house by an octagonal pass-through room, which, from the outside, reminded her of the circular towers of a castle. The walls were stone and there were a couple of chairs and a nice accent table. Being separated from the main house made the bedroom quieter and more private.

The bedroom was large and comfortable with a secluded covered patio that was accessed through French doors. To the left of the doors, a wooden privacy screen stood in front of a small table. Mama or Papa had set the bust of Michelangelo's "David," the one Wendy had bought at the airport, on the table.

There were twin beds and it was obvious that they had originally been pushed together. Wendy could see the fresh indentation marks they had left on the area rug under them. She knew that most European homes didn't have queen- and king-sized beds like in the United States. Most were twin-sized that were pushed together and made up with linens as if they were one bed. When Mama and Papa said they had errands to do as they left the hospital, they must have come back home and rearranged the furniture. Wendy smiled at the thought, even though it saddened her, and wondered if Mama was sending her a subtle hint: the beds were apart, but that didn't preclude her and Gianni from sharing one bed.

There was a full-length mirror, a desk and some beautifully upholstered, comfortable-looking chairs at the other end of the room.

The bathroom walls were adorned with cheerful, blue, hand-painted tiles. Wendy was pleased to see that there was a full-sized tub and a shower. Gianni would need to be able to shower so that he would not have to navigate getting up and down out of a tub. Papa would have to help him with that, she decided. She fairly drooled when she thought about soaking in that tub though.

"I put fresh linens in the bathroom and here are more if you need them." Mama was pointing to a closet next to the bathroom door. "Papa moved your luggage down here. If you need anything, you will ask me and I will see that you have it. Now you must take your bath and when you are finished, you come to the kitchen and we will talk." Wendy thanked her and smiled, wondering if she could survive another "talk." How much more to the story of the birds and bees could there be?

The hot bath was heavenly. Until she felt its warmth soothing the stiffness and aching from her muscles, her thoughts becoming one with the glorious water, she hadn't realized how totally depleted she was. It had been three full days of physical and emotional anguish. But now, with the warm water caressing her body, it was all melting away, leaving her relaxed and sleepy.

She was in the room standing by the sofa next to them as they talked. Gianni was telling Sofia how much he loved her and about how he wanted a sacred love with her. Then he said that Wendy would not forgive him and he was sobbing as he told her. As she watched, her soul ached for the pain it was causing him and she started crying.

Sofia unbuttoned her blouse and offered herself to him. Wendy tried to scream at him, to tell him to stop, that she would *always* forgive him, but no sound came out of her mouth. She tried to go to him, to hold him, but she couldn't move. She was stuck to the floor, unable to comfort him and tell him he was forgiven, her crying so profound that the sound of it scared her.

As he reached for Sofia to kiss her, Wendy jerked free of the force that held her to the floor and bolted upright, the room, the sofa, Gianni and Sofia disappearing before her eyes. She saw the blue tiles on the wall of the bathroom and knew she had fallen asleep.

Her heart was pounding, her body burning from soaking in the hot water. Searing tears washed down her face. She gave in to them, letting them come unhindered, her body convulsing with sobs until she knew she had nothing left. She was empty of all other emotions, except for the love she had for him. It was still there and still living in her, ingrained in who she was. She lay back into the water, closed her eyes and asked God to fill her with more love for him. She prayed for forgiveness for herself.

She got out of the tub, dressed and brushed her teeth. She applied a cool cloth to her face and when she determined that it look as though she hadn't been crying, she headed for the kitchen.

Mama had a pot of water boiling on the stove and something that smelled wonderful simmering in another. Wendy couldn't believe how just the aroma caused her stomach to seize in anticipation. She was weak and needed something to revive her.

"I am making for you Gianni's favorite *lasagne bianco*." She was tasting the white sauce and handed her a small spoonful. Wendy tasted it, letting the sauce linger on her tongue, seduced by its richness and excited by the tantalizing hint of nutmeg. Mama told her that there were two styles of lasagna: one made with a tomato sauce and the *lasagne bianco*, which was made with a white sauce. Now she understood why it was Gianni's favorite.

Papa came into the kitchen, smiling. "Wendy, would you like a glass of wine?" She told him 'yes' and he poured three glasses. Mama drank fairly half of her glass while stirring the white sauce and singing loudly. Wendy had heard the song before and knew it was from an Italian opera, but she couldn't remember the name. She smiled watching Mama and Mama noticed.

"Wendy, good Italian food is made only better when you sing as you cook! You will remember this, I hope, once you are married to Gianni. And if you are lucky, he will join you in the singing. He has a very good voice, not as good as Caruso, but good enough for cooking!" All three of them laughed. Mama winked at Papa and he understood what he was to do.

"Wendy, it is best to leave Mama alone with her sauce. She has almost a love affair with it and she and the sauce like their privacy. Bring your wine and I will show you the olive orchard. It will save us both from Mama's singing!" Mama shot him a scowl and with that, Papa and Wendy left the kitchen.

The orchard wasn't very large, about thirty trees and all of them mostly bare of olives; the olive harvest had been over for a month. She loved the color of the leaves. They were a silvery gray-green and when a breeze would blow on them, the color flashed almost metallic in the sunlight. Papa told her that they used all the olives: some he pressed into oil and the rest he brined. They were seasoned and used for antipasto or just to eat by themselves. Taking care of the olives was Papa's job.

Mama had a garden planted in the back yard with golden sunflowers, herbs and tomatoes. The smell of basil reached her nostrils and she breathed it in as if it were as necessary for respiration as oxygen itself. She loved fresh basil and she loved the olive trees and the bright sunflowers. She loved the Chianti. She loved everything about Italy. In her reverie, another thought intruded: could her love for Gianni erase the bathtub dream forever? Being out here, in the fresh air with the scent of basil floating around her, she believed it could.

"Tell me, are things going well between you and Gianni?" Papa's voice was gentle. From his first hug when she had arrived at the airport, she'd felt comfortable with him, as if she'd known him all of her life. He continued, "Gianni can be difficult at times. He is stubborn like his mama."

She was still upset; not with Gianni anymore, but with herself. She couldn't forget the look of hurt on his face when she'd asked him if he wanted her just to satisfy his lust. Papa put his arm around her shoulder as they walked.

"I want you to know, Wendy, that I look on you as my daughter and I love you the same as I love my daughters and my daughters-in-law. I hope you will come to me at any time you are unhappy or have a problem and tell me. Don't forget, I have known Gianni since he was wearing diapers! Mama and I have tried to raise him to be a good man." She interrupted him.

"Oh, he *is* a good man, Papa! A very good man and I love him more than life itself. I just don't know if I am good enough for *him*."

They had walked back toward the house, past the row of cypress trees and took seats on the patio outside the big bedroom. They both sipped their wine, Papa patiently waiting for her, wondering how she could believe she was not worthy of Gianni. Papa knew it was Gianni that might not be worthy of her.

"Gianni and I were talking at my house once and at that time, I hadn't known him very long. We were talking about sacred love and I always thought I knew what he meant by that, but now I'm not sure. Do you know?"

Papa smiled. He could guess now what might be bothering her. He knew that they were saving themselves for marriage and he knew how difficult that could be. They were both under stress from his accident and from the wedding. There was bound to be tension in their relationship leading to disagreements and hard feelings.

"Sacred love is a complicated thing, Wendy," he began. "I am sure other people would give you different definitions as to what it means to them. But I will give you my definition. I will tell you what I taught all my children." He set his wine glass down on the end table.

"Marriage is a holy thing created by God. In these days, fewer people know how to honor it in the way that God intended, nor do they want to. They rush into a relationship with no thought about the commitment that comes with it and rush out of it when it does not live up to expectations, when life becomes difficult and the thrill of new love wears off."

"God has said that when a man and a woman are joined, they become one flesh. Have you thought about what that means? It means that they now are joined in all things and what affects one, affects the other. If you are sad, Gianni will be sad too. When you are joyful, he will be joyful with you. His only desire is what is best for you and your desire is for him."

"It does not mean that you become something more than human. There will still be times of selfishness and anger, times when you will hurt each other. It does not mean that you will agree on everything or that you will give up who you are and become him, but it does mean that you will work as a single body and heart with the same purpose and goal, even though you may reach that goal in different ways. It means that your love and your body are only for each other."

He paused for a moment and sipped his wine. She sat still, looking down into her wine glass, considering everything he was saying.

He continued. "Sacred love is knowing that true love is more than what happens between a man and a woman in the bedroom, but knowing that your body is the holy gift that God intended be given only to your spouse. Husbands and wives may give each other gifts, like the exchanging of wedding rings, but the gift of yourself, your body given in holy matrimony, is special. It will help you to understand it if you think about Our Lord giving His life on the cross. It was precious and valuable because He had only *one* life and one gift of Himself to give." Papa finished his wine, waiting for her to process all that he had said.

"Mostly, Wendy, it means that you are committed to your marriage and to your husband in the same way you are committed to your body. For example, if your hand was injured, you would not cut it off. You would not hate it because it caused you pain and discomfort. You would care for it and treat it tenderly. You would do anything to make it better and you would be patient for the healing. That is the way that husbands and wives are to treat each other, as part of the same body."

"If our bodies can only be given once, then can our love be sacred again now, mine and Gianni's? We've both been married before, so how is that possible?" There it was, the question she had always wanted to ask Gianni, but hadn't.

"The marriage vows you make before God last only until death. When your husband died, God released you from being one with him. When you marry Gianni, you will consummate your marriage and you will become one with him. It is *marriage* that validates your right to become one with him in sacred love. God has made marriage a very holy thing and many people today do not put much value on it, but God does and He honors it. He will bless you and Gianni and your marriage. He will keep your marriage sanctified, set apart and holy for Him. That is why sacred love is important. That is what many people do not understand."

"Thank you, Papa. You've helped me a lot." They both got up and she wrapped her arms around him. "I love you, Papa. I'm so happy that Gianni brought me into this family."

"We are so happy to have you join us. Now, whatever it was that irresponsible son of mine did to upset you, I hope you will forgive him out of the love you have for him. Someday, you may need *his* forgiveness and he will remember your kindness to him." She hugged him again, knowing that she would never have it again, the dream about Gianni and Sofia.

"Mama will be after us with her big wooden spoon if we do not get to the kitchen for her lasagna!" No sooner had he said it, than they both heard Mama shouting out the back door. "You see, we are one. I know her as well as I know myself!" They both laughed.

Wendy couldn't remember when she had ever had lasagna that good. The white sauce was sinfully rich with cream, butter and cheese and Mama had even made the pasta from scratch. It was the ultimate Italian comfort food and after the past three days, she needed comfort wherever she could find it, calories or no calories.

It was eight o'clock. Papa was digging through his office looking for the family photo albums which were stored in a closet that overflowed with the trappings of a life filled with work, children, family and friends. He told Wendy it might take a while to find what he was looking for, but she didn't mind. She told him she was going to call Memorial Hospital, talk to Gayle in the emergency department and fill her in on what had happened to Gianni.

Six days of their three weeks' leave were gone and even when they returned, Gianni would not be able to work until he could put his full weight on his injured leg. That could be several weeks from now. It could take up to a year until he was fully recovered. She was getting nervous about both their jobs. Would the Board allow them more time or would she and Gianni be looking for new employment when they got back to Cape Narrows?

She was thankful now that she had thought to contact her cell phone provider and purchase an international calling card. She figured it was about eleven in the morning in Cape Narrows, so she would call Gayle at the hospital. She sat in the hexagonal passage room, dialed the country code and Gayle's work number and got her on the second ring.

"Buona sera, Gayle! It's Wendy!"

"Wendy? Wendy! Is that you? What time is it there? Are you married now? Or...wait, your wedding is tomorrow, isn't it?" Wendy could hear the excitement in Gayle's voice, the joy and friendship.

"Gayle, get hold of yourself!" she laughed. "It's eight o'clock here. I'm with Gianni's parents and we've just had dinner."

"Gianni? Who's Gianni? Where's Giancarlo? Tell me what's going on?" The confusion was evident in Gayle's questions, the excitement replaced with uncertainty.

"Take a deep breath, okay? And then sit down."

"I *am* sitting down!" There was a pause. "Okay, I took a deep breath, now tell me what's going on." She seemed calmer so Wendy thought about how she would tell her friend everything that had happened. "Are you still there? Talk to me!"

"First of all, Gianni is Giancarlo's nickname. Everybody here calls him that. Secondly, we aren't getting married tomorrow. There's been a little hitch in our plans. That's why I'm calling."

"Not getting married? What happened? He didn't get cold feet, did he? If he did, he'll have to answer to me personally!"

"Take another deep breath, Gayle, okay? You're not making this easy for me."

"Oh, honey, I'm sorry. It's just that I'm so surprised to hear from you! I'll be good, okay? Go ahead and tell me what's going on."

"First I want to let you know that Gianni and I are fine. So don't worry about us. The wedding has been delayed because last Wednesday he had an accident on his brother's motorcycle and ended up having surgery."

Wendy could her a loud gasp from Gayle. "I *knew* that bike of his would be his undoing! I never liked him riding it! Is he all right? How bad is it?" Gayle was upset. She always ran on like that when something upset her. Wendy decided not to tell her about the attempt on his life.

"Yes, he's okay. He fractured his femur and some ribs. He had a pneumothorax with the chest tube and all that. He was unconscious when they brought him in and was intubated and in a coma for two days."

"Oh, no! I'm so sorry, honey! Are you sure he's okay?"

"Yes, he's fine. It's been a really rough five days, that's all, but he's doing really well now. He was up on crutches this morning and walked in the hall. He used to work in this hospital so most of the staff know him. They've been really wonderful and have given him excellent care. His day nurse, Rosabella, and his evening nurse, Fabiana, are just great. I've discovered that he can be a difficult patient, if you know what I mean."

"Oh, one of those, huh? Doctors hate it when the tables are turned, don't they?" Gayle chuckled.

"Well, he's no different, that's for sure. But Rosabella and Fabiana know just how to handle him. And I've been with him every day. They let me stay with him in the ICU. The doctor in the ICU and his orthopedic surgeon are wonderful. They both know him and I know that everybody makes sure he gets special attention. Everyone has been so good to him and to me. The only bad part about this hospital is having to eat in the cafeteria! I miss Chef!"

"I'll tell him that when I see him," Gayle said, laughing.

"I called because I'm worried about all the time we've used up. I'm hoping that Gianni will be well enough so that we can get married in another week or so. He can't stand for long periods of time. I know he'll be on crutches for the ceremony, but I'm pretty sure he won't be back to work there for several weeks after we return. I don't know what to do about our jobs."

"Wendy, honey, don't even give it another thought. I'll talk to Dr. Hazleton and get it all worked out for both of you. Don't worry, it'll be fine. Trust me, okay? I just feel so bad for both of you that this happened."

"Thanks, Gayle. I don't know what I'd do without you."

"I just want you and Giancarlo to be happy. Is everything else going well? I mean, meeting his family and all?"

"I'm so lucky to love him because his family is wonderful! You would love his Papa and Mama! They already treat me just like a daughter. In fact, right now Papa is looking for family photo albums so that he can show me photos of Gianni as a little boy. Mama is a fabulous cook. She made some white lasagna that was incredible!"

"How is Giancarlo taking all of this?" Gayle was concerned for both of them, for the stress this must be causing them. She loved them both and had hoped all along that they would fall in love. She was overjoyed when she was able to see it happen as they worked side by side at Memorial.

"Of course, he's been pretty miserable. It was traumatic for him, but through it all he's been really great. He jokes with me and the staff and when we're alone together, I have to watch him or his hands are all over me! I'm trying to figure out if it's just him or if all Italian men are like that!" They both laughed.

Gayle was feeling more reassured. "Is there anything I can do for you? I mean, I know I'm thousands of miles away, but I want to help."

"Just being able to talk to you has been so wonderful for me. If you can just let Dr. Hazleton know what's happened and find out how the Board wants to handle our leave. I mean, we can come back at the end of our three weeks, but Gianni won't be back in the ED for several weeks after that. Just see what the Board thinks about that, okay? That would be a great help to both of us now."

"Consider it done."

"Are things okay with you and Memorial? How are the subs doing?" She was curious. It had seemed like so long since she and

Gianni had worked in the ED with Gayle and yet it had only been eight days; eight days that seemed like an eternity.

"The replacements are good, competent, but definitely not you and Giancarlo! Come back to us soon, okay Sweetie? Work is no fun without you two and I want to hear all about Italy!"

"As soon as we can and thanks again. I'll try to call again just before the wedding. Love you."

"Same to you and Giancarlo. Give him a hug for me, would you?"

"Okay, I will! He always seems to have enough energy for that!" They both laughed, said good-bye and hung up.

She was helping Mama with the dishes when the phone rang. Mama answered it, a worried look crossing her face as she handed the phone to Wendy. "It is the hospital. The nurse wants to speak to you."

It was Fabiana. She was worried about Gianni. He hadn't had any pain medication since the early afternoon and it was obvious that he needed it. She had offered morphine several times and every time, he had refused but would not say why. His blood pressure was elevated, he hadn't eaten anything from his dinner tray and he would barely talk to her. He had refused to get up and on his crutches as Dr. DeSanti had ordered.

Apparently, Rosabella had had the same problem with him on her shift. Fabiana had put in a call to Dr. DeSanti when she got Rosabella's report, but was told that he was tied up in surgery and would check on Gianni as soon as he could. If there was a serious problem, she was told to contact the ICU doctor on call.

Would Wendy come and speak to Gianni? Perhaps he would talk to her and she could persuade him to take some morphine or at least some oxycodone. Wendy told her she would come immediately and handed the receiver back to Mama.

"What is wrong? Is Gianni all right?" Mama was almost in a panic, her hands clasped together tightly.

"It's probably nothing, Mama. He's just being difficult and Fabiana needs my help. She wants me to talk to him." Mama was relieved. She knew he could be stubborn when he wanted.

"I will take you, Wendy," Papa offered.

They drove to the hospital with barely a word between them, Wendy looking blankly out the car window, remembering what Papa had told her about becoming one with Gianni.

Fabiana met them as they walked through the doors into the ICU. "Thank you for coming. I have done everything I can to persuade him to have some morphine. Dr. DeSanti wants him to have it and made sure that I understood that. I know that he needs it, but I cannot understand why he will not let me give it to him. Would you talk to him please? Perhaps he will listen to you."

"Yes, I'll talk to him and you have the morphine ready." Fabiana looked relieved and hurried off to get the drug prepared. "Papa, would you please wait here? I should talk to him alone." Papa nodded and headed for the waiting area.

As soon as she came through the doorway, she knew why Fabiana had called her. She was shocked. He looked worse than she had ever seen him, even the morning of his accident when she saw him in the emergency room. His eyes were shut tightly against the pain. His face was ashen, the perspiration beading up on his forehead and he looked positively worn out. His body was trembling, his arms were at his sides, his hands were gripping the sheet so tightly that his knuckles were white.

She was devastated, knowing *she* had probably caused his suffering this time. She had turned her back on him without even giving him the hope that she would forgive him. She shouldn't have walked out on him, shouldn't have left without saying something to him, without making things right between them. Now she was seeing what her selfish anger had done to him.

He hadn't opened his eyes when she'd come in, hadn't acknowledged that she was even there. She picked up a washcloth from the bedside stand and wiped the perspiration from his forehead. She spoke to him softly, trying to sound calm, desperate to find the words that would reach him. "Gianni, what are you doing? Why won't you let Fabiana give you something for the pain?" She closed her eyes for a moment, pushed this vision of him away and instead, imagined his smile and his beautiful eyes. He still wouldn't respond, but she saw tears escape from the corners of his eyes and roll onto the pillow.

"Please, Gianni, talk to me. Don't shut me out." There was only silence. She was terrified that he would never speak to her again and so she laid herself across his chest as she had done before, wrapping her arms around him. With all her strength, she willed him to feel the love she had for him.

"This is my fault. I told you that I had forgiven you, but I hadn't. I know that and I'm so sorry I treated you like that. I love you so much. Please forgive me, please!" Her tears came freely, the sobs leaving her gasping for air.

She felt his hand on her head, his fingers slowly combing through her hair. She raised up and looked at him. "Why are you doing this?"

He opened his eyes, those beautiful eyes that she loved to look at and that could see into her soul. They were bloodshot now and glassy from his tears. "I do not deserve your love, Wendy. I have dishonored and wounded you. I have caused you great pain. How can I take the morphine and let it take *my* pain away and then go to sleep as if I had done nothing?"

Now she looked directly at him wanting to erase what she saw in his eyes. "You're punishing yourself for dishonoring me? You can't do that! Don't you see how much it hurts me to see you like this? I can't bear it! My heart isn't broken because you wanted to touch me; I dream about you touching me. I was hurt because of what happened with you and Sofia. I didn't trust you and I thought that you just wanted to make love to me, that I was just a substitute for Donnatella or Sofia, just someone to satisfy you. I know that was wrong."

He wiped her tears away with his hand. "I am so sorry, my *Bella Donna!* You have *always* satisfied me! Everything you do satisfies me. It makes me hunger for you and want to lose myself in you. Without you I am only half and I cannot live as half a person."

She understood exactly what he was saying because she felt that way too. They were two separate parts of one thing, like a glass and some water. They were complete in themselves, but empty in the greater end, the glass empty of its ultimate purpose of containing water and the water void of form without something to hold it. But when the water is poured into the glass, the purpose of each is made complete.

That's what Papa was telling her: what it meant to be one person, to have a sacred love. It was more than the physical act of loving him. She saw how she had already become one with him through her commitment to love him completely, even when he hurt her, even when it meant forgiving him. She realized that when they did finally make love, it would be the *final* act of becoming one, not the first.

Wendy saw Fabiana standing at the doorway, a relieved smile on her face, and nodded to her. Fabiana came in, said nothing as she injected the morphine into the IV tubing and then left the room quietly.

"Go to sleep now, Gianni. Rest." Wendy said softly. "I will always be your other half and you will always be mine."

Chapter 10

IT WAS SATURDAY, but there was not going to be a wedding today. As she lay in bed watching the room filling with light, she realized that she wasn't unhappy about that; it didn't matter as much as it had before. In fact she was thankful for how things had turned out, not about Gianni's accident, but the rest of it: knowing about Sofia, the talk with Papa and especially now knowing that she and Gianni already had a sacred love. That part she was happy about.

She knew that sacred love was a lesson, one that both she and Gianni needed to learn before the vows were exchanged, before they made love to each other. She understood that whatever problems they might face as the years passed, they would face them together. They would not walk away from them or each other, but come together until a solution was found. Sacred love meant never shutting the other one out, never turning to someone else, no matter how difficult life could be. And now she knew they were already one, joined in their commitment to each other, and that was what was important. The rest would just be icing on the wedding cake.

There was a timid knock on the door. "Wendy?" It was Mama, her voice almost a whisper. She was always loud and animated; Wendy liked that about her. She didn't realize that Mama could whisper.

"Come in, Mama. I'm awake." She sat up as Mama shuffled in wearing some hot pink, fuzzy slippers which seemed so out of place on her that she giggled. She wondered if they had been left behind by one of the grandkids. Mama was carrying a tray and Wendy could smell coffee.

"I make you some breakfast. You do not eat enough. You are too skinny!" She put the tray down, put an extra pillow on Wendy's lap and set the tray on the pillow. Walking over to the French doors, she pulled back the heavy draperies and tied each one with the cord, allowing the morning sun to set the room ablaze with light. Then she sat next to Wendy on the bed. "I make cafe americano for you. It is not so strong as Italian coffee."

Wendy sipped the rich liquid. "It's good, Mama, very good." The scent of a warm roll enticed her and she slathered it with butter. It was not as sweet as American pastries, but it didn't matter. It melted in her mouth as she decided that if she didn't marry Gianni soon, she wouldn't fit into the dress she'd bought for the wedding.

She couldn't understand how Mama maintained her figure. She wasn't fat, but not skinny either. Her hair was still dark, but graying all the same, though not as much as Papa's. Gianni got his wavy hair from her. Even though tied into a bun, her unruly curls popped out everywhere as if they had a will of their own.

It was nice, she thought, to be with Mama away from the hospital, sipping coffee and talking with the bright morning sun warming the room. She had slept soundly all night and was feeling better than she had since before his accident. She wondered if Papa had spoken to her of their talk in the olive orchard.

"You will be wanting to visit Gianni. Papa says whenever you are ready, we will take you." Mama had included a small cup of espresso for herself and sipped it delicately.

"Thank you. I really appreciate how nice you and Papa have been to me. I know that Gianni's accident has been hard on both of you."

"Gianni has been hard on me all of his life!" Mama laughed. "He was a curious boy and always looking for adventure, so he found himself in trouble many times. It was not bad trouble, just the kind small boys always find. I think maybe he did not find trouble, but trouble found him." Mama took another sip of her espresso. "But he always would charm me so that I would not punish him." Mama looked up, making eye contact with her. "You will be careful, Wendy, when you and Gianni are married. Do not let him charm you." She gave her a grin and went back to the espresso.

"I know what you mean. It's those beautiful eyes of his. I can't resist them and how they sparkle when he's teasing. But I'll be careful, Mama. You can be sure of that."

She patted Wendy's hand, her expression soft. "You will be a good wife for our Gianni, Wendy. Papa and I know this. He has been lonely since Donnatella died. He loved her very much and worked hard to make her happy. He suffered terribly when she would not love him and found another man to be with. I was afraid that he was not able to keep his unhappiness inside and that it might get him into trouble. He has needed a good woman and I see how happy he is now and how much love he has for you."

She paused, choosing her words. "He called us many times about you. He wanted to be married again and I knew he wanted you for his wife. He needs to be with you so that he does not get into trouble." She watched Wendy's reaction and saw her cheeks pink up just a little.

"It will take time for him to trust you. He still has pain from Donnatella. Be patient and love him with all your heart and he will make you very happy. I promise this." Mama smiled at her. Yes, Wendy thought, Papa and Mama knew that she and Gianni were working through a problem and perhaps knowing their son as well as they did told them exactly what that problem was.

"I love him with all my heart right now, Mama."

"Then in love you will give him your life and he will give his life to you." She stood up, picked up the empty tray and turned toward the door. "But now, we must go see him and make sure he is not giving trouble to his nurses, no?"

"I'll be ready in just a few minutes. Thank you for breakfast and for talking with me." Mama was humming and Wendy knew the song this time. It was called '*Con Te Partiro: Time to Say Goodbye.*' The singer tells of leaving his past life and starting a new life with his present love; the old no longer exists for him, being replaced with the new.

He was sitting in the large chair beside the bed and all she could do was stand in the doorway, feeling the smile spreading across her face. She wanted to savor the moment, to see him now with color in his face, relaxed and comfortable, the lines of tension in his forehead gone, his eyes dancing again. His IV line was out; there were no more tethers attached to him. It was the total opposite of how she had seen him the night before and it was the first time she'd felt so much hope.

Today they were supposed to be married. All of the family and their friends would have been gathered to help them celebrate. There would have been the scent of fresh flowers and the sounds of soft music, holy prayers and sacred vows, a sumptuous dinner with wine, a wedding cake and singing and celebration into the night. There would have been gifts wrapped in pretty paper and colorful ribbons. But today, there was none of that. The ceremony might have been cancelled, but seeing him now and knowing he was getting better was the best wedding gift she could have gotten and the only one she really wanted.

"*Buon giorno, Bella Donna*," he said, smiling. "*No parlare, beciami.*" His words floated across to her softly, like the wispy fuzz from a cottonwood tree dancing on the air. She rushed to him and kissed him.

"Wendy, you have been learning Italian! You understood what I said!" She had no idea what he had said, except that she recognized the nickname he'd given her, Bella Donna, and she loved it when he called her that.

"No, what did you say?"

Rosabella was changing the linens on his bed and she smiled at Wendy. Everyone on the floor was surprised and happy to see him doing so well this morning, Rosabella especially.

"I said, 'Do not talk. Kiss me!'" She obeyed his command and kissed him again and he laughed. "Is this how you intend on learning Italian?"

"Oh, yes!" she said, "One phrase at a time!" She pulled up a chair and sat next to him.

Rosabella had finished with the bed. "Dr. DeSanti wants you up on your crutches today. I am sure Wendy would be happy to help you and I will be at the nurses' station waiting to see you walk down the hall. Remember though, only a little weight on the leg." She tossed the soiled linens into the hamper and left.

"I'm so happy to see you," Wendy said excitedly. She held both of his hands.

"What did Mama make for your supper last night? Did you sleep well?" He seemed just as excited to see her. Mama was right about her going home so that he would be all the more eager to see her the next day. He wouldn't take his eyes off her and held her hands tightly, kissing them.

"She made your favorite: white lasagna and it was *multo squisito!*" She surprised herself; maybe she was learning Italian one phrase at a time. "And the soak in the bathtub was so nice…" She stopped. It flashed just for a second, her dream of Gianni and Sofia, but then it disappeared as soon as it had come. It didn't hurt this time and she knew it never would again. "And I slept so soundly and then Mama brought me breakfast in bed and we had such a nice talk!"

"Saint Monica, help us! What did she want to talk about *this* time?" He was shaking his head and smiling.

"Relax, Gianni. It wasn't *that* kind of talk this time. It was a nice talk." It was so good to see him feeling so well, she thought, the light back in his eyes, his smile so captivating that she wanted to kiss him and never stop.

"About me? Was she giving you motherly advice about how to handle me?" Those eyes of his were sparkling, drawing her in to himself as they always did.

"Yes, she did give me a piece of advice. She told me not to let you charm me. I intend on following that advice too." She was only fooling herself. She knew there was no way she would ever get used to those eyes and that smile of his. After all, Mama still hadn't. They would always capture her heart and overtake her will, leaving her at his mercy, but she wasn't about to let him know the kind of power they had over her.

"What other advice did she give you?"

"You're so nosey. That's between Mama and I." She saw him put his hand on his nose, feeling its length, a confused look on his face. She laughed. "'Nosey' means it is none of your business. You know, don't stick your nose into my business?" He understood and smiled. "You should get up and take that walk. Rosabella will be waiting to see you."

She retrieved the crutches from the corner of the room and leaned them next to the bed. She helped him up from the chair and once he was standing on his good leg, she gave him the crutches. He seemed to be able to stand much better today; at least he still had color in his face. He tried putting some weight on the good leg, but the pain was intense.

Papa and Mama were sitting in the waiting area near the entrance. They had told Wendy that she should see him alone and that they would wait until she and Gianni had had a chance to talk. She might need some private time alone with him after yesterday, they told her. She was pleased that they seemed to know that there had been a problem, had taken the time to talk to her and give her the benefit of their experience and had done so with such concern and love for her and for Gianni.

Now it was their time to see him and see how much better he was. It was too easy to be selfish and forget that Papa and Mama, along with his entire family, loved him as much as she did, even more, and were as upset and worried about him as she was. She had a medical background at least and knew procedures; she knew what was to be expected, what was normal and when to be scared for him. She knew that Mama probably didn't even know about the attempt on his life. If Papa had told her, Mama hadn't said anything about it.

She watched them for a long while and noticed that Gianni was looking tired. It would take him a while to regain his strength because of the blood loss; he would be weak until his body recovered. "Gianni, you should be getting back to your room now," she said.

"Do you wish to stay longer Wendy?" Papa asked. He could leave her and come back later to pick her up, he said, but Gianni interrupted before she could answer.

"Go home with Papa, Wendy. He will bring you back later this afternoon. You can have a good lunch and then have a nap." That did sound tempting to her, even though she wanted to be with him.

"Yes, you come home with Mama and me. I have some photos of Gianni when he was a little boy that I think you might like to see." Gianni gave his father a hostile look, she saw it and that convinced her; she wanted to see the photos!

While Papa and Mama waited, she walked him back to his room and got him settled in the bed. He was pale, but not nearly as bad as he had been the last few days. She could tell he was tired.

"Are you hurting? I can tell Rosabella that you need something for the pain."

"I am fine, Wendy. It will settle down soon. It is not as bad as the pain of being away from you." He had *that* look and that smooth, buttery Italian accent that told her he was laying on the charm. Sometimes he was so full it, that Italian lover persona. Did all Italian men try to live up to it, to some contrived image of what an Italian man should be or were they all *really* like that? She didn't know, but was she going to enjoy finding out.

She bent down, her face close to his ear. *"Gianni, ardo di amore per te."* She had been practicing that sentence to herself since she'd asked Mama how to say it while they drove to the hospital. Mama had blushed just a little, but she understood. Her future daughter-in-law seemed to be picking up Italian easily, at least the important phrases.

He looked at her in amazement, loving her even more for learning his language. He told her in English that he burned with love for her too and then kissed her, overcome with desire for her. She pulled away, smiling at him and whispered in his ear again. "Mama warned me about how passionate you are. I have to go now. I wouldn't want you to hurt yourself." She smiled and kissed him again, just a peck on his cheek.

"You would leave me so unsatisfied, Bella Donna?" He had that well-practiced, sad-eyed, puppy dog look on his face, the exact look Mama had warned her about.

"The truth is, Gianni, I don't want to hurt *you!*" She heard him laugh as she walked out and the sound of it was like the most beautiful symphony she had ever heard.

Chapter 11

HE SAW THEM leave. He'd been watching the house since before the sun rose and knew that they would be leaving for the hospital to visit him. Giancarlo Giannotti had become his obsession now and Nicolò Amato was determined that his first failure at the hospital would not be repeated. He was going to be successful this time.

He was surprised at how clever he had been in securing an alibi the first time; it was so easy in fact, that he planned to use it again. Sofia had been none the wiser that night when he'd manipulated the clock by the bed so that she would believe that he had awakened her at two, when in fact it was three. Detective Iacopetti had specifically asked Sofia about the time, about where her husband was at two o'clock and Amato had made sure she would remember he was in bed with her. But if he were to awaken her again and she was questioned again as to the time, she might become suspicious. To make sure that she didn't, he was waking her more often than was customary for them so that it would not seem unusual. She didn't mind. She was content believing that Donnatella meant nothing to him now and that Nicolò had turned his affections back to her, his wife.

He knew he would carry out his plan under the cover of darkness, but he needed to know the layout of the house before he came. It was a large house and probably had many bedrooms. He needed to know which room Giannotti would be in and the best way to enter that room. He needed to know if he would be alone in the room or if his fiancée would be with him. That's why he waited until he saw Giannotti's parents and the American woman leave.

He'd checked the hospital computer, had read Dr. DeSanti's progress notes and knew that Giannotti was going to be discharged the next day.

He had to work fast. The hospital wasn't far away and he didn't know how much time he would have before they arrived back at the house. He needed to be certain that this time, Giannotti would pay for causing Donnatella's death.

Peering into the ground floor windows, he could see only one bedroom on the main floor. It was off to the side of the house, separated by a passage area. It was a large room and he could see a private bath at one end of the room and at the other end, through French doors, a patio. He saw separated twin beds and four pieces of luggage stashed in the corner near what was probably a closet. He had no idea if Giannotti and his bride-to-be were sharing the same room; he assumed by the amount of luggage that they were, but thought it was highly improbable that they would be sharing the same room and not the same bed. He knew that women were attracted to Giannotti, knew it from having heard nurses gossip about how handsome he was.

Amato had never considered himself to be handsome. It had always been a source of pride that he had seduced a woman as beautiful as Donnatella away from Giannotti. The night that she had taken the Ducati, they were going away, far away. He was tired of hiding his affair with her. He wanted people to see them together, to see her beauty and wonder how a man like him had captured such a stunning woman. He had told Donnatella to inform Giannotti who the father of her baby was; Amato wanted him to suffer in that knowledge.

Even after he knew who she had been seeing, Giannotti wouldn't grant her a divorce. If she left and went away, she wouldn't need one. They would go somewhere far away and live together. She would love him and he would always have the satisfaction of knowing that he had taken the very thing that Giannotti valued the most.

Walking around to the back of the house, he climbed the few stairs up to the patio. He looked through the French doors. There were heavy curtains held back at each side with drapery cords. He checked the lock, taking a credit card from his wallet and slipping it through the slit in the door. He lifted it up and the door opened. It wasn't silent, but it was quiet enough that it wouldn't waken anyone sleeping inside. He couldn't believe it was going to be so easy.

Once in the room, he checked the names on the luggage tags. He was right. She was staying in the room with Giannotti; at least, her luggage was there. He was more sure now that they were sharing this room and he didn't care if they did or didn't share a bed. It made sense that they would be in this bedroom. As guests, they would be given the best room with the private bath.

There was a full-length mirror near the bathroom door and a desk against the wall. Near the French doors there was a carved wooden trifold privacy screen and behind that, a small side table. He was sure this was the room when he saw the marble bust of Michelangelo's 'David' on the table. It still had the price sticker on it. Amato knew that of all the souvenirs of Italy, this one was a favorite of tourists. It was large, but not too heavy and he was sure the American had purchased it. It was so typical of Americans, he thought, to buy such cheap souvenirs.

He walked quickly through the rest of the house, keeping an eye out the front windows for the returning car. The connecting room led out into a hall. There was a bathroom and an office, then stairs to the upper level. Past the stairs was a very large living room which adjoined the front entry to the house. Past that was a formal dining room with a large kitchen behind at the back of the house. A door from the kitchen opened on to a large, long patio with long tables and more than fifteen chairs. They must entertain often, he guessed.

Just to be sure, he climbed the stairs and checked all the bedrooms upstairs, but saw no sign that Giannotti and the American woman were using any of those rooms. He made his way back downstairs to the main floor bedroom and out through the French doors, locking them before he closed them behind himself.

As he walked back to his car, he thought about the fact that he might have to get rid of the American also. If he had to, if she woke up, he would kill her. After all, she was just like Giannotti. She wasn't supposed to be sleeping behind the curtain at the hospital. Giannotti would be dead now if she hadn't awakened and interrupted his plan. If he had to kill the American woman, then Amato would consider that a bonus.

He wanted to use a large knife. One strong slice to the neck, neat and precise just like a surgeon, severing the jugular vein and carotid artery, and death would be quiet and quick. It seemed fitting to Amato that Giannotti should die like that, the great trauma surgeon suffering the ultimate trauma and unable to save himself. Giannotti couldn't save Donnatella and Amato was going to make sure that he couldn't save himself either.

He got back in his car, more sure now that his plan was good. He went back over what he knew. It would all be quick and sure and he would finally have his revenge on Giancarlo Giannotti. He had the plan for a perfect murder.

❧

Papa called her into his office. It was a large room at the back of the house and, much like the closet, was completely occupied with books, photos and the accumulations of years of life. He pulled up a chair for her next to the desk and opened an album which must have been six inches thick, as close as she could estimate.

He pored over old photos of the children, telling her who they were and what they were like as children. It was so easy to pick out the ones with Gianni in them; his eyes were unmistakable even as a child. Plus, he was the one who was always making funny faces or hand gestures, just being generally goofy as kids will be. In one photo in particular, all the children were gathered around Mama, smiling and perfectly posed. Papa said it was taken on her birthday. Mama didn't look very happy though. She had Gianni by the wrist, trying to hold him while he made a silly face and was obviously trying to get loose from her grip. Papa was smiling, remembering.

"You see now, Wendy. Our Gianni was a rascal, always making with funny faces and causing mischief."

"He hasn't changed all that much, has he Papa?" They both laughed.

"Do you think you can handle such a man as this?"

"What do you think? How am I doing so far?" She was truly interested in his opinion of her. Sometimes she wondered if she really could handle Gianni, if she really knew him as well as she thought she did. Being in love had a way of blinding a person to the faults of others; she knew this. But it took time to really know a person. That must be why sacred love was important, because after years of marriage, the physical passion would cool and when it did, there must be an underlying friendship that carried two people along, kept them in love and committed to each other, kept them 'as one.'

"I think you are doing an excellent job. I think you have the patience, the love and the desire to make him into the best man he can be. He needs that. He did not get that from Donnatella and I know he will do the same for you. A husband and a wife must always strive to build up each other and help each other become the person God meant that they should be. It is a big job and it takes much love. I see you and Gianni together and I know that you have enough love for this job."

He paused a moment, then added, "He drove Mama crazy when he was a little boy and I tell you a secret: we men, we are always little boys! It is the love of a good, strong woman that makes us into men. I see the love you have for him and it makes me very happy."

"Thank you, Papa. I needed to hear that."

"Now, see this photo?" He handed her a formal portrait. It was Gianni's high school graduation photo. Wendy was taken aback by how handsome he was even then. "He had many girls always after him, calling the house for him. He was very popular. He took them out to dances and shows, you know, how kids do. But he was very particular when it came to giving away his affections. He did not give them lightly or often; maybe a hug or a little kiss, but that was all." Papa's face was somber. "I know that Gianni has given himself only to Donnatella."

She needed to know, needed to understand if Papa and Mama knew that Donnatella was her sister-in-law. She didn't want secrets, not with Gianni and not his parents, but she also didn't want to cause trouble in the family.

"Did he tell you about Donnatella's family?" She regretted saying it immediately, regretted that she may have just opened wounds that were better left closed. She should have asked Gianni first.

Papa looked at her, saw her apprehension and smiled. "I know, Wendy," he said, his manner quiet and comforting. "He told us how he found you, that you were married to Donnatella's brother. Do you not think it was the hand of God that brought you and Gianni together?"

"Yes, I do believe that."

"God will always be with you. When you have trouble turning Gianni into the man he should be, you ask God and He will help you. Do you think I am a good man?"

It seemed an odd question for Papa to ask her, but she already loved him as if he were her own father. "I think you're a great man!"

"Now you know why Mama spends so much time in prayer!" They both laughed and she hugged him.

"Come. Let us see what Mama has cooked up for our lunch. After, when you are ready, I will drive you back to the hospital if you like, so that you can be with Gianni. It is not safe to leave him alone for too long. He will get into trouble. Remember, you must grow the little boy into a man."

"I may be a little late for that Papa," she replied, giggling. "Believe me, in some ways he's a man already!"

Papa laughed loudly. "Wendy, *mia bella figlia, ti amo!* My beautiful daughter, I love you! Gianni has chosen the perfect woman to be his wife!" He laughed again as they headed for the kitchen and the smell of minestrone soup and freshly baked bread.

Chapter 12

"YOU HAVE BEEN giving Rosabella and Fabiana trouble." DeSanti checked the incision. It was healing nicely.

Gianni shrugged his shoulders. "Not so much trouble. It was nothing."

DeSanti was looking directly at him, pinning him down. "Nothing? Last night, Fabiana called me out of concern for you. Fabiana never calls me unless it is a big problem." DeSanti wasn't really angry, Giannotti knew that. He was a good friend. "You refused your morphine again. You and I spoke about that and I thought you understood."

He was contrite. "Yes, I understood Allesandro. Please, it is a personal matter and I wish you would not press me to explain. It is done now. I am taking my medications like a good patient."

"You are my friend, Gianni. I am concerned about you, that is all. If I can help you in any way, you will call on me, yes?" He nodded and DeSanti changed the subject. "Your incision looks good. Your lungs sound good. You are eating well and walking on the crutches. I think it is time to get you out of here. How does tomorrow morning sound?"

"*Meraviglioso*! That sounds wonderful!" He wanted to leave right then, leave the bad memories and pain behind and get home to Wendy. He wasn't going to force the issue with DeSanti though. He would be the good patient and follow instructions. It was easier that way.

"Then I will write the order. When you get home, you call my office and make an appointment for, let us say, Wednesday of next week and I will remove the staples. I will give you a prescription for the oxycodone and send you home with some morphine tablets. If you have any problems, you call my cell phone."

"*Grazie* Allesandro. I am indebted to you for all that you have done for me."

"You will let me know when the wedding has been rescheduled?"

"You will be the first to know, I promise." To get out of the hospital, he would have promised anything.

"Ah! Here she is now. Your beautiful bride!"

They were looking at her and smiling when she came into the room. It unnerved her; she never had that effect on men and she wondered what they had been talking about.

"Wendy, you must take Gianni for a walk. He has been in bed too long and needs to get up if he wants to go home tomorrow. Apparently you are the only one he listens to." Gianni knew then that DeSanti had been told that Wendy had been called to help the night before.

She was barely able to contain her excitement. "You're coming home tomorrow?" She couldn't wait to have him home, to be with him, to take care of him. She wanted to put the last week behind them, to move on to the wedding and their new life together.

"I must see to my other patients, so I will leave you both. Remember, Gianni, if you have any problems, call me and do not forget to make that appointment." He looked at Wendy. "And you, *signorina*, if he gives you any problems, you may also call me!"

She laughed. "Oh, you can be sure of that!" she said and DeSanti left the room.

"*Beciami*, Wendy! *La tua bocca mi fa impazzire!*" He grabbed her and held her close, kissing her excitedly. She didn't know what he had said, but she didn't care. Whatever it was though, would be her next lesson in Italian! He was coming home in the morning and that was all that mattered now.

"Did Papa bring you?" He was still holding her as if they were conjoined twins, the strength of his arms reassuring; he was getting stronger.

"Yes, he stopped at the cafeteria for a cup of coffee. I know he has other motives though. He wants us to have some time alone."

"*I* want us to have time alone!" He kissed her again, holding her tighter, feeling her yield to his embrace. "I missed you! *Ti amo più della vita!* I love you more than life!"

"You heard Dr. DeSanti," she reprimanded, pulling away from him. "You need to get up." She broke free of his embrace. It wasn't his forlorn puppy look that she saw on his face this time. It was his unsatisfied, passionate desire for her and it left her overwhelmed. The intensity of his eyes stunned her and she saw the true depth of his love for her. It left her doubting that she could ever love him enough to fill the emptiness left by Donnatella. She shook the feeling away, reminding herself of what Papa had told her: God would help her.

She walked with him in the hallway, noticing that some other patient was now occupying the room where he had first been. She felt her stomach cramp up, knowing that if it was Nicolò Amato who wanted Gianni dead, he was still out there free to try again. How could they protect him once he was home, she wondered? She would call Detective Iacopetti and talk to him before the day was out.

"You look good!" Papa threw his arms around his son's shoulders while Gianni struggled to maintain his balance on the crutches. "When will they allow you to come home? Mama does nothing but talk about you coming home."

"Tomorrow, Papa, let Mama know I will be home tomorrow morning."

"*Ah, multo bene!* She will be so happy! We will all be happy! I will tell her to make something special for your dinner."

"I have missed Mama's cooking," he said and Wendy saw that look that told her he needed to keep moving or sit down.

"Papa, it is my turn to get some coffee. Why don't you take Gianni back to his room and I will join you after I get back?" Papa nodded and they turned and walked toward his room.

After he settled into the large chair, Gianni felt his strength returning. He was taking the morphine less often and substituting oxycodone, but there were times, especially when he was up, that he was miserable with the throbbing in his hip and leg. At least the leg pain took the focus off of his broken ribs.

He continued to need morphine to sleep. At night, his thoughts were as dark as his room and his pain was magnified, his recent memories playing in his mind like a bad song on the radio that he couldn't turn off. He would think about how terrified she must have been, hearing about his accident, waiting in the emergency room for news of his condition and then seeing him in the intensive care unit afterwards. He would picture Wendy waking up when she didn't hear the monitor's beep, picture her watching Amato inject the overdose of morphine into his IV. Sometimes it was the emotional pain, the guilt he felt, that hurt the most. The only memory that had come back to him since before the accident was Wendy asking him not to take Emiliano's Ducati into town and that he'd passed it off as just her nerves.

"Are you all right?" Papa looked concerned. "You are very quiet." His hand rested on Gianni's knee.

"I am good, Papa. I was just thinking."

"You were certainly not thinking about Wendy. Your face lights up when you are thinking about her!" He smiled. Papa had always been very intuitive, especially where Mama and the children were concerned. As a child, he knew that nothing could escape Papa's notice. "Wendy is a wonderful woman. She will make you a very good wife."

"More than anything I want to believe that."

"There is a 'but' somewhere in that sentence. I hear it." Papa was always direct. Gianni knew that and appreciated it in him even if it made talking to him uncomfortable at times. He was quiet for a long moment.

"Can I trust her, Papa? I trusted Donnatella." Papa watched him absentmindedly rubbing his injured leg, trying to ease the pain it caused him, knowing that his physical pain was getting better every day, but the emotional pain was still deep and raw.

"This is not about Donnatella, is it? There is something else that troubles you."

Papa was right, as usual. He did still carry pain from his relationship with Donnatella. He feared being hurt like that again. He thought he'd sorted out all those feelings a long time ago, but now that he was in love with Wendy, those old issues had resurfaced. He didn't want to put that on her; it wasn't fair. But there was the matter of his confession to her about Sofia. Wendy had said that she had forgiven him, but could he really trust her? He couldn't tell Papa about Sofia.

"Gianni, has Wendy done something to make you not trust her?"

"No, she has done nothing." He couldn't look at him because Papa would see his son's transgression.

"Have you given her reason not to trust you?" Papa was sure that whatever had upset Wendy before was the same incident that Gianni was alluding to now. There was no answer to his question, which was an answer in itself. He didn't need to know the details. "How long will it take to heal your leg?"

Gianni was taken aback by the sudden change of topic. "Three or four months, perhaps more."

"As a physician, you know that injuries to the body take time to heal. But I think you forget that injuries to the heart take more time. Pain from a broken heart is very slow to heal. Wendy loves you very much. If you have hurt her, she will heal because her love for you is stronger than her broken heart."

"She told me she had forgiven me, but she lied to me."

"Perhaps she did not lie and she did forgive you, but you must understand that her pain is still there. It can exist with her forgiveness. Be patient with her, give her time and her heart will heal, just like your leg." Gianni was quiet, his head down. He knew Papa was right, that he had hurt Wendy not only with his confession, but by his indiscretion when he had touched her while they were kissing.

"I think there is something much deeper here. I think that before you can trust Wendy, you must forgive Donnatella and how she treated you. And if something you have done has broken Wendy's heart, you must also forgive yourself. I know that she has forgiven you."

"How do you know that? Did you talk to her?"

"Yes, we talked. I could see she was upset about something, but I did not ask her what it was. She wanted me to tell her about sacred love. I told her what I have told all you children and I could see at the end of our talk, that whatever was bothering her, she had decided that her love for you was stronger than her pain."

"Will it always be like this? Will we always hurt each other?"

"All of life is like that. We hurt each other, but when we do, we also hurt God. God is quick to forgive us and wants us to be quick to forgive each other. Then we come together in love again, our love grows in the soil of forgiveness and the times we hurt each other become less and less."

Gianni was smiling. "How did you get so smart?"

"Mama taught me," he laughed and then was serious. "Let Wendy teach you."

Gianni was tired, physically and emotionally. "I need to lie down now," he said and Papa helped him out of the chair. They both saw her in the doorway as he got himself back into bed.

"Well, I will go now and leave you two alone. Mama will be wanting me to come home. She will be very excited that you are coming home, Gianni. When you are ready, Wendy, call and I will come and get you." As he left, she sat down next to the bed.

"Did you and Papa have a nice visit?" She sipped her coffee. It was strong, the norm for Italy, but she was getting used to it, even liking it.

"Yes, it was nice." There was a long pause. He wasn't looking at her, but was absentmindedly running his fingers over the remainder of a bruise on his right arm. The bruise was almost gone, just the yellow-green tint on his skin left behind. When he spoke again, he directed his eyes at hers and began softly.

"I have not been fair to you. Sometimes I forget that you are not like Donnatella and when I forget that, then I do not trust you."

Wendy was suddenly exhausted. Her shoulders sagged as she exhaled slowly. Every conversation seemed to bring up issues that took an emotional toll on them.

It had all been so easy being with him in Cape Narrows. Every day they spent together then was thrilling and fun; they were happy and excited in their new love. There was never any conflict between them, never anything to apologize for and no tears. Now, though, she felt as though they were both on a roller coaster and she was tired and wanted to get off.

"What is this about, Gianni? Do you think I haven't forgiven you for Sofia or for touching me? Is that what this is about?" He didn't answer, but she could see it in his face. Did she have to tell him about what happened between her and Mark? She still loved Mark, loved the memory of him. She didn't want to tarnish that memory, but how else would she be able to convince him?

Maybe it was the accident and the stress on both of them, the pain from which they both shared. Maybe it was something all couples faced when their wedding date approached and the nerves and doubts kicked in and without warning, it all seemed to be happening too fast. Maybe it was part of sacred love, of being open with each other with no secrets, no shame and no guilt and had to be dealt with before they joined as one.

She was thankful at least that he would talk to her, come to her with his doubts and his confessions and at that moment, she knew that she needed to tell him. It was time to end this ride and she was going to pull the brake handle and stop the roller coaster. She wanted to end all the guilt; she was so tired of it.

"Gianni, I'm the one who hasn't been fair to you." This wasn't going to be easy for her, but she wanted peace with him. She wanted to love him completely, without reservations and without guilt.

She put the cup of coffee on the bedside table. Her hands were shaking and he noticed. He took them in his, holding them gently, his eyes so full of love and compassion for her that she didn't think she could finish. He started to speak, but she took her hand and covered his mouth. "Don't say anything please. Just let me say what I have to say to you." She took a deep breath and let it out slowly.

"Mark and I had a good marriage and I loved him with all my heart, but it wasn't always like that. Do you remember when you told me how Donnatella was unhappy when you were in medical school?" He nodded. "Well, Mark and I had the same problem. We hadn't been married very long and he was always gone, always working and going to school. I was so lonely. I just wanted him to spend time with me."

She felt the tears forming. "I was angry with him and I pushed him away. I couldn't tell him what was wrong because it felt so selfish to put my needs above his; he was working so hard for us. When I think about it now, it seems so odd to me that I would push him away when I wanted to be with him so much. But I wanted to punish him for ignoring me. That was what my anger and resentment did."

She was still able to hold back her tears, but she grabbed a tissue from the bedside stand anyway. "Mark was a wonderful man. He was unhappy with me and I knew it. But I didn't think he would ever turn to another woman for comfort." She wiped the tears, now inching down her cheeks and took a deep breath, regaining control for a moment.

"I can't even tell you how betrayed I felt, how devastated I was." She couldn't go on.

He took her in his arms and held her tightly, letting her cry on his chest and feeling her let go of her pain. He could never have imagined that she had been hurt like that, they way he had been hurt by Donnatella. He'd always believed that she'd had a good marriage, that Mark had been faithful to her.

"It was my fault," she said through her sobbing. "I drove him to do it. That's why it hurt me when you told me about Sofia. It brought back all that pain from Mark."

She wiped her eyes with another tissue. She was relieved that he knew. He needed to understand why his confession about Sofia had been so hard on her.

"It took me a very long time to forgive Mark. We still had a good marriage and I did forgive him, but that trust between us was broken and no matter how hard I tried to ignore it, that pain was always there. I don't want there to be any more pain between you and I. I love you so much but I'm afraid. I don't want that to happen to us."

"Your fault was only that you pushed him away, just like Donnatella pushed me away. *He* chose to go to another woman instead of coming to you and giving you what you needed. *I* chose to turn to Sofia when Donnatella would not give me what I needed from her."

He lifted her head, his hand cradling her chin so that he could see into her eyes. "I make a vow to you right now, Wendy, that I will always turn to you, that I will never turn away from you or hide myself from you. You will be my life and my one true love for as long as I live. I promise you this: with God's help, I will never betray your trust."

Sacred Love

He kissed her, his arms ever tighter around her, holding her like she would slip away from him. She could hear the beating of his heart and feel the warmth of his body against hers.

"It's all right, Gianni," she said softly. She kissed him tenderly on his forehead. She was where she wanted to be: safe with him. The roller coaster had stopped and she had stepped off. There was nothing to say, no words needed between them. She stayed with him, lying across his chest, until he fell asleep.

Chapter 13

WENDY FOUND A table in a quiet corner of the cafeteria, took her cell phone out of her purse and then dug around the bottom until she found Inspector Iacopetti's card. She took a sip of the latte she had ordered and then dialed the number. She was surprised that he answered; she was expecting to talk to a receptionist or secretary.

She reminded him of who she was and told him that Gianni would be discharged from the hospital in the morning. She told him she was worried about another attempt being made on his life once he left the hospital.

"How will you protect him? Will you send an officer out to watch the house?" She heard a long exhale before he answered.

"I'm sorry, Signorina, but that is impossible."

"Why is that impossible? Someone wants him dead and I think it's Nicolò Amato. So does Gianni. You say you don't have enough evidence to arrest him, so that leaves him free to try again. His house is not as secure as the hospital and I'm worried." She was also angry, but she wouldn't tell the Inspector that just yet. She would save her anger for later, if she needed to persuade him.

"I understand, but I do not have enough men to guard Dr. Giannotti. It is not something we do. We are not the Secret Service like you have in America, the men who guard your President." That sentence sounded condescending, but Wendy let it go.

"So what are we supposed to do, let Amato try again and maybe succeed?" Now she was seriously thinking of using some persuasive anger; she felt it gathering inside her like ominous, black clouds before a downpour.

"Perhaps you can hire someone to watch the house for you or perhaps there are friends or relatives who can watch for any unusual activity. If there is anything out of the ordinary, then call us. We will come quickly."

Wendy thought about this for a moment. She would much rather have the police watching the house, but she could tell she wasn't going to get any help from Iacopetti and truthfully, she understood his position.

"Could you have an officer drive by the house once in a while?" She was grasping at straws now, but she was afraid for Gianni.

"If I have an officer in that area, I will certainly have him check on the house, but I am afraid that is all I can do for you. I would like to assure you that we have not closed this case. We are investigating the role Dr. Amato may have played in Donnatella Giannotti's death and will continue to do so with the resources we have available. You may call me anytime you are concerned or have further information that you feel would help us."

At least she thought Inspector Iacopetti sounded sincere. She would have to think of something else. Maybe some of Gianni's brothers could stand guard. She would ask him about that and if Mama knew about the morphine incident yet.

She was getting hungry and thought about calling Papa to come get her. She headed for the elevators, her fears for his safety growing in intensity, leaving her nervous and on edge.

Gianni was awake, sitting in a chair when she got back to his room. He was looking better each time she saw him. She pulled her chair next to his, but facing him, picturing the antique S-shaped courting benches used in Victorian times: two lovers could be facing each other, but be side by side.

"I missed you. You were not here when I woke up."

"I went to the cafeteria." She was holding back. She didn't know if he'd thought about his safety once he was discharged and she didn't want to upset him. To hate someone enough to attempt murder seemed a pretty good indication that he was still in danger and Amato would try again.

"What is it, Wendy? You are worried about something." He was getting to be just like his Papa when it came to reading her. His safety needed to be discussed though and now was a good time.

"I'm concerned about you once we get you home. I called the Inspector and he told me that he can't send anyone to watch the house for us." As soon as she had said it, Gianni looked dejected. He let out a long sigh, his shoulders dropping. "Are you upset that I called him?"

"No, not at all," he said, his voice quiet. "I would have called him myself. It is just that I do not want to think about this now. It is hard for me. I am tired and I just want to be with you and talk about happy things."

He wasn't going to tell her he didn't feel well, that he suddenly felt that something wasn't right. It might pass and he didn't want to think about a setback in his recovery that would keep him hospitalized longer.

Sacred Love

She felt bone weary herself. There had been so much pain and stress with his physical injuries and emotionally, she knew they were both worn out from tension. She decided the safety issue could wait a while longer.

"You're right. Let's talk about something nice." They held hands and she remembered the first time she'd noticed his hands, the first time he'd accidentally brushed his hand on hers and how it had excited her. She'd never thought about what a surgeon's hands should look like, but she imagined they would be just like his: long, slender fingers that were strong, but whose delicate movements could repair intricate blood vessels and nerves with the lightest touch.

"Tell me what the angels tell you." His touch still excited her. He was rubbing his thumbs on top of her hands as he held them and she felt a pleasurable sensation race all the way up her arms.

"You know I can't tell you what the angels say," she said jokingly. She saw his weariness. It sat on him like a heavy weight, slumping his shoulders, his eyes downcast and focused on her hands. She was worried; something was bothering him.

"Then make something up, something nice, please Wendy," he begged. She pulled him toward her and they kissed, just a short, sweet kiss, the kind given between pre-teens in the throes of puppy love.

"I'll tell you about the first time I saw you at Memorial." He was interested; his countenance improving. "You came over to my table in the cafeteria and told me your name. I was so surprised and I couldn't get over how handsome you were. Do you remember that you asked me my name and I said it was 'Windy'? That's how much you excited me; I didn't even know my own name!"

He was smiling, remembering. He knew it then, that she was excited. He could see it in her eyes and he remembered how flattered and happy it made him feel.

She saw him straighten up, the weariness leaving him. "I saw you and I knew right then that every fantasy I had ever had about Italian men was true!"

"Did you fantasize often about Italian men?" He kissed both her hands, never letting go of them.

She gave him a look, smiled and decided not to answer his question. She'd let him wonder about that. He didn't need to know what went on in her head, not everything. Not yet anyway.

"Do you remember how I talked and talked and couldn't shut up?" He grinned, nodding his head at the memory. "My heart was beating so hard that I thought you might hear it!"

"Did I truly have such a strong effect on you?"

"Let's just say that it was a good thing I was sitting down because you made me *very* dizzy with excitement!"

They both laughed and she felt thankful that they had decided to put off the safety talk for now. This was a lot more fun and she could see that they both needed something fun, even this little story.

"Did you know that American women have a certain way of describing very handsome men? We say they are 'drop dead gorgeous' and that's what I thought about when I saw you. When I looked at you, at your eyes and your smile, I thought I might drop dead from seeing how beautiful you were!" She paused for a moment, overwhelmed with the memory.

"But there was something more than just your handsome face that attracted me. I felt so comfortable with you, like it was the most normal thing in my life to be with you. When I was finished with my lunch and got up to leave, you said we were friends and I didn't question how you could consider me your friend after having known me only a half hour, it just seemed very natural. You made me *feel* like I was your friend, as if we had known each other all our lives and I liked that very much."

"I am happy you told me this. I was always worried that you were too polite to tell me to…what do you Americans say…to 'buzz off?'" They both laughed. "Tell me what you were thinking about me when I slept on your sofa, when you were drinking coffee and watching me as I slept." He had that look, that mischievous face that she had seen in the photos Papa had shown her.

"I didn't know you were awake, really I didn't. I don't remember what I …"

He interrupted her. "You remember exactly what you were thinking! I know this! When you drank your coffee, I looked and saw your face and I know that what you were thinking, you will remember until you are old and in a rocking chair!" He was enjoying this and Wendy was thankful for that. The past week had been so miserable for him and she wanted him to have some joy before he had to worry about Nicolò Amato.

"At first, I just watched you sleeping for a long time."

"It was a very long time, I know this. I wanted to move because my neck was sore, but I did not want you to know I was awake. Tell me what you were thinking as you watched me," he begged, always probing the intimacy of her thoughts that when shared with him, excited his passion for her.

"I watched you breathe. I felt so calm just watching you breathe! I remember you looked peaceful and that your hair curled at the ends and I wanted to run my fingers through it." She paused, her voice softer as she remembered. "I thought about what it would be like to wake up with you by my side, every morning. I thought about loving you and wondered if you would ever love me."

"Now you know, Bella Donna. I did love you then. I am sorry that it took me so long to tell you. I was afraid you would not want me. I knew that you still loved your husband."

"Yes, I guess I did. I didn't want to let go of him because his memory was all I had. I was afraid that if I loved another man, something would happen and I would be by myself again. I thought I was doing all right, but then I met you and I wanted you to be in my life. I realized how lonely I really was and it made me feel heavy inside and tired. When I saw you sleeping, I knew I didn't want to be alone any longer."

"You will never have to worry about that again. I will always be with you. I will always want you and love you." He kissed her, sealing his vow.

Chapter 14

SOFIA AMATO WAS not being truthful and Giorgio Iacopetti knew it. He had been a police officer for almost forty years and had heard many truths and even many more lies. She was lying and she wasn't very good at it. He could see it in her eyes and hear it in the tenor of her voice. Whenever she would talk about her husband, Iacopetti could see she was nervous and scared. Her eyes would be downcast and she would twist the wedding band on her finger as if it were too tight. He intended to get to the bottom of her lies for Dr. Giannotti's sake.

He admired Giancarlo Giannotti. Although the death of his wife warranted an unprejudiced and complete investigation, he'd never believed that Giannotti had purposefully caused her death. His years of police work told him that Giannotti just didn't have it in him, didn't have the depravity to commit a crime like that and his interviews with the doctor told him the same thing.

Through hours of interrogation, he had exhibited the normal demeanor of a grieving husband. From questioning the staff in the emergency room, he learned that Giannotti himself had treated his wife's injuries and was overcome with emotion. After fifteen minutes in the emergency room, her heart stopped and he would not quit CPR even when it was obvious that she was gone. The staff had to physically pull him away from her lifeless body and he had slumped to the floor from grief and exhaustion. From what Iacopetti was told, every one of the staff present with Giannotti in that room left in tears.

The details of his statement never changed no matter how often Iacopetti's questions were asked or how the same question was rearranged and asked again. He had been truthful about his wife's extramarital affair, but didn't seem vengeful or angry toward her, just hurt, the pain still obvious.

It hadn't taken Iacopetti long to judge that Dr. Giannotti was telling the truth, but without any evidence of direct tampering with the Ducati, either by him or by someone else, the case had been deemed an accident and filed away. Iacopetti however, had kept the case alive in his own mind, trying to fit pieces together, hoping that someday new evidence would present itself and he could bring closure for Dr. Giannotti. Now it had happened just as he had hoped; there seemed to be a new lead and a suspect: Nicolò Amato. That's why the Inspector was now on his way to L'Ospedale Sacra Famiglia to talk to Sofia Amato.

It was Saturday so he'd called the manager of the laundry first and found out that Sofia was there. He wanted to question her away from her husband where she might feel freer to talk. He had questioned her and Amato separately the first time, but just the fact that they had come to the police station together seemed to intensify Sofia's nervousness.

Iacopetti had seen enough battered women to know the signs all over Sofia and he wanted to talk to her again, away from her husband. Now was his chance. He stopped at the information desk in the main lobby and got directions to the laundry.

Sacred Love

It was a large room in the basement with immense tables of clean linens being folded and industrial washers and dryers all spinning like jet engines. It was easy to see the invisible line that divided the area between where the dirty laundry was processed and the clean laundry was folded and stacked. There were large wheeled bins of dirty laundry located near the washing machines. All the machines were tumbling, not one was empty. Other bins held the laundered linens, wet and waiting for their turn in the dryers.

On the other side of the dryers were the long folding tables and mangle irons, ten of them by Iacopetti's count. The ironed and folded linens were stacked on wheeled carts to be taken to the different floors of the hospital. It was hot, humid and noisy. He thought he saw Sofia at one of the folding tables, working on a towel, smoothing it to perfection before folding it and adding it to the cart of clean linen.

He found the manager's office and asked for her. Fifteen seconds after her name was called on the loudspeaker she showed up, the dread on her face evident as soon as she spotted Iacopetti. The manager offered his office, using the excuse that he had a washer that needed fixing, and hurried out the door like a scared rabbit. Iacopetti got that reaction sometimes; he was used to it.

Iacopetti began by suggesting she relax, that he was just checking some facts and that she wasn't in any trouble. That seemed to erase the fear on her face for the moment, but did nothing to quell the trembling of her hands. Iacopetti made a mental note of that.

He offered her a chair. She sat upright, as stiff as the starched uniform she was wearing. Her hair was pulled back and tied with a ribbon. Not a hair was out of place and the ribbon was tied into a neat bow. There was nothing out of place on her. This was a woman who lived and breathed perfection.

He'd seen it before in women who were used to being abused by their husbands; she was no different. He knew that some women believed if they could make everything perfect, be perfect, the abuse would stop. They were brainwashed into believing that they were to blame for the abuse and the usual result was that they tried to live a life of perfection, hoping that it would end the beatings.

"I want to make sure that I understand you correctly," he started. She brushed a piece of lint off her uniform, her hands still shaking. Getting the truth might be easier than Iacopetti expected. "You went to the intensive care unit to see Dr. Giannotti. Is that right?"

"Yes," she answered, now smoothing a wrinkle in her uniform.

"How did you know he had had an accident?" Iacopetti was going to start with simple questions. She would be more apt to tell him something if she were relaxed. It was best not to push too soon with someone like her.

"I overheard people in the laundry talking about it."

"By 'people,' you mean other staff." She nodded.

"So, when you heard that he had had an accident, you were concerned about him." She nodded again. He wanted her talking, not nodding. "I assume then, that you knew him personally." No nod this time and he took that as a 'yes.'

"Were you a friend of his? Is that why you were concerned?" He noticed that her hands were shaking even more and she wouldn't make eye contact with him.

"I know him because he and Nicolò are friends."

"So you went to the intensive care unit to find out his condition, but he was in surgery." She nodded again. "And you spoke with his fiancée, yes?" Another nod. "She told you where he was, is that right?" Again, a nod.

"You told me that you didn't talk to her about seeing your husband tamper with the motorcycle. Am I remembering that correctly?"

"I never said I saw Nicolò *tamper* with the bike. I said I didn't see what he did."

She gasped, the color leaving her face, immediately aware that she was caught in her lie. She lived perfection and her compulsion for perfection took over and she had corrected him, revealing that she had lied when she said she'd never spoken to Wendy about the bike. It had happened in an instant, so fast in fact that even Iacopetti was taken aback.

"Shall we start over again, Signora, from the beginning?" He could see her shoulders drop in defeat. This was a woman who wasn't used to lying. Her eyes were getting red, her entire body shaking now as she pulled a neatly folded tissue out of her pocket.

"I understand why you would not want to get your husband into trouble, Signora. But I must have the truth. You did speak to Dr. Giannotti's fiancée. Is that correct?" She nodded.

"And can you be sure about what time Nicolò woke you up last Friday morning and wanted to make love?"

She sniffed and dabbed her eyes with the tissue. "Nicolò gets called to go to the hospital for emergencies all the time. When he woke me up, I looked at the clock. It was two in the morning. I remember that."

Something flashed in Iacopetti's thoughts. "Did you hear the phone ring when he got the call to go to the hospital?" She thought hard about that question. The phone always woke her, but Nicolò always answered it and then she would fall right back to sleep.

"I do not remember hearing the phone ring that night," she said, undoubtedly as puzzled as Iacopetti was.

"But you assumed he had left to go to the hospital for an emergency?"

"Yes, I thought that was where he went."

"If the phone did not ring or you did not hear it, what made you think he went anywhere?" This question had her very confused and for a while, she had to process it in her mind before she could answer. Iacopetti waited patiently for her.

"I just knew that he had gone to the hospital."

"But what was it that made you think that? Did you feel the bed move when he got up, hear the car drive away?" Here again, she concentrated as hard as she could.

"It was his smell. When he came back to bed, he smelled like the hospital, like the soap we use here in the laundry to wash the uniforms. That was why I thought he had gone there. When he woke me up and we made love, he smelled like the hospital. He always showers before he comes to bed at night and he showered that night, but when he woke me up, he smelled like the hospital."

Iacopetti was excited. He might just have a new lead in this case that would get it solved. "Thank you, Signora Amato. You have been a great help."

Her eyes were pleading with him. "Inspector, you will not tell my husband that I spoke with you, will you?"

He wanted to tell her that he knew she was being abused. He wanted to urge her to leave her husband and never come back before she became another statistic, but his experience told him that most women stayed with their abusive husbands, too frightened or too insecure to take action. "If I must speak with your husband again, I will not tell him where I got the information if that will make you feel better. But Signora, I would suggest that you think about this: if your husband *is* involved in these cases, you may want to take precautions for your safety. He may discover on his own where my information came from."

He hoped that she would consider what he'd said, that she would leave Amato and have a happier life somewhere else. "Thank you for your help, Signora." He turned and left the office.

She'd always known that Nicolò had done something bad to Gianni's bike, but she hadn't ever considered that whatever he had done would end in death. After Donnatella's accident, she'd tried to convince herself that Nicolò just wanted to play some kind of dirty trick on Gianni and the trick had turned deadly. Maybe the accident was really Donnatella's fault anyway. Maybe she didn't know how to handle the Ducati, not like Gianni did. But every excuse she told herself left her feeling more guilty and the guilt nearly buried her.

She wanted to go to the police and tell them what she'd seen, but she knew Nicolò would then be questioned and just like now, if Nicolò found out she had talked, she would end up buried too. So she'd kept quiet, that is until now. She'd heard about Gianni's accident. She was afraid for him all over again, afraid that Nicolò had done something to his bike again and she couldn't let that happen, not to Gianni. In her own way, she loved him.

The Inspector's advice struck a chord within her that she hadn't even known existed, the fear now very real to her. Sofia decided that it had been too long since she'd last seen her mother. A few weeks off, two hundred miles away from Nicolò, might do her good, especially if he were locked up when she returned.

The laundry manager came back to his office when he saw the Inspector leave and as Sofia got up, she asked, "May I speak to you about taking my vacation?"

Chapter 15

GIANNI DIDN'T SEEM to be nearly as concerned for his safety as she did. She told him about her conversation with Inspector Iacopetti, how he could not provide a police guard at Papa's house. She wanted him to ask Emiliano or Cristiano to come stay at the house as added protection, but he didn't think it was necessary. He didn't give in to fear easily; it was the same trait that kept him calm and steady in surgery when everyone else was in a panic. He maintained command of the situation and that was what he was doing now. She loved that about him, but sometimes he was too cavalier about situations she felt were as serious as this.

"What if he tries again, Gianni? What if he comes to the house and this time he succeeds? You promised you would never leave me." She wanted him to understand how scared she was, how vulnerable she felt.

"We will take all precautions, Wendy, I promise you this. I will talk to Papa and we will decide what to do to make the house safe. You will be with me every minute. We are staying in Papa and Mama's room, yes?" She nodded, remembering how he'd laughed when she'd told him that Papa had separated the beds. "I will need pain medication during the night, so we will be awake at times. We will leave some lights on, outside and inside. You will see. We will be safe."

He studied her face, saw her fear there, mixed with her beauty. That he had even found her at all left him amazed, feeling as though he had been given a miracle that he had done nothing to deserve and yet, God had brought her into his life. He couldn't understand how he had survived before knowing her, as if he had been born the very day he saw her in the cafeteria. Sometimes just the thought of her left him without strength. He wasn't about to leave her or let anything separate them.

"Gianni, are you all right?" She was gently running her fingers on his arm, the worry in her face more pronounced. He'd become so quiet, his breathing very shallow. "Are you in pain?"

"You just take my breath away, that is all." He smiled, trying to make light of her concern, but he knew something was wrong. His chest hurt more than it should. The pain from the broken ribs had actually been getting a little better or maybe he'd just gotten used to it; he wasn't sure, but it felt almost as bad now as it had right after the accident and he knew that wasn't right. And for several hours now, he had been successfully hiding the shortness of breath, trying to ignore it, to pretend that it wasn't really there. But it was getting worse too and he had finally resigned himself to the fact that something had to be done; he couldn't avoid it any longer. He was so close to going home. The thought of staying one hour longer in the hospital, of one more night of interrupted sleep, depressed him. He needed to be discharged, but it might not happen tomorrow as planned. That realization hung on him, the heaviness pressing him down, adding to the heaviness he felt in his chest.

"Would you tell Fabiana that I would like to talk to her please?"

Wendy could see it herself now, how shallow his breathing had become. Her heart sank. She saw the look on his face, the resignation, and it scared her. She knew that he didn't tell her everything, that he tried to shield her from the reality of certain situations. He'd done it at Memorial in the ED and she was afraid he was doing it again now.

Fabiana was sitting at the nurse's station, ten feet away from his door. Wendy went to the door and called her name, the concern in her voice obvious, and Fabiana hurried into the room.

"Call Dr. Rossi for me please, Fabiana. I think I may have another pneumothorax." Wendy's heart sank when she heard what he said. If he had a collapsed lung again, it would mean another chest tube and more days in the hospital and she didn't think either of them could take a setback like that, especially Gianni.

Fabiana listened to his lungs with her stethoscope. "I will call him immediately," she said and added "You should get back into bed."

Wendy could hear her dialing the operator, asking that Dr. Rossi be paged as she helped him back into bed. Within a few minutes, the phone at the nurses' station rang and Fabiana answered it, then stuck her head into the room. "Dr. Rossi has ordered an x-ray. I will be right outside waiting for the technician. Call if you need me." With that, she left.

"You're very quiet. Are you okay?" Wendy knew how disappointed she was right then and knew he must be even more so. They just couldn't seem to get a break. They were so close to getting him home. She'd just have to wait and see what Dr. Rossi said.

Gianni looked at her, seeing the concern in her face. He didn't want her to have to ever worry about him again. It grieved him that he had caused her so much anxiety when she deserved so much happiness. "Will you kiss me?" he asked.

"That's a silly question," she whispered. "Of course I will." She kissed him gently, imagining his lips were made of delicate glass and would break from the pressure of hers, but she let the kiss linger as if it could provide him with the air he needed to breathe effortlessly. When she pulled away, he was still short of breath, but he looked more relaxed.

'If that little kiss made him relax, just wait until the honeymoon,' she thought, her face getting warm.

"Tell me what they say, Wendy. Please."

She saw it in his eyes; he longed to know what the angels were telling her. She had never seen it on him before, but now it was so clear. He needed just a small fantasy to get him over this set back. It was just a silly saying anyway, Wendy told herself, something he probably made up that day in the parking lot when they were new to each other, something he said to put her at ease because she was embarrassed. But she had always loved it, always loved the idea that angels were talking to her and she loved leaving him wondering what she was thinking, especially when he knew she was thinking about him. He needed something to lift his spirits and if the angels could give it to him, she wasn't about to deny him.

"I kissed you and you relaxed. They told me if just a kiss made you relax, then you should wait and see what I can do for you on our wedding night."

He thought for a moment and then said, "These angels, they are not going to be joining us on our wedding night, are they?"

"If they do, you will be the first to know about it, don't you think?" He just smiled and hoped the angels never stopped speaking to her.

Dr. Rossi came twenty minutes after the x-ray technician had left. "I looked at your x-ray. It is another pneumothorax, but it is not as large as the first and I think we will be able to aspirate it with a needle. This will be easy to take care of and it should not interfere with Dr. DeSanti's discharge order for tomorrow. You are pleased to hear this?"

"Yes, very much," he answered.

"Then let us get this taken care of so that you may have some dinner and I may go home to my wife and have mine!" He left the room to speak with Fabiana.

"Wendy, perhaps you should leave. I do not want you to be upset." He remembered her face when the chest tube had been removed. He'd always thought it strange how the body reacted to stress, how it was nothing to watch a procedure on a stranger and have no emotional reaction at all, but if it were a loved one, the body would respond with a sudden drop in blood pressure, causing dizziness and fainting.

"I'll go if you want me to, but I want to be with you." She had no worries about fainting this time. She didn't have the energy to be emotionally fragile any more, not with all they had been through. She knew she was getting tough. It was like Gayle was always saying: "Pull up your big girl panties and deal with it!" She'd had a lot of practice pulling up her panties this week, but for all the wrong reasons; not the ones she wanted anyway! Maybe it was tension, she didn't know, but she couldn't suppress a laugh.

Gianni just smiled at her, shaking his head. "I love you so much," he said, her laughter still filling the room. This time, she kissed him with a lot more energy.

❧

The procedure wasn't very complicated, which was reassuring to Wendy because she knew that tough or not, she was anxious about how uncomfortable it would be for Gianni. She needn't have worried as Dr. Rossi used a local anesthetic to numb the area where the needle was inserted into his chest. The air was drawn up into a syringe and then expelled through a stopcock valve. This was repeated until no air could be withdrawn. An x-ray taken at the end of the procedure showed just a very small pocket of air left in the pleural space, but Dr. Rossi felt it would clear up on its own. Another x-ray would be taken in the morning before discharge to make sure the pneumothorax had not increased in size overnight.

Dinner arrived shortly after and Gianni attacked it eagerly.

"I'd better be getting back to the house. Papa and Mama will wonder where I am." She got up to leave, but he caught her hand and stopped her.

"Will you stay with me tonight?" he asked, his voice almost pleading.

"Are you propositioning me?" She was joking with him, but even so, she didn't want another episode like what had happened before.

"It has been a hard day for me, Wendy. I just need you to be with me, that is all." She expected his puppy dog look, but he wasn't using it. He was serious about her staying with him and something about his demeanor told her it had nothing to do with his desire for her.

She dug her cell phone out of her purse. "I'll call Papa and tell him I won't be coming home."

Chapter 16

BEING DISCHARGED FROM a hospital in Italy wasn't much different from being discharged from one in the United States; it took forever. But policy was policy even in Italy and there was nothing to do but wait for all the details to be worked out so that they could be on their way. After breakfast, he'd had the final x-ray done, which added another thirty minutes to their wait while the results were read. Both Dr. Rossi and Dr. DeSanti stopped by his room while making their rounds, to check on him and say goodbye. By the time all the paperwork was done, Gianni dressed, a wheelchair found and all the staff on the morning shift had said their good-byes, they left and would be home in time for lunch.

It was sunny with just a hint that autumn was coming soon. Gianni hadn't been outside since the accident and most of that time had been spent in a windowless room. Wendy hadn't given it a thought until she noticed him enjoying the warmth of the sun coming through the window on his side of the car.

By the time they'd arrived at the house and Gianni had walked into the living room, he was exhausted and out of breath. It was a very large living room with three sofas arranged for easy conversation and Gianni chose to sit on the one in front of the window where he would be in the sunshine. Looking at the smile on his face, his head back and eyes closed, Wendy remembered eating lunch with him in the conference room at Memorial and how she had chosen the chair by the windows for the same reason. She had needed to feel the warmth from the sunshine.

She sat next to him on the sofa while Mama and Papa went to fix lunch. They could be heard in the kitchen, both of them speaking low to each other which was certainly not their usual habit. Wendy looked at Gianni; his eyes were still closed and he was smiling broadly.

Mama called them to the kitchen. Papa was carrying a tray of food out to the back patio and they followed him outside and sat at the long tables. Mama brought out coffee and dishes and sat next to Papa.

It was the typical meal that Wendy had become accustomed to seeing at his house: a beautifully decorated stoneware plate with different cheeses and three kinds of salami, fresh bread, more minestrone soup in bowls that matched the plates and espresso with biscotti.

Papa and Mama were so excited and animated, relieved to have their son home and getting well. They talked about the wedding and about the food and wine that would be served. Wendy watched Gianni enjoying the lunch and how his expression told her he was content and relaxed. It was such a small thing, Wendy thought, to be outside sitting in the sun and eating good food.

Once Gianni had finished eating though, she saw that he was fidgeting and looked tired. He couldn't sit still for very long, couldn't get comfortable in the hard chair. It was time for pain medication.

Sacred Love

Wendy looked at Papa and Mama. "If it's all right, Gianni and I need a nap. Would that be okay with you?"

Papa helped him out of the chair and handed him the crutches. "Of course, of course. You two go ahead. You sleep as long as you like. Mama and I will clean up. We will have dinner when you wake up, so you take a long nap."

Wendy helped him onto the bed nearest the French doors. She got his pain medication out of her purse, poured him a glass of water from the bathroom and handed him the oxycodone.

"Here, take this," she said and was surprised that he accepted it without complaint.

"You see, I am being good. I do not want my nurse to be angry with me." He grinned at her, swallowed the pill and downed the glass of water.

"Your nurse wants you to lie down." She noticed that Mama had put an extra lightweight blanket at the foot of the bed. She unfolded it and covered him, but he grabbed her wrist before she could walk away.

"Lie down with me, Wendy," he said. Though his voice was soft, it felt like a command, compelling her to do as he asked. It was almost as if he had some hypnotic hold on her and she had no power within herself to resist him. That's what she told herself anyway. In reality, she knew she wanted to lie next to him, just as she had wanted to the morning she had watched him sleeping on her sofa. It was as simple as that.

They lay on their sides, facing each other on his bed, each of them with their head propped with one hand, thankful to be alone at last. He took her free hand, imagining the ring that would be on her third finger.

"I want to be like this forever, to look at you and be this close to you. You are so beautiful it scares me." His eyes were locked on hers as usual and sometimes their intensity caused her to be scared too. She was scared now.

"I'm not beautiful. I don't know why you think I am." She was serious. She knew that he thought she was beautiful because he loved her, but it was the way he said it, like she was the most stunning woman in the world.

"I know you are beautiful because I see your heart, Wendy, and it is beautiful. Do you remember a few months ago, when Mr. and Mrs. Hutchinson came into the emergency room?" She would never forget it. Jim Hutchinson looked terrible. His prostate cancer had metastasized throughout his body. He had decided not to treat it after it was first discovered and had gone downhill quickly. He was terribly thin, the cancer eating him bit by bit, leaving him a hollow shell of the man he once was. Lillian had agreed with his decision, but Wendy could see the anguish in her face as she cared for him. Wendy could feel her pain and it hurt just like the pain of losing Mark.

Gianni continued. "You do not know this, but when Mr. Hutchinson got very bad and was admitted, I know you visited him every day after you got off your shift, every day until he passed away."

"How did you find out?" She thought she had been pretty clever at covering up the visits, not that she didn't want anybody to know. It was just that she wanted to be with Lillian, to spend time with her and help her accept the inevitability of Jim's condition. She wanted to keep it private between herself and Lillian.

"Mrs. Hutchinson would come down to the ED after her visits while she waited for her taxi. She would tell me that you were coming to see them every day. She would tell me how much it meant to her and that you would hug her. She loves you very much for doing that."

He stopped, picturing Lillian with Jim during the last hours of his life. "She told me that you kissed Jim on his forehead and told him that is was okay to go, that you would take care of Lillian. That is what I see, Wendy. I see your beautiful heart. And I will not lie; to me, your face is also beautiful."

"Are you trying to make me blush?" She knew he wasn't, that he meant what he said. She could read it in those eyes of his. He closed them for a moment, unable to face her any longer. It was so hard, lying next to her and wanting her the way he did.

"I will tell *you* a story this time," he said at last. "Do you remember when I showed you the photo, the one of you and Mark on your wedding day?"

"Yes, I remember. How could I forget? That's when you told me that you knew about Mark and Donnatella and when you finally told me that you loved me."

"I thought that I loved you the first time I saw you in the cafeteria, but now I know that I loved you even before that."

"You loved me *before* the first time you saw me?" She was confused, but curious. He fingered a lock of her hair that had fallen over her face and then brushed it back behind her ear.

"After Donnatella died, I cleared all of her things out of the house and I found the photo of you and Mark in her jewelry box. That is when I decided to find her family and tell them what had happened to her. I felt I owed it to them. She had told me long before there had been a bad argument with her parents and she had left and never wanted to return. I did not want them to remember her like that. I did not want them to spend their lives wondering if she was all right, if she missed them or thought about them. I had the envelope that the photo came in. Mark had written the return address. It was sent from Eatonville."

"Yes, we lived there," she said, remembering that Mark had told her about the big blowup between Donna and his parents and how distraught they all were.

"I wrote several times to that address, but there was never an answer and my letters did not come back. That is when I decided to quit my job at the hospital and come to America to look for her family. I went to Eatonville and I found that you were the only one left."

Wendy thought about those days after Mark's death. His mother had eventually remarried after his father had passed away and had moved out of Eatonville with her new husband. She was gone now too, having passed away from cancer three years ago.

Wendy had moved to Cape Narrows. There was nothing left for her in Eatonville but sad memories. She had decided to get on with her life, to start somewhere new.

"I looked at that photo all the time because I could see how happy you and Mark had been. Every time I looked at it, I thought about you. I wondered if you were married again and if you were happy."

He looked down at their joined hands and continued softly. "That is when I think I started to love you. The more I looked at your beautiful face and your smile, the more I wanted you. I wanted to have the happiness I saw in your face, but I wanted to have it with you. I prayed that I would find you and that you would not be married again."

When he looked up, he saw a tear in her eye. "I am sorry. I did not mean to bring up sad memories for you."

"No, Gianni, you didn't bring up sad memories. You just touched my heart, that's all. It's so amazing to know that you fell in love with my photo, that you thought about me and cared if I was happy. You didn't even know me."

He turned onto his back. He needed to reposition himself; his leg was cramping, the oxycodone not yet taking away the pain. She laid her head on his chest and listened to his breathing. He was quiet for several minutes.

"What are you thinking about?" she asked.

"I was thinking about Donnatella's jewelry box, about the necklace."

"What necklace?"

"Mark sent her a necklace. I remember it because it was her birthday and she was so excited that he had remembered her and sent her a gift. She loved Mark, I knew that."

Wendy got up on her elbow and looked at him excitedly. "I remember that necklace too! Mark asked me to go with him to pick it out. It was a silver heart and it had two birthstones in it. One was a ruby for Mark's birthday in July and one was an emerald for Donnatella's birthday in May. I remember it because the stones were red and green, like the Italian flag."

"Yes, that is the one. When I told you about finding the photo in her jewelry box, I remembered that the necklace was not there and I do not know what happened to it. I never found it."

"It's okay, Gianni. It doesn't matter now."

"I just wish that I had it to give to you, that is all. But you are right. What matters now is that I did find you." He kissed her, enjoying the feeling of her in his arms, the softness of her body next to his. He was comfortable, relaxed and suddenly very tired.

When she heard his breathing become slow and regular, she knew he was asleep. She thought about getting up carefully so as not to wake him and lying down on the other bed; she thought about it for all of ten-seconds and then decided that she was right where she wanted to be. At that moment, she was more comfortable than she ever had been in years. She yawned and realized that after their nap, they were going to have to admit to Mama that they had slept together. There was no getting around it this time.

Chapter 17

HE DIDN'T USUALLY work on Sundays, unless it was a serious emergency, but Giorgio Iacopetti was eager to follow up the new information Sofia Amato had given him. If he could prove that Nicolò Amato had not been in bed making love at two on Friday morning, he would have caught him in a lie, just as he had caught Sofia.

He could begin there and work toward placing Amato in the intensive care unit at the time Dr. Giannotti was being given an overdose of morphine. Somebody, even at that hour, must have seen him. If he were to bring Amato in for questioning again, he wanted facts he could lay out in front of the doctor, facts that Amato would not be able to refute. He wanted to be able to arrest Amato and lock him up if only to protect Sofia Amato. He hoped that she had taken his advice about leaving town. For now, he would start at the hospital.

He started in the Intensive Care Unit and spoke with the head nurse, asking her if she would have been notified of any emergency that required a call to Dr. Amato on the night shift on Friday. She told him she couldn't remember anything happening, but checked her patient list anyway, hoping that something would jog her memory. No, she told him, there would not have been any calls to Dr. Amato, she said as she looked at the list. He didn't have any patients in the ICU that week. Iacopetti thanked her, feeling encouraged that he was on the right track.

He decided to check the security booth located in the emergency department. He knew that the main doors of the hospital were locked after midnight and any personnel or visitors would have to pass by the security booth in order to have access to the hospital. He got the name of the guard on duty that night, found a waiting room and sat down.

Taking out his cell phone, he called his wife. He had promised he would take her to lunch and he wanted to let her know he would get home on time. Then he dialed the number of the guard on duty that night, who sounded sleepy when he answered the phone and wasn't too overjoyed about being awakened; he'd worked the nightshift last night too, he told Iacopetti.

Iacopetti asked him if he had seen anyone come into the hospital after midnight on Friday. There was a long pause while the guard thought back, then said yes. There had been a pregnant woman in labor, along with her husband, but he had shown them through to the emergency department. The only other person he'd seen was Dr. Amato, who came at about one-fifty. The guard remembered it because he'd asked Amato if he had an emergency, but Amato told him he was just checking on a critical patient. The guard thought at the time that that was a little strange, but let it go. The guard said that he didn't remember Amato coming back out the same way.

Was there another entrance where Dr. Amato might have been able to leave the building, Iacopetti asked him? There were utility doors located in many places around the hospital and they had electronic key pads. There were also the fire escapes. Amato could have left through any of those. He thanked the guard, apologizing for waking him up.

Iacopetti was satisfied that Amato was in the hospital at two on Friday morning, but now he knew it would still be very difficult to actually prove that it was Amato who had tried to murder Giannotti.

He'd put in enough hours for a Sunday, a day he wasn't even supposed to be working, so he called his wife and told her he was on his way home.

Chapter 18

WENDY HEARD VOICES coming from outside. She looked at her watch. They had napped for two hours and she felt very rested, better than she had for a long time. Gianni was still asleep, his breathing regular and deep, which was a relief. She was worried that the pneumothorax would reappear, but for now he seemed peaceful. She started to get up and he stirred.

"What time is it?" he asked, rubbing his eyes. He wrapped his arms around her, bringing her back down close to himself.

"It's three-thirty. Did you sleep well?"

He smiled at her. "I had the most wonderful dreams. They were about you." He kissed her. She was so soft and warm in his arms that he didn't ever want to get up.

"I heard people talking outside. I think your brothers and sisters are here. Didn't you tell me that they all come for Sunday dinner?"

"Yes, they do. They are early this time though. We do not eat until seven or eight o'clock. I think they are early so that they can visit with you. They have not had much time to get to know you."

"I think they are early because they want to see you. I know they have been worried."

"Perhaps we should get up then before they wonder what we have been doing." He smiled at her just as Mama peeked into the room.

"Gianni?" she whispered, sticking her head through the door. "Ah, you are both awake! Everyone is here. Are you coming out?" Of course Mama had not missed the fact that they were both in the same bed. Wendy noticed she wore a slight smile; they were both dressed and her smile reflected her relief. After all, she *had* given them permission and seemed happy that they had not taken advantage of it. At least now they wouldn't have to tell her they had slept together.

"We will be right there, Mama." Wendy got up and then helped him get out of bed, handing him the crutches. "If you get too tired, I'm sure your family will understand if you need to rest and let me know when you need more pain medication. It hasn't even been a week since your accident. Don't overdo this, okay?" There was an uneasy feeling gnawing at her, something she couldn't quite put her finger on. Whether it was Gianni's health or the threat of another attempt on his life, she couldn't say. Maybe it was both.

"I will be fine, I promise." He kissed her cheek. "You take such good care of me, Wendy." He was remembering how angry Donnatella was that it took so long for him to recover from his knee surgery and that he couldn't do all the things she wanted to do.

"Just remember. I'm your nurse and what I say, goes."

The afternoon was just as Gianni had described when he'd told her about Sunday dinners with the family. All seven of his siblings had come with their children, including Marcello and Analisa, who'd both driven about two hours in order to be there. That meant that, counting children, there were forty-four people, plus Mama and Papa, at the house. Wendy couldn't even imagine having a family that large. She still couldn't remember all their names, especially all the children.

Everyone was excited to see how well Gianni was doing. He seemed especially happy spending time talking with the children, who also seemed to enjoy him. Wendy saw that he was really just a boy himself, especially around his younger nephews and nieces: laughing, telling stories and making faces with them. She'd been watching him, making sure he wasn't getting too tired, but he seemed to be thoroughly enjoying himself.

She wondered if any of them knew about the attempt on his life; she hadn't heard the subject come up. She wanted Gianni to ask one of his brothers to stay at the house, but she didn't think that he had talked to any of them about it. That only increased the uneasiness she'd felt since they'd left the hospital.

At six, most of the women were in the kitchen, talking and preparing dinner. The men were filing out to the front porch to have some wine and supervise the children, the younger ones running all over the place, the older ones talking in groups and texting on their cell phones. Gianni called her over and asked her to help him to the bathroom, telling her that he also needed oxycodone.

"Are you okay?" She thought he looked tired and a little pale. She noticed he was slightly out of breath just walking to the bedroom.

"Yes, I am all right. I just waited too long for the oxycodone." She got the medication and a glass of water from the bathroom and handed them to him.

"Are you okay going to the bathroom by yourself?"

He took the pill, drinking the full glass of water. "I do not need your help. I hope that does not disappoint you," he said, a playful smile on his face.

Until he'd answered her question, Wendy hadn't even thought about how it had sounded. She honestly wondered if he could manage with the crutches. As she thought about it though, she felt a light blush, knowing he saw it.

"Watch," he told her as he leaned his crutches against the bed. He balanced on his good leg, pulled her to himself, wrapped his arms around her in a tight embrace and kissed her better and longer than he had ever kissed her. At last, there were no barriers: no lying in a hospital bed, no sitting in a chair side-by-side.

"Okay, you're all right. I get the picture," she said, trying to catch her breath.

When they returned to the living room, Mama met them and told them dinner was ready. They knew it was early, but Mama explained that she had told the family that he needed rest and that they should not stay too long.

How Papa and Mama fit all those people for dinner Wendy would never figure out, but by the time the food was on the table, everyone had a place to sit, though not all together. The eleven adults sat at the long tables on the back porch. The thirty children sat on the larger porch in the front of the house: older children on chairs, younger children at the table. It seemed to Wendy that they all knew instinctively where their places were, which would be natural since this was something they did every Sunday. Sometimes Marcello and Analisa couldn't come, but for the most part, Gianni told her that the entire family would gather on Sunday for the big meal.

And it was just as he had told her: the table full of delicious food and wine, the laughter, stories and the singing. She had never had that, the large family and relationship with brothers and sisters, and she realized just then how much she had missed. She had wanted to think of Donnatella as her sister, to be close to her and share the secrets and stories that sisters share, but Donnatella was gone by the time Wendy and Mark had met. Wendy felt the longing that she'd always known was there, but now was very real to her and instead of feeling the grief of that loss, it made her grateful for Gianni, for Papa and Mama and for being part of their family. She was sublimely happy and content, more than she'd ever been before.

At nine, the dishes were done, all the hugs and 'good-byes' were over and everyone was gone. Papa and Mama were watching TV in the living room. Wendy still didn't think Mama had been told about the attempt on Gianni's life, but then maybe he and Papa knew what was best to keep from her.

She didn't want the joy of the evening to go away, but as soon as the house was empty, Wendy felt her anxiety returning. Gianni obviously hadn't asked any of his brothers to stay at the house and she was hesitant to bring it up, but the picture of Amato injecting the morphine into the IV kept coming back to her.

He was sitting on one of the chairs in the bedroom, trying to get his shoes off. She knelt down and untied them. "Did you ask your brothers if one of them could stay here?" She saw his annoyance and realized immediately she'd made a mistake.

"We have already been over this. I have spoken with Papa and he has made sure all the doors and windows are locked and all the lights are on outside the house." Now he was fighting with the sock on his right foot, unable to remove it because of the stiffness in his leg, which she could tell was bothering him. There were dark circles under his eyes and he looked exhausted. She pulled the sock off for him. She knew the subject was closed, but she needed him to know how scared she was.

"I'm worried about you, that's all. Nicolò tried to kill you twice. Don't you think he'll keep trying until he succeeds?"

"What do you want me to do, Wendy? My brothers all have jobs. I cannot ask them to stay up all night guarding me just because you are worried!" His voice was raised now, his hostility evident. This was the first time he had ever been angry with her and it hurt her deeply. It scared her too. She consoled herself by remembering the pain and stress he'd endured the past week, but that didn't help the heartache that was growing inside.

"I just want you to understand how scared I am," she said slowly, trying to remain calm.

"I do understand how you feel, but I do not want you dictating to me what I should do! I told you I would take care of it and I want you to allow me to do that!"

"How are you going to protect either of us? You can barely walk! You *don't* understand how I feel!" She knew she was going to cry and she didn't want him to see it.

"Do not ever talk to me like that again, Wendy! You are smothering me and I will not have it!"

She looked into his eyes. Those beautiful eyes that always drew her in to him were now so dark they shocked her, forcing her away, blocking her out of his heart. She had to be away from him. She got up and went into the bathroom, slamming the door behind her, the tears coming quickly, the pain in her chest feeling as though he had pulled her heart out with his bare hands.

His remorse was immediate and all-consuming. He'd done it again. He'd treated her like he'd Donnatella and the guilt of his actions toward both of them pressed down upon him until he felt he couldn't bear the weight of it. He sank down into the chair, his head in his hands, the exhaustion overtaking him.

He loved Wendy so much. She was his life and the only thing he wanted, but he kept hurting her and he didn't know why he couldn't stop. Then he remembered what Papa had said about forgiving Donnatella. He understood now why he needed to forgive her; it was the pain of what she had done to him that surfaced raw and new, again and again, causing him to lash out at Wendy. He wasn't going to let that happen any more. He needed her forgiveness but would she give it to him again? Had he hurt her so badly this time that she would not take him back? He was more afraid of facing her than any threat Amato could make on his life and he would have preferred that Amato had been successful with the morphine overdose than to have hurt her the way he had now.

She heard his knock and the door opening. He leaned the crutches against the counter. Turning her around to face him, he saw her wet cheeks and red eyes. He hated himself for his weakness.

"I am so sorry, Wendy, for speaking to you like that. I know that it may not mean anything now, but I promise I will never raise my voice to you again." He waited, praying that he would see something in her face that told him she'd forgiven him, even though he knew he didn't deserve it. Her face was blank except for the tracks left by her tears.

There was nothing else he could say, no words that would erase the tears or the pain he'd caused her, and so he retrieved his crutches and walked back into the bedroom, his remorse swallowing him until he felt nothing but a great sadness and loss, the pain of which was worse than anything he'd suffered physically. Somewhere inside himself, he wanted morphine.

It was all before her now; she could see it clearly, could see it for what it really was. She saw how great the tension and stress had been on both of them, the good and the bad emotions that captured them, holding them hostage for so many months. From that very first thrilling day that he'd walked up to her table in the cafeteria until his anger with her now, their emotions had become open and raw like a wound. She thought about the phone calls, Tanya and Monica, Lillian and Jim, Brantmeier, dinner at Villa Bella, Sofia, his accident. It was all there, consuming their energy, eating away at their patience.

And underneath it all was the enormous difficulty of abstaining, of denying the overpowering desire they had for each other. Mama didn't know how right she was when she told Wendy that she and Gianni might be frustrated. She was now acutely aware of how impossible it was to be so close to him, to love him so much that all she wanted was to give herself to him, but couldn't because of a vow they had made. She knew he felt the same way. She saw it on him every time he looked her. She felt it in his touch and tasted it on his lips. If not for his accident, they would have been married by now and on their honeymoon. She would be keeping her promise to make love to him all night and they would be happy, not angry with each other they way they were now. It was no wonder that they were on edge, irritable and upset.

She turned on the cold water and splashed her face, drying it with a towel. After brushing the hair out of her face, she walked back into the bedroom and saw him sitting on the edge of the bed, his head in his hands. He looked up when he heard her, his eyes red. The softness in them had returned. She sat next to him, taking his hand in hers and held it until she had the courage to speak.

"Waiting is so hard, Gianni. It's hard for me and it's hard for you. That's what is behind all of this." She let out her breath before she continued, wondering how he was going to take what she had to say and afraid he would be angry with her all over again.

"I don't want to wait any longer. What difference does it make anyway? We're getting married. We already know we have a sacred love, so why does it matter?" Her eyes were pleading with him and he saw her longing in them, not so much longing to make love, but a longing for peace between them.

He'd asked himself that question so many times, every time he'd kissed her or held her and felt his desire out of control. He was tired of denying himself and of denying her. Why *did* it matter? Did he even know the answer?

He stilled his thoughts, letting his mind go blank, praying that God would intervene with the words that would answer her, words that would heal the wounds between them.

"Wendy, our waiting to make love is not about us. It is a vow we made to God, the One who created marriage. He is what is important." The words were coming to him slowly, filling his heart and mind, assuring him of their truth and trustworthiness. He breathed deeply and felt himself relax, a peace settling in on him.

"We both believe that God brought us together, is that not so?" She nodded. She knew it was true because of the improbability that they would already have been connected through Mark and Donnatella and that he had come looking for

Donnatella's family and had found her instead. She thanked God for that every day.

"You know that I love you with all my heart. If I bought you a gift for your birthday, something very special that only I could give you, that you had wanted for a long time, would you go behind my back and open your gift before I had presented it to you?"

"No, Gianni, I wouldn't do that because I know it would hurt you." Her voice was almost a whisper.

"We wait because not to do so hurts God. Our love for each other is a gift given to us out of His perfect love for us and it has great value. When we stand together at our wedding, we make vows to God and to each other and we say them in front of witnesses. It is when we are pronounced husband and wife that the gift of marriage is presented to us. We honor God by waiting, as a way of thanking Him for such a wonderful gift. Is that not what we owe Him, to honor Him in that way?"

She understood. All she had been able to think about was the pleasure of giving herself to him and of the fulfillment she wanted him to have in making love to her. She knew how much he wanted her. Sometimes the intensity of his passion astonished her, but now she couldn't bear the thought of how much it would hurt God if she were to submit to him. Gianni had fought his natural desires to maintain his integrity before God and before her and she didn't want to take that away from him even if it meant he was easily angered, even if he took out his frustration on her. In her selfishness, she hadn't thought about what honor there was in waiting: honor not only to God, but to him.

He couldn't look at her now, but kept his eyes on their joined hands.

"Waiting has been very hard. There has been so much stress for us. I know this, Wendy. I am so sorry about my accident and how hard it has been for you, but if it will take away the pain I have caused you, I will make love to you. I will not make you wait any longer." Here he searched her eyes, seeing the love for him reflected in them, knowing that he would do anything to make her happy again.

"No, Gianni, not now and not like this. I can't ask you to do that and I'm sorry that I asked you if waiting mattered, because I know that it does. I can't ask you to break your vow to God and I don't want to break mine. If we honor God when we wait, then He will help us. We'll get through this. And if you never make love to me, I will love you forever just as much as I do now."

He took her in his arms, holding her securely, loving her more than he could ever tell her. The embrace remained for several minutes, each of them knowing that something had changed between them, but that it was something for the best.

Gianni finally pulled back and looked at her. "Do you know what I want?"

"No," she said, "what do you want?" She expected a funny comment. He always said something to make her laugh and to relieve the stress when there was any kind of tension between them.

"I want a shower! Would you ask Papa if he would help me?" She smiled, waiting for the angels to speak to her as they always did, but they were silent.

"I'll go get him," she replied and with that, she kissed him affectionately and left the room.

Chapter 19

He was in bed when she came back into the room and Papa was gone. "Come and sit with me," he said. "I want to talk to you." She sat on the edge of the bed, noticing how well he looked.

"How was your shower?" She remembered how good her hot bath had felt after days of being with him in the hospital.

"It was wonderful," he said, "but Papa almost got as wet as I did! He was afraid I would fall." He was smiling, his hair still damp and his curls much more noticeable, reminding her of Mama's hair.

"Papa and I talked and I have some things to tell you." He held her hands. "Everything is arranged for our wedding. The only thing that needs to be done is to let the guests know the new date. *Mi vuoi sposare?* Will you marry me next week on Saturday?"

Her eyes widened in excitement. "Do you realize that you just proposed to me?"

"Yes, and I know that I have not asked you to marry me before this."

She kissed him several times on his face and then on his lips. "Does that answer your question?"

"No, I am not sure I understood your answer," he teased.

She kissed him again, more passionately this time, loving him for remembering that he'd never asked her formally.

"I want to tell you where we are going on our honeymoon," he said.

She had asked him about where they would honeymoon before they left Cape Narrows, but he'd always been vague about giving her a location, telling her that he was looking into it and would tell her when he'd found a suitable place. As far as she was concerned, as long as they were alone, she didn't care where they were. They could have stayed in Cape Narrows at her house and she would have been happy; she just wanted to be with him.

"Papa made reservations for us at Hotel Mayer in Desanzano del Garda. It is a small, town on the shores of Lake Garda. The lake is in the mountains and is very large and beautiful! The room is very romantic and will have a balcony with a view of the lake! The food is incredible, especially the seafood! You will love it Wendy! Tell me what you think." He had that joyfully expectant, childlike look that she'd seen so many times before.

"I think I would be happy in a barn if you were with me!" He laughed. "I know I will love it, Gianni, and I can't wait to go!"

"Papa is going to rent a car, but I cannot dri—"

She interrupted him. "I'll drive. You just tell me how to get there!" She was looking forward to the wedding now, eager to put his accident behind them and wanting only to be alone with him at last. Maybe this feeling of dread would leave her, she thought, if they could go somewhere else, to a place where Nicolò Amato couldn't find them. Then she would feel more at peace. They would be flying back to the United States as soon as the honeymoon was over and she was sure Amato would not follow them there.

"What are you thinking?" he asked, seeing the look on her face.

She shook her head, not wanting to start another argument with him. "It's nothing. I'm just tired."

"Then kiss me good-night."

She did as he asked, enjoying the warmth of his lips and wondering if Amato would try again. The bad feeling wasn't leaving her; if anything, it was getting stronger. She tried to trust what Gianni had said, that the house was secure, but she was scared and there was no talking herself out of how she felt.

She knew she wasn't going to sleep well, not until they were at Lake Garda and maybe not even until they were back in Cape Narrows. She wished there really were angels talking to her and not just her own crazy thoughts; she needed to hear what they had to say.

She grabbed her pajamas and went to the bathroom to change, deciding that the only way to help the feeling go away was to pray.

ぼ

In her half-sleep, she heard the thump and woke, immediately startled, her heart pounding in her throat. She sat straight up, barely able to see him in the moonlight that filled the room giving it an eerie, haunted appearance. She noticed they'd forgotten to close the heavy drapes on the French doors.

"I am sorry, Wendy," he whispered. "I was trying to be quiet. I did not want to wake you."

"What are you doing?"

"I need my pain medication. I was going into the bathroom to get some water."

She saw him sitting on the edge of the bed, holding one crutch, the other having fallen to the floor. Looking at the clock on her bedside table, she saw that it was one-fifty, well over the time he should have had more medication. She got up, turned on the bedside lamp and righted the crutch, seeing the pain in his face.

"Lie back down. I'll get it for you." She helped him back into bed and then headed for the bathroom.

"I am sorry," he whispered after her.

He swallowed the pill and handed her the empty glass. He'd noticed that she'd given him morphine instead of the oxycodone, but he took it without comment; he knew he would need the stronger narcotic.

"It's okay, Gianni. That's why I'm here with you. Mama wanted me to be here to take care of you. They went to a lot of trouble to move the beds apart, so we mustn't disappoint them." She saw him smile.

She wanted him to beg her to lie with him, not for him, but for her; the bad feeling was sitting on her stomach, making her nauseous. But she told herself that after he had offered to make love to her and she had refused, something had changed and she knew he wouldn't ask her. She wanted it that way.

She kissed him, noticing he kept his eyes closed even after she stood up. It was his way of dealing with the pain until the narcotic kicked in.

It was taking a chance, but she wanted to make sure the French doors were locked and she wanted to close the drapes. She tiptoed over, knowing he wasn't asleep, and checked. Of course they were locked; he and Papa had made sure of that. She was about to close the drapes when she heard him.

"Come here, Wendy," he said. Her heart sank. She walked to him and waited by his bed, remembering his promise about raising his voice, but expecting a lecture at least. He took hold of her wrist.

"You know that I will not ask you to lie with me, but if you would be not so scared, perhaps you are able to move your bed next to mine. Would you feel better if that were so?"

"I wasn't going to ask…"

He interrupted her, a smile forming on his lips. "I know, Wendy, but I need to get some sleep and so do you. If being close will make you sleep better, then move the bed. It will be all right and if you are worried about what Mama will think, you can move it back in the morning before she is up."

It wasn't difficult for her and when the beds were next to each other, she turned off the lamp, noticing that it was chilly in the room. She snuggled under the blankets, then reached for him.

"Thank you, Gianni," she said, her stomach a little more settled.

He squeezed her hand. She didn't let go, instead concentrated on the feel of his fingers entwined in hers while she tried to fall asleep. The bad feeling was still with her.

❧

It was three-twenty when he turned the headlights off. He parked a short way beyond the end of the stone walkway, behind the row of cypress trees. He left the keys in the ignition, assuring he would be able to get away quickly.

He walked along the walkway, until he was near the area of the house he knew was the large bedroom. He crept around toward the back and the patio outside the French doors. There was only one light on the wall outside the doors, which cast a weak glow on the patio. Even so, he unscrewed the bulb, laid it down quietly and then checked his pocket for the knife. He retrieved his credit card from the other pocket and stood to the side of the doors, peering in.

In the dim moonlight, he thought that the beds had been pushed together, was fairly sure at least. That meant that he might be forced to take care of the American woman too. She would surely feel the movement of Giannotti's bed when the knife sliced through his throat. He wouldn't be able to call out, but he might thrash about before he died and wake her. Amato didn't care if she had to die too. What mattered was that nothing came to light about the brake cable on the Ducati being cut and that Giannotti pay for Donnatella's death.

Wendy had been unable to fall asleep right away and when she finally did, she woke with a start. In her half-sleep, she'd heard a car. She went into the bathroom. The window looked out toward the front of the property and she could see the road, but no sign of a car. Remaining for some time, her eyes straining against the feeble moonlight, she saw nothing and decided she'd either dreamed the sound or the car had passed by. She used the toilet, flushed and walked back toward the bedroom, her feet turning cold against the tile of the bathroom floor.

She saw the dark figure, hunched over against the glass of the French doors and a sudden chill encompassed her until her entire body felt as cold as her feet. Her throat closed in terror, her heart beating so hard that it made her ears ring. She was going to call out to Gianni, but stopped herself. The intruder would hear her and if it was Amato, and she was sure it was, he would get away and she would never be rid of worrying about him. She worried that Gianni would try to do something to save both of them and with his injuries, he would end up being a victim instead of a savior. She had to think quickly; she could hear the almost imperceptible click as the intruder tried the door.

The weak moonlight shone on the floor in front of the doors, leaving the rest of the room in sinister shadows. The door was locked, but somehow she knew he would be in the room at any minute. The fear was making her nauseous. As her mind sped through her options, a sudden anger mixed with the fear, adding to her nausea until she could feel the vomit raising in her throat; Gianni should have listened to her, he should have asked Marcello to stay at the house. It was too late now to think about that; she had to do something. But what? She needed a weapon. Then she remembered.

With her back to the wall, she inched her way along until she past the entry door and came to the privacy screen next to the French doors. Slipping silently behind it, she listened for any sound that would tell her she'd been spotted. The only sound was Gianni's deep breathing, the morphine keeping him asleep. Some part of her was grateful for that, even though she was terrified and wanted his help. She heard Gayle's voice: "Pull up your big girl panties and deal with it," and took her advice.

There on the table, she saw the bust of David that she had bought at the airport. It was heavy enough. She was shaking so badly, she had to pick it up with both hands, fearing she might drop it and give herself away. She waited, flashing back to her time in the ED with Gianni when they had discussed skull fractures and brain injury. She hadn't expected she would get a practical lesson.

The door was locked as he expected, but he had to try. He took the credit card and slipped it under the latching bolt, one hand on the knob. It was not opening as easily this time and Amato was getting worried, his first failure heavy on his mind. After a few nervous seconds of trying, he felt the latch give way. He turned the knob and eased the door open slowly.

It took only a moment for his eyes to adjust to the darkness. He saw Giannotti in the bed nearest the doors. He was sleeping on his back, his neck fully exposed, the best position possible. One powerful draw deeply across his throat, deep enough to make sure the jugular and carotids were severed and it would be all over in a matter of seconds. He removed the knife from his pocket and held it firmly in his hand, the excitement now chasing away the fear of failure.

He peered through the darkness, checking the other bed, but couldn't see her. She was probably under the covers; it was cold in the room.

Holding the knife tighter, his arm starting to ache and tremble with the tension, he took the first step toward the culmination of his plan for ending Dr. Giancarlo Giannotti's life.

She waited, holding her breath, afraid that he would hear the air escaping from her lungs. Her head hurt from the blood pulsating in her temples and she was getting dizzy. She could taste the nausea at the back of her tongue now, but kept repeating Gayle's advice. She could do this; she would deal with it.

There was just enough room between the wall and the edge of the privacy screen for her to ease out. When his back was to her, she crept up behind him, raising David and aiming toward the back of his head, willing strength into her muscles.

She swung and as the bust was about to make contact, his head turned toward her, a look of total surprise on his face and his arm bringing the knife up toward her body. Striking him as hard as she could, the flat bottom of the bust landed against the left side of his head. She heard a scream as he crumpled to the floor, his legs spontaneously folding under him.

He hadn't made a sound and he wasn't moving. It was only then that she realized she had been the one who had screamed.

"Wendy! What is wrong?" Gianni was sitting upright, pulling the blankets off his legs, trying to get out of bed. "What happened? Are you all right?" His voice was loud and she could hear the panic in it.

"I'm okay, Gianni! Don't get up! Stay there! Just wait!" There was an authority in her voice that surprised her. She felt strong, still scared to death, but no longer plagued with the bad feeling.

She grabbed both of the heavy cords that held back the draperies. With one, she tied Amato's wrists together behind his back and with the other, she tied his feet. Then, as she had seen Mark do so many times when treating animals, she hog-tied him, joining the cord from his wrists to the one on his feet. It must have been an angel talking to her, because her only thought was that he was trussed up like a Thanksgiving turkey! She would have laughed out loud, but the shock was still too new and she was starting to feel faint.

She rushed to Gianni, his arms folding around her tightly. He had watched her tie Amato up, saw the open door and realized what had happened. "It is okay now, Wendy. I have you. You are safe."

She couldn't talk and was aware only of his voice telling her over and over again that she was safe, that nothing would hurt her now. The fear was leaving her; the nausea subsiding.

She took a deep breath, let it out and felt him release his grip.

"It's Nicolò, Gianni, and I think I've hurt him badly. We need to call an ambulance right away." Nicolò still hadn't moved or made any noise and she wondered if he was dead. Her eyes filled with tears. Gianni hugged her for a long moment, amazed at her strength and will.

"Give me your cell phone and I will call," he told her. She turned on the lamp and retrieved her phone from the bedside table, then heard the tones as he pressed the numbers. She wiped her tears with her pajama sleeve and sniffed hard.

She needed to know how badly Nicolò was hurt. She went to him and noticed the knife a few feet away from where he lay on the floor. It was very large and she trembled thinking about the damage it could have done. She pushed the thought away and saw that he was breathing. Blood pooling on the floor under his face and she saw a deep laceration on his head, the blood pumping in rhythmic spurts, running down his head and matting his hair. She checked his pulse, relieved that it seemed strong and steady; there was no sign of shock yet.

She heard Gianni on the phone talking to the ambulance service, giving them directions to the house. Then he hung up and dialed again, probably calling Iacopetti, Wendy guessed.

As she hurried to the bathroom, she was surprised at how weak her legs felt and wondered if they would support her. Grabbing a couple of towels, she went back to Nicolò and applied pressure to the laceration, feeling the tears run down her cheeks again. She was thinking about Sofia and wondered if Sofia would hate her for what she had done to Nicolò?

Gianni was up on his crutches. He stood over Wendy, watching her with Amato and was overtaken with emotion. She had saved his life again and now she was caring for the man who had tried to kill him and she was crying as she did so. It was her beautiful heart that he saw again and in the back of his mind, he knew that her tears were his fault. He hadn't listened to her, hadn't supported her or honored how she felt.

His strength suddenly left him. He sat down on the bed, knowing that he could never make any of this up to her, knowing that he was alive only because of her. The depth of his sin against her crushed him and filled his eyes until they could no longer hold the volume of his tears.

Wendy hadn't even realized that Papa and Mama had never awakened, had heard nothing until the ambulance came.

Iacopetti arrived about the time the paramedics were taking Nicolò out on a stretcher, still unconscious, his head bandaged. He told Wendy and Gianni about knowing that Amato had been in the hospital the night that Gianni had received the overdose of morphine and that he had been following up on that information.

Several times in questioning Wendy, he'd stopped, looked at her and said something about how incredible it was that she had handled the intrusion so well. His praise for her courage did nothing to make Wendy feel better about Sofia and about hurting Nicolò. Intellectually she knew she was justified in defending herself and Gianni, but her heart ached for the way that Nicolò's affair with Donnatella had caused so much fear and pain to everyone involved, especially Sofia. She saw this as the final result of the broken commitments made by Nicolò and Donnatella.

Then suddenly, it made sense. Sacred love was important in a way even Papa had not mentioned. If Nicolò had loved only Sofia, had valued her, been committed to her and had honored the marriage vows they'd made, none of this would have happened. And that applied to Donnatella as well. If she had been happy with Gianni, had given him the sacred love he'd wanted with her, she would be alive. Wendy and Gianni would not have the love for each other they had now, but he would never have gone through the horror of two attempts on his life and Wendy wouldn't be standing in Papa and Mama's room, looking at the pool of clotting blood on the floor, knowing she'd hurt Amato and Sofia. She wouldn't have to see the depth of guilt in Gianni's eyes; wouldn't have to see him crying.

Wendy thought about Donnatella's innocent baby and felt the pain of that loss so much, she cried openly. There were devastating consequences when marriage was taken lightly, when self-centeredness held sway and commitment was not honored; people got hurt.

She and Gianni were alone at last. He hadn't said anything to her through all the commotion of the paramedics and

Iacopetti's questioning, hadn't held her or comforted her as she cried and she knew why. He couldn't face her; his guilt wouldn't let him. She looked at him, still sitting on the edge of the bed, his face wet. The pain of knowing how badly he must feel made her heart ache and her chest feel heavy. Papa's words came back to her: "When Gianni is sad, you will be sad too." She felt no anger toward him now, only compassion, and prayed that he would be able to forgive himself. She already had. She sat down on the bed next to him, loving him more now than he would ever know and probably wouldn't understand, remembering that Papa had said God would help her.

"Let me see your eyes, Gianni," she said and he turned his head toward her. She saw the beautiful eyes that had first drawn her to him, saw the remorse in them now. "I love your eyes, you know," she said softly. "You told me that you see the beauty of my heart. Well, I see the beauty of your soul reflected in your eyes." She saw fresh tears come, but he didn't hide them or himself from her, just as he had promised.

She took his hands, loving the strength she saw in them, knowing how he used them to heal people. She wanted healing for him, for his body and his soul and for herself.

"This is over now. It's the past and we are moving on to the future, to our life together. We will start something new with each other. When we make love, it *will* be the first time for us; you will see it in my heart and I will see it in your eyes. We *will* have the sacred love the angels promised. I will always love you, Gianni." She wrapped her arms around him, holding him safe in her love.

In their impassioned embrace, they both felt the power of their love erasing what was before and encouraging them with what was to come. There was forgiveness between them and finally the peace they both longed for.

Epilogue

HER FEARS WERE never realized. As she walked down the aisle toward him, she was thankful that Mama's cooking, as good as it was, had not caused her to gain any weight and the ecru lace dress she wore fit perfectly. It flowed gently around her calves as she approached him, the afternoon sun warm on her back. After a frantic week of preparations, the time had finally arrived.

In the old Italian tradition, the women of the family made all the food; catered weddings were something new. All of the Giannotti women had been preparing their own specialties as soon as Gianni had set the date.

Analisa made antipasto consisting of prosciutto with baked stuffed figs. Nicolina's speciality was zuppa di porcini: porcini soup with mascarpone crostini. Giuliana worked on tagliatelle with fresh tuna ragu, while Analisa's speciality was grilled whole black bass with onions, olives and red chard. Mama prepared grilled squab with pomegranate molasses and Marcello's wife, Luciana made short ribs in Barolo red wine. The vegetable, broccoli sautéed in wine and garlic was made by Emiliano's wife Isabella and Cristiano's wife Carla was charged with ordering torta nuziale, the wedding cake, and making the small 'purses' that would hold the Jordan almonds which would be given out to the guests. The only outside cooking would be done by hired culinary help who would do the last minute preparations and grilling, leaving the women free to enjoy the wedding.

Gianni and Wendy had decided to have the wedding at the house. He was still early in his recovery and he tired easily. A church wedding would be hard for him to manage physically and Wendy and Gianni liked the idea of the intimacy of his entire family gathered at their home. Papa and Mama also like the idea and so the plan was to have the ceremony outdoors in the large yard at the side of the house. The weather was expected to be sunny and warm and all of the flowers in Mama's gardens were still in full bloom.

Papa and the brothers had seen to setting up the side yard with rented chairs, arranged in neat rows, and a flowered arch at the front where the vows were to be taken. The large patio at the front of the house was filled with more rented tables and chairs for the reception and the bar was well-stocked. Musicians had been hired and would arrive later.

Father Marcangelo was excited to officiate, having presided over the weddings of every one of Gianni's siblings. He was in his eighties, but spry with a glint in his eye and a ready smile.

She still hadn't gotten over the surprise of Gayle's appearance. Gianni's oldest sister Renata and his brother Marcello had agreed to stand with them as witnesses and Papa had walked her down the aisle, but as Wendy walked toward the flowered arch, Gayle had appeared from behind Renata. Wendy had been so intent on looking at Gianni that she hadn't even noticed until she was standing before Father Marcangelo. As soon as she'd seen her, Wendy had hugged her and greeted her excitedly in the European fashion: a kiss to each cheek. If everything was wonderful before, Wendy knew that this wedding was perfect now.

She couldn't take her eyes off of Gianni throughout the entire ceremony. He was even more handsome than she could ever have imagined in his black Armani suit, white shirt and red rose boutonnière. Without her knowing, he'd practiced standing without his crutches for longer periods of time so that by the time he stood with her before Father Marcangelo, he stood without them, much to Wendy's surprise and admiration.

During the ceremony, the love and joy in his eyes was so overwhelming that Wendy had to fight back tears. With every word they repeated to each other, she remembered how difficult the past two weeks had been for them both and how completely they had learned the lesson of what it meant to have a sacred love. It had tried their patience, forced them to confess their innermost guilt and taught them what it really meant to forgive. They had learned how important commitment was to a relationship and a marriage and she knew they were lessons she and Gianni would not forget. When Father Marcangelo pronounced them husband and wife and they kissed, they both knew they were now complete in each other.

Gianni had told Wendy that typical Italian weddings began at four in the afternoon, but because they had a three hour drive to Lake Garda, theirs had started at two. After the half hour ceremony, they greeted all their guests. They were especially happy to see Dr. Rossi and Dr. DeSanti, who both remarked that they were amazed at how well Gianni was looking and were quick to attribute his recovery to Wendy and her excellent nursing care.

Fabiana and Rosabella had also come and Wendy made sure that they were introduced to Gayle, who seemed to like them immediately and vice versa. The three of them immediately exchanged stories from their work and Wendy could hear Gianni's name being mentioned more than once. She had some time to chat with Gayle, who told her that Gianni had planned for Gayle to come to Italy even before they themselves had left Cape Narrows. As Gayle told Wendy, "Do you really think I would pass up a chance to kiss your groom?"

That made Wendy laugh and she hugged Gayle again and asked "So how was he?"

Gayle's eyes lit up. "*Sorprendente!*" Wendy laughed hard; she knew that word. It meant 'amazing!'

Wendy was introduced to numerous aunts, uncles, cousins and friends of the family; so many names and she still hadn't remembered all the names of his siblings! But she liked them all, liked the way they enjoyed each other, the noisy conversations as they caught up on family news with children giggling and playing in the background. She could not have imagined a better or happier wedding.

At three, the wines were opened and Analisa's antipasto served, followed by more visiting and frenetic conversations. The food courses continued to come out and be served about every hour until seven o'clock, when the main dishes were served: Mama's squab, Luciana's short ribs and Isabella's broccoli dish. Wendy was again amazed at the amount of food served, but true to European custom, when the food was spread out over several hours, Wendy never felt too full. She sat at the head table with Gianni, savoring every bite, enjoying the wine and eagerly kissing him whenever they heard the clinking of the wine glasses as the guests tapped on them, which was very often.

The musicians arrived and the dancing began with Wendy and Gianni dancing the first dance, joined by Papa and Mama after a few minutes. Gianni managed to stand without crutches for the entire dance, although he and Wendy remained in one spot. He couldn't put much weight on his right leg yet, but Wendy enjoyed just being in his arms. When the song ended and the second one began, everyone danced, even the children.

"Are you happy?" he asked her, holding her close to himself as they swayed to the rhythm of the music.

"More than I have ever been," she said. "I can't imagine being any happier than I am right now."

He whispered in her ear. "But Wendy, we have not had our honeymoon yet. I think you will be even more happy tonight!" He smiled and looked into her face, his eyes so intense with passion for her that she already felt naked in front of him. Feeling the warmth of his body next to hers, his cologne exciting her senses, she blushed. This time he said nothing, but kissed her, her lips satisfying and sweet, like the Chianti.

As the last strains of the music ended and he released her, she noticed someone standing alone by the road, almost hidden by the cypress trees and rows of parked cars. She knew who it was.

"Gianni, come with me," she said. He got his crutches and followed her. They walked toward the street, the setting sun casting long shadows across the stone walkway, until they were close enough to recognize her.

"I'm happy to see you again," Wendy said truthfully. She knew that Nicolò was in jail, awaiting sentencing. She had spoken with Sofia at the arraignment hearing and was grateful that Sofia had been so understanding and didn't hold any animosity toward her for hurting Nicolò.

Sofia was uncomfortable in their presence. She and Gianni had a history together and she still felt the guilt of that, especially with Wendy standing beside him. She wouldn't make eye contact with him, but spoke with her eyes downcast.

"I am sorry to come at this time, but I know you will be leaving soon and I have something to give you." She opened her purse and pulled out a small box, the kind jewelry came in. It was then that she looked at Gianni, holding the box out to him. He took it from her as she continued. "I found it in Nicolò's dresser. I think it belonged to Donnatella." She hung her head as Gianni opened the box and saw the necklace Wendy and Mark had picked out for Donnatella's birthday: the heart with the red and green birthstones.

"I want you to have it and to know that I am sorry for what Nicolò did to you, for hurting you." Sofia's eyes filled with tears. In everything that had happened, she had suffered the most and was still suffering. Nicolò had pled guilty at the arraignment and would be sentenced soon. Sofia would be on her own, safe now, but without him. She still loved Nicolò; it showed on her face.

Gianni was at a loss for words. He still carried the pain of hurting Sofia, knowing that she had needed him that night as much as he had needed her. Then he remembered what Wendy had said the night Amato had broken into the house: he and Wendy were moving on to the future; they were starting something new. He handed his crutches to Wendy, took a step toward Sofia and wrapped her in his arms. "Thank you," he said.

Sofia's tears rolled down her cheeks and Wendy let her tears come too. Where the dream of Gianni and Sofia on the couch had hurt so much, now she loved him for holding Sofia; for comforting her. She loved the beauty she saw in his soul. Before either of them could say anything more, Sofia turned and hurried toward her car, driving away quickly.

He stood there, silent for a moment, looking at the necklace in the box. He thought of Donnatella, knowing that some part of him would always love her.

He took the necklace out of the box. "Turn around, Wendy," he said softly. She did as he requested and felt him place the necklace around her neck, fastening it in back. He held her shoulders and turned her back to face him, the light from the setting sun leaving her face radiant.

"You told me that what happened last week was in the past and that we were moving on to the future. You were once one with Mark and will never forget him. You will always love him. And I will never forget being one with Donnatella and I will always love her. I want you to have this necklace and when you wear it, we will remember them and remember our vows to each other. It will always remind us of them and of our sacred love."

He took her in his arms and she felt a presence surrounding them. As brother and sister, Mark and Donnatella had connected her and Gianni. Now she and Gianni were husband and wife and Wendy couldn't help imaging that somewhere Mark and his sister were together now too, that all along it was their plan for her and Gianni to meet. Maybe Gianni was right; there were angels talking to her and maybe their names were Mark and Donnatella.

Acknowledgments

THIS BOOK WOULD not have come into being without an idea inspired by my friend, Wendy Riggs. We met while working in a medical office and had many laughs and good times. It was a comment she made in an email about the intrigue of working in the medical profession that spurred me to make up a fantasy story for her, which became this book. Here I need to say that the Wendy of my story is nothing like the real Wendy except where blushing, blond hair and a beautiful heart are concerned! I want to thank you, my friend, for inspiring this story which has been as much fun for me to write as the time we spent in together in Lori's office. *Mi manchi, Bella Donna!*

A big thank you to my husband Doug. You had to put up with many months of being 'alone' while I sat in front of my computer. You took time to listen to me read every word to you and were as excited about the story and the characters as I was. You gave me great ideas and helped me with the research. You have been my life and my sacred love for forty-five years. *Ti amo come Wendy ama Gianni.*

Thanks also to my granddaughter, Leah. Over a weekend, you sat entranced as I read the story to you, wondering if I had created a story suitable to be read by a fifteen-year-old gi who has already pledged to her parents to 'wait.' You said you'd read it again! You are a joy, a lover of books and my special crafting partner. *Ti amo sempre.*

A special thank you to my daughter Colleen, who is a talented author in her own right. You started me on this journey to get my manuscript published. Now get started on yours! *Ti amo sempre.*

Finally, to Morgan Richter my publisher, my deepest gratitude for all your help, emails, interest and talent. Wendy may have given me the idea, Doug, Colleen and Leah the encouragement, but without the gift of your talents, this book would never have come to fruition. *Grazie molto.*

"Three things will last forever — faith, hope and love — and the greatest of these is love."
1 Corinthians 13:13

About the Author

Writing, art and medicine have shaped Cheryle Fisher's life since childhood. She has been drawing and painting since elementary school and been writing since high school and after graduation, entered nursing school. *Sacred Love* is her first novel and published work. She has been married to her husband Doug for forty-five years, has three grown children and seven grandchildren, with the eighth due in December 2014. She enjoys traveling, volunteering, photography, riding her bike and believes that every good gift comes from God.

Made in the USA
Middletown, DE
19 April 2015